Bewitched & Betrayed

"Once again, Ms. Shearin has given her readers a book that you don't want to put down. With Raine, the adventures never end."
—*Night Owl Romance Reviews*

"*Bewitched & Betrayed* might just be the best in the series so far! . . . an amazingly exciting fourth installment that really tugs at the heartstrings." —*Ink and Paper*

"If you're new to Shearin's work and you enjoy fantasy interspersed with an enticing romance, a little bit of humor, and a whole lot of grade-A action, this is the series for you."
—*Lurv a la Mode*

The Trouble with Demons

"The book reads more like an urban fantasy with pirates and sharp wit and humor. I found the mix quite refreshing. Lisa Shearin's fun, action-packed writing style gives this world life and vibrancy." —*Fresh Fiction*

"Fans can rejoice as ubertalented Shearin dishes up more hilarious mayhem. Snappy dialogue, great pacing, and two seriously sexy heroes ensure hours of nonstop pleasure. Raine is sassy and irreverent, and this book is an auto-buy!"
—*Romantic Times* (top pick)

"Lisa Shearin represents that much needed voice in fantasy that combines practiced craft and a wicked sense of humor . . . A book by author Lisa Shearin should come with a warning on the cover or the pages coated in plastic. You are going to laugh out loud."
—*Bitten by Books*

"The brisk pace and increasingly complex character development propel the story on a roller-coaster ride through demons, goblins, elves, and mages while maintaining a satisfying level of romantic attention . . . that will leave readers chomping at the bit for more." —*Monsters and Critics*

continued . . .

Armed & Magical

"Fresh, original, and fall-out-of-your-chair funny, Lisa Shearin's *Armed & Magical* combines deft characterization, snarky dialogue, and nonstop action—plus a yummy hint of romance—to create one of the best reads of the year. This book is a bona fide winner, the series a keeper, and Shearin a definite star on the rise."
—Linnea Sinclair, RITA Award–winning author of *Rebels and Lovers*

"An exciting, catch-me-if-you-can, lightning-fast-paced tale of magic and evil filled with goblins, elves, mages, and a hint of love interest that will leave fantasy readers anxiously awaiting Raine's next adventure."　　　　　—*Monsters and Critics*

"The kind of book you hope to find when you go to the bookstore. It takes you away to a world of danger, magic, and adventure, and it does so with dazzling wit and clever humor. It's gritty, funny, and sexy—a wonderful addition to the urban fantasy genre. I absolutely loved it. From now on Lisa Shearin is on my auto-buy list!"　　　—Ilona Andrews, *New York Times* bestselling author of *Bayou Moon*

"*Armed & Magical*, like its predecessor, is an enchanting read from the very first page. I absolutely loved it. Shearin weaves a web of magic with a dash of romance that thoroughly snares the reader. She's definitely an author to watch!"
—Anya Bast, *New York Times* bestselling author of *Dark Enchantment*

"Shearin continues to demonstrate her marvelous gift for balancing offbeat humor with high-stakes adventure and paranormal thrills in book two of her high-octane, first-person suspense ride. You don't get much better than this imaginative and hilarious book."　　　　　　　　　　　　　—*Romantic Times*

"One of the best reads I've had in a long, long time . . . If you love an imaginative fantasy romp with a winning blend of laugh-out-loud humor and chilling suspense, this novel is a must-read."
—*The Toasted Scimitar*

Magic Lost, Trouble Found

"Take a witty, kick-ass heroine and put her in a vividly realized fantasy world where the stakes are high, and you've got a fun, page-turning read in *Magic Lost, Trouble Found*. I can't wait to read more of Raine Benares's adventures."
—Shanna Swendson, author of *Don't Hex with Texas*

"A wonderful fantasy tale full of different races and myths and legends [that] are drawn so perfectly readers will believe they actually exist. Raine is a strong female, a leader who wants to do the right thing even when she isn't sure what that is . . . Lisa Shearin has the magic touch."   —*Midwest Book Review*

"Shearin serves up an imaginative fantasy . . . The strong, well-executed story line and characters, along with a nice twist to the 'object of unspeakable power' theme, make for an enjoyable, fast-paced read."   —*Monsters and Critics*

"Lisa Shearin turns expectation on its ear and gives us a different kind of urban fantasy with *Magic Lost, Trouble Found*. For once, the urban is as fantastic as the fantasy, as Shearin presents an otherworld city peopled with beautiful goblins, piratical elves, and hardly a human to be found. Littered with entertaining characters and a protagonist whose self-serving lifestyle is compromised only by her loyalty to her friends, *Magic Lost* is an absolutely enjoyable read. I look forward to the next one!"   —C. E. Murphy, author of *Spirit Dances*

"[An] edgy and fascinating first-person adventure. In her auspicious debut, Shearin populates her series with a variety of supernatural characters with a multitude of motives. Following along as this tough and feisty woman kicks butt and takes names is a most enjoyable way to spend your time."   —*Romantic Times*

"Fun, fascinating, and loaded with excitement! *Magic Lost, Trouble Found* is a top-notch read of magic, mayhem, and some of the most charming elves and goblins I've ever encountered. Enthralling characters and a thrilling plot . . . I now need to cast a spell on Ms. Shearin to ensure there's a sequel."
—Linnea Sinclair, RITA Award–winning author of
Rebels and Lovers

Ace Books by Lisa Shearin

MAGIC LOST, TROUBLE FOUND
ARMED & MAGICAL
THE TROUBLE WITH DEMONS
BEWITCHED & BETRAYED
CON & CONJURE

Con &
Conjure

Lisa Shearin

ACE BOOKS, NEW YORK

THE BERKLEY PUBLISHING GROUP
Published by the Penguin Group
Penguin Group (USA) Inc.
375 Hudson Street, New York, New York 10014, USA
Penguin Group (Canada), 90 Eglinton Avenue East, Suite 700, Toronto, Ontario M4P 2Y3, Canada
(a division of Pearson Penguin Canada Inc.)
Penguin Books Ltd., 80 Strand, London WC2R 0RL, England
Penguin Group Ireland, 25 St. Stephen's Green, Dublin 2, Ireland (a division of Penguin Books Ltd.)
Penguin Group (Australia), 250 Camberwell Road, Camberwell, Victoria 3124, Australia
(a division of Pearson Australia Group Pty. Ltd.)
Penguin Books India Pvt. Ltd., 11 Community Centre, Panchsheel Park, New Delhi—110 017, India
Penguin Group (NZ), 67 Apollo Drive, Rosedale, North Shore 0632, New Zealand
(a division of Pearson New Zealand Ltd.)
Penguin Books (South Africa) (Pty.) Ltd., 24 Sturdee Avenue, Rosebank, Johannesburg 2196,
South Africa

Penguin Books Ltd., Registered Offices: 80 Strand, London WC2R 0RL, England

This is a work of fiction. Names, characters, places, and incidents either are the product of the author's imagination or are used fictitiously, and any resemblance to actual persons, living or dead, business establishments, events, or locales is entirely coincidental. The publisher does not have any control over and does not assume any responsibility for author or third-party websites or their content.

CON & CONJURE

An Ace Book / published by arrangement with the author

PRINTING HISTORY
Ace mass-market edition / April 2011

Copyright © 2011 by Lisa Shearin.
Map by Lisa Shearin and Shari Lambert.
Cover art by Aleta Rafton.
Cover design by Judith Lagerman.
Interior text design by Kristin del Rosario.

ISBN: 978-0-441-02018-8

ACE
Ace Books are published by The Berkley Publishing Group,
a division of Penguin Group (USA) Inc.,
375 Hudson Street, New York, New York 10014.
ACE and the "A" design are trademarks of Penguin Group (USA) Inc.

PRINTED IN THE UNITED STATES OF AMERICA

10 9 8 7 6 5 4 3 2 1

As always, for Derek

Acknowledgments

To Kristin Nelson, my agent. I couldn't do any of this without you. You're simply the best.

To Anne Sowards, my editor. You're amazing to work with. And in my opinion, the best editor in New York. Period.

To Joanne Stapley, an awesome fan. The winner of my Name That Book contest, with the perfect title: *Con & Conjure*.

To David Parker Ross, my first fan who wasn't related to me, and the winner of the Name That Goblin Assassin contest, with "Nisral Hesai" (a clever anagram of "Lisa Shearin").

To my fans. Your support and enthusiasm amaze me and keep me going. All of Raine's adventures are for you.

Chapter 1

There's no sick like seasick.

I knew this from personal experience; but fortunately, I wasn't the one staggering down the gangplank looking like death warmed over and served up.

Mago Benares was a banker, not a sailor. Or as his employees at the First Bank of D'Mai knew him, Mago Peronne. The name Benares wasn't exactly welcome in banking circles, since most people wouldn't want to trust their investments to a member of the most notorious criminal family in the seven kingdoms. Mago had changed his name, but nothing could alter his instincts.

The Benares family didn't get all of their money at the business end of a cannon. To Mago, embezzlement was an art, and he considered himself to be a master. This was one time when I had to agree with Mago and his ego. My cousin was at his con artist best when diverting funds, usually into offshore accounts for his own use and enjoyment.

But this morning, the master was as green as the money he stole. Seasick wasn't a good look for Mago. Or since he was now standing on a dock rather than a deck, I guess that made him just plain sick. I smiled. I couldn't help it. Don't get me wrong, I liked Mago; I liked him a lot. But when my normally impeccably dressed and groomed cousin was leaning over a dockside railing, disheveled, disreputable looking, and about to toss what was left of the last food he'd managed to keep down . . . well, call me twisted, but that was funny.

Mago tossed and Phaelan chuckled from where he was standing next to me. Phaelan's sense of humor was even more sick and twisted than mine. And yes, it's possible.

Though as Mago's little brother, it was Phaelan's job not only to embarrass him, but to make him miserable. I'd never seen Mago looking more miserable than he did right now, and Phaelan didn't have a thing to do with it. My cousins' dad was Commodore Ryn Benares, the most feared pirate in any body of water larger than a bathtub. Phaelan was a chip off the old mainmast. Mago was quite possibly the craftiest weasel I'd ever met—a weasel who couldn't set foot on a ship without feeding the fishes.

I'm a member of the family while not being in the family business. Yeah, I know what you're thinking. No one else believes me, either.

I'm Raine Benares. Like the rest of my family, I'm an elf. Unlike the rest of my family, I have a legal and moral job. As a result, every other Benares makes more money than I do. Hand-over-fist more. Believe me, crime most definitely pays.

I'm a seeker. I find lost people and missing things. Though the only things I've found lately are more ways to get into trouble and almost get myself killed.

And a rock the size of a man's fist is to blame for every last bit of it.

Ever since the Saghred latched on to me like a leech fresh off a hunger strike, I've been attracting the attention of the kind of people I've never wanted to have notice me.

And to turn my predicament from bad to as bad as it can get, the Saghred has taken my magical talents from mediocre to monstrous. I have more power than any living creature has a right to have or need to possess.

And therein lies my biggest problem. Other people want to possess that power for themselves—and to get the power, they have to get me.

That's why I asked Mago to come to the Isle of Mid. Mid was home to the top college of sorcery and the Conclave of Sorcerers, the ruling body for all magic users. I came here thinking that they could help me. It never occurred to me that they would be the ones who I would need protection from.

Conclave sorcerers, elven intelligence, and the goblin king. All wanted me and mine. And since they were funded by wealthy and powerful allies, their pockets were deep enough to make it happen.

Mago was here to help me cut holes in those pockets.

I knew that what could be paid could be diverted. And what could be schemed could be scammed.

My family had been behind some elaborate scams before, but none had involved this much money, government officials this highly ranked—and none had my life and the lives of people I loved on the line.

This time we were playing for keeps.

I was counting on our scam buying me enough time to get rid of the Saghred. Permanently.

Phaelan and I were in the office of a dockside warehouse, looking out of the dirty windows facing the harbor. The windows were a special kind of dirty—no one could see in, but we could see out.

Neither one of us particularly wanted to be seen right now.

In my opinion, Phaelan had made a monumental effort to blend in. My cousin was normally a vision in a scarlet leather doublet and matching trousers. Today his leathers were dark, his boots scuffed, his tanned face unshaven.

His hat had enough brim to conceal his face, not attract attention.

Phaelan took off the hat and ran one hand impatiently through his shoulder-length black hair. "Mago's certainly taking his time."

"He has to see to his luggage," I reminded him. "The man travels with even more clothes than you do."

"I have a reputation to maintain."

"Best-dressed pirate?"

"Someone has to maintain the standard." He took in what I was wearing, sighed, and shook his head.

I didn't need to look down at myself to see where Phaelan was going with this. "I happen to like brown and black," I said. "They're great colors for redheads."

"So are others that you've never tried."

"I've never tried painting a target on myself, either."

I'd adopted the mantra of blend and survive. Thanks to the Saghred, people could feel my magic coming a mile away; I was determined the same wasn't going to be true for seeing me. If wearing brown or black or both helped me blend in with the background and kept me from being a target at least some of the time, then they were officially my favorite colors. Red hair and pale skin made me stand out enough; I was going to camouflage as much of it as I could as well as I could.

Mago would be joining us here shortly. As a vice president at the First Bank of D'Mai, he couldn't be seen associating with criminals, either known or supposed. Mago knew the drill. He'd arrange to get his luggage sent ahead to the Greyhound Hotel, the finest accommodations Mid had to offer, and then we'd have a little private meeting. The warehouse's owner was a friend of the family, meaning he was paid to store stolen goods until they'd cooled enough to be put on the market. That pay also bought us certain benefits like a meeting place that could be counted on to be completely private. These walls only had ears if Phaelan wanted them to.

While we waited, Phaelan used the toe of his boot to push a bucket next to one of the office's chairs. I just looked at him.

"What?" Phaelan asked. "You want Mago throwing up on your boots?"

Minutes later, a miserable groan came from the open doorway.

Mago was your basic tall, dark, and handsome elf. Phaelan shared the dark and handsome moniker with his older brother, but Mago had "tall" all to himself. Phaelan had always claimed that Mago stole all of the height so there'd be none left for him. Probably not possible, but if it were, Mago would have been the one who could have stolen it. Mago Benares was the master. He could rob a man blind and have that same man thank him for his diligent work.

Though right now, the master was miserable. His dark eyes were bloodshot from what I imagine was lack of sleep, he was pale from lack of what he'd last eaten, and most of his black hair had escaped the silk ribbon that always tied it back.

Phaelan looked past him. "Damn, brother. Did you even close the door?"

Mago looked at Phaelan like he'd punch him if he could just convince his hand to make a fist.

I pushed the chair closer to where Mago was leaning shakily against the door frame. After a moment's thought, I pushed the bucket over to the chair. Mago looked at me and nodded gratefully at both.

Phaelan offered him his flask. "Here, this'll help."

Mago glanced distastefully from the proffered flask, to his little brother, and back again. "If that's the vile liquid that you consider to be whisky, I'll pass."

Phaelan shrugged. "Suit yourself. Never let it be said that I didn't try to help."

"By poisoning me."

Phaelan popped open the flask and raised it in salute. "Mother's milk."

"I'm certain that Mother would disagree," Mago said dryly. He gingerly settled himself in the chair, and I passed him my own flask.

"Caesolian brandy," I assured him. "And yes, it's a good year and vintage," I added before he could ask.

Mago took a tentative sip. Apparently he was satisfied, because his second sip was more like a gulp. Mago closed his eyes, and with a weary sigh, leaned his head against the back of the chair. "I may live. My thanks, Raine."

"Hey, you're here to help me stay alive. Returning the favor is the least I can do." I pulled up a chair and sat down. "Was it hard to wrangle the time off?"

Mago opened his eyes and managed a crooked grin. "Actually, I'm here on official bank business. One of my more affluent and private clients has need of some discreet financial services. He normally conducts business through an intermediary, but insisted on an in-person meeting this time. Considering the destination, I agreed to come only after negotiating a raise and a sizable bonus from the bank."

Phaelan laughed, a short bark. "That's my brother." He paused. "Why wouldn't anyone want to come here?"

Mago looked at Phaelan like he was a couple of coins short of a full purse. I think I was wearing a similar expression.

Mago wasn't going to dignify that question with an answer, so it was up to me to remind Phaelan why Mid was presently the next best thing to a hellhole. "Uh, Hellgate opened, demon infestation. Saghred opened, ancient evil mage infestation. Then Sarad Nukpana sucked out people's life forces and turned them into beef jerky."

"The Isle of Mid in its present state is hardly a vacation destination," Mago said. "I wasn't going to set foot on this cursed rock without hazard pay." He looked at me. "Speaking of a cursed rock, how are you doing?"

"Working day and night to find a way to get rid of the damned thing. I'm close. Really close."

I didn't say what I meant by "close." The only way I'd found to destroy the Saghred and break its hold on me was to empty the rock of the thousands of souls it held captive inside. The only creatures who could accomplish this monumental feat were Reapers—Death's minions, gatherers of the dead and dying. I wasn't dead or dying, at least not until they got hold of me. In their soul-sucking frenzy, they'd probably take my soul, too. "Probably" was too close to "definitely" for my taste. Needless to say, I was looking hard for other options.

"Pity the Saghred would eventually drive you insane," Mago was saying. "Do you have any idea of how much money you could make with that much power?"

"Unless it'd be enough to buy back my sanity and life, everyone can keep their money."

A sparkle of life—and avarice—lit Mago's dark eyes. "Until we relieve them of it."

That moment of bringing financial ruin to those threatening me and mine couldn't come soon enough.

"When do we start?" I asked him.

"As soon as I get my land legs under me." Mago paused and grimaced as if his stomach was considering doing something unpleasant. "And once I can keep a decent meal in me."

We all wanted that. Phaelan nudged the bucket closer.

"I'm hopeful that I can attain both states of equilibrium by tonight," Mago muttered. "I'm scheduled to dine with my affluent client this evening."

I frowned. "He's here already?" Call me paranoid, but most of the affluent people on Mid right now had a finger in the let's-get-Raine-Benares pie.

"My client has some financial transactions he wants to conduct, and he will only do so in person. So your request to come to Mid couldn't have come at a more convenient time."

"Well, we wouldn't want you to be inconvenienced on our account," I told him.

Mago glanced toward the office's windows. "His ship was not far behind mine."

Phaelan was already looking out over the harbor. "Would that client be a crazy goblin bastard looking to get himself shot full of holes?"

I quickly joined him. "What crazy bas—" I didn't finish the question; I couldn't. And people said I was nuts.

Prince Chigaru Mal'Salin, exiled younger brother of the goblin king, with a price on his head and every other body part, was brazenly standing in clear view near the bow of a luxury yacht sailing into the harbor. His personal standard was flying at the top of the ship's tallest mast, telling even the most clueless exactly who and what he was.

Phaelan was absolutely right. He was a crazy goblin bastard. Though his last name was Mal'Salin, crazy was in their blood.

Mago looked over both of our shoulders and saw what we saw. "Oh, bloody hell."

Phaelan clapped him on the shoulder. "Think about it this way, brother. If someone puts a bolt in him, you won't have to worry about keeping dinner down."

I didn't like Chigaru Mal'Salin, and unless his feelings had changed, the prince didn't like me, either.

It wasn't easy to forgive someone who had used a friend of mine as bait to kidnap me, and then threaten that friend with torture to get me to find and use the Saghred for him. I couldn't believe that his manners had improved any since then. The prince was cunning, manipulative, ruthless, and conspiracies and plots were recreational activities. In other words, a Mal'Salin. But unlike his brother, Chigaru could be reasoned with and he wasn't nuts.

Well, at least not as nuts as his brother.

I knew Prince Chigaru was coming to Mid; he just wasn't supposed to be here this soon. The prince had made the trip from wherever his last hiding place was for two reasons, and both of those reasons were because of his brother. One was in response to his brother's invitation to bury the hatchet and sign a peace agreement. The second reason was to overthrow his brother's government then bury that hatchet in one of his vital parts. Not directly, mind you. Direct confrontation wasn't the goblin way. Intrigue and subterfuge were the favored methods for two power-ful goblins to settle things once they'd reached an impasse.

Sathrik wanted his little brother dead. Chigaru had re-fused to stand still for any of Sathrik's assassins.

In goblin diplomatic parlance, this was called an im-passe.

In the face of such an impasse, Prince Chigaru's behav-ior was brazen at best, wantonly suicidal at worst.

Phaelan nudged Mago in the ribs. "Shouldn't you go out and greet your 'affluent' client?"

"I would prefer a bath and a change of clothes first."

"And see if he makes it to shore in one piece," I muttered.

"That, too."

Like elves, goblins were generally tall, sleekly muscled, and lithe with elegantly pointed ears. There, pretty much all resemblance between the two races ended. Sure, some elves had large black eyes, though none had a goblin's pale gray skin and sharp white fangs, but those weren't our big-gest differences.

I enjoyed intrigue as much as most of my family. But goblins took it to an entirely different level. For goblins, intrigue was a full-time, full-contact sport, played to the death—or to the win—whichever came first. And that fun-loving nature was multiplied to an absurd degree when goblins got anywhere near the Mal'Salin royal court.

And if a goblin's last name actually *was* Mal'Salin . . . well, you get the picture.

Then I noticed something odd, even odder than a goblin prince making himself into a two-legged target.

Chigaru Mal'Salin was standing alone.

There should have been crew swarming all over the

ship, preparing it to dock. There were crew working, but they were all careful not to cross in front of the prince.

Too careful.

I drew in a touch of power and focused it on Chigaru, to see him through the eyes of a seeker. The prince was shielded against magic and weapons. The spell protecting him was light and subtle, and completely invisible. I only knew it was there thanks to my Saghred-heightened senses. It was incredibly sophisticated work, like a tightly woven steel web that curved out in front of him like a protective shield.

The goblin prince was using himself as bait.

I looked over the crowds beginning to gather in curiosity at his arrival, and the dock workers going about their business. There were a few people—goblins, humans, and elves—whose eyes weren't on the prince and his yacht, but were intently watching others, scanning the crowd.

Just like I was.

Agents of the prince, ready to take down any hopeful assassins.

Agents of the prince's opposition, ready to take out the prince.

Chigaru was still a crazy bastard, but he was also crazy like a fox. Get someone to take a shot at him before he even set foot on dry land, his people pounce on them, interrogate them into revealing any accomplices, and he saves himself the trouble of spending every waking moment of his visit jumping at his own shadow.

Brilliant. In an insane kind of way.

I opened the door from the office and stepped outside onto the dock built adjacent to the warehouse. Phaelan came out with me. Mago stayed inside and out of sight.

"He's trying to get someone to take a shot at him," I said.

Phaelan heard me, but he wasn't scanning the crowd, or even looking at the prince. My cousin's dark eyes were intent on the busy harbor. It was the morning high tide and fishing boats of all sizes were coming in with the night's catch, and merchant and passenger ships were either setting sail or arriving.

I looked where Phaelan was looking. It was a pair of small ships, not much more than boats really, running protectively near the prince's yacht, guiding it in. I recognized them. Mid's harbormaster used dozens of them for patrolling the harbor and escorting larger ships. The pilot boats' sails were full, the canvas straining.

I didn't see anything wrong, but Phaelan obviously did. "What is it?"

"There's only one man on each boat. The pilots. Harbor regulations in every major port stipulate a pilot and two crew. And do you notice anything wrong with the wind out there?"

One boat was running slightly behind the other—intentionally hanging back. No mean feat with all that wind.

I froze. "Wait a minute." My eyes flicked to the goblin yacht's rigging. The crew had pulled the sails in, and what canvas was still up was far from full. The only air moving in the center of the harbor was a light breeze.

There was plenty of wind behind those two pilot boats, but it sure as hell wasn't natural.

A weather wizard. He or she was good, and probably about to split a gut moving enough air to fill those sails.

"And pilot boats keep themselves light, easier to maneuver," Phaelan was saying. "The one out front is riding lower in the water than it should." He scowled. "Way lower."

One man, one laden boat. Another behind, no extra weight. Oh crap.

I reached over and yanked Phaelan's spyglass out of his belt to take a look.

Elves. The pilots were both elves, in boats running alongside a yacht carrying a goblin prince—and the best hope for peace, a peace a lot of powerful elves and goblins didn't want. The extra weight on one boat didn't mean it was a suicide run with a hold full of explosives, but it didn't mean it wasn't.

I handed the spyglass to Phaelan. "I'm going out to take a look."

I couldn't walk on water out to those boats, but as a seeker, I didn't need to.

I'd only done a Sending a few times before. The last time I'd been trying to locate a kidnapped spellsinger. Someone with mage-level talent had blocked me then. Now, the only thing between me and my destination was half a harbor full of water. Water and I had an agreement. I stayed away from it and it wouldn't drown me. I came from a family of pirates and I couldn't swim for shit. Yeah, it was pathetic.

I steadied my breathing and tried to ignore the fact that one of those two boats could go boom within the next minute when it caught up to the prince's yacht, and I could be out there when it did. A Sending involved my essence leaving my body to do something it'd be impossible or ill-advised for my body to do—like hover over a boat possibly packed with explosives. I didn't know whether my essence could be blown up, but I didn't want to find out.

I focused my will on my destination, trying to convince my stomach and nerves that I wouldn't physically be going out over the water. Within moments, I felt myself rise out of my body and flow out over the harbor. As I crossed the hundred yards or so separating me from those boats, I clearly saw the pilot in the first one. Light brown hair, short military cut, chiseled features—everything perfectly clear, almost as if it were outlined.

Too clear to be real. Like a mask. Except it wasn't a mask, at least not one you could buy. It was magic, a glamour. That pilot wanted people to think that he was an elf. I looked closer. He wasn't shielded. The weather wizard would need to be within sight of the pilot boats, and there couldn't be any shield or wards between him and the boats he was moving.

And if your goal was to ram the lead boat into a yacht

and blow it up, there couldn't be shields of any kind between you and your target.

The wind in the pilot boat's sails faltered and so did its forward momentum. For only an instant, I got a look at who and what he really was.

A goblin. A goblin with a blood-red serpent tattoo on his cheek. That meant he was a Khrynsani assassin. The Khrynsani were an ancient goblin secret society and military order, and their assassins were even more fanatical than their merely homicidal brothers. I didn't need to look in that boat's hold; I could smell it, even over the stinking harbor water, I could smell it.

Nebian black powder. Regular black powder didn't have anywhere near the punch that the Nebian variety did. It was literally powder fine, highly unstable, and obscenely expensive. The impact of the boat against the yacht's hull would do the trick. Either the Khrynsani pilot was planning to blow himself up along with the prince, or jump out once he'd steered his boat close enough for impact, then swim like hell for the second boat.

Khrynsani were essentially the goblin king's enforcers. It looked like Sathrik wasn't even going to let his little brother set foot on dry land—unless one of his feet happened to fall there when he got blown to bits.

And the elves would be blamed.

The prince would be one of the first to die, but he wouldn't be the last. I didn't know how much Nebian black powder was actually in that boat's hold, but when the prince's yacht exploded, the flying debris could kill who knew how many. It was morning and the harbor was busy. And on shore, a crowd was gathering to watch Prince Chigaru's high-profile arrival, like sheep for the slaughter.

Countering the weather wizard's spell would take too long. Those boats weren't the only thing that couldn't be shielded while the wizard did his thing. He couldn't have magical obstructions or interruptions of any kind in his way.

That included personal protective shields.

His magical and metaphorical britches would be down around his ankles.

And when you were that focused on maintaining a spell as complex as calling enough wind to fill two sets of sails, broken concentration meant a broken spell. And if I wanted to get really vicious with my interruption, that spell could snap back on its caster. I was feeling particularly vicious right now. But to do it right, I needed to be back in my body.

Speeding across the harbor made me dizzy; coming back to my standing-still body made me sick. Suddenly seeing things through my body's eyes again was one of my least favorite parts of being a seeker. Disorienting at best, nausea inducing at worst. I took shallow breaths and blew them out in short puffs, willing the contents of my stomach to stay where they were. I didn't want to share Mago's bucket.

"Well," Phaelan said, "what'd you see?"

I told him who I saw, what they were disguised as, and what that lead boat was carrying. While I was telling, I was looking for the weather wizard behind all of the above. He didn't have to be behind the ships to push air into their sails, but it'd make his work a lot easier. I was hoping he went for easy.

I helped myself to Phaelan's spyglass again and looked in the direction the boats had come from.

Pay dirt.

There on a pier jutting out into the harbor was a figure in a black cloak with the hood pulled up. If two Khrynsani assassins weren't about to blow a hole in the water where the prince's yacht was, he'd be laughable. Bad guys could get away with a lot more if they'd stop dressing like they plotted world domination for fun. He appeared to be short. I guess he needed all the evil accessory help he could get.

He wasn't shielded or warded. He might as well have been standing there buck naked. There was nothing between him and me but about half a harbor. I could probably use my magic to kick him off the pier from where I was standing, but adding momentum to an already moving object would work even better.

Two dock workers were rolling a barrel down the pier. My best estimate put that barrel about twenty yards from the wizard. An instant later—after a little nudge from me—that barrel mysteriously escaped. The dock workers yelled, people ran, and the wizard stayed right where he was, oblivious, intent on maintaining his spell.

The barrel hit the wizard, the wizard lost his hold on the spell, and his feet lost their hold on the pier. Wizard and barrel hit the water together with a gratifying splash.

The spell stopped, but a sudden gust of real wind kicked in where he left off. The pilot boats actually picked up speed.

Oh crap.

Chapter 2

I estimated about thirty seconds before the prince's yacht was blown to kindling.

Time obligingly slowed to that speed that let me briefly ponder what it was going to feel like to go kablowie. A quick calculation told me that Phaelan and I would probably escape the blast, but odds were good that flying debris—flaming or just airborne projectiles—would do an equally good job of killing us.

I was no weather wizard, but I had to stop those boats. Now. Sinking the things would be the simplest solution, but I knew from nasty past experience that water and unexploded Nebian black powder didn't mix. I wanted to stop one explosion, not set fire to the entire surface of the harbor.

"Raine," Phaelan warned. "We need to get out of—"

"I'm stopping them," I said, my eyes focused on the boat with the black powder, drawing in my will to—

"Are you crazy?"

"Looks that way," I murmured, keeping my eyes on the lead boat. Moving a small object was simple, so was what I did with the barrel. This was going to be like locking on to the back bumper of a speeding coach with my teeth.

The Saghred had given me an obscene amount of strength. Even though that strength was a part of me now and not the rock, I still didn't like using it. It was like spending dirty money that could spend you right back, but I didn't have time to be squeamish. The pilot boat was traveling parallel to me and headed toward the docks and the prince's yacht. I extended my arm and clenched my fingers in the air, using my mind and magic to latch onto the boat near the stern—and braced myself.

I pulled back with every ounce of effort, magic, will, and sheer stubbornness I had.

And someone else did the same.

From the opposite direction.

Two mages using that much magic on the same object at the same time from different directions was tantamount to lighting the fuse on a bomb and then standing there to see what happened. A split second later, I spotted my competition.

Not one, but five goblin mages on the deck of Chigaru's yacht. The prince didn't travel with magical lightweights. They were strong, and worse, they could work together. I had the magical muscle the Saghred had given me. They were trying to push the boat away; I was trying to stop it where it was. A crack and snap of splintering wood sent its recoil up my extended arm. The pilot boat was going to disintegrate under our combined magic. Though if I let go, the mages would push the boat as far away from the yacht as possible, right into the middle of the crowded harbor, where it could run into any of dozens of ships. I was trying to keep the boat where it was to minimize collateral damage. The only lives the mages were concerned about were those of the goblins on the yacht; that their actions could cause other ships and crews to be blown to bits wasn't their problem.

I gritted my teeth. It was mine.

They shoved and I shoved back. Hard. The mages weren't going to stop. Suddenly, I didn't just want to stop them now; I wanted to stop them permanently. Yank them off of that deck and into the harbor. Their robes would weigh them down, but their deaths would be their own fault for refusing to obey—

Shit.

Nausea flipped my stomach, and having just flown over the harbor had nothing to do with it. My breath came in shallow gasps. Steady, Raine. You don't want to kill them, just stop them from what they're doing. Just breathe and do the work. Breathing got rid of the urge to throw up, but it didn't stop my heart from pounding at the thought of what I'd wanted to do, not only wanted, but had justified to myself all too easily. That was the Saghred talking, not you. Shake it off. Worry about it later.

The goblin mages kept up the pressure, pushing the boat away from them. I had no choice; I let the boat go, releasing it slowly to minimize the damage. Still the boat lurched in the goblin mages' collective grip. The planks were coming apart. Dammit to hell. Which was exactly where a good part of the harbor was going to be blown to.

The recoil from even a slow release of my magic threw three of the goblin mages backward like dolls. Even though I was no longer holding on to the boat's stern, I felt the hull shudder and the wood crack under the pressure. If one of those planks snapped the wrong way, the impact against those kegs would—

The world exploded.

I grabbed Phaelan, hit the dock, and threw the best shield I had around us both. I didn't know if it'd hold if a chunk of ship came flying at us, but there was no time to run, and we couldn't get far enough fast enough.

Phaelan covered his head—like that was going to help— and laid out a string of curses that'd make his crew proud. I confess I joined him for a few seconds.

The aftermath wasn't as bad as it could have been, but it

was bad enough. Other pilot boats abandoned their escort charges and became rescue vessels. There were people in the water and once the debris finally stopped raining down, the screams and shouts started. The mass of people on the shoreline had more than doubled.

Great, just great.

Flaming debris had started fires on the decks of at least four vessels, and at least one of them had been carrying something extremely flammable, judging from the panicked activity on deck and some crewmen diving over the side into the harbor.

I looked to the bow of the yacht where Prince Chigaru had been standing.

It was empty.

Empty didn't mean that he'd been injured; empty could mean the goblin was showing some sense and was doing what Phaelan had done—cower and cuss. But the number of goblins leaning over the yacht's railing and frantically searching the harbor below indicated that the prince had taken a swim. I couldn't see that being voluntary or good.

Dammit to hell again.

The thick smoke kept me from seeing the stern portion of the yacht.

"Can you tell if she's taking on water?" I yelled to Phaelan. It was the only way to make myself heard.

"She's not listing, but that doesn't mean she wasn't hit."

I ran down the boardwalk toward the dock closest to Chigaru's yacht. I'd been on Mid for nearly three months, and by now nearly everyone knew exactly who and what I was—or more to the point, what soul-sucking rock I was bonded to—and got the hell out of my way. For some, they threw themselves over the side into the harbor and thought that was the lesser of two evils. Smart people. I'd have joined them if I thought I could actually get away from myself.

I'd almost reached the dock, when a goblin I knew only too well pushed his way through the crowd, shucked his outer robe and dove off the pier after the prince, smoothly cutting through the water's surface like a knife.

Tamnais Nathrach.

Tam was a friend of mine and a former nightclub owner. Now he'd gone back to his old job as a duke and chief mage to the Mal'Salin family. He wanted to kick the king off the throne and put the prince on it, which had resulted in a big bull's-eye on his chest. Though right now, Tam was doing a fine job of killing himself before the king could by diving into flaming, debris-infested waters after a prince who hadn't enough sense to keep his head down when sailing into enemy territory.

If Chigaru survived his fall into the harbor, *I* was going to kill him.

I got to where Tam had taken a swan dive off the pier and looked down into dirty harbor water.

No prince. No Tam.

Phaelan shouldered through to stand next to me. He looked down in the water, shook his head, and winced. "Damn."

"Yeah, they're still under."

"I was referring to *what* they're under," Phaelan said. "I've seen what all gets tossed or dumped in a busy harbor."

"Good riddance to the goblin scum," a man's voice said from nearby.

Phaelan and I turned our heads to find the speaker. He picked that moment to shut up. The comment wasn't loud, but it was loud enough to earn him some mutters of approval from some of the people around us. Elves mostly, some humans. The murmurs spread and my hand inched toward my sword when a different man from farther back in the crowd said, "drown 'em all like cats" in a loud voice.

Some of the goblins heard that.

Great. Just great.

There was enough elf versus goblin hostility in the air to start our own little war right here. A good number of the elves gathered on shore were mages and their guards. If an elf shoved a goblin or a goblin said something to an elf, the boat would merely be the first explosion of the day.

A pretty, petite, and highly pissed goblin pushed her way through the crowd on a dock jutting out closest to the yacht, and frantically scanned the water. I couldn't hear the word she spat, but my lip reading was working just fine.

Imala Kalis was the director of the goblin secret service. Like Tam, she wanted the prince in and the king out, but nothing would put the brakes on a coup faster than the future king and his chief mage drowning.

Tam came to the surface, pulling in as much air as his lungs could hold, his arm locked around Chigaru's shoulders. The prince appeared to be out cold.

"Pakil. Zukat. Help the duke." Imala snapped and two goblins jumped. Literally.

Tam twisted in the water, and I saw it.

A crossbow bolt sticking out of Chigaru's shoulder. The explosion didn't throw him in the water; an assassin's shot did. The explosion must have made the prince drop his shield, just before that bolt arrived. Talk about bad timing.

The crowd on the waterfront was getting bigger by the second. Armed goblins were stalking through the crowd, looking for a hit man that they weren't going to find. Anyone hired by Sathrik to take out his baby brother would have enough sense to be long gone by now. Once he found out that his shot just took Chigaru in the shoulder, he'd be back for another try. But for now, he'd have ditched the crossbow, and was probably having a drink in a dockside dive.

Tam was climbing a ladder that extended from the water to the dock with Chigaru limp over his shoulder. The prince was almost as tall as Tam, and all lean muscle. Yet Tam was climbing that ladder like Chigaru weighed no more than a child.

Imala turned toward the yacht that was now being tied to the dock. "We need a healer!" For such a tiny woman, she had no problem making herself heard over the chaos.

A mage ran forward, leaping like a cat over the distance between the yacht's deck and the dock. He saw me and his lips pulled back from a pair of very impressive fangs in a snarl. Judging from his robes, he was one of the mages I'd played boat tug-of-war with; judging from that snarl, he recognized me, too.

Mage and healer, and both pissed. He clearly wanted to do something about it, but he had a job to do first. He glared at me and then knelt beside Chigaru, turning all of his attention to the prince. The bolt had taken Chigaru in the right shoulder just below the collar bone. I remembered Chigaru as being left handed. It wasn't going to kill him and it wasn't going to slow him down. Much.

"He's not breathing," Tam growled.

What?

Imala pushed her way through to him, while Tam quickly rolled the prince over and worked on getting the harbor water out of Chigaru's stomach. No water came out of the prince's mouth. The bolt hadn't hit anything vital . . . so how did . . .

Maybe all the assassin needed to do was get the bolt in.

"Tam, poison!" I yelled and tried to push my way through the crowd to him. Phaelan was right behind me. Most people got out of my way; the rest I shoved out of my way. Four needlessly large goblin guards rushed in to stop us. There's not really a polite way to lift someone off their feet and remove them from an area, and these guys didn't even try.

The goblin mage/healer glared at me. "She pushed the boat into us."

Instantly, every goblin on that dock was looking at me like I'd sprouted two horns and a tail. Mob mentality promptly took over. I felt the growls of the two goblins who were holding me clear down to my toenails. They clenched their hands around my arms like they were getting a better grip to tear me apart. Phaelan was on the receiving end of the same treatment.

And I couldn't say a damned thing to prove that I wasn't a prince killer.

The weather wizard controlling the boats had probably fished himself out of the harbor and was long gone by now. The pilots were blown up so there was no proof that they were Khrynsani, not elves. And to top it off, Chigaru's people were well aware that I didn't like him, and he didn't trust me.

It was too much and too complicated for anyone to believe.

"No one move!" Tam roared. That order was intended for every goblin on the dock and yacht, but Tam's dark eyes were leveled squarely on our over-eager guards. Their grip lightened. A little.

Imala knelt beside the prince, quickly pulling his long, wet hair away from his neck and throat. She hissed a curse, and pulled a tiny dart from the back of the prince's neck with her gloved hand. She quickly but carefully examined the wound, the dart, and lifted back one of the prince's eyelids.

"Baelusa," she told Tam.

I had no idea what baelusa was, but Imala's glare and Tam's spat curse told me it meant plenty to them.

The goblin healer knelt beside the prince, his healing magic a living, pulsing thing. He placed one hand over Chigaru's chest, holding the other a few inches above the prince's mouth. A spiral tattoo on the back of both hands darkened from blood red to almost black. I felt the steady strength of air being pulled into Chigaru's lungs and being pushed out from his nose and mouth.

The harbor around us was chaos, but no one on the dock moved or spoke.

Suddenly, the goblin prince gasped and started coughing.

Tam's glare went from the guards to the goblins gathered on the yacht's deck—the prince's courtiers, personal guards, and mages. Imala's eyes quickly took in the faces of everyone on that deck, storing them for later questioning.

One of them had just tried to assassinate their prince.

That dart had taken the prince in the back of the neck. The person who fired it had to have been standing behind him. Every goblin on Chigaru's yacht had been standing behind him. One of his own tried to poison him. Khrynsani disguised as elves tried to blow him up. And an unknown assassin armed with a crossbow wasn't about to be left out of the fun and took his own shot.

Someone—or several someones—wanted Chigaru *really* dead. Blown up, shot, and poisoned all in less than ten seconds. I think the goblin prince just set a new assassination attempt record.

Imala stood and carefully wrapped the dart in a small square of cloth. That done, she turned to our guards, who were still dutifully not tearing us in two. "Release them," she told them. "Now!" she snapped when they didn't immediately obey.

They did as ordered. As I straightened my doublet, I noted with satisfaction that she memorized their faces for later, too.

So there.

"Raine," Imala called with a pointed glance back at the fancy goblin courtiers on the yacht. "Would you be so kind as to tell me who fired this dart?"

Imala knew I was a seeker, and that finding or simply identifying someone based on their connection to an object was one of my best tricks. Phaelan and I walked over to her and not one goblin dared to stop us. I carefully accepted the cloth-wrapped dart from her.

I glanced at the healer. "When he removes that bolt, I might be able to tell you who notched it."

The head of the goblin secret service gave me a dazzling smile complete with dimple. "You'll have the eternal gratitude of the goblin people."

I knew of at least two goblin people who wouldn't be grateful—the ones whose faces I'd be describing to Imala.

As Tam stood up, one of the goblin guards picked up

his robe from the dock and respectfully draped it around Tam's shoulders. The robe fell past the heels of his boots, and even sopping wet, Tam looked like a prince himself. Though Tam would have been the kind of prince who could wake a sleeping princess at fifty paces. Just because we weren't involved didn't mean I couldn't appreciate what was there in all of its tall, silvery-skinned, black-eyed wicked sexiness.

Imala nodded to her pair of dripping-wet agents who moved to prevent anyone from leaving the prince's yacht.

"They were only doing their jobs, Raine," Tam said, his voice low. "Something blows up and a Benares is close by." He glanced at Phaelan. "Make that two."

Phaelan snorted. "They do their jobs too damned well. Raine was trying to stop that boat, not push it."

"And I had it until Chigaru's mages horned in on my spell," I said. "There wouldn't have been an explosion if they'd let me finish."

"Let you finish him off!" the healer snarled.

"Chatar!" Tam snapped. "She is not at fault. That will be all."

The goblin thought about saying something, and decided to do as ordered. I knew he wouldn't forget me, and for my own health, I memorized his face, too.

Tam's hand was on my elbow, steering me away from the prince, his trigger-happy guards, and spell-happy mage. Phaelan gave the healer an I'm-not-through-with-you-yet look and followed us.

"You can understand his animosity, Raine," Tam said. "Those pilots were elves."

"Those pilots were Khrynsani," I shot back. "Two of their assassins with glamours."

Tam scowled. "What?"

"You didn't see them when they dropped their glamours?"

"No. They were too close to the yacht."

Oh, freaking marvelous. Even the goblins thought

they were being attacked by elves. No wonder Chigaru's healer wanted to take my head off. The Khrynsani hadn't succeeded in blowing Chigaru up, and the assassin hadn't shot a fatal hole through him, but the damage had been more than done. Within the hour, every goblin on the island would believe that a pair of elven suicide bombers had tried to assassinate their prince. Regardless of which Mal'Salin brother they were loyal to, more than a few goblins would see it as their duty to start sending elves to slabs at the city morgue.

With an enraged shout and some decidedly un-regal swearing, Chigaru expressed his displeasure at that healer/mage removing the bolt. For what I could see, the healer had cut away the prince's leather doublet, revealing body armor underneath. Well, at least the prince wasn't completely stupid and had taken some precautions. The bolt hadn't penetrated far. I turned and looked at the shoreline.

There were a lot of civilians who didn't need to be here, and entirely too few city watchmen and Guardians. With the exception of his own people, Chigaru had sailed into Mid's harbor with no protection whatsoever.

"Why didn't you tell anyone he was arriving early?"

Tam lowered his voice even further. "I didn't know," he said barely moving his lips. Impressive. He clearly didn't want anyone to know that little piece of information. Tam shot an exasperated look in the prince's direction. "I didn't know until Imala told me, and she didn't know until half an hour ago."

Phaelan laughed, a short bark. "The crazy bastard's trying to commit suicide."

I looked at the prince and almost smiled. "Someone's going to get a lecture."

"And then some," Tam promised. "I know what he was trying to do—and I'll be having a long talk with His Highness about never doing that again."

"Playing assassin bait?"

Tam nodded once. He wasn't looking at the shoreline;

he was looking at the windows of the buildings within crossbow-sniper distance of the yacht. There were entirely too many of them, and the shooter was long gone, probably already planning his next attempt.

There couldn't be one.

If Chigaru died, the hopes of preventing the goblins from inciting a war died with him.

The goblin king wanted that war and he wanted the Saghred's power to ensure he'd win it. More than a few elven government power brokers wanted the rock for the same reason. Prince Chigaru might not have sense enough to display himself like a two-legged pincushion, but he drew the line at using the Saghred. He knew the danger and he'd rejected the rock.

That was why it was in my best interests to keep him alive by telling Imala Kalis exactly who wanted him dead.

A guard approached Tam, carrying something wrapped in a piece of cloth. "The bolt, Your Grace."

Tam took and unwrapped it. Black steel with a red band around the shaft below the fletching. Armor piercing. Our assassin wasn't taking any chances. Chigaru starting to fall into the harbor a split second before that bolt was fired was the only reason he was alive right now. Tam closely studied the bolt, but was careful not to touch it, then he handed it to me.

"Did the healer touch it with his bare hands?" I asked.

"Probably."

I looked at the healer, and found him glaring at me again. That one was determined to be a problem. That was fine; I could be a problem, too. I met his glare and raised him a solemn promise. It wasn't good to pick fights with people who thought you were in cahoots with a pair of suicide bombers, but he'd started it. Childish, I know. But I wasn't going to be intimidated, and Chigaru's goblins needed to know that from the start. Though it wasn't the best way to convince them that I was on their side.

I looked away from the healer. I was taking the professional high road. I could always memorize his psychic scent from the bolt for later.

I turned my full attention to the bolt in my hands. As a seeker by trade, I'd done a lot of work for the city watch in Mermeia, where I'd lived until three months ago. More than once I'd been called to a crime scene only to find that the object I most needed to use had been handled by nearly every watcher on-site, contaminating it and rendering it useless for seeking. It was their emotional imprint I'd get, not the perpetrator's. So the only person I'd find was the stupid watcher who'd last picked it up.

I should get three presences from the bolt: the healer, the prince, and the assassin. If any more than that had touched it in the last few hours, that could be a problem, but there was only one way to find out.

Tam glanced around. "You need someplace quiet."

"At least where everyone isn't looking at me like *I'm* the assassin."

Phaelan pointed at somewhere behind me. "How about over there?"

I turned and looked. The office for the harbormaster's men responsible for this dock. That'd work. I made for it, and found my way blocked by a big, burly, and belligerent dock worker.

"Sorry, ma'am. That's for harbor personnel only."

I didn't think he looked sorry in the least, but he was about to be.

As soon as I opened my mouth to say something I probably shouldn't, a familiar presence and voice came from right behind me.

"She's on official Guardian business. Step aside."

Mychael.

Suddenly all the chaos got less chaotic—at least people got a heck of a lot more polite.

A tall elven warrior wearing full battle armor tended to have that effect.

Mychael Eiliesor was the paladin and commander of

the Conclave Guardians, the most elite magical fighting force in the seven kingdoms, protector of the Conclave of Sorcerers, and the top lawman on the Isle of Mid—which essentially meant if it happened on this island, it was his business.

A few weeks ago, we'd become each other's business.

Not many people knew about that, and considering who and what I was, and who Mychael was, that information needed to stay as private as our activities.

"We need to talk," Mychael said. No expression, no hint of what might be going on behind those tropical sea blue eyes, just four words that rarely meant anything good.

I'd just played tug-of-war with five goblin mages and a boat full of explosives. It'd been the first of three assassination attempts on a visiting goblin royal before he even set foot on dry land.

Oh yeah, Mychael definitely wanted to chat.

He looked at the bolt I had in my hands. "Can you find who fired that?"

"If I can get somewhere quiet enough to hear myself think, I should."

Mychael glanced back at the prince and his wall of goblin muscle. "His healer seems to have things well in hand."

"He's working fast so he can come after me."

"Pardon?"

"Nothing."

Mychael nodded toward the harbormaster's office. That had to be the best suggestion of the whole day. There had to be at least one chair in there, and after all the magic I'd just slung around, I needed to sit down. We went in and Mychael closed the door. The only furniture was a table, a couple of chairs, and a cot in one corner. The cot was tempting but the sheets looked like if they'd ever been washed, it'd been in the harbor. With a groan of pleasure, I sank into the nearest chair and treated myself to closing my eyes.

"Are you all right?"

I opened one eye. "What? No 'why are you in the middle of an angry mob?'"

Mychael almost thought about smiling. "The answers to some questions are obvious. There's an explosion, then you and Phaelan are in the middle of an angry mob. Obvious." He took another chair for himself. "That and I had men watching the waterfront this morning."

I did smile. "I thought I detected a tail."

"As you should have since you weren't supposed to leave the citadel without an armed escort—and I told them not to bother hiding."

"I had a meeting," I said. "A private meeting. One that wouldn't have been private if I'd been leading a parade of Guardians."

"Did your meeting have anything to do with that explosion?"

"Not directly." I hesitated. "It was about our family project."

Mychael knew exactly what I was talking about. I'd told him weeks ago that if it was the last thing I ever did, I was going to ruin not only Taltek Balmorlan, but anyone else who had the poor judgment to pick that scumbag for a business partner.

"This is the other cousin you've told me about?" Mychael asked.

"That's the one. Phaelan's big brother. Apparently he's also Chigaru's personal banker."

Mychael blinked. "A Benares banker?"

I grinned. "He uses the name Peronne. But yeah, a Benares banker. Great, huh?"

"And convenient. However, he was nearly the *late* Chigaru's *former* banker."

"Came damned close. You hear what all happened?"

Mychael arched an eyebrow. "My men are trained observers."

"Did they observe that those bombers were Khrynsani assassins?"

"A few were close enough to detect the glamours."

"Too bad most every goblin on the waterfront isn't as gifted." I told him about my role in the boat tug-of-war and the messy results.

Mychael frowned. "Khrynsani assassins and a weather wizard. Was he a goblin?"

"Couldn't tell. He was cloaked, hooded, and gloved."

"He'd have to be a goblin. I can't see Khrynsani assassins trusting a human at their backs. Sounds like I've got a Khrynsani nest to find and clean out." Mychael indicated the folded cloth in my left hand. "Is that something else Imala and Tam want you to look at?"

I nodded. "The dart that took Chigaru in the back of the neck."

"The back?"

"Fired by one of his own courtiers. Imala wants to know who." I carefully peeled away the cloth, exposing what was essentially a black needle that was no longer than my last finger joint.

The dart still had the prince's blood on it, as did the bolt. Any contact with that blood and I'd be sharing Chigaru's shoulder-puncturing, virtually drowning experience. But if I wiped any of the blood off, some of the assassin's residue could be wiped off with it.

"Can you find out who fired it without touching it?" Mychael asked.

I winced. "Wish I could."

Mychael knelt on the floor next to me, and I could sense the heat of his body even through his armor. He wrapped his fingers around my hand holding the dart, keeping it steady to get a closer look.

"I can't see any residue of poison," he murmured. "But that doesn't mean—"

Some things could be resisted, but why?

I closed the distance between our lips. I had a bolt in one hand and a dart in the other and didn't dare drop either one, but my lips didn't need any help; they were doing a satisfying job all by themselves. I pulled away from the kiss only when the terror of nearly being blown up was replaced by wondering how I could get past Mychael's armor, and how long we'd have until someone started banging on the door.

There was nothing more life affirming than lust.

Mychael's grin was slow and wicked. "I would ask what that was for, but it doesn't matter. Thank you."

I felt myself finally start to relax. Sometimes a little lust was not only fun, but needed. "I'm just glad to be alive to do it. I don't go around asking for big trouble, but it's got a tendency to show up when I'm around."

"You'll get no argument from me," Mychael said. Then the grin was gone. "I'm also not going to argue with you about an armed escort."

I met him with silence. He knew how I felt about being stuck in the middle of a crowd of big, armored men. I might as well stay in the citadel, but I had the sense not to say *that* out loud.

I glanced down at the dart and bolt. "Well, the quickest way to get rid of the trouble is to find out who caused it. I don't suppose you'd step outside while I do this?"

It was Mychael's turn to give me the silent treatment.

"You're too noisy," I told him. He knew I didn't mean talking; I meant magical noise. Mychael was one of the strongest battle mages there was, and just being in the same room with him was playing havoc on my concentration. Having him within touching distance was doing the same thing to my control. Neither was conducive to locating a pair of potential assassins.

Mychael stood. "I'll sit on the other side of the room, and you won't even know I'm here."

After that kiss, I seriously doubted that, but I knew from past experience that Mychael could tamp down his magical power to next to nothing. Within five seconds, he'd done just that. It was as impressive now as it had been then.

"Are you going to stay in that chair?" Mychael murmured.

"Good point."

I got out of the chair and found myself a nice corner. With my shoulders wedged against a pair of walls, that'd be at least two directions I couldn't fall. The impressions I got from an object could be jarring, and since I was trying to find a pair of assassins, the hit from those links could very well put me on the floor. That didn't even factor in what it'd be like to feel Chigaru's impressions coming off of that dart and bolt. I'd done seekings before using items ranging from a bolt or blade to a necklace and hairbrush. The most recent use of the object was the one felt first. If a person had been killed with what I was holding, I'd get the treat of feeling what it was like to die right along with them. Chigaru hadn't died, but taking a crossbow bolt in the shoulder and falling overboard had to have hurt like hell.

Just do the work, Raine. Do the dart first.

The problem with touching a poisoned dart was not knowing how much poison was left on it. However, since Chigaru was still alive, the dunking in a harbor full of water must have been what'd kept the poison from killing him. Still, it wasn't a theory that I was eager to test, especially not on myself. The dart was tiny so I took a big chance and placed the tip of my index finger very carefully on the flat, non-pointed (and hopefully non-poisonous) end.

In the blink of an eye, I was seeing what the poisoner saw. I'd never had a connection that immediate, which meant this person was close by, very close by. Well, we knew that they were on the yacht, but what I was seeing now wasn't the yacht. It was the dock, or more precisely on the dock.

Kneeling at Prince Chigaru Mal'Salin's side.

Oh hell.

Chatar, the goblin healer/mage.

No, that couldn't be right. Chatar might be a jerk, but he was a jerk who'd just saved the prince's life. Why would he poison the prince and then save him? That went beyond not making sense, even for an intrigue-loving goblin courtier.

The dart showed me something else. When Chigaru was hit with the dart, he started falling to the left. Apparently this baelusa stuff was fast acting. *Then* the bolt took him in the right shoulder. If the prince hadn't been shot with that dart, he would have been standing straight when that bolt arrived, and it would have taken him right through the heart and he'd have been dead before he hit the water.

Saved by poison.

I carefully rewrapped the dart and set it aside. Mychael didn't say a word, and neither did I. I had my concentration and I didn't want to lose it.

I picked up the bolt and wrapped my fingers around it in a fist. A connection with Chigaru Mal'Salin was strong and immediate. The crazy goblin had *known* that he was going to get shot. He was counting on his people in the crowd to catch whoever was firing the shot. The prince had nearly fifty agents in and around the waterfront. Mychael didn't know that, and he needed to. His job was to keep the peace on Mid. Certain elves and goblins were spoiling for a war. Just because Chigaru's people were there to protect him didn't mean that the prince didn't have them here for other purposes.

A goblin seldom had only one motive.

A Mal'Salin could juggle dozens.

I'd been shot with a crossbow before, so I could anticipate some of what I'd feel. The jolt of the impact followed by white-hot burning, like what was sticking out of you wasn't a bolt, but a heated fire poker. The disorientation of falling backward off of the yacht, and pain of hitting the water. Chigaru's neck and shoulders had borne the brunt of the impact.

I blew air in and out between my clenched teeth to keep myself from doing the same, only falling against a filthy wall rather than in an even-more-filthy harbor.

Chigaru's unconsciousness severed my connection to him. I held up my hand to keep Mychael on his side of the office. He didn't like it, and he didn't need words to tell me so. I felt it. It took a few minutes for me to manage to sit up straight, but once I wasn't seeing two of everything, I searched further for the man—or woman—who'd held the bolt and loaded it into that crossbow. I followed the line that the bolt had taken, back to an open second-floor window. I saw a pair of hands first. The assassin was a man, and his hands weren't gray, so he was either an elf or human.

Then I saw his face.

My eyes flew open and I almost choked on my own breath.

Rache Kai. The deadliest assassin in the seven kingdoms. Our paths had crossed—and rubbed together.

Rache was my ex-fiancé.

I broke up with *him*. Let's just say it could have gone better.

Chapter 3

I looked at Mychael and felt a little sick.

Telling the man you were in love with that the man you used to be in love with was here on business was one thing. When your present love was the top law enforcement officer, and your past fiancé was the kingdoms' top assassin . . . well, the thought made you queasy.

"Well?" Mychael asked. A man of few words.

"I found both of them."

I stood and went over to the dirty window. Prince Chigaru was being carefully lifted onto a litter, loyal snake-in-the-grass Chatar by his side no doubt waiting for another chance.

Or was I wrong?

I knew I wasn't, at least I didn't think so, but it just didn't make sense.

"Raine," Mychael was saying. "Who is it?"

"Chatar."

"Who?"

"The healer out there working on Chigaru."

Mychael was instantly at the door, opened it and called to Tam. I didn't share Mychael's urgency. Chatar wouldn't try anything with Imala and her agents watching his every move, and guessing his next one. Tam stepped through the doorway and I told him what I'd seen.

"Raine, Chatar has been the prince's personal physician for three years," Tam said. "Are you certain?"

"It was fired from a small dart gun," I told him. "Chatar's hands loaded it. I saw the tattoos on the backs of his hands."

Tam glowered. "Damn."

"Ditto."

"I'll have to handle this carefully," Tam murmured. "Chatar is one of the prince's closest confidants." He left the office and gestured to Imala. You could have heard a fish scale drop on that dock as Imala crossed to him, and Tam leaned down close to Imala's ear. Her expression gave absolutely nothing away as she looked to me. When I nodded, Imala's eyes hardened, but she made it a point not to look at Chatar. Instead she tilted her head up and spoke quickly to Tam. He turned and came back to us.

"Imala will post agents with the prince and Chatar to keep another attempt from being made. She will question those on the yacht to get Chatar's whereabouts from the time the yacht entered the harbor until I brought the prince out of the water. His cabin will also be searched." He looked at me, eyebrows lifted.

"Yes, I'm sure. I don't know how he did it, but he did."

"What about the crossbowman?" Mychael asked.

"Well . . ." I started.

Phaelan had walked over to the doorway, and saw what had to be a sickly look on my face.

"I found our crossbowman," I told him. I paused. "I love it when my past comes back to bite me in the ass."

Phaelan knew precisely who I was talking about. "Tell me you're kidding."

"Wish I was."

"Dammit."

"And then some."

"Is he here for anyone else?"

"Don't know." And I didn't really want to know since that other person on Rache's to-kill list could very well be me. As angry as he'd been the day I broke off our engagement, he'd off me for free.

Mychael was looking from one of us to the other. "Who?"

"Want me to tell him?" Phaelan asked.

I sighed. "Might as well."

"Rache Kai," Phaelan said. "Heard of him?"

Mychael nodded. "Assassin. The best."

"That's the one." Phaelan looked expectantly at me.

I waved my hand. "Go ahead, tell him."

"He's also Raine's ex-fiancé."

"I broke up with him nearly a decade ago," I told a stunned Mychael. I did a little cringe of my own. "It really could have gone better."

Mychael's expression didn't give anything away. He quietly asked, "Where was his shooting perch?"

"I broke off contact once I knew it was Rache, but I can track him to the ends of the earth."

"She knows him *very* well," Phaelan added helpfully.

I shot my cousin a withering look.

"I didn't know who he was back then," I hurried to add. "I mean, of course I knew *who* he was. I didn't know *what* he was. I broke off our engagement when I found out. 'Young' and 'stupid' pretty much sum up my early twenties." I stopped blabbering, taking Mychael's continued silence as an accusation, when it was probably just an inability to get a word in edgewise. "Or didn't you ever do anything stupid when you were young?"

My fist had a death grip on the crossbow bolt. I wanted nothing more than to let it go, but I knew I wasn't finished with it yet—though no doubt the killer elf on the other end would gleefully be done with me. A bit of advice: before you get involved with a man, make sure he's not a killer for hire; and if he is and you decide to ditch him, make sure he's a crappy shot.

Mychael looked at me for a moment, a hint of a smile on his lips. "It's a wonder I lived to see thirty."

"I'm continually amazed that I lived through my teens," Tam muttered.

Phaelan grinned. "Hell, it's a good day for me when I live past breakfast."

Imala quickly strode over to Mychael. "I need transport through the city for the prince with a Guardian escort."

"Done."

"And I need a perimeter set up around the Greyhound Hotel."

"My men are already there." Mychael frowned. "Preparing for the prince's arrival, in *two days*."

Imala glanced at the prince and I swear she growled. "I didn't know." She said it like she'd already said it a couple dozen times today and knew she'd say it dozens more. Chigaru was going to get a lecture from the head of his secret service, too.

At least something good was going to come from all of this.

Chigaru's guards managed to get their prince into a coach and on his way to the Greyhound Hotel. The coach was surrounded by goblin guards, and the goblins were surrounded by Guardians. Mychael wasn't taking any chances that any of Chigaru's guards might be tempted to make a slight detour to take down any crossbow-toting elves. You could carry pretty much any weapon you wanted to around Mid; you just had to fill out reams of paperwork. Phaelan claimed that if your hand survived all the name signing, it'd be worthless for wielding the weapon you went to all the trouble to be able to carry.

Mago felt safe enough joining the prince at the hotel. Yes, he was an elf, but he wasn't carrying a crossbow, the prince knew him—but most importantly, the prince didn't know him as a Benares. A cover of a respectable mild-mannered banker definitely had its advantages, especially now.

Me? I had no cover and no hope of obtaining any anytime soon. If Sathrik had hired Rache, Rache had to know that I was on Mid. For all I knew, Sathrik probably slipped Rache a little something extra to turn me into a crossbow cushion, too. After I'd broken up with Rache, I went to a lot of trouble to get as much information on my professionally homicidal ex as I could. Sometimes survival just meant knowing more about your adversary than they thought you knew. I'd been ignorant about Rache once; I swore never to be that way again. Our paths had crossed several times since then, but never with fatal results. Though I'd always known that Rache was the patient sort.

"Rache prefers upscale accommodations," I told Mychael. "But he's willing to sleep in the dirt if his client pays him enough."

"Sathrik has always been willing to pay for what he wants," Tam said.

The goblin king was generous and giving—just what I didn't want to hear.

"At least he can't glamour," Mychael said.

"Not a spark of magic to his name, thank . . . what did you say?"

"Rache Kai can't glamour."

"And you know this, how?"

"I know Rache."

"Apparently not as well as you know Rache," Tam chimed in.

I wasn't going to dignify that with a response. Though Mychael's bombshell wasn't going to go unnoticed. "Personally or professionally?"

"What do you mean?"

"You know exactly what I mean."

Mychael was the Guardian commander, but in his former professional life, he'd also been a Black Cat. Officially, they had no name, though were called Black Cats by certain criminal elements who had the bad luck to come into contact with one. Like a black cat in a dark alley, you might catch a glimpse of one, but if you blinked, it was gone. Black Cat operatives had reported to the elven throne, were trained to do what was needed, where it was needed, and to whom it was needed, going where the law couldn't go.

Mychael had been one.

And Mychael knew Rache.

"I've had to stop him on more than one occasion," Mychael was saying.

"Has he seen your face?"

"Not my real one."

Rache couldn't glamour, but Mychael could; and as one of the best spellsingers there was, he could also alter his voice. A master of disguise was my Mychael.

"Did your 'not real self' piss Rache off?"

Mychael grinned. "Just every chance I got. We often found ourselves at odds."

Phaelan spoke up. "He'd been hired to off someone you'd been asked to keep alive?"

"Something like that." Mychael turned to me. "Which is why I want you off the streets as soon as you can tell me where he is."

"We know he's been hired to assassinate Chigaru," I said. "I've been walking around this island for three months now. Word spread pretty quick that I was here with the Saghred. If Rache had wanted me, he could have come and tried to get me anytime."

"You said Rache wouldn't kill a fly unless someone had paid him," Phaelan said.

I resisted the urge to punch my cousin. "I'm personal. Rache knew I was in Mermeia. He didn't come after me then, and he won't come after me now."

At least I hoped not.

"Unless you try leading every Guardian on the island to his hideout," Phaelan continued. "I don't know about Rache, but I'd take that personally."

And I was thinking about personally yanking my cousin behind the harbormaster's shack and kicking his ass.

I shot him a look that said just that. "We can stand around here talking, or we can go and get ourselves an assassin."

"Absolutely not," was Mychael's response when I said I needed to be there when they caught him.

"Mychael, just because I tell you where he is, doesn't mean he's going to stay put for you. By the time your men get there, he'll be gone. Rache can smell someone coming after him."

"And he won't be smelling you. I've caught him by surprise before."

"And he's still alive."

"So am I," Mychael countered.

"And so am I. You know I have to be at the front of your hunting party for this to work."

His frown told me he knew it and he didn't like it.

That made two of us.

I knew that finding Rache wasn't going to be easy. He knew me and he knew how I worked. Yes, I'd learned a lot as a seeker since I'd last seen Rache, but no doubt he'd been keeping up with me just like I'd been keeping up with him. And even though my seeking skills had been multiplied by a factor of a hundred thanks to the power boost I'd gotten from the Saghred, the rock had merely enhanced the skill set that I already had.

Rache knew that skill set. He'd volunteered to let me practice my tracking spells on him. He'd gotten entirely too good at staying one step ahead of me. I usually found him. Eventually. That was then and for practice. This was now and for keeps.

It didn't take me long to pick up Rache's trail. The impressions from the crossbow bolt had reminded me of any details that I had forgotten. I hadn't forgotten much, and it didn't take me long to recall every last bit of it. We found that he'd been staying at an inn in the entertainment district. It had the benefit of a lot of people coming and going, and no one really paid attention to anyone else. Everyone was focused on their own pleasure—unless their pleasure involved finding someone else. Rache had the knack for making people either not want to be anywhere near him—or to be very close to him.

Yep, I'd been young and stupid.

And I'd been in love. My first and, I thought, my last time.

Until Mychael.

When I was in training to be a seeker, I'd thought that tracking Rache was just good practice. Though if I'd been paying attention, I'd have noticed that he was way too good at staying one step ahead of me. Rache claimed to be a merchant, which explained why he traveled a lot. That he was a successful merchant explained why he would bring me such expensive presents when he returned. That certainly explained the travel, money, and the uncanny ability to avoid detection and capture. Not a skill set often seen in your average merchant.

But downright critical in your above average assassin.

"Anything?"

Mychael was about twenty paces back, giving me enough room to work, but when you share some kind of mysterious magical bond with someone that lets you talk to each other without speaking, personal space changes into something that's neither space nor personal. I hadn't minded until now. Being able to talk without speaking to the man I was sleeping with was fun, and being able to do it in public took it a couple of steps and a leap over from fun and into naughty fun. But having the man I loved inside my head while I was hunting the man I used to love took awkward to a whole new level.

"He's ahead." It was all I said because it was all I knew. Rache was still ahead of us. I couldn't sense that he was moving, but we didn't seem to be getting any closer to him,

either. The Rache I'd known and broken up with wasn't a magic user; he wasn't even a magic dabbler. Though maybe he'd lied to me about that, too. I didn't want to find out now that Rache followed our breakup with an extended period of self-improvement.

Just in case, I quietly muttered my personal shields into place. They'd deflect a crossbow bolt—or a novice magic user's attempt to fry me.

The farther toward the city center we got, the more uneasy I became. There were plenty of places for an assassin to hide—but only one was protected by wards, guards, and diplomatic immunity.

The elven embassy.

And guess what? That's where Rache's trail went cold.

The elven embassy was located half a block from the goblin embassy. And judging from the guards in full battle armor punctuating the walls around both compounds, everyone knew everything that had happened in the harbor. Everyone also looked entirely too eager to find a reason to retaliate. Retaliation of the painful, bloody, and deadly kind.

Neither Mychael, his Guardians, nor I shared the same homicidal need.

All of us were presently standing between the two embassies, but across the street from either one. I wasn't comfortable with our proximity to either embassy's range of fire. I think some of Mychael's boys were beginning to reach the same conclusion.

"This isn't a good place, sir." Leave it to Vegard to say what we were all thinking.

Mychael's stony gaze went from the elven embassy to the goblin embassy. "Which one?"

I knew that question was for me, and I also knew that I had no idea how to answer him. I stood a fifty-percent chance of being right—or wrong. Truth was, I didn't want to go into either place. I'd been inside the elven embassy once, gotten trapped, damned near died, and didn't want a repeat of either experience. I hadn't been inside the goblin embassy, but if the exterior trappings—sharpened black iron stakes for fence railings, and blood-red wards sizzling on the gates—were any preview of what waited inside, I'd rather stand here in the street. Not to mention, I was an elf, a member of the race that all believed just tried to kill a goblin prince.

Embassy Row was normally crowded with coaches and pedestrians this time of day.

There wasn't a living soul to be seen.

People knew what had happened. They were smart enough to stay away from the elven and goblin embassies. If someone fired a shot or launched a spell, Embassy Row would turn into ground zero for the beginning of a war.

Unless they were crazy, people usually stayed away from war zones.

We were standing right in the middle of the street. I guess that made us several kinds of crazy.

The elven embassy looked like it was expecting a full-scale attack at any moment. The guards appeared ready to shoot anything that moved wrong. And to put the paranoia icing on the cake, the embassy actually had battlements complete with armed and patrolling guards. Some of those guards had partners—nearly waist high, dark, sleek, and red eyed. Werehounds.

Rache had tried to kill Prince Chigaru—a goblin. There were plenty of goblins who wanted him dead, but so did a lot of elves.

Left or right. Elf or goblin.

Take your pick.

I didn't want either one.

"This is a quandary," Vegard noted.

My Guardian bodyguard had the gift for ultimate understatement.

I looked back toward the elven embassy. A man I knew only too well stood on its marble stairs, watching me, wearing the same smarmy and smug expression he usually did.

You could see Taltek Balmorlan in a room and look right past him—which was exactly what the elven inquisitor wanted. The word that described him best was average. His hair and eyes were an unremarkable shade of dull brown. He was of average height with average looks. There was absolutely nothing remarkable about his appearance.

It was perfect camouflage for the predator he was.

Balmorlan wanted war with the goblins. Balmorlan would want Prince Chigaru dead.

Taltek Balmorlan wanted me.

He was an inquisitor for elven intelligence. That was his job title. What he actually did was deal in weapons, and in a world of magic, mages were weapons—so Balmorlan dealt in mages. I called it kidnapping; Balmorlan called it doing business. Guess who was at the top of his shopping list?

I stepped out into the street.

"Ma'am," Vegard cautioned.

Mychael didn't say a word either out loud or inside my head. He knew what Balmorlan had planned for me.

Unable to get his hands on the Saghred, the elven inquisitor had found a way to bond other mages to me, which would allow them to tap and use the Saghred—by using me. He'd had a warded cell built in the elven embassy with Level Twelve wards, detainment spells layered for strength, and magic-depleting manacles bolted to the walls.

All he was missing was me in those manacles.

I was Balmorlan's target.

And he was mine.

Rache's trail ended here. With all the wards and spells protecting both embassy compounds, he could be in either one, though I was leaning toward the elves as Rache's latest clients. Taltek Balmorlan and his elven government allies had access to more money than was in the elven royal treasury.

He could afford Rache. Easily.

Besides, Imala Kalis was firmly in control of the goblin

embassy. She was working every waking hour to plan the coup that would kick Sathrik off the throne and put Chigaru on it, not put the prince in the Mal'Salin family crypt.

I stood there, letting Taltek Balmorlan get an eyeful. It was all he was going to get, and I gave him a smug smile of my own to let him know it.

"Is he in there?" Mychael asked out loud and from right behind me, then he stepped up to stand by my side. I felt a surge of satisfied delight. Mychael and I were in the middle of Embassy Row. Vegard wasn't with him, so he'd obviously asked him and his men to wait on the other side of the street.

Mychael beside me was an obvious challenge to Taltek Balmorlan—or Rache. Mess with my woman, and you mess with me, his posture said.

"I want you now," I murmured.

"Right here in the street?" I heard the smile in his voice.

"What's wrong with that?"

"You're a bad girl, Raine Benares."

"You bet I am."

"Can you sense him?"

"Not with all the distortion."

"Those aren't the same wards the elven embassy typically uses," Mychael told me.

"Heavy-duty mage work?"

He nodded. "They're blocking anything from getting out."

I didn't need three guesses as to what—or who—that something was.

"Can you get in?" I asked.

"Not without a warrant, and by the time I got one, Rache Kai would be long gone."

That was when the shot came. It didn't come from the elven embassy or the goblin embassy. It came from the building behind us.

I heard the whistle of an incoming bolt.

Everything went into slow motion. Mychael shoved me

away from him and twisted his shoulders and chest sharply to the right. The bolt glanced off of Mychael's breastplate with a metallic spark.

Armor-piercing bolts.

Rache wasn't aiming at me.

That shot was intended for Mychael. If his reaction time had been any slower, he'd be dead.

I clearly saw Rache in a third-story window of the building behind us. The bastard wanted us to see him—wanted me to see him kill the man I loved. Then in a blink, Rache was gone and the window empty.

So were the stairs of the elven embassy.

No Rache. No Balmorlan.

No answers.

Chapter 4

I thought I would be the one sharing Rache's crosshairs with Prince Chigaru.

I was wrong.

We searched the building Rache had used for a killing perch, which conveniently for my homicidal ex was a Conclave office building that was being renovated, so there were no occupants who would have been very-much-needed witnesses. Even more frustrating, the workmen who were there had been on the lower floors and hadn't seen anyone.

Right now I didn't know if someone had paid Rache to kill Mychael, or if he was making this hit a personal vendetta. The potential who, why, and how much didn't matter. The bottom line was that Rache wanted Mychael dead, and if no one was paying him that meant that in some twisted way, it was my fault.

And to make the situation worse—if that was even possible—I hadn't known he was there until his bolt hit Mychael's armor. That meant a veil of some kind. Rache didn't have magical talent, but it was possible that his employer had given him an amulet personally keyed to him whose purpose was to veil his presence. I'd encountered them before, but they were obscenely expensive. But if Taltek Balmorlan could afford to fund the start of a war and retain Rache's services to help that war happen, he could certainly afford a custom-made magical trinket.

We were walking quickly back to the Greyhound Hotel. Mychael had set the fast pace. He wasn't trying to put distance between him and the man who tried to turn him into roadkill. Mychael wanted to get back to the scene of what he considered the bigger crime and Prince Chigaru as quickly as possible. There were plenty of Guardians there, and a senior knight to act in Mychael's stead, but when a hopefully future head of state was poisoned, shot, and nearly blown up, that was a situation that needed to be handled by the paladin himself.

Mychael's scowl mirrored my own. We'd chased Rache halfway across town, and now we were coming back empty-handed. Mychael took that personally.

So did I.

Rache had gotten away from me twice in one day, and that pissed me off. Though Rache had missed his target twice, and I *knew* that would piss him off. Rache didn't miss.

Though what bothered me the most was that for all intents and purposes, Mychael completely blew off the fact that Rache Kai had just tried to kill him. And Vegard and the other Guardians didn't seem all that bent out of shape about it, either.

I nearly had to run to keep up with Mychael's long strides. "So world-class assassins take shots at you every day?" I snapped.

"What?"

"Rache just tried to skewer you and you don't care."

"Trust me, I care."

"You don't act like it."

"Because I have a worse situation on the waterfront and at the Greyhound. We didn't catch Rache, and my time was wasted."

"And your life was damned near ended."

"Damned *near*. I won't forget the attempt, but it was just that, an attempt."

"So you're not concerned?"

"At the moment, I'm more concerned with keeping Prince Chigaru alive. And with three assassination attempts before he even set foot on dry land, I think we can count on everyone who tried before trying again. *That* concerns me."

We went around the next corner and the voices coming from the waterfront were like a solid wall of sound. That was one of the things you could always count on from a crowd that's just seen a big explosion—the smart ones had gotten away, leaving the morbidly curious and the brainless gawkers, and the only thing either group did was get in the way of everyone who was trying to clean up the literal and political mess.

Mychael apparently trusted his men to deal with it all. He didn't even pause, but headed straight for the Greyhound Hotel.

Prince Chigaru Mal'Salin had reserved nearly the entire hotel—a palatial structure in the center of the Judicial District built to accommodate visiting dignitaries and obscenely wealthy mages and students' parents. I was used to inns where the smoke was as thick as the coffee. In my opinion, all the polished marble and gilded woodwork was a bit much, but I wasn't the one footing the bill.

What I saw filling the entire wall behind the registration desk caused a twitch to take up residence in my right eyelid.

A mirror.

I looked around the room. More mirrors, ridiculously large and abundant mirrors.

Some people were content to merely ask for trouble; the hotel's owner was on his knees begging for it. All kinds of nastiness could get into a room through a mirror. Assassins, spies, black mages, demons. Prince Chigaru had dodged death three times already, and it wasn't even lunchtime.

I couldn't believe this. "Who the hell thought those were a good idea?" I asked Mychael.

He looked where I was looking. "I'm not fond of them, myself."

I couldn't believe what I was hearing. "Not *fond*? They're unwarded mirrors. What kind of lunatic would—"

"I had my best mirror mages check them. They're completely warded."

"But they aren't all"—I made a wavy motion with my hand—"nauseatingly ripply."

Warded mirrors rippled; rippling mirrors would make a lot of hotel guests sick. I could see where that would be bad for business.

"It's a special kind of warding," Mychael said. "I had a mirror mage friend of mine check them again last night. He assures me that nothing's coming in that way."

Imala was waiting for us in the lobby, though waiting normally implied patient and calm. Imala was neither. The head of the goblin secret service was pacing, and judging from the floor space available all around her, her people were very smart.

They were staying out of her way.

She spotted us and closed the distance. "Well?"

"He tried to kill Mychael, too," I told her.

Imala's expression didn't change. "And?"

I didn't think anyone could be less concerned than Mychael about Rache's second target, but I was wrong.

"And we didn't get the bastard," I told her.

Imala didn't say a word; instead she closed her eyes and inhaled slowly. Yep, the lady was frustrated to the point of violence. We had three assassins and only one of them was in something resembling custody. Imala's day was far from over.

"Raine, I know you did your best," she told me.

I was sure Imala meant it, but what she said wasn't what I heard. "You did your best" ranked right up there with "I'm disappointed" as far as I was concerned. Both sounded nice enough, but it didn't make me feel any better about failing. You couldn't sugarcoat failure. The only thing that would cure that was having Rache trussed at my feet. Feet that would kick him a few times before anyone official could haul his sorry ass away.

"And it wasn't good enough." I paused. "I know him, Imala. I'll find him."

"Know?"

I told her exactly how well I knew Rache Kai.

She laughed, and a few of her people backed away even farther. "For many goblins, such a relationship would be cause for boasting, not shame."

"What have you found out from the healer?" Mychael asked her.

"That he's telling the truth; or at least he thinks he is."

"Meaning?"

"Chatar was with the other four mages attempting to push the boat away—"

I started to explain that I didn't shove the boat into the yacht, but Imala held up her hand.

"Tam told me what truly happened. Thank you for your attempt. You risked much to make it. Our mages misunderstood what they saw and counteracted your efforts."

"The mage was telling the truth . . ." Mychael prompted, encouraging Imala to continue.

"I have witnesses," Imala said, "the trustworthy kind, who say that Chatar was on the stern of the yacht with the other four mages. However, I also have equally reliable witnesses who place Chatar near the prince when the attack came."

"So who's lying?" I asked.

"Neither. All honestly believe that they are telling the truth. Tam and I have questioned them ourselves. Both of us are quite adept at discerning falsehood."

"Was there any magical hanky-panky with your reliable witnesses' minds?"

"None that we can discern."

"Did you find the weapon?" Mychael asked.

Imala shook her head. "Nothing was found on Chatar's person or in his cabin." She shrugged. "But that means little considering it could have been easily disposed of in the harbor following the explosion."

"Where is Chatar now?" I asked.

"In his room. He's being guarded, but for the moment, that is all." Imala smiled, very slightly. "He claims you accused him because he and the other mages stopped you from assassinating the prince."

I snorted. "And what about his own colleagues pointing the finger at him?"

"He says he was framed by rivals."

"So, let me get this straight. Everyone on that yacht considers themselves to be loyal to the prince, yet there are rivalries strong enough that they'd frame each other for murder?"

"These are goblin courtiers, Raine. Rivalries start in the crib. Intrigues begin when we can walk."

"Damn."

She shrugged. "It's the way of our people."

"It's a wonder anyone sleeps at night."

"We sleep mostly during the day." Imala's smile broadened until her dimple showed. "And then we find it advantageous to be light sleepers."

Mychael needed to see Prince Chigaru—and Chigaru wanted to see me.

Just when I thought my day couldn't get any better.

Imala escorted us up to the prince's suite herself. It was protocol and polite, but mainly it kept two elves from being met with drawn steel and bad attitudes. Imala knew at least I would respond accordingly. That was what she really didn't want—any of her people to get themselves permanently dead because they were momentarily cocky.

Tam met us in the sitting room in the prince's suite. He was dry and once again perfectly groomed. His robes were mostly raw black silk with velvet trim. They swept the floor but were slit up the sides to show fitted leather trousers and boots. Tam shared my opinion about robes—they were fashionable deathtraps. Trying to fight or run away from someone or something bent on killing you was best done with unencumbered legs. I'd imagine that was ten times as true in the goblin court. Tam's hair fell in an ebony sheet down his back, and was held away from his face by a silver circlet set with a single ruby. A silver chain of office was draped over his broad shoulders.

We told him what happened with Rache, what nearly happened with Mychael—but most importantly, what didn't happen. No Rache Kai in chains. Tam hissed a particularly descriptive obscenity in Goblin.

"I couldn't have said it better myself," I told him.

Chigaru Mal'Salin was sitting up in bed and doing a fine job of holding court for someone who'd survived three simultaneous assassination attempts just a few hours before. His shoulder was bandaged; his waist-length hair spilled over the opposite shoulder in a blue-black wave. His smooth and leanly muscled chest was bare. A silk bed jacket lay on the bed beside him, untouched.

No doubt some of the prince's confidence came from the fact that his suite was packed with guards and retainers—all armed, all eager to use their weapons. Some of the goblins in the room with him also wore their black hair loose, while others wore theirs in braids, elaborately entwined with silver chains and caught at the base with jeweled clasps. They wore earrings with fine chains linking them to cuffs attached to the ear near the pointed tip. All were stylishly attired in dark silks and velvets, though some wore intricately tooled leather and blued steel armor in addition to their finery.

The prince smiled fully, exposing a pair of pristine and sharp fangs. "Mistress Benares. Paladin Eiliesor. I'm delighted to see you."

"Too bad you weren't able to tell your guards that down at the docks," I said.

The prince waved a dismissive hand. "They are merely protective of me. Please excuse their behavior if you found it disquieting."

"Call me rude, but I have a problem excusing behavior that involves threatening to rip me in half."

"They meant no harm. Their reaction was not part of my plan—and neither was your interference."

Interference. Not "thank you for saving me from my own stupidity." Or "I'm sorry that my self-absorbed behavior could have killed hundreds of people." Or even "my sincere apologies that you risked your life to save my selfish skin."

Interference.

I didn't say any of those things out loud. I wanted to. Badly. I thought my restraint was nothing short of amazing. Going down that path wouldn't accomplish a thing. Goblins thought differently from elves. Hell, goblins thought differently than any other race. To them a threat of murder was simply overprotective and harmless. And if Chigaru's guards had succeeded in offing me, the prince would have referred to it as an unfortunate misunderstanding. A misunderstanding for him that would be unfortunately permanent for me. As Imala said, murder and intrigue were merely another way to pass the time at the goblin court; neither was met with much, if any, concern.

And now, Prince Chigaru was pissed at me, or at least regally annoyed. I saved his life and he blamed me for interfering with his plans.

"Did this plan of yours involve getting yourself shot, poisoned, and blown into fish food?" I asked mildly.

All signs of amusement vanished and the prince waved his courtiers out of the room. Tam, Mychael, and two guards remained. From Chigaru's unchanging expression, he gave them no more regard than he did the furniture. What a guy.

Just before the last courtier closed the door behind him, I saw the curious and smugly knowing faces in the adjoining sitting room. I was in the prince's bedroom; he was in bed half-naked—or maybe even all the way naked under those covers. His servants probably knew, but I didn't, regardless of what the courtiers' smarmy faces implied. I had a sudden urge to go out and punch some goblin nobles.

"My plan was to take any assassin alive—not have them blown to bits," Chigaru told me.

"Which would not have happened if your mages had let me finish what I started."

"They were under the impression that you were there to finish me. After all, you are an elf."

"And everyone knows that we're all chomping at the bit to kill every Mal'Salin we can aim explosives or a crossbow at, right?"

"You have to admit that the vast majority of your people would not pass up the chance to kill a member of my family."

That did it.

"Contrary to what you may believe, Your Highness, the vast majority of elves don't plot your demise on a daily basis; in fact, I'd be surprised if any of them gave you a second thought—or even know who the hell you are."

Chigaru didn't move. Neither did his two guards. In fact, they didn't even blink. I resisted the urge to further insult the prince to see if they were real.

"Tamnais tells me that I've had the dubious honor of being shot by the infamous Rache Kai, and that I have you to thank for identifying him."

That was as close to gratitude as I was likely to get.

"Thrilled to help," I drawled.

Apparently Tam hadn't mentioned that I knew said

killer and had nearly married him. That was one detail I could go without the prince knowing.

"And once you reached Embassy Row, you lost his trail."

"The magical distortion around the embassies kept me from following him any farther." I wasn't about to tell him that he'd taken a shot at Mychael. He didn't need to know that, either.

"But you believe him to be in the elven embassy," Chigaru pressed.

Mychael spoke. "We have no proof of that, Your Highness."

"Ah, but that is what you believe."

"It's probable," he replied. "Considering that Director Kalis is in control of the goblin embassy, I doubt any of her people would welcome an elf—let alone an elven assassin—with open arms."

"Your Highness?" Tam cast the barest glance at the two guards flanking Chigaru's bed. Chigaru might consider them furniture, but Tam knew that anything and anyone could also be ears.

Chigaru spared a quick glance at each of them. "I will be quite safe with the chancellor, paladin, and Mistress Benares."

As the two guards left, I gave Tam a bemused look. "Chancellor?" I mouthed silently.

Tam shrugged. "It's a title."

The door closed and the prince's full attention was on us. "There, is that better?"

"Very much so," Tam told him. "Until your power is secure, the fewer people who are privy to your meetings, the better."

Chigaru leaned back against the pillows, getting comfortable and taking his sweet time doing it. "I would like your opinion, Mistress Benares."

That was going to get real old, real quick. "Let's just make it Raine, and get it over with."

The prince flashed a smile full of fang. "If you insist."

"No, I don't insist. I can only take being called 'Mistress Benares' so many times. Raine is my name, so you might as well use it."

Chigaru flashed a smile that most women would have swooned over. "And it's much more friendly."

"I can assure you, friendly is the last thing I feel about you; but if believing that makes you happy, go right ahead."

"Tam tells me that the men who tried to blow up my yacht—and me along with it—were goblins, not elves."

"That's right. When they realized that they were going to be blown up along with it, they dropped their glamours. Staring death in the face can make you lose your concentration."

"They were Khrynsani assassins."

I nodded. "Apparently your brother cares enough to hire only the very best to kill you."

"Others wish my death as well, Mistress—" He gave me that swoon-inducing smile again. "Raine. Some I know of. Others I suspect—and others remain hidden from me."

"They were Khrynsani," Mychael said. "That means your brother or Sarad Nukpana, probably both."

"The services of Khrynsani assassins can be purchased."

That was surprising. "They freelance?"

"Virtually any goblin in Regor will sell something they value for the chance to be owed a favor by a powerful member of the court," Tam told me. "That includes assassins."

"A wealthy court noble could be trying to buy his or her way into my brother's good graces by proving that those assassins acted under their orders," Chigaru said. "Sometimes favors or putting another in your debt is more advantageous."

And framing the elves while they did it. The elves were going for the straightforward approach of hiring Rache.

"I know you didn't ask me here to tell me all about goblin court politics," I told Chigaru. "I have an assassin to track down, so if you don't mind too terribly, can we just get on with it?"

I swear the prince squirmed, and if possible, he actually looked more arrogant. Someone was feeling a tad defensive. This could be fun. I was long overdue.

"Raine has had a long day, Your Highness," Tam said. "Sometimes the easiest way to do something is to simply ask."

The only thing Chigaru looked like he was going to do was simply be sick. "I would like . . ." The prince stopped as if he were about to choke on the words.

Tam sighed. "Chigaru, we have spoken of this on more than one occasion. To make such a request is not a sign of weakness, but one of strength."

"I require your help. In Regor." The words weren't exactly rushed, but the goblin prince did get them out before he managed to gag on them.

I wasn't letting him go that easily. "*Require* my help?"

"I . . . I need your help."

I kept my expression blank. It wasn't easy with the snicker lodged in my throat. I think Tam wanted me to make Chigaru squirm. That was the kind of help I was only too happy to give. "I see. And does this need include me beside you in this Execution Square I've heard so much about from Tam and Imala? Because being pulled apart by four horses isn't the way I plan to die."

The prince spoke through gritted teeth. "If we do not fail, there will be no executions."

"I'm not talking about failing. I'm talking about not going to Regor. Period."

Chigaru drew himself up regally; at least he tried. Not easy to do with all those bandages. Oh yeah, here comes the royal proclamation. I had news for him, I wasn't—

"Thousands of people will die if you do not help."

Ah, the good old guilt trip. There was nothing like the classics.

"They need you . . . *I* need you."

Damned if he didn't look sincere. I shot the barest glance at Tam, and got the barest nod in return. Dang, playtime was over; just when I was starting to have fun.

"I came to Mid early for a reason," Chigaru told me.

"Other than setting yourself up for use in target practice?"

"Actually Raine, he does have a reason. Mychael, you need to hear this." Tam shot Chigaru a chastising look. "It would have been better if this intelligence had been communicated to us earlier. Much time has been needlessly lost."

Not only was playtime over, so was waiting for the prince to remember his manners and invite me to sit down. The only chairs in the room were those fragile things ladies perched on while drinking tea from absurdly dainty cups. I sat down, crossed my arms, and gave the prince my best glare.

"Word has reached me from agents in my brother's court that Sathrik and Sarad Nukpana have begun preparations for when the Saghred is in their hands."

Talk about putting the cart before the horse.

Mychael frowned. "The Saghred is in our citadel, defended by over five hundred Guardians. It's buried, spellbound, and warded."

Chigaru shrugged. "My agents say that Sarad Nukpana prepares as if that is of little consequence." His dark eyes narrowed to black murder. "And my brother prepares to force the woman I love to marry him."

That was more than a little concerning. Nukpana's confidence, not the woman-I-love part. Sarad Nukpana wasn't one to be confident without a reason. If he thought he had a way to steal the Saghred from underneath the Guardians' collective nose that meant that he had one. We had enough problems on our plates right now without Sarad Nukpana coming up with some secret, sinister, and ultimately successful plan.

"Mychael, he's building the base for a Gate," Tam said.

Oh, holy hell.

A Gate is a mage-made tear in the fabric of reality. You could walk through a Gate like stepping through a door, except that doorway could cover miles instead of inches. A Gate is conjured with magic of the blackest kind, fueled by terror, torture, despair and death—the more the merrier.

It was right up Sarad Nukpana's dark alley.

I'd seen him use one before. If there was one thing Nukpana was good at it was torturing and murdering people to do black magic.

"Sathrik has a portion of the goblin army working outside of Regor, constructing the base for what my sources say will be the largest Gate ever built."

I had a sinking feeling in the pit of my stomach. "Let me guess, big enough for an army."

Tam nodded, his expression grave. "The entire army and more."

"And another wild guess has Nukpana planning to have that Gate open in Pengor somewhere near a major elven population center—an unarmed one."

"At this point, all any of us can do is guess, but I think it's safe to say that Pengor would be among his first targets."

Nukpana would have plenty of sacrificial victims to keep the Gate open—or to feed to the Saghred to power the stone. And once he'd killed, sacrificed, or enslaved the elves in one area, he could simply redirect the Gate to open in another place. There would be no warning, no time to prepare. The elven armies couldn't be everywhere at once. It was slaughter on an epic scale waiting to happen.

Imala's agents in Regor had reported to her that Sarad Nukpana was lurking behind Sathrik's throne, whispering sinful somethings in His Majesty's pointed ear about vengeance most sweet and a stone most powerful—and how by killing me, they could have both.

"This is why I need your help," Chigaru told me. "For my people—and yours."

"Your people aren't the ones about to be invaded."

"They're the ones about to be killed to open that Gate."

Damn.

"And as you know, magically powerful victims are best not only for powering a Gate, but for keeping it stable."

Mychael scowled. "I take it Nukpana has sent his Khrynsani out to capture goblin mages."

Tam nodded. "Goblin mages and nobles have been vanishing from their homes and estates for the past two months."

"Vanishing as in kidnapped," I said.

"Those mages and nobles were chosen with care," Tam said. "If you oppose King Sathrik or are a powerful mage, you'll find yourself and your family being dragged from your beds. They're being held in the Mal'Salin palace dungeons."

Chigaru spoke. "And to prevent a city-wide panic, or a coup breaking down the palace gates, Sathrik has publically announced that these mages and nobles are traitors who fled rather than face the consequences of their criminal actions. The truth is their only crime was to oppose my brother's rule, and support mine."

And any chance Chigaru had of overthrowing Sathrik—and Sarad Nukpana—would die with them.

Unless somebody stopped them.

Last time I checked, I was someone.

Tam looked at Mychael. "Sarad has made it known that he needs more mages to keep that Gate stable."

Mychael stood in silence, a muscle working in his jaw. "They're coming here first."

"There is one thing that will prevent a full-scale invasion," Chigaru told him. "Giving them the Saghred." The goblin prince looked at me. "And you, Raine. Most of all, my brother wants you."

Chapter 5

*You'd think being told an evil king and his even-more-evil quasi-*demigod minion want you at their mercy or thousands of people would die would be as bad as anyone's day could get.

You'd be wrong.

The Seat of Twelve had to be told.

The Seat of Twelve was the ruling council for the Conclave, which was the governing body for every magic user of consequence in the seven kingdoms. These were twelve of the most powerful mages, period. Thanks to the Saghred, I now had more power than any of them. This bothered them.

A lot.

In their collective opinion, anyone with that much power needed to be watched very closely. Which meant if I so much as blinked wrong, I'd find myself in a citadel containment room. And if I completely cut loose with the power the Saghred had given me, my head and shoulders would soon be parting ways.

Before the meeting, Mychael needed to meet briefly with Justinius Valerian, the archmage, the supreme head of the Conclave of Sorcerers, the commander in chief of the Brotherhood of Conclave Guardians, and a crafty, foul-tempered old man.

I loved the guy.

Even better, he was right fond of me, too.

Vegard and I were in the citadel on our way to Mychael's office to wait. His office had wards and a well-stocked bar. I needed the former and wanted the latter.

Naturally, we didn't make it there.

From the end of the hallway came a cool and crisp voice. "I hoped I would find you here, Mistress Benares."

Crap in a bucket.

The voice belonged to an elven mage who thought he was about to get me right where he'd wanted me since the day I set foot on Mid.

A tall figure stepped into view.

Magus Carnades Silvanus was a pure-blooded high elf who wasn't about to let anyone forget it. White-blond hair, glacier blue eyes, pristine porcelain complexion. His black and silver robes were elegant and expensive, and emphasized his cold beauty. Gleaming against the silk of his robes was a mirrored disk dangling at the end of a silver chain. I'd never liked mirror mages, and I'd never like Carnades Silvanus.

As the senior mage on the Seat of Twelve, Carnades Silvanus saw himself as the champion of the elven people. I saw him as a self-righteous, narrow-minded jerk. Unfortunately, he also had the influence to convince a lot of powerful and dangerous people to see things his way.

Two others stepped up behind him. Elves. Mages. Two mages on the Seat of Twelve. I'd seen them before with Carnades. Always standing a step or two behind, their deference to Carnades made it clear to anyone who cared to notice that they were nothing but lackeys. Lackeys who were probably two of the top mages in the kingdoms, but were still Carnades's flunkies and hangers-on. As Carnades grew in power and influence, they moved up the ladder with him without doing a thing except what he told them to.

Vegard came to reluctant attention. The Guardians' main duty was the protection of the archmagus and the mages of the Seat of Twelve. Carnades was second in command only to the archmagus, and he was convinced that my involvement with certain goblins not only made me a goblin sympathizer, but a traitor to the elven people.

He smiled, a dazzling white flash of insincerity. "I understand that your visit to greet your precious prince didn't turn out as you planned."

I flashed him a smile of my own. "I don't think anyone got what they paid for this morning. Too bad assassins don't give refunds, isn't it?"

That wiped the smirk off his face.

Carnades and Taltek Balmorlan had become the best of friends, and friends didn't keep secrets from each other—especially not secrets that involved hiring the deadliest assassin in the kingdoms, who conveniently happened to be an elf.

"You used your Saghred-spawned power to defend a Mal'Salin—a creature who would go to any length to kill an elf, any elf." Carnades's voice was a self-satisfied purr. "Except you, of course. Merely a continuation of the relationship that began in—"

"Relationship?" Maybe I'd hit my head when I fell against that guard shack wall.

"Your clandestine meeting with the prince at an estate in Mermeia was—"

"A kidnapping. Mine. Prince Chigaru wanted me to find the Saghred for him. I refused."

"A second encounter was more public. An embrace at the goblin king's masked ball two nights later."

"If your snitches had looked closely enough they would have seen that the prince had a dagger to my ribs. Stepping away from him wasn't just ill-advised, it was impossible."

I took two steps closer to Carnades, close enough to make him flinch. "But I could hardly expect you to be concerned with facts." I lowered my voice to the same purr. "You just want an excuse."

"Guardian, I want to speak to Mistress Benares alone." Carnades said it without even looking at Vegard. He knew Vegard's name; he just refused to use it. Just one more way to belittle Mychael's knights.

"It's all right, Vegard," I said. "I *want* to have a private chat with Magus Silvanus."

Vegard and Carnades's two yes-mages moved down the hall and out of earshot. However, I did notice that Vegard stayed within his ax-throwing range. I gave him a knowing wink.

"Let's stop playing games, Mistress Benares," Carnades said.

"Works for me. I'm tired of this one anyway. For starters, stop with the 'Mistress Benares' act. You hate my guts; I hate yours, so why waste perfectly good dislike on acting polite when neither of us wants to. I know there's another five-letter word you'd love to call me, but for now let's just go with 'Raine,' shall we?"

Carnades's mouth twisted with distaste. "That would imply familiarity."

"Yeah, it's offensive to me, too. But let's try just this once." I crossed my arms over my chest. "Okay, you've got your privacy. Talk."

"I want to see you dead."

"That's nothing new, but you are dispensing with the small talk. I like that."

"The ideal end for you would be on an executioner's block before sundown. That won't be for another two hours. In my opinion, that's two hours too late. Unfortunately, for the good of many, the desires of the few must be pushed aside."

"Meaning you don't get to see my head lopped off before you go to dinner."

"That would be a much better start to my evening." Carnades's lips curled into a mocking smile. "Though from what the Saghred's history has shown us, I won't have much longer to wait."

"So now you're entertaining yourself by rewriting history?"

"There's no need to alter the truth," Carnades said. "You've read Rudra Muralin's journal. He was the Saghred's bond servant, exactly like yourself. No doubt you've realized that you're following in his footsteps."

"I am not now, nor will I ever be like Rudra Muralin," I said, my voice tight with fury. The goblin was a thousand-year-old, seriously psychotic mage who'd used the Saghred to slaughter thousands and enslave thousands more. He was dead now. Permanently, thanks to Sarad Nukpana. In several pieces then reduced to ashes, thanks to Imala Kalis.

"You have used the Saghred more than a few times now," Carnades continued as if I hadn't said a word. "It becomes more a part of you each time. You don't see this, but others can. I can. Soon its desires will become your own. When that happens, you'll have become too dangerous to live. It's only a matter of time." His long fingers toyed negligently with the jeweled chain lying against his dark robes. "It will happen quite soon, I think." His eyes gleamed in triumph. "If it hasn't already."

My breath froze. Carnades hadn't been at the harbor this morning; and even if he had, he'd have had no way of knowing about the goblin mages—and how the Saghred had made me want to kill the lot of them.

"If that little dream makes you happy, keep having it." My voice was steady, but the rest of me wasn't.

"Isn't it odd that you claim to want to be rid of the Saghred and the power it has given you, but you have yet to expend any real effort toward achieving that end? The stone's influence over you goes deeper than you will admit."

I forced a smile. "I've been a little busy. It's hard to

work on my own problems when more pressing issues keep coming up. Many of them were your fault; the others you kept sticking your nose into and making them worse. And on at least three occasions, if it weren't for me, your own arrogant stupidity would have gotten you killed. I saved your life, and what thanks do I get?"

The smile grew. "A chance to save your pirate cousin from probable torture and certain execution."

I went perfectly still.

"You don't believe me," Carnades murmured.

"Why wouldn't I? Threatening innocent people with violence to get what you want. It's the ultimate villain cliché, but from you, I believe it."

"Good. That will save me the effort to prove my sincerity. I assure you my associates and I would be doing nothing illegal."

"So torture and execution aren't illegal in your little world?"

"Neither I nor any of my associates would harm one hair on Captain Benares's head. We would merely be apprehending a known criminal."

"Mychael and the archmage have granted Phaelan immunity while he is on Mid."

"That immunity ceases to exist once he is out of Mid's waters," Carnades noted.

"Phaelan's not leaving Mid anytime soon."

"I never said it would be his choice."

"That's kidnapping."

"Not at all. Like yourself, I am merely warning you of the impending actions of others. Not that they would be committing a crime. They would merely be apprehending a known and wanted criminal. There are countless warrants for the infamous Captain Phaelan Benares's arrest. Some of the rewards being offered are quite exorbitant. Your cousin must be exceedingly proficient at his chosen calling. They can't all have him, of course. I understand there are plans to award him to the highest bidder. It would be the only fair way to settle any conflicting claims. And with such a wanted man as Captain Benares, there are certain to be conflicts."

"What do you want?"

Carnades stepped closer. "I want nothing, Raine. In fact, I am offering you an opportunity to save the life of your cousin and help your own people."

"An opportunity. I don't believe I've ever heard it called that before. And let me guess, all I have to do is walk through the gates of the elven embassy of my own free will."

"Would that be so difficult?"

"Then a certain elven intelligence inquisitor will escort me to a warded cell made just for me, and clap me into a set of custom-made manacles. Have I missed anything?"

"In exchange for your cooperation, your family will not be harmed."

The Saghred twisted in my chest, my rage awakening it.

Carnades knew. He laughed softly and his voice dropped to a bare whisper. "You want to obliterate me, don't you, Raine? The urge is almost more than you can bear. How many nights have you lain awake wondering how much longer until you lose what little control you have left? Knowing that the instant you do there will be no going back."

"And all I have to do is let Balmorlan's sicko mages get their hands on the Saghred by getting their hands on me, so you and yours can destroy every goblin breathing your air."

"Before they do the same to us," Carnades hissed. "Before you further betray your people to help our enemies. Enemies who at this moment are planning our race's destruction."

"Destroy them before they can destroy us. Brilliant. It never occurred to you to work with the goblins who have no interest in killing a single elf. Who want to bring down the goblins who do want the elves' collective neck in a noose."

"There are no such creatures. Goblins kill. It's what they are. Consumed by evil from the moment they are spawned."

"You want to see what evil really looks like?" I snarled. "Take a look in the mirror hanging around your own neck."

Carnades stiffened. You'd think I had slapped him. Believe me, I wanted to do a lot more than that, and the Saghred was eager to help.

"You refuse my offer?" Frost rolled off his words.

"And toss it back in your face."

"Very well. I offered you the chance to surrender voluntarily. Enjoy your last few hours of freedom—and if you see your cousin, tell him to do the same."

Surrender or thousands die.

Don't surrender, the goblins and/or elves will come and get you, and thousands will still die. I really didn't want to think about what was going to happen to me in either one of those scenarios.

I hate no-win choices. In my book, if you don't have a chance of winning, then it's not a choice. But either way, I was screwed and innocent people died. I didn't believe for one second that King Sathrik would stay home and play nice—or Carnades and Balmorlan would crawl back under their collective rock—if I served myself up on a silver platter. But that's exactly what the Seat of Twelve wanted to do with me as soon as they could vote on it.

I'd been in this room before. Nothing good had happened in it then, and I didn't see that changing now.

In my opinion, it wasn't a room for the Seat of Twelve to meet—it was a star chamber for passing judgment. I'd been in the hot seat last time, too. The dais was still there, but the throne-like chairs were around a massive table instead. Marginally less imposing, though it still said loud and clear that this group took themselves and their power way too seriously. No low self-esteem here.

"What are the terms for the surrender?" Carnades asked.

To Carnades, saving his own lily-white patrician ass and those of his yes-mages was his first priority, the rest of the island's inhabitants and students be damned, or in this case destroyed.

"There are no terms, because there will be no surrender." Justinius Valerian gave Carnades a look that said loud and clear that he would not say that again. As far as he was concerned, there was nothing to debate.

Unfortunately the old man was in the minority.

The Seat of Twelve was shaking in their designer robes. Scared mages meant trouble of the fatal kind for me.

Fighting never occurred to men and women who depended on fancy magic and political maneuvering more than they did standing their ground and defending what was theirs. To them that was what they hired guards for. Actual fighting was barbaric and beneath them.

Which was exactly what Sathrik Mal'Salin and Sarad Nukpana were counting on.

Justinius was the top dog in this well-dressed pack. The old man had teeth and he knew how to use them. The same couldn't be said for most of the others. Just because you were a mage-level talent didn't mean you could use that power for fighting.

That's why they had established the Guardians.

Five hundred knights against tens of thousands of goblin warriors, and at least a couple hundred of those warriors were mage-level talents—in black magic. And with Sarad Nukpana coordinating the invasion, I'd be willing to bet that there would be major-class demons among those numbers. I didn't care how much magical ass Mychael's boys could kick, outnumbered was outnumbered.

If I surrendered, all I would do is buy Mychael and his Guardians some time, but when the goblins did attack, it would be ten times worse.

King Sathrik Mal'Salin and Sarad Nukpana would have the power of the Saghred at their beck and call.

They would have me.

If they had me, they didn't need the rock. They could use the Saghred through my link with it, and sacrifice victims the same way. Nukpana had the power to open the Gate. He was planning to use me to keep it open.

I was a weapon, a conduit to cataclysmic power, and the goblin king was going to invade the Isle of Mid to come and get me.

A human mage sat a little apart from the fray, calm and aloof—mainly from the borderline panic among her colleagues. I remembered her. She'd been the only one not in favor of throwing me in a containment room and throwing away the key the last time I was in this room. That didn't make her a friend, but right now I'd take what I could get.

"Not that I am questioning Prince Chigaru Mal'Salin's word, but what proof do we have of this?" Her voice was strong and cut right through the din. "He desires his brother's throne. No doubt he would have an equal desire in getting Mid's help to destroy his brother."

A voice of reason. Always a good thing to have.

"I have people getting that confirmation now, Magus Cagilian," Mychael told her with a slight bow. "I hope we find no such evidence; but if an impending invasion is confirmed, we must be ready to begin evacuating the students."

Another mage spoke up; actually, it was more of a whine. "But the goblin king said that if we gave him Raine Benares they would not invade."

"And you believe him?" Justinius barked, a short laugh minus the humor. "He and Nukpana want the Saghred. They'll use Miss Benares to get enough power to come and take it. If they get that far, we're all toast."

Carnades strode across the room in a swirl of robes and sat on one of the ornate chairs. Naturally it was at the front of the room with the dais behind him and facing me. A nice dramatic backdrop.

"No one has voiced the obvious solution," he said. "When the goblins attack, we use the Saghred to strike."

My eyes locked on his. "You mean use me."

"For all intents and purposes, you and the Saghred are now one and the same, so there is no difference."

"Even if I knew how to destroy an army—which I don't—the rock hasn't had a decent meal in hundreds of years. That's hardly enough juice to take on an army."

Carnades didn't even blink. "Then feed it."

There it was. So much for confirmation whether Carnades was in on Balmorlan's plan for me.

No one in the room said a word; no one even breathed.

You could have heard a fly fart.

Some of the mages were appalled. Others started nodding in agreement. Too many.

Mychael broke the silence. "You're advocating murder," he said, his voice tight.

"I'm advocating saving the lives of our citizens," Carnades countered.

"And yourself," I snapped.

Mychael walked slowly toward Carnades. "By sacrificing our citizens, damning their souls to eternity trapped inside the Saghred, their souls used to fuel a black magic that shouldn't exist, let alone be used. You want that."

"I want survival."

"The price is too high."

"In your opinion," Carnades said smoothly. "The Conclave accords say that you only have one vote in this or any other matter brought before the Seat of Twelve." He smiled in a flash of perfect teeth. "I don't make the rules, Paladin Eiliesor."

Justinius's smile looked more like a shark that'd just spotted lunch. "If any proposal you put before this council for a vote is deemed of questionable sanity or criminal intent, you will find yourself on the other side of those doors, stripped of your vote—and your position on this council." The old man's bright blue eyes glittered in anticipation of that moment. "So says the accords. I don't make the rules, Carnades, but I'll enjoy the hell out of enforcing them. Now, do you want to make that proposal of yours official?"

Carnades looked around the room. He didn't have the votes and he knew it. Yet. The elf wouldn't act until he was sure he had the backing to toss me outside the city walls with a bow around my neck for the goblins and slam the gate behind me—or onto the elven embassy's front steps. We weren't under siege yet, but the men and women in this room would get a siege mentality real quick. Survival of the strongest; or in this case, the politically strongest.

Scary thing was, in another day or two, Carnades Silvanus would have his votes. He knew that, too.

"Not at this time, Archmagus Valerian." The elf mage was the very picture of civility. No one who just walked in would ever think that he'd just calmly suggested killing hundreds of people to save his sorry hide. "I merely ask that this council be open to all solutions to the dire situation we find ourselves in." He inclined his head to Mychael. "Though like Paladin Eiliesor, I sincerely hope that the report is false and there is no need for alarm." Carnades looked at me. "However, we all must be prepared to make sacrifices."

"Son of a bitch!"

We were in Justinius's office. I was pacing and cussing, Mychael was standing in the center of the room, and the old man was pouring liquor for all of us.

The only thing I wanted more than a stiff drink was Carnades's face in front of my punching fist.

Repeatedly.

I was more than furious at Carnades. I was furious at myself, my situation, and that whatever I did, I was going to die and die horribly. Die knowing that an untold number of people would be following me in the war that would result, and nothing I could do would stop the killing.

I didn't say a word between the Seat's council room and Justinius's office, but I was thinking plenty. There was a solution, the only solution that might not involve my immediate death.

Call a Reaper. Let it draw out all of the Saghred's souls through me. It'd probably take mine with it, but at least the stone could be shattered once it was empty.

In theory.

I didn't know any of this for certain. What I did know for certain was that Sarad Nukpana wouldn't turn around and go home when he was told that "The Saghred's been pounded to dust. No power to be had here. Nothing to see. Move along." Nukpana would move along, all right. Getting his hands on that rock had been his lifelong obsession. Then I'd tricked Sarad Nukpana into touching the Saghred with his bloody hand and the rock slurped him up as a sacrifice, destroying his body and imprisoning his soul. The goblin fought his way free, and when he couldn't regenerate his body by consuming the life forces of mages, he claimed the freshly killed body of his uncle for his own.

Sarad Nukpana wanted me dead. He wanted me worse than dead. And he'd destroy every elf he could hunt down, because an elf had deprived him of his ultimate prize. Out of spite, the goblin would destroy everyone I loved, but I'd already be dead. I snorted. Yeah, lucky me.

"Son of a bitch!" The phrase was getting a bit old, but nothing expressed frustration like repetitive swearing.

"We won't use the Saghred and we won't use you."

Mychael said it like a solemn promise, and I knew he would do everything in his power to prevent either from happening, but this was something he wouldn't be able to stop alone.

"And we sure as hell aren't slaughtering our people to feed the damned rock," Justinius said. He flashed an evil grin. "Though if Carnades is so keen on pushing that proposal of his, the smarmy bastard can be first in line. The Saghred finds magic users especially tasty."

Normally, my sick sense of humor would like the idea of Carnades paying the price for his own evil plot. But "the front of the line" meant the first to have his soul sucked into the Saghred through me, after I'd been coated in his blood.

Nothing to laugh at there. Screaming for the rest of my soon-to-be-terminated life would be more like it.

Justinius handed a drink to me, then gave one to Mychael. "My predecessor exiled . . . excuse me, *assigned* Carnades to be the Conclave emissary to the goblin court. I think he hoped Carnades would have what goblin courtiers call an accident, but the bastard came back to Mid just like a rash on my bony ass."

"I saw Carnades before the meeting," I told them.

Mychael's eyes narrowed. "What?"

"I expected the usual threats, but he's getting creative." I told them what Carnades had threatened to have done to Phaelan unless I took a stroll over to the elven embassy, knocked on the door, and asked to move in. I didn't mention the five goblin mages at the harbor this morning—and my sudden urge to stop their interference by permanently stopping them. I hadn't killed anyone, therefore it wasn't a problem. Yet.

Justinius set his glass on his desk. It was empty. "You need to let your cousin know that he's a target."

"So he can do something stupid like come on shore after Carnades?" I countered.

Mychael's lips turned up in a slow grin. "Just tell your Uncle Ryn. He's told me some stories, and several of them ended up with him literally sitting on Phaelan. He knows how to keep his son in line."

I nodded. "And Uncle Ryn can keep his temper. He won't go after Carnades—at least not directly." I chuckled, and it sounded a little evil, even to me.

Think, Raine. Yes, you're tired. Yes, you're scared out of your mind. Yes, you've got so many people who want you dead or worse that they're going to have to start taking numbers. And to top it off, you nearly married one of them. You want to live to see next week? Then get a grip on yourself. If you're going down, take some of those people down with you.

"How long until you have confirmation of what Nukpana and his pet king are really up to?" I asked Mychael.

"Sky dragon flight time between here and Regor is two days. I've told my men not to get too close. Any closer than three miles and Nukpana will be able to sense them even with the veils they're using. All they're looking for are signs that a lot of magic is building up. In my opinion, that would more than prove Chigaru's claim."

The three of us didn't need proof. We knew Chigaru wasn't lying. Though the human mage was right; it'd be a great way to get an island full of mages to help take on his big brother. And one way or another Sathrik Mal'Salin and his army were coming. At least the goblin army was coming. I really couldn't see Sathrik stepping through that Gate until he was sure that no one was left standing who could so much as ruffle his hair. And if we were in that condition, Sarad Nukpana could just stroll into the citadel and scoop up the Saghred. If I were dead, the stone would bond to him like a starving newborn.

Unless the rock was dust.

"Solutions, gentlemen?" I really wanted another one other than my soul in the stomach—or whatever—of a Reaper.

Justinius didn't hesitate. "We fight."

I raised an eyebrow. "Against an army."

The old man grinned. "I never said *how* we would fight."

I looked at Mychael. He was already looking at me. He also knew what I was thinking.

"Absolutely not," he told me.

"We can't let Nukpana get his hands on the Saghred." I said. "You know how obscenely strong he is now. If he gets the Saghred, no one or nothing will be able to stop him." I hesitated. "Which means we have to stop this now."

"Reapers?" Justinius asked.

I looked at him in surprise.

"I know what's going on in my own citadel, girl," he said with a trace of a smile. "You've been working with Vidor Kalta. Find out anything?"

Kalta was a nachtmagus. He was human, and a great

guy for someone who worked with dead people for a living. A nachtmagus could control the dead—in all of their forms. Communicating with the dead was the least of what they could do. I'd heard that given enough time, money, and motivation they could raise the dead. Reapers weren't dead, but like Vidor Kalta, they worked closely with them.

"Through my link to the Saghred, I'm also connected to the souls trapped inside," I told him. "And since I'm also a conduit for the rock's power, I can serve the same function for its inmates. Reapers calm panic. If I were dying on a battlefield, I could see where a cool, soothing calm would be a good thing. The souls they've already drawn out of me wanted to leave the rock. Too bad for me it felt like someone was dragging my insides out through my chest. Multiply that a couple thousand times . . . if it didn't kill me, I'd be wishing that someone would."

"Is that all he could tell you?" Justinius asked.

"No, but none of the rest of it does anything to help me." I raked my fingers through my hair. "He's sent out some carefully worded queries to a few colleagues that he trusts. Some of them specialize in Reapers and their behavior—a few of them are actually still alive and didn't get eaten by their own homework." I looked at Mychael. "How much time do we have until that Gate's ready?"

"Judging from what Chigaru's spies said, we have about five days. It'll be enough time to get the students off the island—and anyone else who wants to leave." He paused. "I want you to be one of them."

"We've had this discussion; I've given you my answer and it's still the same one. If anyone needs to leave, it's you. I'm not the one who got shot at this morning."

Justinius raised one bushy, white eyebrow. "Now *that* I didn't know. Care to fill me in, son?"

Mychael did, but left out any mention of my relation to said killer.

"That tells me who, what, and when," Justinius said

when Mychael finished. "But why did he pick you for a target?"

I spoke right up. "I can answer that one, sir." No use trying to hide it. I laid it out for him, simply and directly.

The old man whistled. "Damn, girl. And here I was thinking that your knack for finding trouble started with the Saghred."

I sighed. "No, sir. Unfortunately, trouble is what I find best. Always has been."

"You do a fine job of it."

"Thank you, sir." I tossed back the rest of my drink. "Though I'm working on something that could take care of Rache's itchy trigger finger and suck the wind out of Carnades's sails at the same time."

"We believe that Rache Kai was paid by Taltek Balmorlan to assassinate the prince," Mychael said.

Justinius glowered. "Balmorlan also wants to get his hands on our girl here." If Balmorlan had been in the room right now, I had no doubt that the old man would have turned him into the cockroach that he really was and then stomped on him. I had to really resist the urge to kiss the old guy.

"And Carnades is Balmorlan's newest best friend—and investor," I told him.

"You have proof?" Justinius asked.

"Let's just say that I know someone at Balmorlan's bank."

Justinius smiled slowly. "Is this someone willing to help?"

I grinned. "Willing and eager."

"You know that Carnades isn't going to wait until he gets the votes he needs."

"That's fine," I said. "Neither am I."

Chapter 6

Carnades had tossed down the gauntlet, and I was only too happy
to pick it up.

Either I cooperated or my family would pay the price.
It wasn't the first time a Benares had been threatened like
that, and the family had several favored forms of retaliation.

I was about to set one of those in motion. I'd be doing
what a Benares does best.

Scheme and scam. Or in my case, con and conjure.

Time to find Mago.

Setting up Phaelan and paying Rache to kill Chigaru
and Mychael took money. A lot of money. I knew for a fact
that Rache wouldn't kill a fly without being paid, and Carnades's lackeys wouldn't go after Phaelan without having
their pockets well lined. The best way to stop them would
be to stop their money, then see what I could do about taking every coin they already had.

Prince Chigaru hadn't reserved the entire hotel, but
he'd come close. There were goblins at every opening that
could even remotely be considered a way in or out. I'd been

taught since childhood how to get around virtually any obstacle an opponent could throw at me.

It wasn't easy, but I got into the hotel without anyone seeing me. No goblin in this hotel knew that Prince Chigaru's personal banker was a Benares, and there was no reason why I would know Mago Perrone.

So, I snuck in.

Almost as difficult as getting into the hotel undetected was convincing Vegard to wait for me at a bar across the street. In no way could a big, blond Guardian blend in with a hotel full of goblins. I was small and fit through openings Vegard couldn't get his head into, let alone those shoulders of his. I thought about telling Tam and Imala about my little trick, but decided against it for now. I might need to sneak back in before all this was over.

I couldn't exactly walk up to the front desk and ask where Mago Perrone's suite was. I mean I could, but it would be ill-advised. Hotel staff generally wanted to know personal details that are best not shared in my kind of situation, like your name and what business did you have with the hotel guest in question. Then they would oh so politely offer to send a bellboy up with a message. Pretty much everyone knew who I was, and having me connected in any way, shape, or form with Mago would have scuttled our plan before we got a chance to break even one law.

Over the years, we'd worked out a sign in our family for letting another family member know where we were. For an inn or hotel, the tip of a handkerchief discreetly visible in the upper right corner of the door said that a Benares was in residence. To keep me from wandering suspiciously from floor to floor looking for his door merely took a little deductive reasoning. Mago never stayed on the ground floor, to prevent anyone from breaking in. Someone stealing from Mago would be the ultimate irony. My cousin also never stayed on floors too high up to prevent him from easily getting out. Escape was a good option for a Benares. He always carried a ladder woven out of Caesolian silk; it was light, fit neatly in his luggage, and could be pulled down quickly after him. That ladder had seen a lot of use over the years. It would reach three stories, no more. Chigaru was on the fifth floor—naturally the top floor—that would put Mago on the third. He'd want to be close to the prince, but close enough to the ground so that his getaway ladder would reach.

Unlike Prince Chigaru's floor, there were no guards on Mago's hall; in fact, there was no one in the hall except for me. The golden glow from recessed lightglobes set into the walls at regular intervals revealed a faint gleam at each end of the hall. Sentry beacons. Sometimes magic was a major inconvenience. Hotel security could see everything going on in every hall. Though one of the first spells I learned as a seeker was for disabling any magical device that let anyone see me when I didn't want to be seen.

Focus, a touch of will, and a muttered spell later, all the security guard downstairs would see was a lot of empty hall. There would be no record that I'd been here.

I found the tip of a pale blue handkerchief peeking out of the door of the suite closest to the stairs—another prudent Mago precaution. I used the knock that would tell him it was me, and my cousin answered the door a few moments later, drink in hand, color back in his face.

I slipped quickly into the room so Mago could step up to the threshold, look both ways in confusion, shrug, and close the door.

Mago's hair was still damp from a bath, and he was wearing a dark blue silk lounging robe. Most of a meal was still on a small dining table by the window. I stayed by the door and Mago crossed the room and closed the drapes. Standing on a floor that didn't pitch and roll definitely agreed with my cousin.

"You're looking almost lifelike," I noted.

Mago raised his glass in salute. "You're a silver-tongued flatterer, as always."

I nodded toward the table. "Still can't keep anything down?"

"I ordered more than I wanted." Mago smiled. "I knew either you or Phaelan would put in an appearance and would be ravenous from one nefarious activity or another." He raised a flawless eyebrow. "And what sort of trouble have you escaped this afternoon?"

I glanced down at myself. No blood that I could see. "What makes you think I'm in trouble?"

"I don't think anything. I *know* you."

I grinned. "Touché."

"Quite so. Would you care for dinner? The poached salmon is excellent."

"You don't have to ask me twice." I sat down and fell to.

I was sure that Phaelan would put in an appearance later in the evening, but he would be more interested in refreshment of a liquid variety while he and Mago regaled each other with stories of monetary acquisition that, if heard by an officer of the city watch, would land them both in jail. Naturally, the stories would embellish reality to an obscene degree, but it was the telling of the stories and the drinking until neither of them could find the door that was more important, not that trifling thing known as the truth.

I regaled Mago with a story of my own, first about Carnades's threats against Phaelan unless I surrendered myself to the elves, and then about the pending goblin invasion unless I gave myself up to the goblins.

By the time I'd finished, Mago had drained his glass and was at the suite's bar pouring himself another.

"Don't worry about Carnades," Mago assured me. "This isn't the first time someone came up with the bright idea to sell my little brother to the highest bidder." He laughed. "One time, I was the winning bidder."

I was incredulous. "You actually *paid* someone for Phaelan? You're slipping, cousin."

Mago raised a finger. "Ah, there's a big difference between 'bought' and 'paid for.' I made the purchase, acquired the merchandise, and double-crossed the seller, leaving her with no Phaelan and no gold. I think the entire operation went exceedingly well."

"Her?"

Mago nodded. "Phaelan protested that I purchased him far too soon. He was about to make headway of an intimate nature with the lady in question."

I blinked. "He was going to boff his own kidnapper?"

"Phaelan considered the bidding process a novel kind of foreplay."

"I don't think I need to hear any more."

"It's a very entertaining story. You should really let me tell it to you when you have a few hours." He gave me a reassuring smile. "Raine, don't worry about Phaelan. He'll be coming here later tonight and I'll tell him."

"Can you also keep him from doing anything stupid?"

He laughed. "I'm incredibly good, but I have yet to work an actual miracle."

"Then do what you can."

"That much I can promise."

"Okay, back to the goblin part of my problem. You can siphon all the money out of Taltek Balmorlan's account into one to fund Prince Chigaru, but it'll be too late to help anyone if Nukpana gets that Gate built."

"Due to the prince's injury, my meeting with him has been postponed until breakfast tomorrow. King Sathrik keeps an absurdly large amount of imperial goblin gold on deposit at our bank, but he rarely makes withdrawals from it, only deposits."

"How much is in there?"

"The last time I checked, it was in the area of thirty million kugarats."

I whistled.

"The goblin army is doing most of the manual labor on the Gate?" Mago asked.

"As far as I know."

"Do you know how the goblin army is paid and from what source?"

"No, but I could find out. Or better yet, you could ask Tam—and tell him precisely who you are. That'd make me coming to visit you a lot simpler."

Mago looked like he'd swallowed a bug. "You're quite serious, aren't you?"

"Deadly serious. After what happened this morning, we don't have time for your prim-and-proper banker act. If necessary, keep it going for the prince, but Tam needs to know the truth."

"And you know Chancellor Nathrach how well?"

"*Very* well." I proceeded to give Mago the shortened version of meeting Tam two years ago in Mermeia, up to sharing an umi'atsu bond with him until a month ago. The only person who knew Tam better than me was Imala Kalis and Tam himself.

"And having been chief mage to the goblin queen for five years, Tam would know where Sathrik gets his money right down to the pocket change he keeps on the royal nightstand."

"Men—even disciplined soldiers—will work only so fast if their pockets are empty," Mago said. "It won't matter what psychotic goblin mage is cracking the whip. But first I need to know where the king keeps the money that he uses to pay his army. No doubt he pays them from the palace treasury, but he has to replenish that from somewhere."

"If you don't know about it, chances are it's not from your bank."

Mago took a sip and smiled like a man with a secret, the fun kind. "I have friends, in banks all over the world, who would be only too glad to help a colleague in need. In fact, they might even be willing to help with our noble cause." He winked. "Especially if there was something in it for them."

I knew I shouldn't be surprised, but I had to ask. "Does everyone in this business need their palms greased?"

"Only if you need something from them in return."

I pushed the now empty plate away from me and sat back in the plush chair with a satisfied sigh. I'd been hungrier than I'd thought. "I need to know the details of your plan for Taltek Balmorlan and Carnades Silvanus. Intercepting Sathrik's payroll is critical, but I need Carnades's wings clipped. Now."

"I take it from that vindictive gleam in your eyes that the trouble you encountered this afternoon involved Silvanus's colleague Inquisitor Balmorlan?"

"Correct." Though at the thought of who Balmorlan had been hiding and paying, my face did a little wince and cringe. Mago most definitely knew about Rache Kai. They had been friends and Mago had been the one who introduced us. He'd never forgiven himself for that—or Rache. I hadn't been the only one Rache had fooled. Mago swore that no one would ever fool him again, and no one ever had.

Mago sat perfectly still, the firelight glinting on his spectacles. "What is it?"

I told him.

You don't usually think of bankers as being the types to cuss a blue streak, but there weren't that many bankers with the last name Benares, either.

Let's just say that Mago did the family name proud.

"You think Balmorlan hired Rache?" he asked.

"I don't have proof, but Rache's trail went cold on Embassy Row. Both the elves and goblins had defensive wards up and at full power, but I can't see Imala's people taking out a hit on the prince."

"Unless she has some double agents in her midst," Mago countered. "I'm not saying you're wrong, but why would Balmorlan want the prince dead?"

"Simple. Balmorlan and Carnades want war; Chigaru in power means peace."

Mago set his glass aside and stood up. "Well, let's see

what we can do to put Inquisitor Balmorlan up to his eye-brows in hot water."

"More beautiful words were never spoken. And if you can pull it off, consider it my birthday present for the next ten years."

"The satisfaction of a sting well done and no shopping for ten years." Mago smiled broadly. "How can any man refuse such an offer?"

I grinned. "That's my offer, now what is your plan for after you've drained Balmorlan's account?"

"I opted not to pursue that option."

I couldn't believe what I was hearing. "*Opted* not—"

"Never commit yourself to one course of action when a better one may have just come available."

"May have."

Mago held up a hand. "Hear me out, cousin. I don't do anything without a reason—or at least a hunch I can hang my hat on." He sat down in the chair next to mine. "Phaelan tells me that you have an impeccable glamour."

Oh crap. "Not impeccable, just decent."

"From what he told me, you could fool anyone, any-time." Mago had a wicked gleam in his eyes. "Including a man's wife."

"I'd really rather not glamour myself into a man again."

"You want Taltek Balmorlan to hoist himself on his own petard?"

"Of course I do, but—"

"But nothing."

He was right. I didn't like it, but he was right. When I said I'd do anything to put Balmorlan out of commission, I'd meant it. It just didn't occur to me that would involve acquiring dangly bits again.

"Any chance I could do this glamoured as a woman?"

"None. Two weeks ago, Taltek Balmorlan requested a meeting with a D'Mai banker. An obnoxious little worm named Symon Wiggs."

"Sounds like someone Balmorlan would want for a banker."

Mago smiled. "True, except Symon isn't his banker. Like myself, Symon Wiggs has various profitable outside interests. In Symon's case, he represents a Nebian criminal cartel. When these men need money handled, shall we say 'cleanly,' Symon is their go-to man."

"So what does this have to do with Balmorlan?"

"Balmorlan wants to make the cartel an offer, something he seems to think they would be salivating to acquire."

I didn't like where this was going. "What is it?"

"I don't know; but I do know that for him to contact Symon and request a meeting in person, there's a great deal of money involved. In fact, Symon would have been on the same ship as me."

"Let me guess, something came up at the last moment and he couldn't make it."

"Just me intercepting the invitation. After reading it, I arranged for Symon to do an audit at our Jebas branch." Mago lowered his voice to a conspiratorial whisper. "A vice president there owes me a favor, and I called it in."

"Clever." I gave him a tired smile. "Thank you, Mago. I can't tell you how much I appreciate—"

Mago actually blushed a little then waved me off. "You would have done the same for me."

"Except I don't have bank vice president friends in tropical resorts."

"I'm sure you could come up with something equally creative and effective if I needed it." Mago reached forward and selected a chocolate from the dessert tray. "And after the audit, my friend will reward Symon with a week in the Jebas's most notorious pleasure palace and casino." Mago popped the chocolate in his mouth. "He'll be calling in a few favors to make *that* happen."

"So you're going to owe him even more."

Mago sat back with a satisfied sigh. "No, that's the

simple beauty of the plan. My friend will be arranging for Symon's nocturnal activities to be captured on a scrying crystal for future viewing. My friend's colleague is brokering a deal that Symon has to sign off on but is known to be opposed to. My friend thinks Symon will be more agreeable to signing the papers if he knows that his wife will discover that his business trip wasn't all business. So when you think of it that way, by putting Symon Wiggs into my friend's clutches I'm actually doing him a favor." Mago gave me a pleased little smile. "He says *he* owes *me*."

I think my mouth may have fallen open. "You're better at this than a goblin."

"Why, thank you, Raine. What a lovely compliment."

"I'm not sure I meant it as one, but I'm glad you're on my side. So I take it I'll be glamouring myself as an obnoxious little banker?"

Mago arched a brow.

"Hey, you called him obnoxious; I didn't."

"True. Yes, you will."

"Do you have a scrying crystal with you to show me what he looks and sounds like?"

"Naturally." Mago went to a suitcase on a stand in the corner of the room, peeled back a small section to reveal a padded and hidden compartment. He extracted a small box that would easily fit in my palm.

"I've never seen a crystal that small."

"The advances in spy magic are indeed wondrous." Mago handed it to me. "Take it with you and study it. You'll be having a late lunch with him tomorrow at the Swan Song. Balmorlan had initially wanted to meet in the elven embassy, but I knew you weren't about to set foot in that place again."

I closed the box on the scrying crystal. "I'd really rather not. I'd also really rather not have to perform in front of the hoity-toity crowd at the Swan Song."

Every high-ranking mage and Conclave bureaucrat had a favorite table at the Swan Song. If you were even going to try to make a reservation, you'd better have made sure the chief waiter recognized you and your name, otherwise there would mysteriously be no tables available at any time you wanted to dine. The Swan Song was all windows along the street side on Mid's major thoroughfare. The owners wanted anyone passing by to see only the crème de la crème of magical society at their tables.

"Not to mention, I can look and sound like Symon Wiggs, but that doesn't give me any knowledge of a criminal cartel, their money, or any banking knowledge, period."

"Don't worry, cousin. You have the perfect coach right here."

"Uh, I'm a quick learner, but I don't think—"

Mago's dark eyes sparkled. "You don't honestly believe I would let you have all the fun?"

"You're going with me?" I asked hopefully.

"Of course. Balmorlan has never met Symon Wiggs in person. Plus, it's perfectly normal for men such as Symon to bring along a colleague as a witness—or protection—when dealing with less than savory characters. Besides, I wouldn't miss seeing you out in public with . . ." He wiggled his fingers downward. "Now, what did Phaelan say you called them?"

"Dangly bits."

"Oh yeah, dangly bits. I wouldn't miss that for the world. No worries, Raine. After my incomparable tutoring, that meeting will be the most fun you've ever had with your clothes on."

That night, I had the most fun I could have with my clothes off.

When I'd told Mychael that I'd be meeting with Mago and Taltek Balmorlan the next day, he hadn't reacted quite the way that I'd expected.

I nestled against his bare chest and smiled. Actually all of him was bare.

"What is it?" Mychael murmured.

He must have felt me smile. His words rumbled in his chest and against my ear. Nice.

I snuggled closer. "You took my meeting better than I thought you would. I should have more meetings." I raised my head so I could see his eyes. "Is this the way you're going to react every time I do something dangerous?"

Mychael smiled sleepily. "You didn't like it?"

"Oh, I liked it; I just don't understand it."

"I don't want to lose you." He gently pushed the hair back from my face, his fingers lingering on my throat. "So anytime you do something where you might get hurt, I'm going to do this beforehand."

"Send me off to my doom with a big grin on my face?"

Mychael's hands did some delicious things under the covers. "Something like that."

The sparkle in his eyes told me he wanted to do it all again. I started to say something, but Mychael closed his lips on mine and I suddenly had no idea what I'd been about to say.

"Sneaky tactics," I said when he let me come up for air.

"I never claimed to play nice."

I ran my fingers lightly down his taut stomach, and Mychael's breath caught in response. "I noticed that," I murmured, "and I want to say that your behavior has my complete approval." My hand moved up to his chest and stopped. "So, what *do* you think of Mago and me meeting Balmorlan at the Swan Song?"

Mychael gave me a level look. "It doesn't matter because what I think won't change your mind."

"No, it won't. It can't. Believe me I'm not chomping at the bit to sit across a table from Taltek Balmorlan unless I get to stick a piece of cutlery in him. Mago's got a good plan; better still, it lets me play a big part in taking Balmorlan down—even though I have to glamour myself as a man." I smiled up at him. "Will you still love me when I'm a short, scrawny, pompous jerk?"

Mychael made entirely too much of a show of thinking

it over. I took a pillow and let him have it. He wrestled the pillow away from me and let me have it. Wrestling, tickling, and giggling followed. I was the giggler; Mychael was the tickler. Mostly. I grabbed the back of his neck and pulled his head down to mine, capturing his lips and taking my sweet time with a long, deep kiss. That put a stop to the tickling.

"I'll know it's you underneath that pompous banker exterior," Mychael said when I let him up for air, his voice husky. "So I might not be able to control myself." His lips curled in a slow, wicked grin. "I might just have to kiss you right in the Swan Song."

"Oooo, I've never been kissed there before."

"Then I'll have to change that."

I looked up into his eyes. "You're going to be there, aren't you?"

His lips were on my throat. "Closer than you ever imagined."

"You're as good with a glamour as I am. Nothing you'd show up as would surprise me."

"Not nearly as good. I have to stay the same sex that I was born as."

"And I can't tell you how glad that makes me."

Mychael laughed. "I think you just did."

"You did say your walls are soundproof, right?"

"They've never been tested to your extent."

My eyes widened. "Then the Guardians outside your door could be—"

"Envious as hell," Mychael finished for me.

Crap.

"How many of your 'envious as hell' Guardians will be at the Swan Song tomorrow?"

"Enough."

"Enough for . . ."

"Whatever trouble you manage to kick up."

"And if everything goes perfectly to plan?"

"Then they'll be envious *and* stunned."

"Here's hoping for stunned."

I piled the pillows on my side of the bed against the headboard and sat up against it, pulling the sheet up with me. Talking about tomorrow had made me think about Mago, which led me to my family, which made me think about criminals, which led to Rache Kai. Thinking about Rache effectively pulled the plug on my playfulness.

Mychael didn't know the landing place for all my mental gymnastics; he just saw that I'd covered up all of my toys. He got the hint that playtime was over, or at least suspended for the time being, and sat up in bed next to me. The seconds ticked by and neither one of us said a word. Mychael probably knew what was wrong. I definitely knew what was wrong. I also wasn't about to be the one to bring it up. I didn't want to talk about it, argue, or analyze it—all I wanted was for it, namely Rache, to go away. Preferably without killing anyone.

The knowledge that Rache was on Mid and Mychael knew that he'd once been engaged to me was kind of like a dragon hulking in the middle of the room. You could try to ignore it, but that didn't change the fact that it was there, it was big, and it wasn't going anywhere.

I'd never been good with tension, so it didn't take much longer for the dam of words building inside of me to break. "Yes, falling in love with Rache was stupid. *I* was stupid. I should have known better, known he was lying to me, making a fool—"

"Raine."

"—out of me. I was blind as a bat, and—"

"Raine."

"—he didn't even—"

Mychael reached over and hauled me, sheets and all, across the bed to him. His lips closed on mine in a long, deep kiss that made me stop thinking about Rache or criminals. Eventually the contact from his lips lightened into small, teasing nibbles.

"What was that for?" Air was suddenly in short supply. "Not that I'm complaining."

"It's the only way I can get a word in, and because I wanted to." He gazed down at me, his sea blue eyes searching my face, reading me. "Raine, being involved with a criminal doesn't make you one."

"It's not that."

"And I don't love you any less because of it. How could I?"

It was kind of that. Okay, it was mostly that.

"He's an assassin," I said, "and you're . . . most definitely not."

"Raine, you were young and in love with the man you thought he was. That's nothing to be ashamed of. So you fell for a guy because he was good-looking, a smooth talker, and treated you like a princess."

"But he was a—"

"And *you didn't know*. You also don't have any reason to worry about us now. I love you, and your ex-fiancé trying to puncture a goblin prince isn't going to change that."

"And you."

His brow creased in puzzlement. "And me, what?"

"He's trying to puncture you, too."

"My plan is to arrest him before he gets another chance." Mychael lightly ran a finger down my cheek. "His lies hurt you then and he may want to physically hurt you now. I'm going to keep both from happening."

"How?"

"Not all of my Guardians are based in the citadel and in uniform. In fact, a few of them get arrested on a regular basis by the city watch to keep up appearances. They'll find Rache. In the meantime, I want you to start wearing a mail shirt under your clothes."

I laughed. "You mean you're not going to try to lock me up in your bedroom?"

His eyes glittered. "Tempting, but unfortunately impossible right now."

"We have elves to con and an assassin to catch," I said. "Which brings up another question. You said Rache has never seen your real face. Is there any other way he could have found out who and what you used to be?"

Mychael didn't respond immediately.

Damn.

"If you have to think about it then it's possible," I said.

"It's highly unlikely."

"Pardon me if I ignore the 'highly' part of your 'unlikely.' If Rache even suspects that you're the same man who kept gold out of his pockets by snatching hits out from underneath his nose, he'll perch on every building in this city to take you out. That's probably why he's trying to kill you."

"I've always had a target on me, and a few of those times have been from Rache Kai. Incoming bolts and blades come with the job."

"That was before the Saghred was part of your job—and me."

Mychael made a sound that was something between a sigh and wry chuckle. "We've been over this before. Anything that happens to me is not your fault."

He pulled the sheet down far enough to plant a light kiss between my breasts. I let out a little gasp.

"It's your job," I managed.

"Absolutely." Mychael kissed my stomach.

"And you enjoy your work."

"Most satisfying." He kissed my belly button.

"And getting to kick Rache Kai's ass is—"

"A welcome bonus." The tip of his tongue swirled a hot trail around my belly button.

"But if it hadn't been for the rock—"

Mychael looked up at me. "If it hadn't been for *you* tricking Sarad Nukpana into touching the Saghred that night in Mermeia, he would have the rock and I'd probably be dead."

Along with some of the other people I loved most in the world.

"It's been three months since you found the Saghred."

I nodded once. "Seems like longer."

"Three months is enough time for Sarad Nukpana to have done everything he wanted to do. So all this being your fault turns into you've saved every man, woman, and child Sarad Nukpana would have sacrificed, slaughtered, or enslaved if he'd had the Saghred during those three months." Mychael's smile was slow and wicked as his fingers traced the still tingling trail of his kisses. "So if you ask me, everyone in the seven kingdoms owes you a big thank you."

His kisses went lower. "I'll thank you now."

Chapter 7

The face looking back at me out of Mychael's bedroom mirror wasn't mine.

I glamoured as soon as I got up, just for practice. I couldn't leave the citadel looking like Symon Wiggs, but I didn't want to change into him for the first time just before my meeting with Taltek Balmorlan.

One of the more useful enhancements the Saghred had done on my previously meager magical skill set was the ability to do an anatomically correct glamour, to make myself look and sound like someone else. The mechanics of doing a glamour weren't all that difficult, but I'd seen someone get stuck halfway through a transformation a couple of years back, and I knew that failure now would hurt a lot more than my ego.

I'd studied the banker's portrait in the scrying crystal. There was no room for a screwup or even a wrong step. Even though Balmorlan had never met Wiggs in person before, he could have seen his image in a scrying crystal just like I did. Balmorlan had to believe without any doubt that

I was Symon Wiggs. Failure wasn't an option; there was too much at stake. Literally everything I had or would ever have was on the line.

I focused on Symon's image, committing it to memory little by little, internalizing the smallest detail. When I had it firmly in my mind's eye, I released the slightest touch of my power into the image in my mind, projecting it outward, feeling the glamour solidify around me.

I saw Mychael standing behind me, reflected in the mirror. He checked me out from head to toe, started to say something, then stopped.

"Well, what do you think?" Even my voice was Symon's. Mago's spy crystal had sound as well as images, and I'd taken full advantage.

Mychael made a face. "Don't take this the wrong way. I still love you, but I just can't touch you right now."

I grinned, and on Symon Wiggs it came out as a smirk. Oh yeah, definitely the kind of guy who would act as a front man for a cartel. "No offense taken. Believe me I won't be staying in this skin one second longer than I have to."

"I just got a message for you from Prince Chigaru requesting a meeting early this afternoon."

I meticulously straightened my frilly cuffs. "Inform His Highness that I have a previous engagement." I smiled Symon's oily little smile. "Disappointment builds character, something the prince seems to be lacking. Being told no a few times will be good for him."

I glanced back in the mirror and straightened the fussy black doublet Mago assured me would look similar enough to the one that Symon wore. I felt his/my chest and grimaced. Then I quickly unbuttoned the front enough to take a look. The man had a bird chest. I flexed my right thigh against my left and then my left against my right.

"Ah, hell with it." I pulled my trousers out from my waist and looked down.

I snorted. Symon Wiggs's chest wasn't the only thing that was bird-sized.

Mychael chuckled from behind me. "That bad?"

"Well . . . everything's there, but let's just say that walking isn't going to be much different than when I'm myself."

"Ouch."

I grinned at him. "Wanna see?"

"I'll pass."

"You're sure?"

"Raine, that's just not done."

I put Symon's trousers back where they belonged, and there was no need to adjust anything when I did. "To have to live with this would just be embarrassing. No wonder Symon's such a jerk."

Noon at the Swan Song gave a whole new meaning to the term "power lunch."

The place was wall-to-wall mages packing enough magic to light the entire island.

Taltek Balmorlan's elven mages weren't willing to bond with me and the Saghred out of the goodness of their hearts or any kind of racial loyalty—they wanted money and lots of it. Part of the Saghred's legend was that it made its bond servants insane. Balmorlan's mages would be facing the same fate, but for enough money, they'd risk it.

I was about to find out what Balmorlan was selling to get the money he needed.

Mago and I were at our table and had already ordered drinks.

Mine was untouched.

One, I don't drink before noon. Okay, you got me there, but I don't make it a habit, especially when glamoured as a banker about to con an inquisitor who wanted me worse than dead.

I lowered my voice. "Okay, Mago, let's hear the high points one last time."

My cousin sighed theatrically and rolled his eyes. I knew what the plan was. He knew what the plan was. But I wanted to make sure that what I knew was what Mago was still going to do. My cousin had a tendency to get creative once a scam was underway. I had no problem with spontaneity; I just wanted to know about it first.

Mychael was right; I definitely had control issues. But I was still alive, so it was a good thing.

Mago's voice was loud enough to reach my ears, but no one else's. "Symon Wiggs told Balmorlan—"

"Actually, *you've* told Balmorlan."

Mago waved a dismissive hand. "Yes, yes, whatever. That I'm here because a transfer of any substantial amount must be authorized by another senior bank officer. And to expedite the process—"

"And as far as Balmorlan knows, you're not Mago Peronne, you're Magar Benick."

"Correct."

"Doesn't all that ever get confusing?"

Mago just stared at me like I'd asked the most ridiculous question ever.

"Right," I said. "Of course, it doesn't."

"Do you want to go over this or not? Because he'll be here any minute."

"No more interruptions," I promised.

"I'll believe that miracle when I see it."

There was a muffled guffaw from the next table. I turned and saw a red-haired, bearded mage whose robes looked like they'd once been covering one of the restaurant's windows. The man was big, brocaded, and belligerent. He sat ramrod straight, his bright eyes scanning the room in challenge. I'd seen his type many times before. He liked the way he was dressed, didn't give a damn what anyone else thought, but wanted nothing more than for someone to insult him and give him an excuse to pick a fight.

He saw me looking at him and winked.

I knew that wink, even if it was from another man's eye. It was Mychael.

Not only was it a perfect disguise, the entertainment potential was virtually limitless.

I told myself that I could smack him for that guffaw later. A banker turning and hitting a mage in the height of the lunch hour at the most exclusive restaurant on the island would raise a few highbred brows, to say the least. And I had a feeling I'd be raising more than eyebrows before I left; no need to start the show early.

Mago had ignored the exchange and lowered his voice even further. "I have all the information I need to empty Balmorlan's account—the one he holds jointly with several partners. The account and access numbers were child's play to obtain."

"Child's play for you."

Mago's lips twitched in a crooked smile. "That goes without saying. But last month Balmorlan set up a private account, and the naughty boy has transferred more of that money than is probably his into this new account."

"His partners would love to hear that he's stealing from them."

Mago meticulously realigned his silverware. "All in good time. Since Balmorlan has no problem with taking their money, I don't, either. So anything he offers to sell you today, you'll be eager to buy—but not too eager. Symon Wiggs is known for driving a hard bargain. And to pay for the purchase, I'll siphon the money directly from Balmorlan's partners' account."

"We'll be buying what he's selling with his cronies' money. Screwed by his own greed. I love it."

Mago nodded once. "The more money he demands, the more he and his partners will lose."

"Okay, we're paying him with his own money. He'll want it deposited into this new account of his."

"Correct."

"So . . . how does all this gold end up in your affluent client's account?"

"Balmorlan's new account is private. That means it's only identified by numbers; there's no name attached. I don't know which one is his. I could find out, but it would take too much time. Balmorlan will give you the account transit number to transfer the money. With that I can get everything else I need to empty the contents of his new account into the prince's."

"A goblin prince who wants peace with the elves, not war."

Mago took a sip of his drink to hide a small smile. "No doubt his elven partners will be very disappointed in him. And if elven intelligence *somehow* discovers that he's funding the enemy, or if his war-monger partners find out he's donated all of their money to a peace-loving goblin prince . . ."

I cracked my knuckles meaningfully. "Taltek Balmorlan will be taking a long swim with a rock and rope."

"You're as barbaric as Phaelan."

"Thank you." I toyed with the cutlery, too, most notably the knife which had an acceptably sharp edge. "So instead of merely draining the old account Balmorlan has with his partners as previously planned, we'll be draining his partners' account into his new account—"

"Then emptying the lot of them. Thanks to my colleagues back in D'Mai, there will be an abundant and obvious paper trail, so Balmorlan's partners will have no trouble discovering exactly where their money went—and to whom that account belongs."

I grinned. "His partners will come after him with a vengeance."

"No doubt they'll be extremely upset with him."

"And after he gives us the account transit numbers, your banking friends will be able to tell you exactly which bloated account is his—"

"And will empty every last coin Inquisitor Balmorlan has into a poor, exiled goblin prince's account." Mago raised his glass. "Here's to a generous elven benefactor whose largesse will soon be the talk of the seven kingdoms."

I clinked my glass to his.

Mago took and savored a sip. "Now do you understand everything?"

"I always did."

That earned me an annoyed look. "Then why did you make me say it again?"

"To make sure it hadn't suddenly sprouted a new twist. Symon doesn't strike me as the type who would like surprises. I know I don't. I've had enough surprises since this whole crapfest started to last me a lifetime." Then I remembered something we hadn't actually covered. "Are we eating lunch?"

"I beg your pardon?"

"Lunch. Are we eating?"

Mago's expression came perilously close to appalled. "Of course. Inquisitor Balmorlan made the reservations—and he is paying."

I grinned. "Then what's the most expensive thing on the menu?"

Mago flashed his teeth in a predatory smile. "I have no idea, but whatever it is, I'll have what you're having."

Three men came in. One was Taltek Balmorlan; the other two were protective muscle. These boys looked like they were good at being big, but that was about it. Speed, either in thought or action, didn't appear to be a burden that either one carried. However, there were others outside: lean, armed, and alert. The muscle-bound bookends were merely decorative. Balmorlan didn't expect trouble in here. His elven guards were outside to keep the trouble from coming inside.

I had news for Taltek Balmorlan—the worst trouble he'd ever had in his life would be sitting right next to him.

I felt myself smile. I'd make the bastard curse the day he'd ever heard the name Raine Benares.

"Symon doesn't gut business acquaintances with a spoon," Mago whispered in a singsong voice.

I looked down in surprise at my clenched hand. A spoon. I knew how to do all sorts of unpleasant things to a man with a spoon. I calmly set it down, reluctantly forced the homicidal grin off my face, and stood to greet the man I was about to ruin.

Once introductions were complete, we all sat down. Time for small talk. As a result of my newfound vindictive confidence, it was amazing how relaxed and talkative I was.

After a few minutes I sensed someone standing at my left shoulder, patiently waiting for me to finish what I'd been saying. I turned to look and damned near lost it.

Vegard was a vision of servile propriety in black tunic, poofy black knee breeches, black hose, and . . . did my eyes deceive me? Nope, they knew what they were seeing—black shoes with darling black silk rosettes on top. The big Guardian's blond hair was pulled back and tightly braided, his beard was closely trimmed in dandy fashion, and a pair of delicate gold-rimmed spectacles were perched on what was definitely not Vegard's real nose.

"Hello, I'm Marc, and I'll be your server today."

As I looked up at him, I had to bite my bottom lip as tears welled up in my eyes. Fortunately, my back was to Balmorlan so he couldn't witness my facial contortions.

Vegard, the consummate professional, didn't bat an eye—which were now green, by the way.

"Would you like to hear our chef's specials?" he asked.

"Of course," Mago told him, knowing that I was well past the power of speech.

I got myself under control as Vegard—excuse me, Marc—prattled on about the sauce for this fish or the glaze for that steak, and even went so far as to make wine recommendations for each. Impressive.

Mago ordered the best cut of beef in the largest portion the restaurant had. Mid was an island and a rocky one at that. Fish were plentiful, but beef would most definitely be an import—a pricey one.

I handed my menu back to Marc with a bright smile. "I'll have what he's having."

Balmorlan ordered the fish.

I proposed that we not talk business until after we'd eaten. Balmorlan didn't like it, but then Balmorlan wasn't going to like much about our meeting, though he wouldn't know it until the results jumped up and bit him on the ass.

As we chatted and ate what was quite possibly the best meal I'd ever had, I became painfully aware that Taltek Balmorlan wasn't what one would call a scintillating conversationalist. Mago, on the other hand, was well educated, well traveled, well-heeled, and well . . . interesting. Everything Balmorlan obviously was not.

I knew there had to be an accepted way to discuss buying something of questionable legality with money that was not your own. Since I had no clue what that was, I went with the direct approach. It seemed to be the way Symon would handle it. And since Balmorlan apparently accepted me as the genuine article, I just cut to the chase.

"You didn't ask me all the way here from D'Mai for lunch."

"I would have preferred a more private meeting location."

"Such as your embassy, which is considered elven soil and is subject to elven law." I dabbed my lips with my napkin and laid it carefully on the table. "I'm not an elf and the people whose interests I represent aren't elves. So you can understand my suspicion of your elven privacy."

"Symon, Symon, you misjudge me. Have I ever gone back on my word or not delivered what I'd promised?"

I had no idea what Balmorlan had promised or delivered, so I went with a stony silence. It seemed like the right response.

Balmorlan pursed his lips in annoyance and lowered his voice. "You can't still blame me for your operation in Tamir."

"Can't I?"

"Your associates got what they paid for. However, it was beyond my control that the intelligence I was given reported that the garrison was empty. There was no way I could have known that your partners' men had been set up for an ambush."

"Your intelligence was obviously lacking."

Balmorlan shrugged. "The loss of life was regrettable, but unavoidable given the circumstances."

"And now you ask me here to attempt to sell those I represent yet another disaster in the making."

"Ah, but you came. And I can I assure you that your employers will be delighted with their purchase."

"Their delight has yet to be seen, and I came only because I was ordered. This meeting was not my choice." I gave Balmorlan what I hoped was an oily smile. "Though it is my choice whether or not I reject your offer." I sat back in my chair. "What do you want? And don't waste any more of my time. The quicker I can get off of this cursed rock, the better."

"I'm offering them power."

"Pardon me?"

Balmorlan leaned forward. "Power. I'm offering you and your associates a chance to eliminate those who oppose you once and for all. No more risks, just profits and unquestioned power."

I gave him a scoffing laugh. "For once and for all *and* on your word. An amusing proposition, but not one I'm inclined to accept." My humor vanished. "I require proof. Tangible proof."

Balmorlan smiled the smile of a man with a secret. "I can provide it. Proof of how with one strike, your associates will be in unopposed possession of all southern Nebia."

One strike. I forced my breathing to remain even. He couldn't mean—

"I can provide this for you and your associates," Balmorlan was saying.

"Now?"

"By this time tomorrow."

"For a price." I forced the words out.

"Naturally."

The son of a bitch was selling the Saghred's power. Power he didn't have.

Yet.

Unless he got his hands on me, and he was giving himself one whole day to get the job done. Cocky bastard. Simply killing me wouldn't get him the Saghred's power. The rock was locked and guarded in the citadel. The only thing my death would do would be to let the Saghred latch on to the first mage it could lure within touching distance. Taltek Balmorlan couldn't steal the Saghred, but he seemed confident that he could steal me.

Within one day.

I didn't say anything. I didn't trust myself to say anything. However, I did trust myself to put the steak knife that had found its way into my hand to good use. I toyed with the handle.

Mago cleared his throat. "Considering the history of my colleague's dealings with you, his associates can hardly be expected to accept any claims at face value."

Balmorlan bristled. "You're saying that I'm a liar?"

"Not yet," I said smoothly. "My associates now find it prudent to proceed with caution to any offer you make." I paused. "They will only tolerate being burned once," I said with quiet menace. "They will not allow it to happen again."

Mago spoke. "You seem confident that you can deliver the promised results, Inquisitor Balmorlan. But you understand that we cannot share your confidence, let alone assign monetary worth to it based on a few words—"

"Meaning we want to know precisely what you're selling," I broke in. I knew the answer, but I wanted to hear the son of a bitch say it.

"Very well," Balmorlan said. "By this time tomorrow, the Saghred's power will be mine."

I didn't move. "From what I've been told, the Saghred's bond servant is an elven seeker by the name of Raine Benares. This Benares woman is a magic user; you are not, so I fail to see how you could not only claim to possess and wield such power, but offer it to others."

"By possessing Raine Benares," Balmorlan replied smoothly. "My own mages will be able to wield the stone's power through her. And best of all, my claim to the woman will be perfectly legal."

I leaned forward, hopefully the very picture of a skeptical negotiator, not a banker about to dive across a table with a steak knife. "To claim is one thing, to gain cooperation is quite another."

"Her cooperation is not needed," Balmorlan said. "Once she's in custody, I have a specially constructed cell waiting with magic-neutralizing restraints. I've retained the services of mages eager to taste the Saghred's power for themselves."

Mago's eyes were the flat black of a shark, his voice cold. "If the woman is chained and can't access the stone's power, how can these mages—"

"The Saghred is hungry," Balmorlan told him point-blank. "It'll bond with my mages like a starving demon being offered fresh meat." He paused and smiled. "Except in the Saghred's case it will be fresh souls. The stone will have to be well fed before it can be properly used. We'll feed it through the elf woman, and once the Saghred is satisfied, my mages can put the stone's power to good use." He tossed back the remainder of his drink. "Raine Benares is merely a conduit for souls and power. She'll be used as long as she remains useful. You're aware of what the Saghred can do?"

I knew the answer to that one. "I am."

"Then you know that my offer is genuine. I've arranged a demonstration of the Saghred's power that will more than prove the validity of my offer."

Demonstration? That would be some trick since I was sitting right here.

"Where and how?" I asked.

Taltek Balmorlan grinned. "Let's just say I've taken the liberty of moving your luggage from the Greyhound Hotel to a safer location."

Chapter 8

Mago didn't move a muscle. "Safer?"

"It's also safe to say there will be no need to pay your hotel bill." Balmorlan smiled, showing us his teeth.

Teeth I wanted nothing more than to knock out.

"There's a tavern on the corner of Hobwell Street that will provide us with a splendid view and adequate protection," Balmorlan continued. "I've arranged a table by the window. As soon as we arrive, the show will begin."

"That's nearly two blocks from the hotel," Mago noted. His voice was calm, his posture nonchalant. He always had been a good actor.

When hundreds of lives depended on it, I could fake calm, too. "I'm not fond of surprises," I told Balmorlan. "Just what is this demonstration of yours?"

"There will be an attack on the Greyhound Hotel, but the primary target is its occupants. At this moment, Raine Benares is in the hotel meeting with her goblin prince."

I froze. A meeting I'd canceled to be here.

A meeting Taltek Balmorlan knew about. Who the leak

was or where it was didn't concern me, not now. Snarling and lunging across the table for Balmorlan's throat wouldn't save Prince Chigaru, his court, or any of the hundreds of innocent people staying or working in or around the hotel. If it was only safe outside of a two-block area, there was going to be collateral damage. A lot of collateral damage.

Balmorlan didn't care about any of that. It was simply a way to make his point. The smirk the smarmy bastard was wearing told me that he had something we wanted, something we couldn't resist. He was right—he had his life and I wanted to take it.

"She'll hardly stand by while the prince, his retinue, and every other living thing inside are annihilated," Balmorlan continued. "However, to have a chance of saving anyone, she'll have to use the Saghred."

Mago's face was expressionless. "And if this Raine Benares is 'annihilated' along with the others?"

Balmorlan waved a dismissive hand. "She'll be the only creature who will survive. The Saghred would hardly allow its bond servant to be killed before it has found a suitable replacement. And after having used the Saghred, my associates will see to it that Raine Benares is arrested as a public menace." He chuckled. "Someone with that much power can hardly remain on the loose among our citizens. So you gentlemen will have your proof, while my associates eliminate a political inconvenience. And if you're experiencing any guilt at the unavoidable loss of life, don't bother; my associates had already planned this. It would have happened whether you had accepted my invitation or not."

I had no doubt that every time Balmorlan said "associates" he meant Carnades Silvanus.

There would be no Saghred demonstration. I was here and so was the rock's power, but that wouldn't stop Balmorlan from having everyone in that hotel killed. The only thing there would be was death and a lot of it. Deaths that in Balmorlan's opinion only the Saghred's power could stop. I didn't doubt his opinion. Balmorlan wasn't a mage, but he knew what mages could do, couldn't do—and what was beyond their power. I was betting he'd arranged a demonstration of the latter kind.

And I wouldn't be sitting in a tavern while it happened.

Balmorlan pushed back his chair and stood. "The bill has already been taken care of, gentlemen. I have a coach waiting for us. We'll begin negotiations after you've seen the obvious value in—"

"What do you mean you're out of lobster bisque!" roared the red-haired mage (aka Mychael) at the next table.

Marc/Vegard visibly cowered. "Sir, if you will allow me to—"

"To what? Explain why you brought this vile—"

Vegard gasped in indignation. "Sir, the ingredients are the finest—"

"Swill!"

"The chef assures me that it surpasses even the—"

Vegard/Marc didn't get a chance to finish; the gaped-mouthed mages around us didn't get the chance to regain their composure. Mychael's fist came up and knocked the bowl from Vegard's hands, hands seemingly desperate to catch the bowl, not to direct the fishy contents onto Taltek Balmorlan's head, down the front of his doublet, trousers, and probably into his boots.

It was a really big bowl of soup.

It was beautiful.

Hotel destruction delayed.

I had to fight the urge to kiss that redheaded mage smack-dab on the lips.

Vegard/Marc stared at Balmorlan in abject horror. "Sir, I am *so* sorry." He grabbed a pair of cloth napkins from a nearby table and began dabbing at the soup covering the elf's silk doublet; the napkins doing nothing but spreading the fishy mess around. Balmorlan was trying to stop Vegard from dabbing; Vegard was determined to stop Balmorlan from leaving.

We had quite the commotion going, and within moments an impeccably dressed man came running out of the back near the kitchens, took one look at the scene in all of its sogginess, took a deep breath, and strode toward us. "Sir, if you will allow me to assist," he told Balmorlan. His voice was the very essence of professional calm. "I'm the manager, and on behalf of the owners, I offer you our sincerest apologies. Come with me and we can take care of this." He lowered his voice. "The fish sauce will be difficult to get out, but not impossible. We have something in the kitchen that will take care of it without too much damage to your clothing." He smiled with every bit of charm he could muster. "We've had worse stains," he whispered. The manager gripped Balmorlan's upper arm with both hands, not giving the inquisitor any choice except to go with him.

I really hoped there were cats in the alley behind the kitchen. Fish-loving, hungry cats.

*Our coach was waiting just down the street. The city watch nor-*mally wouldn't let a coach park on the street, but coaches didn't normally have plainclothes Guardian drivers and outriders, either.

I ran to the coach as quick as Symon's scrawny legs would carry me, spitting curses the entire way. If any of Balmorlan's spies reported back to their boss, he'd think I was just pissed at having to clear out of the best hotel in town, or not getting the best of the son of a bitch in our first meeting. The Guardian "footman" saw us coming and got the coach's door open fast. They had no idea I was a glamoured Raine Benares. Mychael had given them an assignment and they did it without asking questions. All they saw was the pissed off little man they'd driven to the restaurant who now desperately wanted to hurt someone.

No doubt Taltek Balmorlan would wonder why we didn't wait for him at the Swan Song or show up at that tavern.

No doubt I didn't give a damn.

Mychael was waiting in the coach, his mage glamour gone and the Guardian paladin back in spades.

I pulled myself inside and quickly sat down; Mago was right on my heels.

Mychael tapped twice on the wall behind him and the coach quickly moved out into traffic. "You two are getting out at watcher headquarters."

That was only halfway to the hotel.

"No deal, I'm—"

Mychael's eyes blazed. "Raine, I'm not making any deals with you. He's set you up—"

"And people are going to die unless I'm there," I shot back.

"You're not going to be one of them."

"Damn right, I'm not. I'm also not getting out of this coach until it gets to the hotel. I can't hide, Mychael. Not now."

"Balmorlan said the show wouldn't start until we joined him at the tavern," Mago said.

"With this many lives at stake, that's a chance I can't take," Mychael replied.

"What could he do that we'd need to be two blocks away?" my cousin asked him.

"Magic of the worst kind."

"Balmorlan collects mages, remember?" I said bitterly. "The more lethal, the better." I didn't say that he'd be paying any black mages, supernatural assassins, or whatever was waiting at the hotel, with the money we were supposed to get with the transit numbers that we didn't have. Mago didn't need me to remind him.

Mychael glowered. "Which is why you won't be there," he told me.

"Balmorlan already thinks I am there." I leaned forward in my seat. "Mychael, it's me he wants; whatever he's about to do is *my* fault, so what I do about it is *my* decision. And if it's something that only the Saghred can handle, then I'll handle it." I felt my glamour start to waver. I stopped and steadied my breathing. I knew from experience that pain wasn't good for a glamour, apparently neither was rage. I couldn't go back to being myself, not yet. If there was any chance that I could get out of this without taking the lead role in Balmorlan's horror show, I owed it to Mychael to keep my head down. But if the bastard forced my hand, I'd have no choice. I leaned back in the seat and forced myself into a calm I didn't feel. "Don't worry," I told him. "Balmorlan won't get a chance to have me hauled off. If I'm caught, I'll die of embarrassment first. That'd ruin his day."

"My men can handle anything Balmorlan has planned," Mychael assured me. "It's what we train for. My men are inside the hotel, outside the hotel, on rooftops around the hotel, and hell, they're even on sky dragons patrolling above the hotel."

"Balmorlan seemed sure that I'd have to get involved."

"No, he just knows that if people are in danger you'll do something about it."

Mago braced himself against the jostling of the speeding coach. "You said what's going to happen will involve the worst kind of magic. Can you be more specific?"

"It would have to be something that would catch the prince's mages off guard; that is if the assault came from inside the building. If it's outside, he's hoping to catch my men flat-footed. It'd take a hell of a lot for either one to happen."

My cousin exhaled. While not as uncomfortable with magic as Phaelan, Mago would rather not have to deal with it head-on. Neither would I. "I imagine the prince hasn't lived as long as he has by not being able to anticipate and counter any attacks," he said, as if trying to make himself believe it.

Mychael's mouth turned into a firm line. "Let's hope today's not the exception."

• • •

Mychael had the driver pull the coach around to the back of the hotel. He wanted to get everyone who was inside the hotel to safety, but at the same time, he needed to catch the bastards, bitches, or creatures waiting for Balmorlan's signal. Jumping out of the coach in front of the hotel and screaming that the world was about to end would incite panic in the public and hiding in the bad guys. Both were undesirable for obvious reasons.

Mychael had the door open and was out before the coach stopped. He turned and looked at me. "You wouldn't consider staying here, would you."

He didn't ask it as a question, because he didn't seriously consider it one. I was going with him. He knew it, and so did I. I dispensed with a verbal response and jumped out of the coach with Mago right behind me. Mychael and I just looked at him.

"Hey, don't even think about leaving me here alone," my cousin told both of us. "You're the Guardian paladin, and you're the lady with the killer rock. If anyone's getting out of this alive, it'll be the two of you." He flashed a grin. "So I'm going to be harder to get rid of than bad credit."

We entered the hotel.

I was going with Mychael because I thought I could help find whatever or whoever it was that was about to unleash doomsday in the Greyhound Hotel. However, I was at a serious disadvantage considering that I had no clue what I was looking for. True to his word, Mago was staying close enough to qualify as my second skin.

I was wearing my own skin now, not Symon Wiggs's. I was bonded to the Saghred; Symon wasn't. I couldn't tap my magic and hold onto an anatomically correct glamour at the same time. So it was Symon or the Saghred. I liked Symon more than I did the rock, but I needed the rock more than I did a scrawny banker.

I dropped the glamour.

If I was going to locate Balmorlan's surprise before it happened, I'd need every bit of my magic. And if the elven bastard pulled something truly nasty—and I had no doubt that he would—I'd need the Saghred to stop it.

Mago and I would have opted for stealth when going into a building with heavily armed men not in our own employ. Mychael was the chief lawman on the island; he barged right on through the hotel into the lobby.

My eyes and magical senses were trying to see everywhere and everyone at once. The lobby was filled with armed goblins and Guardians. Neither was growling at the other, but that was as far as niceties were going to go.

While Mychael went to speak with a Guardian officer and a goblin senior guard near the front doors, Mago slipped behind a potted plant and pulled me with him, whispering urgently, "Do you see what I see; or more to the point, what I don't?"

I blinked. "Cousin, I don't even know what the hell you just said."

"No elves."

"What?"

"There are no elves at the front desk," Mago told me. "They were there when I left for the restaurant, and the senior staff on duty this morning were all elves."

Now they were all humans, every last one of them.

Oh no.

I could smell the setup from here. "Every elf in this place was probably an intelligence agent."

"And now they're gone," Mago said. "Told to leave, I imagine."

"So Balmorlan values his people," I muttered, "but doesn't give a damn about humans. What a guy."

If the elves at the reception desk had been agents, they would also know exactly who was in what room, which would make it a lot easier for assassins to get in and do their thing.

The goblin guards who had seen us were giving yours truly some seriously belligerent looks.

"I'm here to try to save their collective ass and they're

looking at me like I'm something they'd like to scrape off their boots."

"Should we tell them?" Mago asked.

"That elven intelligence is plotting to wipe them all out and they should run screaming into the streets?"

"You know, that sounds implausible even to me."

I wish I could say the same. I'd seen Balmorlan's destructive handiwork entirely too up close and personal. A couple of weeks ago, he'd arranged for half a dozen or so crates of Nebian grenades to be stacked in the basement of a house Markus Sevelien was staying in on Embassy Row. When those grenades blew, so did Markus's house and nearly us along with it.

The Saghred couldn't stop explosions from happening. Well, maybe it could, but I didn't know how to do it.

Balmorlan would arrange something guaranteed to be deadly to an entire hotel full of people, but something that he knew I could stop and survive.

My eyes were drawn to the wall behind the registration desk. People weren't the only things the Greyhound Hotel had too many of.

Mirrors ran a close second.

Mychael's mirror mage friend had said the hotel's mirrors were warded as of two days ago. Were they warded now? Without the ripple, I couldn't tell. But a mirror mage could.

Carnades Silvanus was a mirror mage.

This was starting to stink like last week's garbage.

The Guardian and goblin officer Mychael had been speaking with were now giving orders to their people, and the hotel lobby suddenly got really busy. Good. Message received; threat believed. I didn't want to think about what would have happened if Mychael hadn't been with us at the Swan Song. If I'd come running in here yelling the same thing, no one would have believed me. And disbelief would have been the best reaction I'd have gotten; I didn't even want to consider other more likely scenarios.

"Let's go!" Mychael called to us.

He took the stairs at a run, four at a time. I could only manage two, which put Mychael one flight ahead of me, which is exactly what he was counting on. If there was danger on the prince's floor, he wanted to get to it first. That was fine; I needed the space around me clear of any magical distortions. Mychael's power definitely qualified. Mago was a few steps behind me and didn't affect what I was doing.

My feet weren't the only things running as fast as they could. My magical senses were wide open and racing, searching anywhere and everyone, looking for an anomaly, someone who looked out of place or a hotel staffer or guest who was packing some serious magical mojo and trying to keep it quiet. I knew Mychael was doing the same.

"Feel anything?" I asked in mindspeak, saving my breath for running, and for what I hopefully wouldn't have to do all too soon—kick some serious supernatural ass.

"No." His curt response sounded in my head. He was conserving energy, too.

I didn't know what I was looking or listening for, but I hoped I found it before it found me.

We reached the top floor and our way was blocked by a quartet of the prince's guards.

"Move!" Mychael bellowed.

They did.

There was no spellsinger compulsion in that word, just the voice of a man that other men obeyed without question.

Apparently so did goblins.

To my surprise, no one tried to stop me, either.

Imala was in the hall, a pair of wickedly curved short swords in her hands and the nimbus of a protection spell forming around her.

"Get the prince out of here," Mychael told her, his voice low and intense. "Get everyone out."

"What is it?" said a deep voice from right behind me.

I damned near jumped out of my boots, and Mago helpfully yelped for me.

It was Tam.

"Within the hour, this building will be destroyed," Mychael told him.

Tam didn't even blink. "How?"

"Unknown."

To Tam and Imala's credit, that was all the proof they needed.

I thought getting goblin aristocrats out of a building would be like herding cats—big cats. That wasn't the case. Apparently when you were courtiers of an exiled and renegade prince, you learned to move fast. Not only were they quick about it, they moved in complete silence, no talking other than what was absolutely necessary, and those words were whispered.

My estimation of goblin courtiers went up a few notches.

"Uh, Mychael, they can't just go out into the street." I kept my voice down, too. I didn't need to tell him that I was thinking about snipers.

"There's a door in the basement leading to a short tunnel," he told me. "It empties a block away from the hotel."

Balmorlan had said *two* blocks over would be safe. Well, when it came to saving lives, you took the best option you had.

I gave Tam and Imala a quickie rendition of why Balmorlan was having the hotel destroyed.

"Two birds with one stone," Imala noted dryly. "Kill the prince and every goblin who supports him. Then a war with Sathrik will merely be a matter of who fires first."

Tam looked at something over my shoulder. "Your Highness, we need to leave immediately."

Prince Chigaru Mal'Salin was on his feet. Barely. A pair of guards stood just behind him, far enough for protocol, close enough to catch the prince before he hit the floor if he happened to pass out.

The prince was actually smiling. "I must run for my life, and Raine Benares is involved. How shocking."

"And once again, it's you they're trying to kill," I retorted. "Shocking."

At least Chigaru was wearing trousers and boots this time, and he was almost wearing a shirt. It was completely open down the front, exposing his bandaged shoulder. His right arm was in a sling.

One of his guards turned, went back into Chigaru's suite, and quickly returned with a cloak, which he draped over his prince's shoulders and fastened with the clasp at his throat.

Tam nodded. "Let's move."

The main staircase was full of panicked guests and staff from the lower floors.

"This way," Tam said.

"Service stairs?" I asked.

Tam flashed a quick grin full of fang. "Rule one in the goblin court is always know the nearest exit."

I was standing still, but the skin on the back of my neck wasn't. Tam looked perfectly calm, relaxed even. Many of the goblins I could see were the same.

"Either being exiled has made running for your lives old hat, or you all risk your lives for fun."

Imala smiled. "Yes."

"I'll never understand how goblins—" The tiny hairs on my arms joined the skin on my neck in trying to run away. A scent—no, a sensation—drifted through the air. It held the slightest hint of foulness, corruption . . .

. . . of brimstone.

Black magic.

"Mago, stay close," I said quietly. "Mychael, how many men do you have outside?"

He stopped, and I felt the magic he instantly held in readiness. He sensed it, too. We all did.

I swallowed. "We need them inside."

The lights went out and the screams began.

Chapter 9

Screams came from the main stairs and the floor below us. For the first few seconds, those screams were because of the dark, the base fear we all have of the unknown. But panic in a pitch-dark building—where getting out meant going down flights of stairs—could be bad, worse than bad. I'd seen the aftermath before.

I couldn't see my hand in front of my face. How far was it to the service stairs door? Twenty steps? Thirty? The goblins around me went completely silent, and no one drew a weapon. Good. Blades in the dark and in close quarters meant accidents of the fatal kind. Goblins wouldn't be scared of the dark because they could see in it. I couldn't see, and I was scared. I also wanted to see where I was going and what might be coming after me almost as badly as I wanted to get out.

I wanted out, but this was only the beginning of what Balmorlan had set in motion because I was in here. And I was in here because he knew I could handle it.

But only with the Saghred.

I backhanded that thought out of my mind.

Light, Raine. One thing at a time; get yourself some light.

I held my hand at what I thought to be level with my face, palm up, and summoned my magic. Normally, a bright lightglobe would instantly spin itself into existence. All I got now was sputtering sparks, their light going only a foot or two in front of me, but it was enough for me to see that the lightglobe set into the wall nearest me hadn't gone out.

It'd been smothered.

Just like the next one and the one after that.

A black fog covered everything, sliding against my skin like an oily darkness. The air quickly grew cold and thick; trying to lift my arm was like being under water.

Muffled magic, smothered lightglobes, greasy air. Only one thing could do that.

Magic of the blackest kind.

Who or whatever was behind this spell didn't want us getting out of the hotel.

Who or whatever could bite me. I gritted my teeth and pushed my way through the murk toward Mychael.

I could barely see Imala at the edge of my light. She spat out a low curse. "What the hell is this? It doesn't smell like smoke."

"It isn't," Tam said, his voice tight. A red lightglobe struggled to life above his outstretched hand. More red orbs of light bloomed as the goblin mages followed suit. None of them did much to cut through the oily murk.

"Where's it coming from?" Mago's breath came on a plume of frost.

Only then did I realize that I was shivering. I thought I was just scared. I was, but I was also freezing. "It's cold enough to hang meat in here."

That earned me a dark chuckle from the goblin guard closest to me.

"We're out of here," Mychael told us. "Now."

A goblin was pushing his armored shoulder against the stairwell door. "Sir, it won't open."

A second guard joined him. They were big, but that door wasn't budging.

With a visible effort, Mychael waded through the magic-thickened air and the goblins made way for him. "It shouldn't have a lock." He laid his hand flat against the door's wood and the iron bands that wrapped them and I could literally see the surge of Mychael's power go into the door, power that should have blown the thing off its hinges.

It didn't budge.

It should have done a lot more than budge. I'd seen Mychael disintegrate doors sealed shut with Level Twelve wards.

The door began to glow and hum, getting brighter and louder.

Oh hell.

"Down!" Mychael shouted.

He shoved the guards away from the door and flung himself down the corridor and against the wall. I covered Mago and me with the best shield I could manage on short notice.

The door exploded outward in a scream of tortured iron hinges, its splintered wood now deadly stakes flying down the hallway.

Doors couldn't absorb magic and spit it back. That was impossible. Though the smoking black hole where the door had been clearly said otherwise.

I scrambled to my feet, pulling Mago with me.

Whether the door had been blown out, blown in, or blown up didn't matter. It was gone and we could run through the hole that was—

Filled with a monster. Not just filled, packed.

Even in the dim light, there was no mistaking what that thing was.

A buka.

The nine-foot-tall, hairy, long-fanged, and longer-armed mountain monster out of goblin legend.

The creature had to duck and twist to get its thick body through the door opening. Its roar was deafening in the confined hallway, drowning out any shouts or commands. For the first time ever, I heard a goblin scream.

The buka was fast, faster than any living creature had a right to be. Goblins were quick, but for the ones closest to the door, the only thing they did quickly was die. With two swipes of one of the buka's long arms with its claw-hooked hands, screams became feral shrieks as dark goblin blood spattered against the walls and ceiling.

The buka had appeared, attacked, and killed in less than five seconds.

The goblins instantly went from forced calm to near hysteria, but they didn't stampede. The cries and shouts from the lower floors redoubled, probably at the sight of their own bukas—or things even worse.

A panicked scream came from the main stairs. A man was scrambling up them, his face a terrified mask. An enormous gnarled hand reached up from the gloom below and grabbed the man by both legs at once, jerked him off his feet, and snatched him down the stairs. There was a quick, wet snap of bone in the dark, and the man's screams rose to an inhuman shriek. Two more snaps and the shrieks stopped.

The buka looked directly to where Chigaru's guards supported the prince against the wall, one on either side. The buka roared, baring fangs the length of my fingers, and lunged toward him. Mychael threw himself between the monster and the prince, the steel of his sword infused and glowing with magic. Tam was next to him, his unseen power adding to Mychael's strike. Between the two of them, they gave the bastard something to really roar about.

Or they should have.

The thing ate Mychael's magic like candy and Tam's like a sugar topping. Absorbed. Gone. The sword didn't even part its fur.

"Raine, get him out of here!" Mychael shouted.

I knew he meant the prince. "I'm not leaving without—"

"We'll follow!"

"If we can" went unsaid.

Imala shouted to the prince's guards. One got in front of Chigaru and the other behind, and pushed their way through the courtiers, toward Imala and me.

I looked down the stairs. Just because I couldn't see the giant hand and the nightmare it was attached to, didn't mean that it wasn't down there waiting with its closest monster friends. Terrorizing a hotel packed with people wouldn't be a solo effort. The sounds of screaming, running, and panicked people coming up from below proved it.

Imala, Chigaru, and his guards reached us.

Mago clutched my arm. "I have a ladder in my room. If we can get there, we can get the prince out through the window."

I had a surge of hope. Mago's escape ladder, in his luggage . . .

Luggage that Balmorlan had ordered taken.

I swore. "It's not there. Balmorlan took—"

Mago bared his teeth in a fierce grin. "I keep it under the mattress in case of emergency."

If this wasn't an emergency, I didn't know what was.

Make it down two floors alive instead of four. Sounded like better odds to me, though it depended on what hell spawn was waiting on the fourth and third floors. Mago's room was at the end of the freaking hall. One death trap at a time, Raine. One at a time.

"Let's go!"

We went down the stairs as quickly as the darkness and probable presence of monsters would allow. Imala and Mago were on either side of me. Chigaru was moving on his own, but his guards were sticking close, as were two of his mages. Other goblin courtiers brought up the rear. I didn't see Mychael or Tam.

Chatar was one of the prince's mages.

Great. Monsters weren't bad enough, now I had a mage

accused of murder because of me close enough to shoot one of his poisoned darts into the back of *my* neck. There needed to be a revenge timeout until we were out of here.

Mago tripped, the gilt railing the only thing that kept him from falling into the stairwell. "What the hell is—" He looked down at the carpet and sucked in his breath with a hiss.

A foot. A man's foot.

The shoe was still on, but the rest of the body was gone, though not without a trace. Blood and gore soaked the carpet in a dark trail down the next dozen or so steps.

Visuals to go with the sounds we'd heard.

Chigaru stepped up beside me. "What lies below, seeker?"

The prince was simply calling me what I was. No insult or slight intended. He was standing beside me, in the glow of what light I had.

He was a target in more ways than one and he knew it.

"Whatever waits for us was sent here because of me," he said quietly.

He was only partly right, but I wasn't going to be the bearer of that bad news.

The prince's ramrod straight posture told me more. He wasn't going to let any more of his people be killed trying to protect him. When he had stood on the bow of his yacht, he had been trying to draw out his assassin. Now, he was using his body as a shield for his people, some of whom were probably plotting to kill him—and one of them was standing not five feet away.

A noble Mal'Salin.

Icicles must be forming in the Lower Hells. Big ones.

Focus, Raine. Bukas and monsters with giant, people-snatching hands didn't just jump out of a black mage's twisted imagination. I picked up the pace as much as I could in the thickened air. The slower we moved, the faster we could find ourselves eviscerated and eaten, and not necessarily in that order. One of Chigaru's guards walked directly in front of him, so the prince didn't have to force his way through the air. Having to slow down for the prince—or worse, having to stop for him—could be fatal for all of us.

Imala's red lightglobe reflected off one of the hotel's mirrors. Mine shone on what was sprawled at its base.

The mirror may have been warded before, but it wasn't now.

At first glance, someone might think the body had been torn in half. This was worse, if that was possible. From the waist up, the man was on the floor. From the waist down, he was inside the mirror, wherever the monster that had grabbed him had come from—and where it had gone back to, trying to drag its prize with it.

Imala snatched some kind of metal sculpture off a small table next to the mirror. "Shield your eyes," she ordered. With one smooth move, she hurled the sculpture into the mirror, shattering it, and exposing nothing but a wall behind it—with half a body lying at its base. That shut one door to Hell or wherever that thing had come from, but it left entirely too many more on this side with us. I swore if I lived through this I was going to shatter every mirror I saw for the rest of my life.

Mago swallowed with an audible gulp. "So much for where the buggers are coming from."

I hustled our little party the rest of the way down to the fourth floor. Chaos reigned. Judging by the screams coming from down the darkened corridor, a lot of people hadn't made it past the doors to their rooms before they were attacked.

Imala hissed in frustration.

If we stopped to help, we stopped to die. She knew it and she hated it. The odds of us making it out of here ourselves weren't too gre—

Pain, like a hammer to the chest, sent me to my knees.

My mouth was open, but no air was making it in or out. I tried to speak, struggled to breathe, my hands joining my knees on the floor. Pain, sharper than the first, sent me facedown on the carpet. Power surged in my chest, alternating with the pain. At each surge, I gasped a little air. The power was the Saghred.

So was the pain.

I knew it. I didn't know how, but I did.

The Saghred twisted and jerked against my chest. It wanted to stay here. Badly. To stay and to feed. Dying people released souls, souls the rock wanted, needed like it needed nothing else.

Its need became mine.

I raised my head and saw them. Souls fleeing dying bodies, their last moments of life spent in terror and screaming, in a hotel turned hunting ground, a slaughterhouse for the demons and nightmares that came out of mirrors, through walls and up through the floors.

"Raine?" I heard Imala call as if from far away. "Raine!"

All I could manage was a head shake, which was what the rest of me was doing. I forced myself to breathe slowly. In. Out. Just keep the air moving. All I got was a lot of rasp and too little air.

"You!" She shouted to someone, sounding closer now. "Help me."

Strong hands locked around my upper arms, pulling me to my feet; another arm went around my waist, supporting me. Mago's arm.

"Are you all right?" he asked, even though he knew I wasn't.

I couldn't answer. I hissed air in and out between my teeth to keep control. The rock wasn't taking me, not now. Another punch to the chest made me stagger, but the pain was milder. The surging, swirling power was taking its place. The pressure on my chest suddenly lifted, and I sucked the cold air into my burning lungs, cooling, calming. "I'll be fine . . . when we get out."

Imala's small hands gripped my upper arm; Mago took over where one of Chigaru's guards had hauled me to my feet.

"I'm here, Raine," Imala said. "We're getting out; just keep moving."

I managed a nod, my vision starting to clear. My steps were like lead; I didn't know if it was the spell-thick air or the Saghred's desperation to feed. It coiled tightly inside of me, its rage building. I knew what it was about to do, but I couldn't speak, couldn't warn Imala.

The Saghred struck her. Its power surged down my arm and into Imala.

She screamed, but she didn't let go of me. Exactly the opposite—she tightened her grip. The rock had bitten Justinius Valerian before; he'd held on to me, and like Imala, he didn't let me go until he was ready to. The old man was the most powerful mage in the world. Imala wasn't. But latching on harder when the Saghred struck sure as hell qualified her as one of the most gutsy.

The rock could have killed her—could have done worse than kill her—but it didn't.

"Sorry," I managed.

The goblin flashed a pained smile. "That rock's not going to tell either one of us what to do."

What felt like an eternity later, we reached the third floor.

We weren't going to get anywhere near Mago's room.

It was on fire.

That entire end of the third floor corridor was engulfed in flames, flames moving so quickly even the smoke couldn't keep up.

There was nowhere to go except down.

The fire rolled its way across the ceiling beams, tongues of blue and gold flame licking their way around the wooden columns, the gilt paint melting in the heat, running in golden rivulets down the scorched wood.

"That's not just fire," Imala said.

"No, it's not." It was magic, magic of the most exotic and deadly kind.

A wall of flame parted, revealing a man standing in front

of the mirror on the third-floor landing. His robes were on fire, spirals of flame licking his face, his hair . . .

And not consuming, not burning any of him.

Oh hell.

A firemage. An elven firemage.

The demons and monsters were just to trap us in the hotel while a firemage burned it down around us.

Some mages could use fire, but firemages could morph themselves *into* fire, into living torches. They could burn a building from the inside out, walking through flames of their own making, spreading the fire, the death.

Shouts and screams—and heat—swirled up from the lobby below. The entire hotel was on fire.

"Run!" Imala shouted.

Downstairs, the lobby was a hysterical mob scene. Those who had lived long enough to get downstairs were surging for the front doors, crushing, trampling in a blind panic. Flames covered the carved banisters, blackened the edge of the pale marble staircase, but the center was still clear. We ran for it.

Imala turned toward me and shouted something.

Her words were lost in a roar of fire from overhead. A support beam cracked and broke, showering us with sparks. Mago yanked me toward him; Imala dove in the other direction as the beam and a chunk of the ceiling crashed to the floor.

We couldn't get to Imala and Chigaru, and they couldn't reach us.

Dammit.

Mago pulled on my arm. "This way!"

A shriek came from the front doors as a javelin of fire struck a goblin in the chest, burning a hole completely through him. A second fire spear sent the goblin behind him up in flames.

There was another firemage outside, probably on the roof of an adjacent building, and the bastard knew what he was doing—if killing everyone inside the hotel was what he wanted.

If you tried to escape, he just killed you faster.

There weren't but a handful of true firemages in the entire world, and Balmorlan had brought at least two of them here.

I couldn't stop the fire. The Saghred probably could, but I had no idea how.

I could stop those firemages. Under their flames, they were just as killable as the rest of us.

Mago and I ran toward the back of the hotel, to the door we'd used to get in. He got there first and pushed against the door, flinging it—

"No!" I screamed.

A fire javelin missed him by no more than an inch, slamming into the wall behind us. The fire instantly caught and spread. We couldn't go back. This door, covered by another firemage sniper, was our only way out.

I knew what I had to do.

People were dead. They were being murdered, slaughtered by nightmares made real. Unless I killed the killers, it wouldn't end until they ran out of victims. I had no choice. I didn't know what would happen to me, what the Saghred would do to me.

Taltek Balmorlan was about to get his show.

The Saghred's power pulsed eagerly inside of me. Eager to kill, to destroy.

Mago met my eyes and he froze. I didn't know what he saw, and I probably didn't want to know. He probably saw power, raw and primal. And deadly.

"Raine, no. Don't do th—"

"Stay behind me." My voice was tight. It was all I could do to hold the rock back.

Then I stopped trying, stopped fighting. I didn't struggle against its power.

I embraced it.

Smoke poured out of the hotel. Out on the street, people ran through the smoke, blinded, choking.

I did neither.

I could see through the smoke as if it weren't there. I knew where each firemage was, the paths of their magic a glowing, pulsing line from their targets right back to them. There were four firemages in sniper positions in buildings in front of the hotel. I didn't have to see them; I knew where they were. Three were on either side of the building, and one had just tried to kill Mago.

Eight outside, at least one inside—and all of them were elves.

If I didn't stop them, hundreds of innocent people, including Mychael, Tam, and Imala, would be burned alive inside the hotel.

That had been Taltek Balmorlan's plan all along.

If I stopped the firemages, Balmorlan got his show. If I failed, every goblin who threatened his war with Sathrik died. The bastard won either way.

No.

It stopped and it stopped now.

I stepped through the door and right into the sights of the firemage sniper on the roof. I felt her gathering power, gathering fire to incinerate me and Mago where we stood. She took her best shot.

It was her last.

The Saghred's magic surged through my body and out of the fist I punched skyward at her killing perch. I didn't know how to take down a firemage, but the magic inside of me did.

The bitch had it coming.

My body blazed red with the Saghred's power, its magic and mine slamming into the mage, turning her body into a screaming ball of fire arching out over the roof's edge and down five stories to the street below.

When I'd used the power the Saghred had given me before, it felt like the power was using me. Not this time.

We worked in perfect partnership; I visualized what I wanted to do and it happened. Immediately. No thought, no hesitation.

No mercy.

I heard screaming. It was me. I knew it was me, but I couldn't stop. I wasn't screaming in fear at what was happening or horror at what I was doing.

I was screaming in pure exultant triumph, the joy of battle, of power unfettered.

"Raine!"

I felt the heat coming before Mago screamed my name. My magic met the flaming javelin sent down from the roof of the next building, met it and rode the firemage's power back to the mage who'd launched it, engulfing him in his own fire and mine. His body fell like a flaming comet to the street.

Time was a blur, so were the screaming people in the streets. There were other firemages. I couldn't see them, but my Saghred-fired senses knew they were near, that they still lived.

I hunted them down.

A firemage was in a building directly across from the hotel's entrance. I couldn't see him, but I didn't have to. His magic heated the air, leaving behind a wavy trail, leading from the hotel doors to the window on the fourth floor. I used his magic's trail like a fuse to a bomb. The firemage was gathering his power for another strike. I didn't know if he realized Death was coming for him.

I didn't care.

I lost track of the next few minutes.

The other firemages tried to escape.

I couldn't stop if I had wanted to.

And I didn't want to.

I only stopped when the last firemage was dead. By my hand, my magic.

People in the hotel streamed out of the front door, out of the door Mago and I had come through, and from around the far corner. No firemages had them pinned inside.

They were all dead. Burned. Destroyed.

And I'd done it all.

I took two steps back from the curb and threw up. The smoke started choking me, strangling me. Strong arms scooped me up.

Mago.

People were drawn to the fire, the chaos; their curiosity drew them in, shouting, jostling. Mago went around and through them. They took one look at the two of us and got out of our way.

I started shaking, tears running in hot trails down my face.

"Easy, cousin," Mago said against my hair. "We're getting out of here."

"Mychael." I coughed. "Tam . . . Ima—"

"I'm sure they got out." The only person Mago was worried about was me. He was scared for me.

I was terrified of me.

Chapter 10

We had to get off the streets. Now.

I'd used the Saghred—and the Saghred had used me.

I hadn't just used the power the stone had gradually given me over the past three months. I had used the stone itself, chosen to use it, and reveled in the death I'd caused. In front of hundreds of witnesses.

Exactly as Taltek Balmorlan said I would—and just as Carnades had predicted.

I'd just signed my own death warrant with firemage blood.

It didn't matter that I killed those who were killing innocents. I'd let the Saghred take me so that I could take lives.

We were in the center city, so there was only one place I could go. Mago didn't know about it, but considering the circumstances, Mychael would have no problem with me taking my cousin to his hideout.

With our bond, I would have known if Mychael were hurt. I wasn't going to say dead; I wasn't even going to think it. I would know if he was . . . I would know it. He wasn't. He was fine, and he had his hands full right now being paladin in a disaster zone. He'd probably heard by now what I'd done. Torching nine firemages with their own fire would kind of indicate that I was on my feet and healthy. Oh yeah, I was healthy all right, a fine specimen of a Saghred bond servant. I'd given the rock something it'd wanted from the moment it latched on to me—complete control.

I was back on my feet. I was leading; Mago was my shadow. We didn't run like we were guilty, but we sure as hell didn't dawdle. There were a lot of city watchmen headed for the Greyhound Hotel, and we ducked out of sight every time we spotted one. Fortunately, most Guardians would be coming from the citadel. If Balmorlan and Carnades were having wanted posters printed right now with my picture on them, I wasn't taking any chances on an overzealous Guardian determined to do his duty, regardless of who I was—or what I was to his commander.

I stopped at an intersection, amazingly empty at this time of day. People were either rushing toward the hotel or running away from it. Mago laid his hand firmly on my shoulder. There was no one anywhere near us; I knew that and so did he. That hand on my shoulder wasn't a warning, it was a question, and he wanted an answer. He was worried about me and no doubt was wondering if I was in my right mind right now. He wanted to know where we were going.

"Almost there," I murmured.

Mago gave my shoulder a quick squeeze and released it.

I stopped at a boarded-up building. Its best days had come and gone long ago. But it had never been more useful than it was now. I ran down a short flight of stairs that went below the street level to a door without a knob. Mychael had told me the spell to get in. I laid my hand flat against the wood and murmured the incantation. The door opened on silent, well-oiled, and maintained hinges.

I shut the door behind us, and with a word, wove a lightglobe into existence that floated above my open palm. This time it worked flawlessly. The Saghred was probably responsible for that, too.

Mago's dark eyes instantly took in everything in the room.

The basement room looked like some of the more comfortable hideouts Uncle Ryn had in every major port city. It had the basics: table, a couple of chairs, and weapons. Lots and lots of weapons.

And a bed in the far corner.

I felt a flush creep up my neck until my ears were burning. Oh yes, I definitely remembered that bed.

"What is this place?" Mago asked.

"Mychael's home away from home."

That didn't clear things up for Mago; if anything, he went from confused to concerned.

"Mychael's been doing some work for Justinius, and no one but Justinius knew about this place until a few weeks ago when he brought me here." I didn't mention that Mychael and I hadn't exactly used the bed in the far corner to plot strategy.

I was here now because the Saghred had just made me its bitch.

And I'd let it.

"Raine, you should sit down."

"Do I look that bad?" I tried for a quip; it didn't come out that way.

"Actually you should lie down."

"I'd crawl under that bed and stay there if I thought it'd do any good." I went and sat on the bed and leaned my head back against the headboard with a thunk. I rubbed a hand across my eyes and left it there.

I heard Mago twist the cork from a bottle on the table. He took a sniff and, apparently satisfied with what was inside, poured two glasses. Mychael only kept the good stuff here. I guess he figured if you need to hide badly enough to be here, you wanted good liquor keeping you company.

That meant I needed the best that had ever been distilled. Mago crossed the room to the bed with nearly silent footfalls; I put out the hand that wasn't over my eyes, and the cool glass slid into it.

"Thank you," I muttered.

"There appears to be plenty more where that came from," Mago said. "We need to let Mychael know that you're safe."

I laughed, but without the humor. "As long as that rock is anything but dust, I'll never be safe again. I can't let Mychael know where I am; this place is spellproof. I can't communicate with him unless I'm outside, and I wouldn't advise that right now."

"Won't Mychael assume that you're here? Since it's apparent that you know about this place."

"After the show I put on, who knows where he thinks I am." I swallowed past a lump that'd suddenly taken up residence in my throat. "Tam and Imala—"

"Are either fine or they're not."

"It's the 'not' that I'm worried about."

"Either one is out of your control."

"Have you always been such a cold bastard?"

"I couldn't do what I do if I weren't. I do what I have to." His dark eyes were still and calm as he looked at me. "The same as you just did." He paused. "And the same as you'll have to do if you want to survive this."

I got off the bed and stalked the length of the room. I could swear the damned thing had shrunk.

"Do things that will get me locked in a containment room until Carnades gets around to lobbing my head off?" I tossed back the rest of the whisky. "Or until Balmorlan chains me to a wall and lets his pervert mages have me?"

"Raine, you know better than anyone that the right thing isn't always the legal thing . . . you did what you had—"

"'Legal'? I don't give a damn about legal. I'm talking about a rock using me to slaughter—"

"Men and women who deserved it. Killers of innocent people."

"But I enjoyed it; I *wanted* to do it. I couldn't stop myself."

"Couldn't you? If the Saghred had tried to use you to kill Mychael or me—or Tam or Imala—could you have stopped yourself?"

"That's not the—"

"That's precisely the point. You killed those mages because they needed killing, and you enjoyed it because you've had too many people after you for no other reason than you have power that they can't control or have for themselves. You got a chance to cut loose—to use everything you had in your arsenal to destroy them—and you took it." Mago studied my face in silence for a few moments. "Did you imagine one of those mages with someone else's face? Balmorlan perhaps? Or Silvanus?"

I didn't meet his eyes. "I don't remember."

"Meaning, yes," he said in a quiet voice. "Raine, you did what needed to be done."

"If a member of the Conclave had torched those mages, they wouldn't get locked in a containment cell or put on trial for being a danger to society. They'd be a freaking hero."

Mago didn't say a word. He knew I was right.

Carnades Silvanus wanted an excuse to lock me up, but he needed proof—and I'd just handed him both on a silver platter.

Dammit to hell.

If I'd been thinking straight, would I have done the same thing? Yes. People were dying; I could help, so I did. End of story. Unfortunately, it could also be the end of me. I hadn't been in control. I let the power inside of me take over. It had been the only way I could stop those firemages. I had the power to do it, and I used it. I didn't care what Mago said. I'd enjoyed it so much that I wasn't just shaking in rage. I was terrified. I wanted to scream and curl up in a dark corner and hide. I wasn't afraid of Carnades Silvanus and what he could have the Conclave's Seat of Twelve do to me.

I was afraid of myself.

I'd let myself be taken over by something stronger than myself. Nothing sent me into a panic quicker than being helpless. Yes, the Saghred had used me as its bitch, and I probably couldn't have done anything to stop it once I had started killing those firemages. But what terrified me the most was that I hadn't wanted to.

I let it have its way with me, and I enjoyed—no, I relished—every second of it. No doubt, every single witness who had seen me in that street thought I was a power-crazed maniac. And they were right. I had control of myself for the moment, but how long would it last? Until the next time another power-crazed maniac tried to slaughter innocents? Then I'd slaughter them. That made me no better than the Sarad Nukpanas of the world.

If the Saghred got that much control over me once, it could easily do it again. The rock's power was coiled quietly inside of me, patiently waiting for its next chance. Gloating in triumph at what it'd just made me do.

I'd just played right into the hands of everyone who wanted to get their hands on me. Carnades and Taltek Balmorlan shared more than the same race—they shared the same ideology. I'd just used the Saghred's power twice in as many days, both times in defense of a goblin prince and his people. I would have saved them if they'd been elves, humans, or purple polka-dotted ogres. I valued life.

They valued power.

Sarad Nukpana and Sathrik Mal'Salin wanted me dead. Locked in the citadel, they'd know right where to find me. Or just wait for Carnades to get his ultimate wish—my head separated from my body. With me dead, the Saghred's power would fall to the first mage-level person—elf, goblin, or human—to get their hands on it. It would be the beginning of the end of the world as we knew it. If the elves got it, they'd destroy the goblins. If the goblins got it, they'd destroy the elves. Either way, every living thing was screwed.

Mago was seated at the table, his fingers steepled in front of his face, watching me. I'd never even noticed that he'd moved.

His gaze continued to search my face. "The question you have to answer for yourself is what are you going to do about it?"

I wasn't going to hide here. They weren't going to win. I couldn't let them. Raine Benares couldn't set foot on the streets.

I couldn't be seen, but Symon Wiggs could.

A very slow smile crept across Mago's lips. "I don't know what you're thinking, but you obviously like it."

"The best place to hide is in plain sight of those you don't want to find you, so I'll put myself in the last place Balmorlan will think to look for me. Sitting right across the table from him." I smiled and it was fierce. I made this choice, not the rock, and it felt good. "He's not going to get me, and he's not going to get away with what he just did. I say we stick with the plan—we bring the bastard down. That'll bring down his allies, too . . ." I paused. I didn't like what I was thinking, but I saw no other option. "And if that doesn't work, I'll take him out."

"You mean kill him."

"I don't see any other way to stop this, do you?"

"Not really."

"You don't approve."

"Phaelan would. But I rob, not kill."

"Well, robbing clearly isn't my area of expertise. Killing is. I just proved that."

"You only proved that you care about people."

"Killing Taltek Balmorlan would go a long way toward protecting everyone."

Mago gazed at me a moment, his expression unreadable. "Whatever you have to do, I'm behind you all the way."

The lump in my throat was back. I wasn't sure if it was from Mago's support or the thought that I was ready to murder someone in cold blood. Taltek Balmorlan definitely had cold blood, and his death would keep hundreds of thousands, perhaps millions from meeting the same fate from the Saghred should he gain control over it—and me.

"Thank you," I managed. "Can you get a message to Balmorlan telling him that we saw his display, were very impressed, and want to do business?"

"Without difficulty."

"I don't like the idea of you being on the streets, but—"

"My name and face isn't all over the city. Yours is. I also feel confident in saying that no one who matters saw us together; in that smoke, no one could see anything. As to my personal safety, I slink along back streets just as well as I move among the gentry." He stood and walked over to the wardrobe.

"What are you looking for?"

Mago thoughtfully flipped through the clothes hanging there. "I was thinking something more appropriate to slinking." He stopped and with a flourish, pulled out a heavy midnight blue cloak. "Something perfect for a cloak-and-dagger evening."

I rolled my eyes. I had to admit it felt good. Anything I could think about rather than what I just did was good.

Mago swirled the cloak to settle it on his shoulders. "I don't believe anyone could identify me as the man with Raine Benares; but in my business, there are acceptable and expected risks, and there are foolish risks. I would rather not have the word 'fool' appear on my gravestone. A hooded cloak will go a long way to ensuring my prolonged life. Like my little brother, I highly value my hide."

My vision blurred. "I highly value your hide, too."

"Is that your way of telling me to be careful?"

"And to come back."

Mago crossed the room and kissed me on the forehead. "Nothing will prevent me, dear cousin."

After I'd closed the door behind Mago, and reactivated the wards, I went over to the bed and essentially collapsed on it. Mago said he'd use the family knock when he came back, but that he wanted me to try and get some sleep.

Sleep. Like that was going to happen.

My eyes welled up with tears. The last time I'd been in this bed had been with Mychael. I'd been warm, cherished, loved. I was walking the fine line between being a felon on the run for the rest of my life or losing my life—or my soul or sanity—in the next few days.

If the Saghred had taken a big bite out of my sanity, would I know it? Crazy people—especially cackling-crazy villains—never thought they were nuts. They could justify everything they did.

Like I'd just done.

I bit my bottom lip to keep from crying. I curled up into the tightest ball I could, folding in on myself, protecting what little the Saghred hadn't torn away from me and used. I buried my face in the pillow and the sobs came, racking and uncontrolled.

In the next few days I had to ruin Balmorlan or kill him, stop my former fiancé from killing the man I loved, keep a goblin prince alive, and prevent a full-scale racial war from ending life as we knew it. All while keeping myself alive, sane, and unarrested.

My time was literally running out.

Chapter 11

Mago returned a few hours later, told me his plan, and after I picked my jaw up off the floor, I had to admit that it was brilliant.

No one but a Benares would be crazy enough to do this.

I was standing in a cathouse, glamoured as a puny banker. In the next hour, I would be having a late supper with an elven inquisitor. For dessert, I would con or possibly kill said inquisitor.

The best thing about the entire scheme was that as long as I was glamoured as Symon Wiggs, I couldn't use the Saghred.

And the Saghred couldn't use me.

"Tell me again why we're here?" I asked Mago.

"We need information before our meeting, which is conveniently at a restaurant across the street. If you want to know every secret, scandal, or just catch up on the day's news, go to the best house in town, have some drinks and a cigar in the madam's parlor, throw some money around . . ."

He spread his hands and smiled. "And the news will come to you."

"Could we find out what happened to Mychael, Tam, and—"

"Most assuredly."

I let out a sigh that was half relief, half anxiety. I had to know what happened; right now ignorance wasn't bliss, it was torment. You'll know when you know, Raine. Try not to think about it.

Yeah, right.

"You know the madam here?" I asked even though I was hardly surprised.

"As a matter of fact, I am on the most cordial of terms with the madams of the finest houses in most major cities. You would be surprised how many business deals are made in a madam's parlor."

"No, I wouldn't."

"Cultivating such relationships is the most advantageous mixing of business and pleasure." He dipped his head toward my ear and lowered his voice. "How long can you hold that glamour?"

"The longest I've had to hold one is three hours."

"Could you hold it for longer if you had to?"

"I don't know how much strength it takes to hold an anatomically correct glamour. And I hope I don't have to find out."

The Satyr's Grove was exactly as I'd remembered it. Well, as much as I could remember from running through it, chasing then fighting the specter of an ancient elven sorcerer who'd possessed one of the customers. The Night of the Naked Possessed Guy definitely ranked up there as one of my less dignified.

I didn't know what Symon's usual odds were at getting laid, but I was willing to bet the ladies at the Satyr's Grove would charge him extra.

Not that I was going to find out.

At least I didn't plan on finding out.

I was a man on a mission. And that mission had nothing to do with what little was between my legs.

Once inside, Mago didn't hesitate, but walked straight through the front reception area to a large door flanked by matching muscle. One was human, one an elf, both were big. Not the big that came from working out, but the big that came from throwing out—anyone who caused trouble in the house.

One smiled at Mago and the other opened the door for us.

Traveling in Mago's wake had its advantages.

The madam's parlor looked like a really nice gentlemen's club—dark wood, fancy furniture, rich men. Though not particularly attractive rich men. Ugly might be taking it a bit far, but let's just say that Symon Wiggs wasn't the homeliest guy in the room. But the job of every sleek, yet curvaceous woman in that room was to make every last one of those men feel like leaving a sizable chunk of their wealth here before they left.

A woman was essentially holding court on a low sofa in front of the fireplace. She was a sultry brunette, all curves with most of them on display. Not out, mind you; just strongly hinted at. She saw Mago, and my cousin was the recipient of a dazzling smile. She rose from the sofa and crossed the room in a seductive sway of silks and hips. She and Mago did that double-cheek-kissing thing, then the woman's smile turned naughty and she kissed my cousin long and deep.

I felt safe in saying that she and Mago knew each other.

"It's been far too long," she all but purred. "It's not nice to keep a lady waiting."

Mago's rakish smile was the twin to the one I'd seen many times on Phaelan. "Last time I was here, I don't recall you being much of a lady."

The madam languorously ran a lacquered nail down the

center of Mago's chest. "You bring it out in me." She gazed around the room. "Unfortunately, I won't be able to give you a repeat performance this evening."

"Business seems to be good," he murmured approvingly.

Her smile was almost demure. "Very good. Patrice is still with us; I'm certain she would be available for you."

"Perhaps later," Mago told her. "Right now my friend and I would like to bemoan our newly homeless state with your best brandy and two of those splendid cigars."

"Homeless?"

"The Greyhound Hotel. We escaped with only the clothes on our backs."

The madam made sympathetic sounds while her hands went from Mago's chest to his shoulders, clearly enjoying the journey. "Do you have a place to stay?"

Mago didn't hesitate. "We have a small room available to us. Please tell me the tailor on Capron Street still lifts his needle for the common man, and hasn't been snatched away yet by the Duke of Brenir. I'm here on business and I can't attend every meeting wearing the same doublet. I'd never live down the humiliation."

She laughed. "He's still here, though the duke still hasn't stopped trying to lure him away. In fact, he'll be here later this evening. I can send him up to your room."

"Room?" I squeaked.

"Ah, Camille, this is my friend Symon Wiggs. A colleague of mine from the bank. In town with me on business when the unfortunate tragedy took place."

"Room?" I repeated.

Madam Camille reached out and ran her hand down my—I mean, Symon's—chest. The little banker didn't have much by way of equipment, but if what I felt a split second later was any indication, all of it was in perfect working order. Holy crap. I think that horrified realization must have shown on my face.

Camille smiled and stepped in closer, brushing her ample charms up against me.

Oh yeah, perfect working order.

"I could hardly turn you two gentlemen out into the street," she said. "Master Peronne has always been a *fine*, *upstanding* client of my humble establishment." The emphasis she put on those two words clearly indicated that she wasn't referring to Mago's superior moral fiber. "I have a small suite on the top floor that would keep you out of the cold for a night—or two."

Mago took Camille's hand and bestowed a gallant kiss just above an enormous diamond ring. "Such a *generous* and gracious lady."

Providing room and board wasn't the kind of generosity Mago was talking about, either. And I think parts of Symon Wiggs were hoping for some of that generosity.

I had to get out of here.

"My pleasure," Camille replied, with a sloe-eyed glance at me.

Get. Out. Now.

"On behalf of myself and my colleague, we most gratefully accept," Mago was saying. "But only until we can make other arrangements. I wouldn't want to interfere with such a profitable enterprise."

All I could make was a strangled sound.

"You'll have to excuse my friend," Mago said. He lowered his voice. "He's a little shy."

"Oh." Those eyes were on me again, looking me up and down, assessing. What she was assessing, I had no clue. "I have a girl who would be perfect for you," she said. "I guarantee after a night in her bed, you won't remember what shy is."

"Maybe later," I managed. I shot Mago a murderous look.

If Mago didn't get to laugh soon, he was going to explode.

I just growled.

A growl that stuck in my throat when I saw Rache Kai strolling by the open door with a working girl on his arm.

A girl that bore a more than disturbing resemblance to me.

Mago saw what I'd seen, and didn't even bat an eye. "An old friend of mine." He smiled in a show of teeth that didn't look at all friendly.

"Yes, Master Winters arrived a little less than an hour ago. Another of my best customers when he's in town."

Mago accepted a cigar offered by a girl who'd appeared at his elbow. All she wore was the bow in her hair. As she lit the cigar, Mago spoke around puffs. "If he's not too busy, I'd like to catch up with him later."

"I could send up a message that you're here."

"No need, my dear." Mago leaned in conspiratorially. "I'd like to surprise him."

Camille laughed. "Understood."

"Do you know how long he'll be, ah . . . indisposed?"

One corner of the madam's mouth turned up in a sly smile. "He paid for the entire night, as usual. He'll be on the top floor as well, conveniently next to your suite."

Mago exhaled in a puff of aromatic smoke. "How wonderful."

My hands itched to get around Master Winters's throat. Yes, how wonderful.

"I'll have Milette get your drinks." Camille's hand lightly brushed the front of Mago's trousers before she left.

My cousin sighed with unabashed pleasure. "There goes a truly lovely woman, with an uncanny head for business."

"You . . . *you*—"

His eyes sparkled with mirth. "Be grateful, Symon."

"Grateful?"

"Quite so. I could have told her the truth—that you don't like women and were once engaged to Master Winters."

Sitting in Camille's parlor let us hear all the news there was to hear and then some.

And see even more.

I don't care what they say about women gossiping, give men some juicy news and they'll leave women in the dust.

All of this news came to us while being served drinks and little, fancy sandwiches by women wearing next to nothing—or in some cases, nothing at all. One of them bent over to light my cigar. I swear a man could suffocate in a pair of those things. I choked on the first puff. I'd had cigars before, but not with a side order of breasts. Mago saw and winked at me. He was enjoying this way too much.

"So we're staying here," I muttered after the cigar lighter and her bounty had moved on. I think my less-than-enthused reaction had hurt her feelings.

Mago took a puff and smiled appreciatively at a blonde sauntering past. "I can't think of a more perfect hiding place. Would anyone ever think to look for you here?"

"No, but—"

"But nothing. We get rest—and perhaps even consolation." Mago looked at me, a wicked gleam in his eye that looked entirely too much like Phaelan. "Are you quite certain you wouldn't like to try some of the consolation offered here? I imagine that few people have the enviable opportunity to become the opposite sex for a night and find themselves in one of the kingdoms' finest establishments. You've literally had the day from hell. You could use something to help you relax."

"No."

"A chance to satisfy a curiosity, perhaps?"

"No."

Mago sat back and took a thoughtful sip of his brandy. "No doubt, Madam Camille will be sending up a lady for the bereft Symon Wiggs." He shrugged. "I'll let you decide how to not satisfy your curiosity. Though you could think of this as a bachelor party of sorts. The last fling before you settle down with your paladin."

"No."

"Suit yourself. As a man who is a man all the time, I can truthfully tell you that you're making a mistake." Mago stood and fastidiously straightened his doublet. "At least I know you won't go running off to a room with some young beauty while I'm gathering information."

"That's happened?"

Mago sighed the sigh of the long suffering. "Just every time I've taken Phaelan anywhere. By the time I've realized that he's no longer in the room, he's usually on his second girl—no pun intended."

"None imagined."

Mago engaged several of the men in conversation, and I sat back and listened. Symon's squeaky voice coming out of Symon's thin-lipped mouth was about more than I could take right now. So I listened and I learned.

Mychael was alive and unharmed.

I had to bite the inside of my lip to keep myself from reacting. Raine wanted to cry, laugh, and cheer all at once. I had to settle for doing what Symon would do—I tossed back the rest of my brandy and waved a girl over for another.

Tam and Imala had escaped with Prince Chigaru, though Tam was probably in the last place he wanted to be. The prince's retinue had moved into the goblin embassy. It didn't matter that Imala was in charge. Having to stay there would have Tam sleeping with his eyes open, if he slept at all.

Mago gestured me over to a relatively empty section of room.

"According to the gentleman with the redhead on his lap, Raine Benares is a very wanted woman."

"And who's he to know?"

"The chief magistrate."

"He would know."

"So one would surmise."

"Who's she wanted by?"

Silence.

"Okay . . . who's she *not* wanted by?"

"It's been my experience that when there's an arrest

warrant out there—with a substantial reward—pretty much everyone is looking, each for their own reasons."

Shit.

"The watchers would like to question her," Mago said. "The elven ambassador is feeling keenly embarrassed that one of the elf queen's subjects is the source of such public concern, and has offered to take her into custody."

"I'll bet."

Ambassador Giles Keril was cozy as could be nestled in Taltek Balmorlan's pocket.

"Guardians?"

"Patrols are out looking."

"Damn."

Mychael didn't know where I was or what had happened to me. As long as I was glamoured as Symon Wiggs, I couldn't use my magic, so I couldn't contact Mychael with our link, and I didn't dare unglamour. I'd find a way later to let Mychael know that I was safe, or as safe as I could be. Right now I was ready to make the world a safer place for everyone by having a really meaningful chat with Rache Kai.

I put out my cigar in the nearest ashtray. "How about before dinner we go talk to our old friend Master Winters?"

I'd been on the top floor of the Satyr's Grove before. That's where the more expensive girls were, and apparently Rache had decided to splurge. Maybe he was consoling himself for missing not only Prince Chigaru, but Mychael as well. That had to affect a man's confidence. I smiled. If there was any justice in the world, Rache's sudden lack of confidence meant he probably wasn't scoring any better in the suite at the end of the hall.

"My, what a dastardly grin," Mago murmured.

"Just thinking happy thoughts."

"Vindictive?"

I shrugged. "You have your happy; I have mine."

Mago flashed a smile and nimbly twirled the room key between his fingers. "Let's see how thick the walls are between our suite and Master Winters's."

I shivered as we walked down the hall, and it wasn't from cold. The last time I'd been on this floor had been when I'd cornered the naked cathouse client and the evil, ancient elven sorcerer who had possessed him. The sorcerer had escaped from the Saghred and his first order of business had nothing to do with plotting world domination and everything to do with getting laid. I guess when a man spends thousands of years imprisoned inside the Saghred, it gives him a lot of time to think about what he'd do first if he ever got back on the outside.

The Saghred had wanted to take him back, and it'd come way too close to making me do the taking.

I'd resisted that time—with Mychael's help.

The suite Madam Camille had given us was clearly meant for activities other than eavesdropping on the man in the next room, though I imagine it'd been used for that purpose before, too.

Red satin and black leather pretty much summed up the decor. Most of the leather covered the room's furniture, but there was a table with leather . . . accoutrements. I only recognized a few of them, and didn't want to know about the others.

Rache Kai was most definitely in the next room.

Mago knew Rache, so he could identify Rache if he were talking.

I knew Rache in an entirely different way. I could identify him based on what he was doing right now.

Mago and I were sitting on the bed, facing the wall our room shared with Rache's, waiting for him to finish.

It was taking much longer than I remembered.

It was damned awkward and borderline embarrassing. Especially with Mago sitting on the bed next to me—the man who'd introduced me to Rache and had regretted it ever since.

I'd debated just barging in, but seeing that the goal was to persuade Rache not to kill Mychael, Chigaru, or me—interrupting him at that particular moment would go beyond rude straight into suicidal. But sitting there listening while my ex-fiancé did what he used to do with me with another woman who looked like me, while I was sitting on a bed with my cousin next to a tableful of accoutrements?

Definitely awkward and embarrassing.

In addition to being rather homely and ill equipped, Symon Wiggs was short. This left me sitting on the edge of the bed, swinging my legs, and trying to look anywhere but at my cousin while the headboard thumped against the wall in the next room. There were other sounds as well, but I was doing my best to ignore them.

"And just how do you propose to keep Rache from putting a nice, neat hole through both of us?" I asked, desperate to change the subject, careful to keep my voice down.

"Actually, I've done this sort of thing before."

"Busting into a room in a cathouse to have a heart-to-heart talk with an assassin in the midst of postcoital glow? Cause I can guarantee you, the moment we step into that room Rache's glow is gone—and we're next."

"One, I don't 'bust in' anywhere. Two, this isn't a cathouse; it's a bordello."

"Same thing."

"No, it's not; I don't patronize cathouses." A corner of his mouth turned up in a quick grin. "Though I don't believe I've ever walked in on an assassin before."

"Which is why we need a plan so our first time isn't our last. We want Rache reasonable, not raging." I thought of something, something that could put a serious crimp in an already questionable plan. "What happened between you and Rache the last time you saw him?"

"Meaning?"

"Meaning what terms are you on—speaking or killing?"

Mago had to think about that one; and I saw a flicker of doubt in his eyes.

I grunted. "Yeah, that's what I thought. Why don't you let your puny—and completely harmless-looking—banker buddy handle this one?"

"Need I remind you that you're wearing a puny banker body? A dagger in his chest is a dagger in your—"

I waved my hand dismissively. "Trust me; I know all about feeling pain while wearing a man's body." I carefully slid off the bed until my feet silently touched the floor. "Got any lock picks on you?"

"Of course, but—"

"Give them to me. Rache will have that door locked. If I was wearing my body, I could shield myself with magic." I grinned. "Symon's going to shield himself with stupidity."

No one was in the hall. Good. Two men at a door to a room not their own, one picking the lock while another stood watch would look suspicious even in a cathou—excuse me, bordello. It would be beyond embarrassing to get kicked out of a bordello before we got what we came for, which wasn't even sex.

I glanced at Mago, pointed to the wall on the left side of Rache's room, then pointed emphatically to the floor. I was telling Mago to stay. My cousin didn't like it, but he did as told. I'd told Mago my plan. He didn't like that, either. But it was a lot safer than his idea. Rache knew Mago, and if their last encounter was anything less than friendly, chances were good that Rache's reaction would be bad.

Symon Wiggs was the personification of harmless and helpless—at least physically. The man's mind was that of a scheming little rodent. Rache wouldn't put a hole in him, at least not immediately. One, he hadn't been paid to; and two, a professional assassin just didn't go around killing random people. It was bad for business. Those rich enough to hire someone of Rache's caliber wanted to retain the professional services of an assassin, not turn loose a nutcase.

And if there was anything I'd learned over the years of keeping tabs on Rache Kai, it was that he was the consummate professional.

The door opened with the softest of clicks. Dammit. Rache knew I was there; better start the show.

"Patrice," Symon slurred in a singsong voice. "Patrice?" I opened the door.

"Wrong room," Rache barked loud enough to shake the rafters.

I jumped. Not because he'd scared the crap out of me. It's what Symon would have done. Just staying in character. Yeah. And the knife glittering in Rache's hand, ready to throw, didn't bother me, either.

I squinted and peered into the room. Rache and the girl were sitting up in the bed. Neither one made any move to cover themselves. Rache Kai had the tall, dark, and handsome thing down to an art, complete with a body that still looked like it belonged on a pedestal in a museum somewhere. The woman had long red hair, pale skin, and I couldn't tell what color her eyes were. She looked a *lot* like me. Though what didn't look like me were a pair of large breasts that didn't quite go with her tiny waist. Apparently Rache had decided to enhance his memory of me.

"You're not Patrice." Symon's voice cracked.

"Wrong room," Rache repeated in a still, deadly voice. "She's not here, and unless you close that door, you're not going to be here, either."

I did as told. I closed the door.

With me on the inside.

I kept my hands in clear view, and dropped the drunk act. But I kept the glamour. I wanted Rache to know who I was, but not the girl in bed with him.

"Long time, no see, sweetie pie," I told Rache. I glanced at the girl. "It's like looking in a mirror."

Rache sat frozen for a moment, then his eyes widened in

recognition. The corner of his lips turned up in that crooked grin that used to get me every time. Now it just pissed me off.

"You're not here to talk about old times," Rache said.

"The past should stay where it belongs." I lowered my voice further. "So should you."

"A man's got to work."

"Do it somewhere else."

"I go where the money is. Because you know I'm nothing but a low-life bastard who murders for pay, with no conscience and no regret. Wasn't that what you said?"

Damn, over a dozen years ago and Rache remembered it word for word. He wasn't just carrying a grudge; he was nursing it like a newborn. Great, just what I never needed.

"Meant it then, mean it now," I said. "You lied to me. Nothing you ever said was the truth. You probably even lied when you said you loved me."

The girl froze, eyes wide, sheet now clutched to her ample chest, looking from me to Rache and back again. "Uh, I don't want to get in the middle of . . . whatever this is."

Rache's shoulders shook in silent laughter. "And now you're here to ruin my reputation," he told me.

"You've missed twice since you got here. I think you're doing a fine job by yourself."

"Twice? I missed once, and that was your fault."

"Mine?"

"Try nailing someone who—"

The redhead jumped out of bed and pulled on a robe. "I'll just step outside until you two . . . ah . . . settle things."

Rache reached for her. "Kara."

She stepped nimbly out of his reach. "I don't do threesomes, and I don't get in the middle of lovers' spats."

Rache blinked. "*Lovers?* Is that what you think this—"

"There's nothing wrong with it; it's just not my thing." She quickly gathered her undergarments, such as they were. "There are girls here who specialize in this sort of thing, really like it. I can let Madam Camille know your new preferences and—"

Rache raised his hands in protest. "No, no. You think that he and I . . . because he said—"

The girl stepped back to the bed and placed a finger on Rache's lips. "You don't have to explain a thing. There's nothing wrong with it. I just . . ." She looked me up and down, and gave me a look that I'm sure Symon had plenty of experience getting from women. "He's just not who I'd expect you to be with." And she left. Fast. There was no surprised squeal from her when she stepped out into the hall, so Mago must have ducked back into our room until she'd gone.

Rache glared at me, and lowered his hands.

"Don't go for the dagger under the mattress or under the pillow," I told him.

Rache smiled. "You don't trust me."

"Not as far as I can throw you."

"You may not be able to throw me, but you were always good for a wrestle."

I gave him my best eat-shit-and-die look.

Rache put his thin-bladed knife on the bedside table and slid his long legs over the side of the bed and stood. Naturally, he made no effort to cover himself. I made an effort not to look.

"Afraid you'll like what you see?" he asked.

I barked a small, harsh laugh. "No, I'm afraid Symon will. I'm finding he doesn't have much control."

Rache just stood there, naked. His crossbow at his right hand, and the knife at his left. He made no move toward either—or toward the trousers that were on the floor at his feet.

"Why are you here, Raine?"

"For starters, Mychael Eiliesor."

"Ah, yes." There was a world of meaning in those two little words.

"Ah, yes, you tried to kill him. Did you get paid for it—or is it personal?"

"Darling, I must honestly say that I don't know what you're talking about. Though you'd like for me to say it's personal, wouldn't you?"

"I don't have that much of an ego, Rache. I don't need to have men wanting me years after we parted ways."

"There hasn't been anyone else since us."

I could say the same thing, but demons with pitchforks couldn't poke it out of me. I'd gotten burned by Rache. Badly. I hadn't exactly gotten in line for seconds after that. In fact, I stayed far from anything that could be remotely called a relationship. You could say I had a few commitment issues. That and trust and abandonment. Yep, thanks to Rache Kai, I was a veritable bundle of neuroses.

"Rache, I want Mychael alive and I want you gone. At the same time, I have no reason to want you dead."

His eyebrows lifted in surprise.

"Did someone pay you to use Mychael for target practice?" I asked.

"I'm here for a job, but that job isn't Mychael Eiliesor."

"I saw you on the third floor of the building across from the elven embassy. You took a shot at Mychael. Fortunately you missed."

"That wasn't me."

"Prove it."

"I don't miss."

"You're lying."

"Which one? That I tried to kill him, or that I don't miss?"

I'd never heard of Rache missing before, but there was a first time for everything. Though this definitely wouldn't be the first time that Rache had lied to me.

"There's nothing wrong with my eyes," I told him. "I know who I saw."

"You saw me."

"I believe I just said that."

"That's your proof right there." Rache took a step forward, so that his body was all too visible in the flickering firelight. "I know I have competition. Whoever hits the prince first gets paid; the poor bastard who doesn't hit the mark doesn't get the money. No one ever sees me unless I want to be seen. That wasn't me, ducky."

"Just like that wasn't you trying to assassinate Prince Chigaru Mal'Salin on the waterfront."

"Oh, that was definitely me."

"You admit it."

"Of course. And thanks to your interference, I hit my target, but I didn't kill him. By the way, very impressive work on your part. I didn't know you had it in you." He indicated the glamour. "Or that, either." He chuckled. "If you ever wanted to be a man, he wouldn't be it."

"You won't tell me your business, I won't tell you mine."

"Raine, you know that the identity of my clients is strictly confidential. If I went around spouting off who hired me, I wouldn't have any clients left."

"And that would be such a calamity."

Rache shrugged. "I'm a jack-of-one-trade, Raine. I am what I am, and I'm not going to apologize for it. And you know that I only take one hit at a time. I'm here to bag a goblin, not a paladin. I like to give a hit my full attention, and my clients their money's worth."

"You're a sweetheart."

Rache may not be bothered much by morals, but he did have professional standards. Those were sacred. He wasn't going to reveal the name of his client.

"Okay, fine. I wouldn't want you to compromise your ethics on account of killing the goblin or the elf who can keep the seven kingdoms from literally going to hell in a handbasket." I leaned forward and dropped my voice to a quick, hissing whisper. "And if said kingdoms do end up in said handbasket, you'll be out of a job. People will be killing each other for free. War is like that."

I glared at him. He glowered at me.

"I deliver results, Raine. Not refunds."

"There's a first time for everything."

"Not this time. My pockets haven't been this well lined in years."

"What if you found out that your client couldn't pay the rest of your fee? What if he suddenly went broke? Would you finish the job?"

Rache laughed. "What do you think?"

I think I'd just gotten new motivation to fleece Taltek Balmorlan. I couldn't see his client being anyone else now.

I smiled. "I think—"

Glass shattered out in the hall, and the screaming started.

Chapter 12

I ran to the doorway.

A broken bottle of wine and a pair of shattered glasses were on the floor at the feet of the source of the screaming.

A girl wearing a robe so sheer she shouldn't have bothered was standing in front of the open door to a bedroom, hands that had been holding the wine and glasses now clenched in front of her mouth. The screams had died to whimpers.

Mago came up behind the girl, took one look at what was in that room and swore.

Rache took one look, saw Mago, shoved me out into the hall, slammed the door behind me, and threw the deadbolts. A few seconds later came the sound of a window being wrenched open.

Dammit.

I turned and pounded on the door. I knew it wouldn't do any good, but I did it anyway. I'd rather have been pounding on Rache. Those deadbolts could only be opened with a key. And Madam Camille would be the only one who had them. I wasn't even going to bother trying to get them.

Rache was gone, and I didn't know much more now than I did before, other than he'd taken one shot at Chigaru, and taken no shots at Mychael. I believed him on both counts. I didn't think Rache was lying, at least not this time. So basically the only thing I'd gotten from all that was one more question without an answer. Who was trying to kill Mychael?

"You'd better look at this," Mago called down the hall.

I did, and what I saw was something I really didn't want to see.

A dead goblin. A mage. Chatar. Previously under suspicion for trying to poison Chigaru Mal'Salin. Presently dangling from a small iron chandelier set in a ceiling beam, a chair kicked out of the way beneath his gently swaying legs. He was naked.

I didn't want to see that, either.

"Damn."

Mago nodded in agreement. "And then some."

The watch would be here soon, and while Symon Wiggs wasn't wanted by the watch, they'd wonder what an elven banker was doing snooping around a newly dead goblin, because that was exactly what I was about to do. Obviously, Chatar had escaped the hotel fire, and what was equally obvious was that he'd decided he needed some consolation afterward.

Or maybe his motives weren't so obvious.

We were here to hide out, get news, and kill some time before a clandestine meeting. Perhaps Chatar had been here for similar reasons. We drank brandy and smoked cigars to pass the time; Chatar decided to get naked and do something else. A matter of preference, nothing more. Besides, the goblin mage didn't strike me as the desolate type. He'd said he wasn't guilty and he'd stuck to it. I wasn't buying the "overcome with guilt and hanged himself" story that was sure to come. There was more here than met Symon's beady eyes, and I'd better find it before the watchers got here.

Mago knew what I was about to do and gave me a quick nod.

He put an arm around the girl's shoulders that were now shaking with barely contained sobs. "My dear, come sit down." He guided her to a settee at the end of the hall, and away from seeing what I was about to do.

I had two minutes at the most and I took full advantage.

Windows were locked from the inside. There was no sign of forced entry on the door. The girl had probably only been gone for a few minutes at the most, but I could confirm that by asking her some questions, though Mago was probably taking care of that right now. I studied the body, but was careful not to touch anything. The city watch had seekers, too. I'd rather not be added to their list of suspects, though it wouldn't be me, it would be Symon.

Chatar's fingernails were clean, the knuckles unscuffed. No sign of defensive wounds anywhere on his body, and I do mean anywhere.

No sign of an assailant, either.

I heard the sound of voices coming up the stairs. I looked at the goblin's neck. The noose was red silken rope. I glanced at the bedposts. Matching rope was tied around three of the four bedposts. Kinky. Someone had put the fourth rope to another use. I said someone, because there was no way Chatar had died by hanging. He was killed and then strung up to look like he'd done it himself. I'd only seen a few hangings, but I'd been given a tutorial at a crime scene by my old friend Chief Watcher Janek Tawl back home in Mermeia.

Chatar's feet were only about a foot off the floor, not far enough for the weight of his body to break his neck when the chair was kicked out from beneath him. There was a reason why gallows had a trap door and a long drop. Weight and velocity broke necks. When suicides tried to hang themselves using the chair and rope method, they often died from slow suffocation, probably not the quick death they'd planned on. If Chatar had strung himself up, he'd have strangled, and his face and neck would have been dark red and congested with blood.

Neither body part was in either condition.

It was murder, dressed up to look like not-murder.

I got out into the hall before Madam Camille and her bouncers cleared the last few stairs. I went to Mago and the girl.

"She was downstairs for ten minutes at the most," Mago told me. "Came back upstairs and found him like that."

"Did he lock the door behind you?" I asked the girl.

She looked up at me with wide blue eyes, the scent of wild roses wafting from her pale, spun-silk hair, her full young breasts pressing firm and taut against the gauzy fabric of her—

I shook my head to clear it of the flood of images that followed. How the hell did men get anything done when everything made them think of sex?

"I . . . I don't know," the girl stammered.

I blinked. "Excuse me?"

"Your question. Did he lock the door behind me?"

I cleared my throat. "Oh, yes. That question."

"I guess he could have left it unlocked," she said.

And a murderer had let himself in, killed Chatar, made a half-assed effort to make it look like a suicide, and made his escape.

"No one was in the hall while I was here," Mago said. "And if anyone had gone down the stairs, he'd have been seen."

I looked down to the other end of the hall, more specifically at a blank wall that I knew wasn't so blank. I stepped away from the girl and motioned to Mago to follow me.

"Not if he didn't go down those stairs," I told him.

"There aren't any others."

"Oh, yes, there are."

I told him about the hidden staircase on the other side of

the wall that emptied out into the street behind the bordello next to a perfectly respectable bakery.

Mago raised an eyebrow. "There's a story there."

"There is, but not now."

Madam Camille looked in the room and had much the same reaction as Mago and me. One distinct word that summed up her feelings perfectly. Prostitution was legal in the city. Murder was not. Suicide was bad for business—so was murder. Either one meant the law would soon be crawling all over this place. And if Camille didn't notify them now, she'd be sorry for it later. An investigation into a death meant losing business for a night; covering up a crime meant losing business permanently.

She half turned to one of her bouncers. "Notify the watch."

Camille was smart.

Mago spoke up. "And the goblin embassy."

"What?" Camille and I asked at the same time.

"The victim was one of Prince Chigaru Mal'Salin's mages. Whether suicide or foul play, he's a subject of the goblin crown and has diplomatic privileges. The prince's chancellor and the acting goblin ambassador must be notified."

That would be Tam and Imala.

I bit my lip against a smile.

My cousin was smart, too.

The goblins would know a murder when they saw one; the watch may or may not. I could find out exactly what happened in that room, but only if I dropped my glamour. But if I dropped it, it would take who knew how long to get it up again. No pun intended. As I'd experienced before, frayed nerves equaled no glamour. It'd happened before, and I couldn't risk it happening again with watchers on the way—watchers who had been told to arrest Raine Benares. I was stuck as a short, woefully unendowed, mild-mannered banker until we could get out of here. In the meantime, Symon Wiggs's identity was the only protection I had.

A pair of watchers arrived first. That made sense considering that next to the entertainment district, the red-light district was one of the heaviest patrolled in the city. They did little more than secure the room and wait for their superiors. This was the Satyr's Grove, the most exclusive bordello in the city. A crime here would have repercussions up the watcher chain of command and the Conclave. Prostitution may be legal, but that didn't mean that certain high-ranking officials wanted their names on a police report as possible witnesses to a murder or suicide of another high-ranking official. I imagine Camille had conveniently neglected to ask her clients to stay for police questioning. In five more minutes, we'd be the only people in the house.

The murderer could possibly be one of the horde of high-class clients pulling up their trousers or pulling down their robes and hightailing it out of here, and there was nothing I could do to stop them—or identify them—as long as I was wearing a banker glamour. I'd give every coin of Symon Wiggs's ill-gotten gains for one spark of magic right now.

Mago and I were doing what people who were the first on the scene of a murder do—stand around, then stand around some more waiting to be questioned. The girl had already told them that the hall was empty and that when she screamed, Mago came out of one room and I came out of another, but seeing that said murderer was in the Satyr's Grove, these two watchers weren't about to potentially put their badges on the line by letting anyone leave who'd seen that body. At least not until their superior told them they could. And that the victim was a goblin made it even more of a career-risking move. The watchers weren't just playing it safe, they were playing it paranoid. I didn't blame them, but I didn't like it.

Mago leaned his head in close. "You could track him?"

I nodded once.

Mago knew the source of my frustration. Unglamour and I could find a murderer. Unglamoured would also get me a pair of magic-sapping manacles and a trip to watcher headquarters—until I could be transferred to either a citadel containment room or Taltek Balmorlan's specially built cell.

I glanced down the hall to Rache's room and stifled a growl. He was gone and I had nothing to show for finally cornering the bastard except a denial and a now-empty room.

I stopped and thought. Maybe that room wasn't so empty. Rache said he was a jack-of-one-trade. That trade wasn't dressing in the dark and climbing out a window. I'd be willing to bet he'd left something behind. Something he'd worn, something with his essence that I could use to track him.

I had to get into that room.

There was a ring of fancy golden keys hanging on Madam Camille's belt. It was the only practical thing about her entire outfit.

"Mago," I said on the barest breath.

"Um-hmm," Mago responded without moving his lips.

"I have to get in Rache's room. Keys are on her belt. Charm your way in?"

The look my cousin gave me said that question wasn't worth dignifying with an answer.

Mago sauntered over to Camille, and bent his head close to her ear. A question, a nuzzle, and a discreet grope later, Mago walked back over and gave me the keys. I pressed my lips together against a smile. Not everyone in the family used cannons to get what they wanted.

Most of the clothes on the floor in Rache's room were the girl's. I guess she figured she could get them later. Rache just wanted to get out; he wasn't worried about leaving anything behind.

He should have been. I found just what I needed.

A glove.

If I'd been wearing my own skin, I could have determined that it was Rache's by using my seeker skills, but as it was, I recognized it as Rache by the scent. He still wore the same cologne, and it was on his glove.

At least one thing had gone right tonight.

"I'd like to interrogate—excuse me, I mean *interview*—any witnesses."

I froze. Mago froze. And we both looked out Rache's door and down the hall.

A goblin. Black armored and armed with enough bladed weapons to discourage anyone from asking any questions—and to encourage everyone to give him answers.

Oh crap.

"I'm certain that Masters Peronne and Wiggs would be glad to give you a statement," Madam Camille told him.

Oh, hell no, we wouldn't. I shot a glance to the window and thought that a three-story drop wouldn't be all that bad. A turned ankle would be the worst that could happen, right?

"Recognize them?" Mago whispered.

"Nope. You're the prince's personal banker. Fix this," I hissed.

"I manage the prince's money, not the murders of the prince's officials."

"Money, murder—they're related."

The big goblin spotted us and smiled until his fangs showed, and in no way, shape, or form was it friendly. He had good reason to smile. His witnesses were a pair of elven bankers. Easily intimidated, easy pickings. Give him half an hour and he'd have *us* confessing to murder. I could read it off of him as clearly as if he were saying it. Symon was good at reading people. Nice gift to have. To this goblin we were just two elves who had been in close proximity to a newly dead goblin courtier. We were suspects. I could smell his suspicion from here.

"Gentlemen," the goblin said, his voice deep and silky soft. "If I might have a few minutes of your time."

Mago straightened his doublet and strolled down the hall to the goblin. I had no choice but to follow.

"But of course, we'd be glad to help in any way we can," Mago said. "But first I need to know your name and rank."

"I will be asking the questions . . . Master Peronne, is it?"

"Yes, it is. But I cannot answer any questions without first knowing to whom I am speaking," Mago said, his tone cool. "When I report this to Prince Chigaru, I want to be certain that I can correctly recall any names."

"Report?"

Mago bowed from the waist. "Mago Peronne, personal banker to His Highness Prince Chigaru Mal'Salin. I've come from D'Mai at the prince's express invitation to oversee some pressing financial matters. We were to have our second meeting tomorrow morning. I gather that His Highness is unharmed after the tragedy at the hotel?"

"His Highness is well." The goblin wasn't happy with this little turn of events. Not only did he just lose his interrogation fun, now his name would be mentioned directly to the prince.

And to Tam and Imala.

The goblin responded to Mago's bow with one of his own, though his was stiff and clearly reluctant. "Captain Sokanon at your service, Master Peronne." When his head came up there was a sparkle in his eye that had nothing to do with being at anyone's service. "Did you have the misfortune of staying at the Greyhound Hotel as well?"

"We did. A tragedy."

"They're going to stay here for the evening," Madam Camille chimed in, "until they can make other arrangements."

"I thought as much." The gleam in his eyes said he knew a pair of bankers couldn't be here for women. As a puny banker I took great offense at that.

The gleam in the goblin's eyes turned into a grin on his lips. I knew what was coming. Oh crap, crap, *crap*.

"Then on behalf of His Royal Highness, Prince Chigaru Mal'Salin, I would like to extend the hospitality of the goblin embassy to you both."

Crap and dammit.

I knew what this guy wanted, I knew that goblins hated Raine Benares with a passion, and I knew I couldn't hold this glamour much longer. In fact, I'd never held one for this long. Yes, Tam and Imala were probably at the embassy, but they just as easily could still be at the hotel, or what was left of it. I knew for a fact that the elven embassy had subterranean levels with prison cells where the bureaucrats upstairs wouldn't be bothered with any unseemly screaming. I let Mago know in no uncertain terms exactly how I felt. I pinched him. Hard. He stifled a yelp.

"I thank you for your generosity, Captain Sokanon, but Master Wiggs and I will be quite content here."

"We'll have to close the Grove for the night," one of the watchers told us. "No overnight guests allowed."

The big goblin clapped his black leather-gloved hands together in undisguised glee. "The prince would not want you turned out on the streets at this time of the night. Since you have a meeting scheduled with His Highness in the morning, I must insist."

Yeah, I was sure he must.

The goblin addressed the watchers. "And should you have additional questions for these gentlemen, you will know where to find them."

The street in front of the Satyr's Grove was packed with people. I guess a murder dressed like a suicide made an interesting change from the entertainment offered in the district. Some of the finest restaurants in the city happened to be in the red-light district. I guess a man—or woman—could work up one heck of an appetite there.

The goblin captain had left some men behind to investigate and to bring Chatar's body back to the embassy. The captain and his men would escort us to the embassy. It was obvious which coach we were expected to get into. Black and sleek with matching horses with coats so black that they absorbed the lamplight. I tried not to be obvious about it, but I was looking for some way, any way, any reason to avoid getting into that coach.

I spotted a reason. A reason to dive *under* the coach.

Taltek Balmorlan *and* Carnades Silvanus were getting out of a coach at the front door of a restaurant directly across the street. Mago and I were in the company of goblin embassy guards, being treated with exaggerated courtesy, and being helped into a goblin embassy coach.

They saw us.

Oh no.

Mago and I had run out of the Swan Song, never shown up at the tavern for Balmorlan's Saghred demonstration, and now we appeared to be the goblin embassy guards' new best friends. An embassy that the alive-and-well Prince Chigaru Mal'Salin controlled.

Our cover wasn't just blown, it was royally screwed.

Chapter 13

The goblin captain sat on the coach seat opposite me and Mago.
Now that we were inside a goblin coach going to the goblin
embassy, apparently the captain no longer felt the need to
be polite or even attempt to make small talk.

That was fine with me. I couldn't spare the energy. I
wasn't even in the embassy yet, and I was trying to think
of ways to escape. Though my most pressing concern was
how to hold on to my Symon Wiggs glamour. Up until an
hour ago, I hadn't felt the weight; I sure did now. Just because I wasn't physically carrying anything didn't lessen
the sensation that I was hauling Mago around on my back
rather than sitting next to him.

I had to carry it myself; and if I dropped it, I'd drop my
glamour.

That would be ill-advised to say the least. As long as I
was glamoured, I couldn't use my magic, but the Saghred
couldn't use me. That was the best reason I'd ever heard of
to keep a death grip on Symon's glamour.

I could trust Tam and Imala, but any and all other goblins were suspect. So until I got the lay of the land in the embassy, I'd hold Symon's pasty skin around myself like the ultimate security blanket.

The outside of the goblin embassy looked much like the two embassies on either side of it, and was built with the same white stone as most of the government buildings on Mid. However, the black iron fence and gate were pure goblin. Taller than the coach we were in, the fence surrounding the embassy and grounds was made of intricately twisted wrought iron with the tip of every other post ending in a sharpened point.

A really sharp point.

The ones that weren't an impalement waiting to happen were topped with a blazing red ball of flame that was far from natural. I could tell just from looking at it that anything that touched them would fry. At least that was my theory, but I wasn't about to put it to the test. Apparently no one here was taking any chances that another attempt would be made on the prince's life. We were going in through the front gates, gates that quite frankly, made me doubt that this was anything other than my painful death waiting to happen.

Woven in steel into the massive embassy gates and glowing with the same blazing red wards was the Mal'Salin family crest of two serpents battling for dominance, both surmounted by a crown.

To top it off, the banner of the House of Mal'Salin was flying over the embassy and every goblin guard was armed to the fangs and on high alert.

And we were going inside.

The gates closed behind the coach with a heavy—and rather unnerving—metal clang. An armed goblin guard opened the coach's door and folded down the steps.

"After you, gentlemen," Captain Sokanon said.

My feet were smarter than the rest of me; they'd decided that they weren't going anywhere. Mago realized this and got out first. Then I had no choice. I stepped out of the coach, tripped on something, and damned near landed on my face. Strong, gauntleted hands gripped both of my arms, catching me, keeping me from falling, but taking their sweet time letting me go afterward.

I looked at those glowing gates and swallowed. I didn't care that the goblins wouldn't kill the prince's banker and hopefully not his puny friend; I still didn't like any of it.

"So we go in, hide out for the night, you meet with the prince, then we leave," I muttered without moving my lips.

"That's the plan," Mago said.

I didn't want to remind him that most plans I'd been associated with lately had gone to crap. He knew.

Mago and I waited as the embassy's massive doors opened on eerily quiet hinges. The guards in the courtyard were completely silent. All I could hear was the crackle of wards on the gate. I think I knew how mice must feel in a room full of cats. Big cats. Hungry cats. We were elves and we had an armed escort into the goblin embassy two days after what appeared to be elves tried to blow up the prince's yacht and an elven assassin tried to turn Chigaru into a pin cushion. And only mere hours after elven firemages torched the hotel the prince was staying at.

It didn't matter that we hadn't been involved in any of this. Well, not directly anyway. To these guards, two elves represented all elves. They wanted us dead and they wanted it to hurt. For the cherry on top of our situation, I had nothing but a boot knife to my name. What I wouldn't have given for a pair of Nebian grenades. Not that those would have saved my bacon, but it'd give goblin guards a whole new respect for elven bankers.

The interior of the goblin embassy was pretty much what I expected. The drapes were heavy velvet, floor to ceiling, and they were drawn against any glimmer of light getting in. Goblins were nocturnal by preference bordering on necessity. In cities where there were large goblin populations, the shops and businesses owned by goblins or those catering to them were open during the day, but kept extended hours in the evening for the convenience and comfort of their patrons. During the day, the windows were kept shuttered against bright sunlight.

Soft blue lighting glowed from recessed pockets in the walls. Supposedly the color was soothing to sensitive goblin eyes. What furniture I could see was dark wood covered in dark fabrics. A line of chairs against one wall—presumably for people waiting to see an embassy official—was covered in a shade of red that was disturbingly close to that of fresh blood. The floor was black marble. Oh yeah, that was cheerful and welcoming.

And we were only in the entry hall.

"Kijika, turn up the lights for our guests."

The goblin bowed. "Yes, Captain."

"Is His Highness still awake?" Mago asked.

"The prince has given strict orders that he is not to be disturbed—for any reason." The words were polite and so was the tone, but with goblins you had to listen to what was going on beneath and between those words. Mago and I received the message loud and clear: the prince may or may not have given that order, but Captain Sokanon had no intention of telling the prince we were here—for any reason. I had news for him: if anyone tried to force Symon Wiggs into a subterranean cell, they wouldn't be dealing with a puny banker anymore; they'd have a very pissed Raine Benares and her Amazing Destructive Rock on their hands.

Mago knew and cleared his throat before I let my fantasy become reality right here in the embassy foyer.

"Are either Director Kalis or Chancellor Nathrach available?" I asked.

The guard raised an eyebrow at that, clearly surprised. "You are acquainted with the director and chancellor how?"

"Through our previous meeting with the prince," Mago said smoothly.

"Are they in the embassy?" I persisted.

"The last report I received had them at the hotel continuing the investigation of the fire." The goblin was only too glad to deliver that piece of information, which meant that it was more than likely true. Just our luck.

"But I know they would want our guests to be made comfortable." He gestured to the imposing staircase, also made of black marble. "I will show you to your rooms. You may rest and refresh yourselves for a while. We will question you presently."

They showed us to two rooms, on the second floor, right next to the guard station, and conveniently across the hall from each other. In other words, we were going to be watched like hawks, not allowed to talk to each other, and probably taken for interrogation one at a time.

Great. Just great.

"We appreciate your generous hospitality," Mago said, "but Master Wiggs and I would prefer to be in the same room."

"But each room only has one bed."

Mago stepped up to me and slipped his hand in mine, intertwining our fingers.

Oh crap in a bucket.

My cousin gave the captain a dazzling smile. "The sleeping arrangements won't be a problem."

Realization dawned, and one of the goblin's fangs bit into his bottom lip to keep from laughing. Two of the guards at the station didn't try as hard, but at least they muffled their snickers with one cough each.

I looked anywhere but at Mago. In response, he gave my hand an affectionate squeeze. So help me if he tried to solidify this with a kiss . . .

"Understood, Master Peronne. One room it is. I will have refreshments sent up."

One of the guards on duty unlocked the door, and then locked it from the outside once we were inside. I'd have been shocked if they didn't.

"Did you have to do that?" I kept my voice low. This was the goblin embassy; the walls most definitely had ears—and eyes.

Mago removed his doublet and tossed it on the entirely too prominent bed. "Yes, I'm afraid I did," he replied in Myloran. "I won't allow them to separate us."

I raised an eyebrow at his language choice.

"Very few goblins speak or understand Myloran," Mago explained. "They don't feel it's worth the bother."

Good enough for me; I switched to Myloran. "I'm not saying your idea wasn't brilliant, but—"

"It also stopped any further inquiry." He flashed a quick smile. "There are some things those goblins wouldn't want to know more about. This was one of those things."

I sighed. "Thank you."

"My pleasure."

I chuckled weakly. "Those goblins think it's your pleasure, too."

"Raine, you need to sit down."

"I need to drop this glamour."

"Then drop it. Hold on until the guards return with food, and then drop it. You can't hold it forever."

I nodded. He was right. "If things get ugly, I'll need every bit of my power, and I'll need rest to use it." I glanced over at the bed. It didn't have any drapes that I could pull to block the inside from view. Though I'd hide under the covers if I had to. As a kid, I used to think that bad things couldn't get me if I hid under the covers. At least here, the bad things wouldn't be able to see me. Yes, the majority of goblins in the embassy were loyal to Chigaru, but some of them had to be working for Sathrik Mal'Salin and Sarad Nukpana. That captain could be one of them. If so, he'd have a vested interest in keeping the prince from meeting with his banker.

I looked out the barred window. I'd been in a bedroom like this only a few months before, in Prince Chigaru's hideout in the district of Mermeia called The Ruins. That time I'd officially been the prince's prisoner. He had wanted me to find and use the Saghred for him. I snorted to myself.

If he knew I was here, he'd probably want the same thing right now. Armed and armored elves patrolled the walls of the embassy next door. The wards and shields and number of guards told me they were on high alert. The goblins were putting on a similar display. Though the goblins were nocturnal with night vision to match. Their high alert at nearly two bells was more alert than the elves. And if all the lights suddenly got extinguished and the goblins were feeling playful, those elves were toast and they knew it.

"Whose flash of brilliance was responsible for putting the elf and goblin embassies next to each other?" I asked.

Mago leisurely pulled a cigar from an interior pocket in his doublet and lit it. "The maze that is the bureaucratic mind is a mystery best left unsolved."

A key turned in the lock and one of the guards wheeled in a cart with several covered dishes and a bottle of wine. He nodded to both of us and left. Of course, he locked us in.

We looked at the food, then at each other. We couldn't touch any of it. Drugs were favorite goblin interrogation tools.

"It would smell divine, wouldn't it?" Mago said. "Goblin torture is indeed cruel."

"Our excuses for not eating?"

"This afternoon has been quite traumatic and we have nervous stomachs."

"Which nicely complements the nervous rest of us."

"Indeed. I've developed an unfortunate case of indigestion."

I looked at the tray. "Better than a fatal case later," I muttered.

Mago was studying me intently. "For a moment I could see you," he whispered.

He wasn't talking about Symon Wiggs. I got up and went to the bed, which conveniently was in the shadows. I was shaking. From exhaustion, but mostly from fear. I was an elf in a goblin embassy, a wanted and hated elf. This glamour was the only protection I had and I was about to lose it.

Literally and figuratively.

"Why don't you get some sleep?" Mago said. "I'll keep watch."

"I can't go to sleep. I'll wake up as me."

Mago smiled gently. "Would that be so bad?"

"It was this afternoon. When I'm Symon, the Saghred can't get to me."

"As Symon you can't defend yourself." Mago pulled back the bed covers. "Raine, you can't run from who you are."

"Or what."

"You're not a what. The only way that would ever be true is if you start believing what others say—others who want what you have for themselves."

"They're welcome to it."

"They're not and you know it. You're defending that stone as fiercely as you're protecting the rest of us. You know what'll happen if anyone other than you gets hold of it. You won't let that happen."

I snorted. "I'm just all kinds of noble, aren't I?"

His smile was back. "Yes, you are," he said softly.

I tried to think of a glib comment for that; but truth was, I was too exhausted to make the effort.

Mago helped me off with my boots, but first I took the boot knife and stuck it under the pillow. I lay back with an exhausted sigh.

"Mago?"

"Yes?"

"I'd rather sleep in a cathouse than a house full of cats," I managed before I couldn't keep my eyes open any longer.

I woke up in the same place where I fell asleep. I loved it when that happened.

I was also me again, wearing the same singed, torn, and bloodstained clothes I'd had on at the hotel. That was the thing about glamouring—when you let go of one, you not only got yourself back, you got the clothes you'd been wearing. I guess it beat the hell out of popping out of a glamour naked.

Mago was standing by the window, the drapes pulled wide open, letting in the morning sunlight, anything he could do to make it uncomfortable for any goblins to try to come and get us for some pre-breakfast interrogation.

I dragged myself out of bed and actually managed to stay on my feet. Amazing. "You stayed up all night."

Mago shrugged. "Wouldn't be the first time. Though I'm usually engaged in a more entertaining activity than watching you sleep."

"When did I lose—"

"About five bells," he replied. "The hour before that you phased in and out." He smiled slightly and shook his head. "Even in your sleep, you were determined to hold on."

The key turned in the lock. I took a breath and held it. Well, Raine, you'll see what happens when it happens.

The same guard who had brought our food opened the door. "Both of you will come with me," he said, his tone brusque. The guard saw me and his eyes widened in shock.

I couldn't run, and I sure as hell wasn't going to hide. I went with a glare instead. The guard quickly stepped back into the hall and closed the door. No key turned in the lock this time. We heard him talking quickly in hushed, hissing tones with others.

"I do believe you've put a slight crimp in their morning," Mago noted. "Bravo, cousin."

The bravo had yet to be proven, but if anyone tried to take me anywhere I didn't want to go, and tried to force me to tell them anything I didn't want to say, their morning wasn't going to be crimped, it was going to be ruined. "If there's anything I'm good at, it's ruining someone's day."

Mago chuckled. "Too true."

The talk ceased outside our door. The door opened again, slower this time. The guard cleared his throat, and respectfully inclined his head to me. "Would you both please accompany me?"

Mago turned to me and smiled. "Such a polite young man."

Chapter 14

I didn't know where we were being led, but I was determined to make an impression.

I succeeded.

I'd made no effort whatsoever to clean up. My leather doublet was singed with multiple black stripes where some of the firemages' bolts had breached my shields. The goblins we passed in the embassy's corridors knew that everyone else who those bolts touched had been instantly vaporized. I only had singed leather.

When walking among predators, don't act like prey. Mago walked, but I stalked. It was a little something I'd picked up from Tam. That man could wear blood like a fashion accessory. Goblins admired that. When a goblin killed an enemy or a rival, most of the time they didn't hide it; they flaunted it. So I figured that the best way for me and Mago to stay uninterrogated was to act like it would be the last mistake anyone here ever made if they tried it.

Our escort stopped at a closed door. Nothing fancy, no guards posted outside to keep a screaming prisoner from running out. Just a door. The goblin opened the door and stepped back for us to enter.

I looked before I stepped.

Imala Kalis stood behind a desk. Her dark eyes widened briefly in surprise. "Hekai, you may go."

Mago and I came inside, and the guard closed the door behind us.

My cousin let out the breath I didn't know he'd been holding. "Director Kalis, you are the most breathtaking vision I have ever beheld."

I opted to collapse in a chair.

"Well, we aren't going to be tortured," I muttered. "That's always a good start to the day."

Imala came running around her desk and did something most ungoblin-like. She hugged me. Not easy to do with me sitting down, but she managed. "How did you get—"

"Last night, your boys brought in a skinny elven banker named Symon Wiggs from the Satyr's Grove—"

Imala did the math in an instant and beamed. "A glamoured witness to a murder. Perfect."

"I wouldn't go so far as to call us witnesses," Mago told her. "We saw the 'after,' not the 'during.'"

"Regardless, you were one of the first to see Chatar's body. And I'll wager the first to investigate the room."

"Guilty as charged," I said.

She raised a quizzical brow. "Why a banker?"

I negligently waved the hand that wasn't holding my head up. "Just another iron I have in the fire."

"Raine, know that this is the highest compliment I can give—it's a shame you weren't born a goblin. Though if you had been, my job would be in danger."

"And make a career of being scared out of my mind?" I snorted. "You can have it and keep it. There's not enough money in anyone's treasury to pay me to do it."

Imala was looking closely at Mago.

My cousin hadn't shaved, hadn't bathed, and quite frankly looked as if he didn't give a flying fairy about either one. Personal elegance was not his primary concern right now. Mago looked a little shady and a lot disreputable.

"And you, sir, the prince's banker, now bear more than a passing resemblance to another dark-haired elf of my recent acquaintance—Captain Phaelan Benares. And here are the two of you, fresh from a night of adventure." Imala's dark eyes shone. "I thought it odd yesterday that the two of you were not only together, but knew each other. Now I can clearly see that your last name isn't Peronne."

Mago may have been up all night, but he swept her a bow that would have been perfect in any court. "Guilty as charged. Will you keep my secret, gentle lady?"

Imala laughed, a delighted sound. "I've never been called 'gentle,' but I keep secrets for a living, Master *Peronne*. Rest assured; your true identity is safe with me." She turned to me. "Mychael's worried sick about you; he and his men are tearing the city apart."

Mychael was alive. My vision blurred and I quickly closed my eyes to stop them from going further. "No doubt with Carnades right behind him."

"So you know about the price on your head."

"It's only the latest gossip at the Satyr's Grove." I ran a hand over my face. "Can you let Mychael know I'm safe . . . well, at least alive and that I'm here? Without anyone else knowing?"

Imala's lips quirked at one corner. "Private goes without saying," she assured me. "I'll take care of everything." She shook her head in wonder. "Including you. You took on at least five firemages."

"Nine."

"The Saghred?"

I nodded. "Apparently the rock was having too much fun to let me die."

"Do you require a healer?"

"Mychael would be nice," I said with a sudden lump in my throat. "Though just food and some more sleep would do, but I don't think I have time for either one."

"Time?"

"Price on my head, assassins to find. I have a busy day planned."

Imala's expression softened; something I hadn't seen it do very often. "Raine, there are many others in this city qualified to track down assassins. As to the price on your head, you're safe here. This is my embassy," she assured me. "Anything you want is yours."

My eyes got misty again. "Thank you."

"None necessary. We'll get you fed and then a bath and clean clothes."

"And if Carnades and his Seat of Twelve henchmen find out that I'm here? I don't want to make trouble for you."

Gentle was instantly replaced by a glower. "No one can force you to leave; if they try, it's an act of war."

"And if Carnades claims that I'm being held against my will?"

"Unless you tell them otherwise, our keeping you here would be a goblin act of war against the elves."

"Don't worry, Imala. I have no intention of lying to anyone. Right now, the goblin embassy is the safest place for me." I started. "Where's Tam?"

Imala raised her hands in a calming gesture. "After he claimed Chatar's body and had it sent back here, he was to meet with the island's chief watcher. He should be back within the hour." She got the chair from behind her desk and pulled it up next to mine. "What happened from the time we were separated at the hotel?"

I let Mago tell Imala about our day and night of adventure. My cousin was an excellent storyteller and he didn't disappoint.

"So that's how we ended up here," I said when he finished.

Imala smiled until her dainty fangs showed. "From elven banker to hero of the goblin people."

I blinked. "Hero?"

"Hero. For an elf to act in such a courageous fashion in

defense of so many goblins, putting her own life and future at risk without thought—"

"Uh . . . it wasn't like the Saghred left me much time for thinking."

"But you directed its power at those who were killing my people."

"I definitely did that."

"Do you have regrets?"

"None. I did what I had to do, and now the Seat of Twelve has put a price on my head. Though I'm probably not the first or last Benares to get that dubious honor."

"From the reports I've received, the elves among the Twelve are responsible for the bounty on you."

"Carnades Silvanus probably knocked a couple of them over so he could sign his name first to my arrest warrant. But it was a friend of his in elven intelligence who was directly responsible for what happened today, though I'm willing to bet Carnades's money paid for some of those firemages."

"That would be Taltek Balmorlan."

I nodded. "Also known as my other iron in the fire. If one of your people gets him in their crosshairs—take the shot. We'll all be better off." I glanced at Mago. "Our chances of taking him down our way are pretty much shot to hell after he and Carnades saw us getting into a goblin embassy coach."

Mago's smile was borderline mischievous. "Nothing's been shot to hell yet."

I raised an eyebrow. "You have another plan?"

"Let's just say I haven't given up."

"Speaking of not giving up." I pulled Rache's glove out of the front of my doublet. "This belongs to Rache Kai. I took it out of his room at the Grove last night."

Imala raised one flawless eyebrow. "My, you do have other irons in the fire."

"Rache was a bonus. We didn't expect him to be there, but while we killed time waiting for supper with Balmorlan, I wanted to have a talk with my ex. He admitted to being hired to assassinate Chigaru. He wouldn't spill who did the hiring, but Taltek Balmorlan is the front runner."

"Well, there are two suspects I can remove from the list," Imala told me. "Sathrik didn't hire Rache Kai; neither did Sarad."

"Distaste of hiring an elf?" Mago asked.

"That and they would hire the assassin they thought best qualified to complete the job. I am more than familiar with Rache Kai's qualifications. However, goblins prefer a more personal touch. They have someone on the inside and it appears that someone has gone to a great deal of trouble to make it look as if the threat to the prince's life has now ended his own."

"Chatar didn't commit suicide," I told her.

"I would be surprised if he had. As you no doubt remember, he never shied away from confrontation of any kind."

Like wanting to obliterate me that day on the pier. "I got that impression."

"That included being accused of the assassination attempt. Chatar vehemently maintained his innocence, and he didn't seem to feel the weight of any guilt. Hardly the behavior of a man about to commit suicide." Imala was silent for a moment. "You have done so much for our people already, but I have to ask—"

I knew where this was going. "If I could tell you who the murderer was by touching the corpse?"

"Yes. I'm sorry, Raine. If there was any other way—"

"I'll do it." My voice said the words, but I wasn't eager.

I still had nightmares about a corpse I'd touched to find how and where he had died. It'd been one of Sarad Nukpana's victims whose life force he'd fed on to regenerate his body. The goblin had left a surprise message for me, delivered by a corpse who grabbed me and didn't let go until Nukpana had promised to do the same to everyone I loved and then me.

No, I wasn't eager to have a repeat of *that* experience.

But Sarad Nukpana hadn't infested Chatar's body.

At least not that I was aware of.

Way to be paranoid, Raine.

"Thank you," Imala said.

"You might want to hold off on those thanks. The last corpse I touched reached up and touched me right back. There was unsightly screaming involved."

"I would have done the same."

I smiled, my first real one of the morning. "Somehow I doubt that."

"You believe the murderer to be here, among your own people?" Mago asked Imala.

"It's likely that they're here in this very building at this very moment. Now that they have eliminated Chatar, they would again be focused on their primary task."

"The prince is well protected?"

"By my most trusted agents. His Highness is quite safe." Imala smiled in a vicious flash of tiny fangs. "His potential killer is not."

Mago chuckled. "You do appear to be a lady who enjoys her work."

"What the lady will enjoy is catching the bitch or bastard who's made themselves so inconvenient."

"And he—or she—tried to make Chatar's death look like a suicide so you wouldn't dig any further," I said.

"I've got news for them; I haven't even begun digging yet."

"If someone felt Chatar needed killing, it was in all likelihood because that someone wanted him quiet," Mago noted.

I glanced sharply at Mago. "Think he might have said something to the girl? You know . . . pillow talk? You'd tell your bartender your troubles. Is the same true for working girls?"

My cousin smiled. "I make it a point not to share my troubles with anyone outside of the family. One can't be too cautious." He turned to Imala. "Did Chatar make it a habit of frequenting bordellos?"

"Not that I am aware of," Imala replied. "He has a mistress in Regor who he hasn't seen in some time. With the prince being in exile, his retinue hasn't exactly stayed in places where such . . . creature comforts are available. Since they arrived, more than a few have visited the finer establishments Mid has to offer." She smiled, her dark eyes shining. "We are a most passionate people."

I slowly pushed myself out of the chair. "Well, hopefully I can get Chatar to tell me what his last trouble was."

Imala led us into what looked like a ballroom. There were a few chairs against the walls, but a table in the center of the room had my full and complete attention. There was a body on that table—Chatar's body. It was covered with a long piece of black silk. I don't know what that table's purpose had been before it'd been drafted into service as a funeral bier, but if it'd ever been used to serve food, I sure as hell wouldn't eat off of it ever again.

The goblin guards' hands went to their sword hilts at the sight of me and Mago. I couldn't blame them, considering I still smelled like scorched leather, and Mago didn't look any less disreputable.

"Stand down," Imala ordered. "Mistress Benares and Master Peronne are here at my invitation. Leave us for a few minutes. Mahet, I want you to stay. I will tell the rest of you when to return."

All but one of the black leather-armored goblin guards left. Imala closed the massive doors.

An amused voice came from a shadowy corner. "I'd hug you from behind, but I'd probably get a knife in the ribs."

Tam.

Goblin guard be damned. I ran across the room and wrapped my arms around him in a crushing hug. I got the same in return. Considering that I'd last seen him battling a buka that wouldn't die on the top floor of a hotel on fire, I thought it was an entirely appropriate response.

I raised my head and grinned up at him. "You're alive."

"Of course I am. Didn't Imala tell you that I was at—"

"Yeah, but being told and seeing for myself are two different things."

Tam chuckled. "It wasn't like you left us all that much more to do."

"Just kill a buka."

"Well, there was that. Mychael and I finally managed to dispatch the thing, then all we had to do was haul our asses down burning stairs. We met Imala and the prince at the basement door." His hands tightened on my shoulder. "I heard what happened outside . . . what you did. Thank you."

"You should be thanking the rock."

He studied my face, his dark eyes solemn. "I'm thanking the lady *in charge* of the rock. I had an easier time fighting the buka than I did wrestling Mychael into that tunnel. The ceiling was caving in and he was still determined to get to you."

"Then I'm the one who should be thanking you."

"Mychael already did." Tam grinned. "That is after he apologized for trying to knock my head off."

"Ouch."

"And it still does."

Mago cleared his throat from behind me. "I'd rather not stand next to a dead body for any longer than I have to."

I didn't like being in rooms with dead bodies, either. "Well, once we see what secrets Chatar here can tell us, we can all get the hell out of here."

Without any ceremony at all, Imala stepped over to the table and pulled down the covering. Chatar was still naked, but thankfully Imala had only pulled the sheet down to just above his waist.

I didn't give myself the chance to think about what I was about to do. I went to the end of the table where the goblin mage's head was, placed my palms on either side at his temples, and tried not to think that I was touching cool, lifeless flesh. Chatar's mind no longer functioned; but while he lived, it had been the center of his life force and his memories. Standing at the head of the table also had the benefit of putting me out of reach should his corpse suddenly get grabby. I knew that would probably never happen to me again, but I'd taken enough unnecessary chances lately.

The first image I got wasn't an image at all, but a scent. Wild rose. The girl. I remembered her perfume from standing near her at the Satyr's Grove. The girl was lying on the bed; the scent of her perfume in the air was like a freshly gathered bouquet. She was smiling and stretching like a cat that had been on the receiving end of a most proficient petting. Apparently Chatar was good in bed; something I really didn't need to know.

There was a small table with a dish of candied fruit. Chatar selected a pair of chocolate-covered strawberries and bit into one of them. An instant later he gasped and jerked upright, his throat closing, unable to speak, unable to breathe. The mage's limbs were paralyzed; he couldn't move or fight back as his vision went dark, the strawberries dropping from his dying fingers.

Poisoned.

Death by after-sex snack. Damn.

As he fell, strong hands caught him around the chest and lowered him quietly to the floor.

Hands that definitely didn't belong to a girl.

Chatar had only turned his back on the girl for a moment; there was no one else in the room, and certainly not a man strong enough to hang him from that rafter. He knew there was no one there. He knew because he had checked, searched every corner of that room.

Chatar had known that someone would try to kill him.

I moved my right hand down to his chest, where the killer's hands would have grabbed him.

A man . . .

How the hell had he gotten in the ro—

I froze. A man smelling of wild roses.

Oh mother of hell.

That girl had changed into a man—into the assassin. Mago and I had comforted the killer right there outside the room.

A master glamourer. Very rare, but not unknown. Able to instantly morph from one form into another, one sex to another. Even with the Saghred's power, I needed time, concentration, and an exact image to work from. The assassin didn't need any of those.

He or she could literally be anyone. Anywhere.

Here.

Chapter 15

Imala sent her two most trusted agents to the citadel with the message for Mychael, with the explicit instructions to deliver it to Mychael and no one else.

All I could do was wait.

I usually wasn't good at waiting.

Unless I was taking a much-needed soak in a tub of steaming water. My predator impersonation had been a success, so I didn't have to stalk around the embassy anymore in burned clothes. As to waiting, as long as the water stayed hot and no one broke down the door with the intention of killing me, I could probably wait forever.

I sighed and leaned back. I didn't go so far as to close my eyes. The trust of a naked elf in a goblin embassy only went so far. There was a master glamourer on the loose, not to mention the walls of my room probably still had eyes. In fact, once word got around that Imala had ordered a tub and hot water brought to my room, I imagine there were a few more pairs of eyes watching. I didn't care. I didn't have anything to be ashamed of, and I was too exhausted to go around the room, poking my fingers into everything that might be a spy hole for goblin Peeping Toms. If they wanted to see a naked elf, let 'em look.

And if anyone should make the mistake of trying anything more hands-on, Tam had provided a pair of sleek, curved goblin swords and enough daggers to make me feel warm and cozy almost anywhere. Imala had found clothes for me.

Those did *not* make me feel warm and cozy.

It was a goblin secret service uniform. Imala had a number of female agents among her people, and one of them was just my size. Lucky me. I glanced over at the sleek black leather ensemble on the bed. I had to hand it to Imala; she knew how to dress her agents. Carnades would love to see me wearing that. To him, it'd be the proof of everything he'd been claiming since I'd set foot on Mid—that I was not only a goblin sympathizer, but I was working for them. And if I set foot outside of the embassy wearing that, I'd be putting the last nail in my coffin.

I wasn't taking one step outside the embassy's front doors. If I did, I not only wouldn't be wearing a goblin uniform, I wouldn't be wearing my own skin. The assassin wasn't the only one who found it easier to roam around town incognito.

I wasn't the only one lying low. I could feel the Saghred's presence inside of me like a rock on my chest. Solid, immovable, but for the moment, quiet. Through me it had killed nine firemages. The rock was used to destroying, but not on an empty stomach, or whatever the Saghred had. It had expended a hell of a lot of strength in the streets outside that hotel, and it hadn't gotten any souls to replenish itself. No wonder the thing damned near killed me to get at the souls fleeing the bodies of the dying in the hotel. It wouldn't surprise me if the Saghred had known about the firemages, and what the two of us would have to do to stop them.

At that cheerful thought, I sank down farther in the

water and added it to the list of my other potentially fatal problems.

Someone glamoured as a girl in the Satyr's Grove to kill Chatar. Had the killer also morphed into Chatar to try to assassinate the prince, then had to kill the mage to cover his tracks? Until I learned otherwise, that convoluted mess sounded not only plausible, but highly likely.

There were reliable witnesses who confirmed that Chatar had been near the stern of the yacht when the assassination attempt had taken place. I'd seen him myself after Tam had fished Chigaru out of the harbor. He didn't act like a man who'd had his evil plan foiled. He was pissed at me for interfering with his attempt to keep the pilot boats from ramming the yacht. I'd felt his magic; it was strong. He'd used every last bit of his strength against those boats. He didn't suddenly stop doing that, run to the bow, shoot the prince, and then threaten to vaporize me for ruining both attempts.

I glanced over at the glove that I'd been carrying around under Symon's doublet and then mine. It was on the bed with the uniform.

I had no doubt in my mind that I'd seen Rache in that window overlooking Embassy Row. He'd let me see him after he'd taken a shot at Mychael. He wanted me to see him.

Now I knew why. It hadn't been Rache. He'd never been there, but his competition had—glamoured as Rache.

The unknown assassin had glamoured as Chatar to try to kill Chigaru, and had morphed into Rache to take a shot at Mychael. Then the nimble little minx had changed into a working girl at the Satyr's Grove to poison Chatar—that is after they'd had some kinky fun. A man who'd turned into a woman to have sex with another man, kill him, then turn back into a man to hang his victim to make it look like a suicide.

This guy was a real go-getter in every sense of the word, no wonder Sarad Nukpana hired him.

Rache said he knew he had competition; competition he referred to as a bastard, not a bitch. I knew Rache well enough that if a woman was trying to steal his hit, he definitely wouldn't hesitate to call her a bitch. That meant the assassin was a man.

The question I had now was did Rache know his name?

My best bet for finding that name was to find Rache. Though I knew I'd never get either one unless I got some sleep. I didn't have time for it, but I had even less time to screw this up. When I was in the same room with Rache again, I couldn't be anything but at the top of my game. If that meant a couple of hours spent studying the insides of my eyelids, so be it.

If it had been the goblin assassin who'd taken that shot at Mychael, why would he want to frame Rache? Rache was an assassin. Why would someone glamour as Rache and try to kill people? Though not just people. Mychael. If Nukpana hired this guy, why would he want him to go after Mychael? Unless the assassin wanted what was happening right now—every law officer on the island was hunting for Rache Kai. If Rache got arrested, the assassin would get rid of his competition. And by killing Chatar, the assassin killed someone who may have been able to identify him. I was seeing a pattern here, sick and twisted, but still a pattern.

I resisted the urge to slide down underneath the water. This was getting way too complicated.

I must have dozed off. You don't jerk, gasp, and choke on bathwater unless you'd been asleep. I also wasn't alone. My hands went over the sides of the tub, grabbed the swords, and I came to my feet with much splashing and sloshing.

"Now that's a vision I haven't seen lately—last time you had a dagger and a towel."

Mychael was in uniform. I wasn't in anything except a tub. After more splashing and sloshing, I'd ditched the swords and jumped into his arms.

His sea blue eyes had a naughty gleam. "But I was about to join you."

"We have an audience."

Mychael grinned. "I could fix that."

"I know you could, but right now goblins are the only people on this island who almost like me."

"I like you."

I smiled and shifted against him. "Yeah, I kind of got that feeling."

I stepped back and looked Mychael up and down. While the scenery was more than nice, that he was wearing his formal uniform was not.

"Let me guess," I said, switching to mindspeak. *"Carnades likes his death warrant signings formal."* I didn't mind goblins seeing me naked, but I wasn't about to let them know the rest of my business.

Mychael's next words echoed with tense fury in my mind. *"Justinius has two votes. I have one."*

My heart stopped for a few beats. *"Carnades bought all the votes he needed."*

The look on Mychael's face told me that Carnades had a lot more.

"How many?" I asked.

"The rest of the Seat of Twelve voted unanimously."

My mouth fell open. "What!" I said out loud. I dropped my voice to a whisper. "All of them? But you and Justinius—"

"Were the only ones who voted against them. It didn't matter that you saved hundreds of lives. They believe you're out of control."

"I only killed firemages." But that didn't matter; none of it mattered. The Twelve would see me taken into custody and then they would see me executed.

"They claim it's for the safety of the citizens and for your own protection."

"I bet Carnades added that last part." I stood very still. *"Are you here to bring me in?"*

"You know I'm not."

"That's treason."

Mychael smiled fiercely. *"Yeah, it is."*

"You know how I feel about you putting yourself in danger because of me."

"I love you and I've sworn to do everything in my power to get you out of this, and if that means taking you off this island and running for the rest of our lives, then that's what I'll do." He handed me a towel. *"And as much as it pains me to have you cover up, you might want to do it before some of the men behind your walls hyperventilate and pass out."*

I tossed the towel aside. *"Let 'em pass out."* I ran my hands up his chest and laced my fingers behind his head, pulling him down to me. I kissed him hard, with a passion born of the fear of losing him—first in the fire and now by choosing sides and choosing me.

In one swift move, Mychael tightened his arms around me and lifted me off my feet. I wrapped my arms around his neck, deepening the kiss, my mouth demanding, taking. Mychael's breathing had a ragged edge as he held me hard against him with one arm while his other hand ran down my body and back again with some gasp-inducing detours.

Our lips parted and I looked into his eyes as we stood pressed together, breathing fast, our hearts beating faster.

"That's not helping the poor bastards watching us." Mychael's voice was a husky whisper. "But it's doing wonderful things for me."

"I'd like to have you do some wonderful things for me right now. Might help curb the terror."

Mychael's wandering hand cradled my lower back. "I won't let anyone hurt you."

"You might not be able to stop them."

His smile was that of a man with a secret. *"I won't be alone,"* he said in mindspeak. *"And you won't be, either."*

"Meaning?"

"After what the Seat of Twelve just did, Justinius is of a mind to tell them—and the entire Conclave if necessary—to bend over and do something to themselves that I know to be physically impossible."

I grinned. "I just love that old man."

"I'm rather fond of him myself." Pride gleamed in his eyes. "And of every Guardian who said they would stand with us."

I just hung there in his arms, stunned. "Us? Both of us? Us as in including me?" I managed.

"Yes, to all of the above."

"Balmorlan will try to flush me out again. Piaras. Phaelan. Carnades has already threatened to—"

"That's been taken care of. Justinius is personally overseeing Piaras's security, and your Uncle Ryn is essentially sitting on Phaelan."

"Sitting on?"

"He wants to find you and get you off of the island now." Mychael reluctantly set me on my feet. "Quite frankly, I think that's the best idea your cousin's ever had."

I smiled, more like a baring of teeth. "I'm not going anywhere," I told him. "I have too much unfinished business. Carnades has signed his way into a higher spot on my list. Has Imala filled you in on how and where I spent my evening?"

"She did."

"Then you know we're close, so close to bringing down Balmorlan, Carnades and his yes-mages. Close to stopping Rache and that glamouring assassin. I'm not going anywhere as long as there's a chance to make any of those things happen. It's not just about me and the rock. It's about the elves and goblins who will fight a war that no one will win, because they've been forced to fight, or to swallow the lies that men like Taltek Balmorlan or Sarad Nukpana feed them. I can run, but thousands of innocent people won't be able to. So I'm not going to, either."

I reached for the goblin secret service uniform on the

bed, my lips curling up at the corners. *"So, how do you like skintight black leather?"*

"Imala, when Chatar last left the embassy, did he take anything with him?" Mychael asked.

Mychael and I were in Imala's office with Tam and Mago.

She shook her head. "I've had him constantly watched. Everything he brought with him from Regor is still in the room he was assigned."

"I need access. Now. And so does Raine."

I agreed completely. "Go through his stuff and see if I get any seeking vibes that match the assassin?"

"It's a good place to start." Mychael turned to Imala. "As paladin of the Conclave Guardians, I'm formally requesting full access to the goblin embassy."

Imala's lips were thoughtfully pursed, but her eyes were gleaming. "Don't you need a warrant signed by the archmagus?"

"I do, but time is critical and lives are at stake, so I'm not going to do it."

Imala raised her hands. "Just a little test, Mychael. I could never do business with a man who wouldn't dispense with the law in favor of expediency." She smiled fully. "As acting ambassador, the goblin embassy is open to you."

In most embassies, the reception areas were on the main floor, offices on the second, and any floors above that were living quarters for the embassy staff and any guests.

We made our way upstairs, and as we went, the lights brightened seemingly by themselves. Spooky.

An elderly goblin was standing at the top of the stairs, looking down at Tam with a fond smile. His long hair was completely white against his dark robes.

"Tamnais, my boy. I'd heard you were here."

"Dakarai." Tam grinned and took the rest of the stairs two at a time and shook hands.

"We'll have none of that," the old goblin said, and gave Tam a hug that made it obvious that he wasn't as brittle as he looked. Then he stepped back, his hands on Tam's upper arms, and looked at him. "It's been too many years. You're looking well." He laughed. "I can't tell you how glad I am to see you alive."

"Every time I wake up, I'm glad for the same reason. It's good to see you, too, Dakarai."

The old goblin's eyes sparkled. "The court isn't the same without you."

"I'm sure it isn't."

"You are sincerely missed by many."

"And everyone else wants my head . . . or heart, or viscera."

Dakarai dismissively waved a palsied hand. "Jealousy."

"The deadly kind."

"The court is an ever-changing creature, and times are changing again. You should keep your options open, my boy."

"I always keep my options and escape routes open," Tam assured him. He turned to us. "Dakarai Enric, allow me to present Raine Benares and Mychael Eiliesor."

He shook Mychael's extended hand. "Paladin Eiliesor I've had the honor of meeting." He turned those sparkling eyes on me, and I was treated to a most proficient hand kiss. "Mistress Benares I've only had the pleasure of hearing about. You have many devoted admirers among our people."

"Devoted to taking my head or just staking my heart?"

Dakarai laughed again, a sincerely happy sound. "Neither, I assure you. You tricked Sarad into the Saghred, kept the Khrynsani chasing you in vain, and have enraged and frustrated our king to the point of incoherent screaming."

"It's nice to be appreciated."

"You are looking for our elusive assassin?" he asked Mychael.

"We are."

Imala spoke. "They thought that searching Chatar's room might yield some clues." She inclined her head down the hall. "His is the last door on the left."

That would be the one with the two really big goblins standing guard.

They greeted Imala with snappy salutes, opened the door for her, and stepped back.

"Where are the safes, false floors, and hollowed walls?" Mychael asked her.

Imala showed him.

I cleared my throat. "There's also the inside of cushions, fake bottoms in drawers and chairs, behind picture frames, the insides of boots, under the mattress, and the ever popular under the bed. Obvious—yet often overlooked—places for hiding something you don't want found."

Mychael gave an amused chuckle. "Do it."

I conjured a tiny lightglobe and got to work.

No fake bottoms in drawers, and the cushions in the chairs felt like they didn't have anything in them except stuffing. Crawling around under Chatar's bed was most definitely not my idea of a good time, but it turned out to be productive. Tucked inside the bed frame, resting on the slats, was a worn-looking wooden box. The floor under the bed was dusty, except in the area where the box was. Someone had been squirming around under here recently. It had been my experience that bad things came in bad boxes, and if this one were a snake, it'd be hissing at me right now. I could feel the malevolent magic oozing from the wood's grain. As long as I didn't touch it, I doubted it would bite.

Probably.

I wiggled out far enough so that my head was sticking out from under the bed.

"Found something?" Tam asked.

"Oh yeah, and I don't think it likes me."

"What is it?"

"A box. It's not big, but it's got an attitude."

"Spells?"

"Of the bite-off-my-face kind."

Mychael was instantly on his knees next to the bed.

"Forget it," I told him. "There's no way you'd fit under here."

"Shit."

"Yeah, I thought the same thing. And I think it's a goblin spell."

"Let me take a look." Imala Kalis dropped down on her belly next to Tam and started wiggling under the bed.

Tam grabbed Imala's ankles. Imala kicked Tam.

He didn't let go. "If Chatar wove that spell, you can't deactivate it."

"But I can tell you what it is, and you can tell me how to do it."

"You can't—"

A heavy sigh came from under the bed; and there was probably some eye rolling to go with it. "I've been studying since you left," Imala told him. "How do you think I've survived all the assassination attempts against *me*? Everyone who wants me dead has brought out the big guns. Believe me, I can identify damned near every nasty spell and ward there is. Let me go."

Tam gave a sigh of his own and shook his head, but he released Imala's ankles.

A few seconds of silence passed.

"Shit," Imala said.

A woman of few words.

"Well, that's three votes for shit," I said. "That means we've got a nasty one. And if it's nasty, it means Chatar is hiding something he doesn't want us to see, which means we need to see it."

"Imala, can you tell if it's only touch activated?" Mychael asked.

"Appears to be that way."

"Come out from under the bed," he told her. "You, too, Raine."

I wiggled out. "What are you—"

"I'm going to move the box to the side of the bed without touching it. Once it's within reach, based on what it's protected by, either I or Tam can deactivate the spell."

"What if it doesn't like being moved by magic?"

"I'm sure it'll let us know."

I was sure it would.

"Dakarai, sir," I said, brushing the under-the-bed dust off of myself. "You might want to step outside. Literally. Across the street might be far enough."

"Absolutely not. I wouldn't miss this for the world."

I almost said "your funeral," but if it was his funeral, it'd be ours first—if there was anything left after the blast, boom, or whatever.

I hated boxes.

Mychael slid the box to the side of the bed and within reach without any unsightly explosions, though I could still feel the thing hissing in my mind.

Mychael bent down to look at the box and I could have sworn the hissing got louder. "Tam, do you recognize what he used?"

Tam and Mychael were on the floor. Imala and I were standing a few feet away. Not that the boys would have a chance to get up and run if the box suddenly got mean, but we thought it was a good idea to be out of their way.

Tam put out his hands and they slowly began to glow red. He started murmuring a spell in Old Goblin that made the hair on the back of my neck stand on end and the skin between my shoulder blades want to crawl and hide.

Dark magic.

Tam wouldn't use it unless he had to. The box was warded with dark magic, so Tam had to use the same kind. Dark calls to dark.

When he'd completed his incantation, Tam calmly reached under the bed and pulled out the box. I could swear it was vibrating in his hands. Tam hissed a single word at it and it stopped. I no longer had any sense of a ward, spell, or plain old booby trap.

Tam opened the box and we all held our breath.

He saw what was inside and his hands gripped the box so hard I heard the wood creak.

Three narrow, elaborate bottles were nestled in thread-bare gold velvet. A red liquid half filled each bottle. There was an indentation for a fourth bottle, but it was missing.

Mychael's hand tightened on Tam's shoulder. "Is that poison?"

In response, Tam carefully pried one of the bottles loose from its velvet nest and removed the stopper. I'd expected him to take a sniff, not pour a drop onto the floor. It was vivid blue and didn't spread into the floor as you'd think a liquid should. Then in a blink of an eye, it became as clear as pure water. Somehow I didn't think the word pure applied to this stuff.

"Malanarda," Tam said quietly, his face set like stone.

"No," Dakarai said in disbelief, crossing the room to take a look for himself. "It can't be."

"Is that what was used on Chigaru?" I asked.

Imala stepped forward and ground the liquid into the floor with the toe of her boot. "If it were, we'd no longer have a prince to protect."

"Malanarda is legendary goblin poison," the old man told me. "Some claim it doesn't exist and never did. I've heard it called the perfect poison—tasteless, odorless, you didn't know anything was wrong until it started killing you, and once it did, there was nothing to be done. The formula was lost nearly two hundred years ago, so no more has been made."

"That loses none of its potency," Imala added.

Mychael's lips thinned into a grim line. "No formula, no antidote."

Dakarai nodded.

"Sounds like what killed Chatar," I noted. "Quick, dead, and done."

"You could be right," Imala said.

" 'Could be'?"

"Except Chatar wouldn't have poisoned his own strawberries, then eaten them."

The possible plot twists and turns to this setup were starting to hurt my head. "Then what's this malanarda stuff doing here?"

"It appears the occupant of this room may not have been the real Chatar."

The goblin master glamourer.

I blinked. "Can't goblins do *anything* straightforward?"

One corner of Imala's lips turned upward. "Rarely."

Mychael spoke. "Imala, did either you or your people have Chatar in sight from the time you got out of the hotel until you got here?"

"That's precisely the point," she said. "I did not. I was more intent on the possibility of another firemage attack against the prince."

"Regardless," Tam told us all, "we have a casket of malanarda here with a missing vial. That we do know, and that is the danger."

Meticulously attached to the gold velvet interior of the box's lid were small portraits, six in all, all of them goblin. One was a woman. Tam reached in and reverently removed the tiny painting.

Horror choked my words. "The bastard keeps trophies."

Imala saw the painting. "Oh, Tam," she breathed.

I stared at Tam. "Who—"

"My wife." His eyes were haunted. "Calida."

The tiny portrait didn't show much more than her face, but Calida Nathrach had been beautiful. Her face was fine-boned and delicate, but her eyes, even in so small a painting, sparkled with humor—and with life.

"We knew Calida had been poisoned, though after her death, no sign of it could be found," Dakarai said. "Tam was accused by her family, but we all knew he was innocent."

"Chatar killed your wife?" I asked Tam.

"Chatar wasn't at court then," Dakarai told me.

Tam's hand that held the box was clenched almost white. "Sarad Nukpana was."

"Some of those portraits look older than Sarad Nukpana."

"But not older than his mother and grandfather," Dakarai said. "I recognize those pictures. The first two men died while Sarad Nukpana's mother and grandfather were both serving at court."

I was not believing this. "A *family* poison?"

"Sarad sent the assassin who tried to kill the prince, and who did murder Chatar," Imala said. "So it stands to reason that he armed him as well."

There were two small pieces of parchment carefully folded and inserted in the crease of the box next to where the missing bottle had been. I knelt down next to Tam and pulled them out. The first was a sketch, hastily drawn, but I could see who it was.

Chatar.

The second sketch had been done with more care. Someone had taken their time to make sure they got it right.

An eighth portrait. An eighth victim.

Me.

Chapter 16

An assassin had a poisoned dart or chocolate-covered strawberry with my name on it.

The Seat of Twelve had essentially signed my death warrant. Though I knew what Carnades had planned would be worse than death—turn me over to Taltek Balmorlan and his Saghred power-hungry sicko mages.

I couldn't stay in the embassy, and I couldn't set foot outside. At least not wearing my own skin.

Everyone was looking at me.

"Raine—" Tam said, giving me the look. He knew me well enough to know when my wheels were turning.

"Yeah, yeah, I know. Go to my room, lock the door, and hide under the bed."

"But Sarad wants you alive," Imala said. "Why would he—"

"Or dead and the Saghred in his hands," Mychael said, his tone grim. "A few of my Guardians have shown themselves to be less than trustworthy over the past few weeks."

Tam snorted and shut the box. "Nice way to say 'traitors.'"

Mychael grunted, but he didn't disagree.

I thought of Carnades, Balmorlan, and every elf who did their dirty work. "Traitors come in all shapes, sizes, and colors," I reminded them all.

"The Saghred is being guarded by only my most-trusted men," Mychael said. "I also have defensive spells on the room; if anyone sets foot in there, I'll know it."

"Which means you need to stay close to the rock," I told him. "When the thief makes his move, you have to be ready to jump on him."

Mychael gave me his version of the look. The one that said I was right, he knew I was right, and he didn't like it one bit.

I raised my hands in a mollifying gesture. "Hey, I'm just stating the facts. And those facts mean that I can't stay here, and I definitely can't go back to the citadel with you."

"Just where do you propose to go?"

"Hunting. Do what your boys haven't been able to do. Find Rache."

"So you're going to stay safe by finding one of the world's best assassins," Tam said. "The man whose black heart you broke."

"The man who probably knows the name of this goblin master glamourer."

"How does he know—"

"Because he told me last night," I said. "He knows he has competition to kill Chigaru; and when a big payday is at stake, Rache makes it a point to know all about anyone trying to take it away from him. Though if it'd make you all feel better, send a few of your people with me. Just have them stay back; I don't want Rache spooked."

"What makes you think you can find him?" Mychael asked. "He completely dropped out of sight at the elven embassy."

"Because that wasn't him. By the time we got there, Rache was already inside the elven embassy."

"I spotted Rache following me again last night," Mychael said.

I froze. "What time?"

He told me.

"That was about the same time Rache arrived at the Satyr's Grove," I told Mychael. "He's good, but he has yet to be two places at once."

"That doesn't change the fact that he's in all probability working for Taltek Balmorlan," Mychael said.

"Balmorlan's probably the man filling Rache's bank account," I said. "He wouldn't tell me who had hired him, but I can connect the dots. For Balmorlan's plans to work, he needs Chigaru dead. A peace-loving goblin doesn't do him a damned bit of good."

Imala cleared her throat. "Uh, Raine . . . if he's working for Balmorlan, then he's the last man you need to find."

"Rache doesn't 'work for' anyone," I told her. "He's only 'paid by.' No one can buy Rache's loyalty, if he even has any. And if Balmorlan had paid him to grab me, he would have tried in the Satyr's Grove. He didn't grab; he ran." I turned to Mychael. "The man who took a shot at you wasn't Rache Kai." I gave him the short version of our go-getter, glamouring assassin.

"He gets close to his marks by glamouring as anyone he wants," I said. "This time I won't be tracking someone who looks like Rache; I'll be tracking the real Rache."

Mychael looked at me in silence for a long moment. "Won't the traces of Rache on that crossbow bolt be too old to use?"

"They would," I agreed. "Which is why I'll be using this." I grinned and held up the glove. "A man who has to jump out of a cathouse window *always* forgets something."

No one liked what I was going to do, and that went double for me, but I didn't have any choice if I wanted to know that assas-

sin's name—and get a chance to talk Rache into taking his toys and going home.

Vegard would be going with me along with two other Guardians who I knew and Mychael trusted. No goblins. I didn't have a problem with any of Imala's people, but Imala's people had a bigger problem with Rache Kai than the Guardians did. He'd shot their prince once, and it was their job to keep Rache from shooting him again. The goblin secret service took great pride in doing a thorough job, and in this case that would mean thoroughly killing Rache Kai.

Though they needed to know the assassin's name as much as I did, and instead of asking Rache nicely, they'd opt for torture. The only thing I could see torture accomplishing with Rache would be pissing him off. Pissed did not equate with cooperative.

Mago said he had some things to take care of. I knew that meant finding another way to tighten the screws on Taltek Balmorlan, so I was all in favor of Mago's continued clandestine activities. My job was to neutralize two assassins. Mago's job was to neutralize two crooked elves. I wasn't sure whose job was the most impossible, or at least improbable, but mine would get me deader quicker.

Though right now, I had something almost as challenging as getting an assassin's name out of Rache Kai—getting the scowl off of Vegard's face. Though with the dandy beard he still sported from his turn as Marc the Waiter, Vegard's scowls had lost a lot of their impact. I had no intention of mentioning the beard. No doubt some of his Guardian brothers had done it, and Vegard had no doubt made them regret it.

"It couldn't be helped," I told him for what felt like the umpteenth time.

"I know it couldn't, ma'am, but that doesn't mean I have to like it."

"I know, I know. You were worried sick."

"And awake. I haven't slept in two bloody days."

"If you're going with me, you'll be awake for at least one more."

"As long as I get to do something besides look for you all over the city, I'll take it."

"The way my luck's been running, that's guaranteed."

"Will you be going out as that banker fellow?"

I chuckled and shook my head. "I think I've gotten the real Symon Wiggs in enough trouble. I have to find Rache, and I don't have time to screw up."

"Meaning?"

I grinned. "Have you ever met Rache Kai in person?"

"No, ma'am."

My grin got bigger. "You're about to. For an assassin, the best way to find your quarry is to think *exactly* like them. The same works for seeking. I know Rache."

"Reportedly very well."

"Yeah, that's something I like to forget; but for now, it's a good thing. Not only do I know him, but while glamoured as him, I'll be able to pick up nuances I wouldn't normally get, such as where the real Rache is. Like calls to like. Combine all of that with his glove—and my determination to find the bastard—how can I fail?"

What I didn't tell Vegard was what safer way to repel every lowlife on Mid than to glamour myself as one of the world's best assassins? Of course I'd have to hide my face most of the time. The last thing I needed was to get arrested for being someone else. I could get locked up just fine by being myself.

Vegard had come to the goblin embassy with Mychael wearing his Guardian uniform. He wouldn't be leaving that way. When Imala came to Mid, she had brought plenty of her agents with her. And with secret service agents came disguises. A table in my room was covered in just about anything Vegard might need to go from upstanding Guardian to a disreputable thug about town. I'd originally thought to go with the deadly look, but we didn't want to get ourselves arrested before we even got to do anything to deserve it. That would more than suck.

My Saghred-fueled glamours were correct in every way—including some of their thoughts. I just needed a solid image in my head to do one. Rache Kai had been my first lover. I literally knew every square inch of him.

Within moments, all of those square inches were looking back at me out of the mirror—and yes, it was a specially warded mirror. Guaranteed not to spew demons. I resisted the urge to smash it to bits anyway.

Vegard stepped up behind me. "So this is him."

"Yep."

I could see Vegard's reflection in the mirror. Tan leather, embroidered linen, and with a fur mantle thrown in for good measure. Just your typical Myloran raider looking for a good time. I shook my head and smiled. "You look good being bad."

He gave me a roguish smile. "That's what the ladies tell me, ma'am."

"Once I get clear of the embassy wards, I'll need to find a quiet place to zero in on Rache," I said. "When we have it, do you have a man to send to Mychael with our location?"

"He's standing by."

"Good. When a Benares is about to do something definitely stupid and possibly fatal, it's smart to let someone know where to collect your body."

Vegard just stared at me. "That's a joke, right?"

"Let's hope so."

Tam took us out through a tunnel that ran under the embassy, under the building behind it, opening out onto a small side street, conveniently empty. Vegard may not have been in a Guardian uniform, but he was packing his favorite Guardian weapon—his double-headed battle axe. It was in its sling over his shoulder, the leather-wrapped grip within easy reach over his left shoulder.

"This is as good a place as any for you to locate the bastard," Tam said.

"Bastard? I thought you said you never met Rache."

"I haven't. He hurt you, he's hunting Chigaru, therefore he's a bastard. The goblin language has much more accurate terms, but that one will do for now."

"Do you mean jak'aprit?" Vegard asked helpfully.

Tam inhaled with intense satisfaction. "The very word. Well done, Vegard."

The big Guardian grinned. "I believe in knowing how to insult a man in every language."

"A fine talent to have."

Tam went back into the embassy, though not of his own choice. I was still borderline exhausted, so maintaining Rache's glamour was enough of a challenge, but add a seeking to that and the least magical interference I got, the better. Tam knew how critical it was to get to my destination, get that name, then get the hell out. All quickly.

Vegard was standing farther back in the tunnel to ensure that his magic didn't interfere, either. I leaned against the wall at the tunnel entrance, pulled on Rache's glove, and put all of my focus on the leather encasing my hand. The leather was soft and supple with a snug fit for each finger, especially Rache's trigger finger. Sewn into the leather at the knuckles was a nice layer of metal. I made a fist and the metal pressed against my knuckles in a perfect fit. Oh yeah, I liked that.

I didn't force the contact, but rather let it come to me. Concentrating too hard would just make me even more tired than I already was. I was willing to sacrifice a few minutes for that.

The connection came in clear and strong. Rache wasn't that far away. He was standing at a bar with two glasses in front of him: one empty, one halfway there. That was more than a little concerning. Rache didn't drink while working. Sorrows to drown? Or his competition? In that case those drinks might be celebratory.

Only one way to find out. Go and ask the man.

•   •   •

Finding Rache was easy. It was like he wanted me to find him.

Sometimes easy wasn't good. I'd learned through experience to be wary of easy.

Now that Rache was less than a dozen feet away from me, keeping my hands from around his throat was going to be a challenge, if not damned near impossible.

He was sitting on a stool at the far end of the bar. There was a door at his back, probably a storage room. Rache wouldn't be sitting next to a doorway unless it led quickly to the outside and a dark alley. You'd think assassins would prefer to sit in a shadowy booth. Many might, but Rache had never been one of the many. If anyone was to walk through the front door of that bar with violent intentions, Rache liked to have plenty of room to play. He wasn't shy about making a scene—or a mess. A little bag of gold tossed on the bar went a long way toward mollifying any barkeep's annoyance at having to mop blood off the floor, or toss a body out his back door.

I pulled the brim of my hat a little lower over my eyes and stepped inside. There were six other men in the small bar. It was connected by an open double doorway to a tavern that wasn't rowdy yet, but sounded like it would be soon. Here in the little bar, one of the men was facedown on a table, muttering to himself. The smell and empty bottle in front of him testament that this wasn't his first stop of the evening, just the place where he happened to pass out. Three men were huddled over drinks in the aforementioned shadowy booth. Four empty bottles shared the space with them. They were armed, but with that much liquor in them, the worst trouble they'd cause would be falling over their own feet trying to stand up. And the fact that the bottles were still there said that customer service wasn't the barkeep's strong suit. He was human, thick-armed, with hard eyes. He gave me a terse nod, and I returned the gesture. The two others sitting at the other end of the bar were more interesting. They sat perched on the edges of their stools so that their swords hung loosely from their belts, no obstacles to making a quick and clean draw. Foam-topped tankards of ale sat in front of them. These boys didn't appear to be thirsty. Either that or they were disciplined. In a place like this, both could mean trouble waiting for the signal to happen. They turned their heads when I came in, sized me up, and turned back to their ales and quiet talk, sitting up a little straighter than before.

Great.

Just great.

I went to the bar and sat down two stools away from Rache.

"What'll it be?" The barkeep's voice was gravelly, and his sleeves were rolled up to expose scarred forearms. Knife fighter and good at it. His scars didn't tell me that—that he was still upright and breathing did. No one came away clean in a knife fight. Winners got scars; losers got dead.

"Whiskey, neat," I told the barkeep. It wasn't my voice; it was an exact copy of Rache's.

Rache's own drink paused halfway to his lips. He finished the movement, took a swallow, and set the glass back on the bar as one hand dropped to his side where he'd always kept a stiletto. It was small enough to hide, large enough to get the job done. I didn't know if he still carried it there, but I think I was about to find out.

He looked at me out of the corner of his eye, and I pushed back the brim of my hat just enough to give him a good look.

"We meet again," I said.

The corner of Rache's lips twitched in a grin. "Get tired of the banker?"

I shrugged. "He wasn't my type."

My voice carried, and the barkeep stopped wiping glasses, frozen in place, his eyebrows raised. All conversation in the bar had ceased, even the muttering drunk in the corner.

Rache chuckled. "You're ruining my reputation again."

"I'm not here to ruin anyone's reputation, just to finish the talk we started last night."

"That would be the talk that *you* started. I had other things I'd much rather have been doing. I don't want to talk about it here." He waved the barkeep over. "Tom, can I use your office?"

The man tossed him a ring of keys and Rache nimbly snatched them out of the air.

"I like it here just fine," I told him. "I like company."

Rache shrugged and tossed the keys back to the barkeep. The man caught them without even looking.

Rache half turned to face me. "All right. What do you want to know?"

"Your competition. I need his name."

"So you and Eiliesor can take him down."

"Something like that."

Rache snorted and raised his glass in a half salute. "I wish you luck."

"What's that supposed to mean?"

"Exactly what I said—good luck if you think you're going to catch that one flat-footed."

"I'm good."

"He's better."

"Tell me why, give me his name, and let me be the judge of that."

"And in return, I get . . ."

"We get rid of your competition for you."

"And as soon as I leave here, the men with you are going to try to get rid of me."

"What makes you think I didn't come alone?"

"Eiliesor and that goblin friend of yours, Nathrach."

I raised my own glass. "Well played."

Rache didn't move, but his eyes took in the men around us in various stages of consciousness. "If all of these fine gentlemen hadn't been here when I arrived, I'd think that one of them was the paladin." He lifted his glass and took a sip. "The two down the bar have been entertaining themselves for the past half hour watching me drink."

"Who are they?"

Rache shrugged. "The gut on the short one tells me they aren't Guardians. Could be watchers. Could be something else."

The last thing I needed was something else.

I knew I was wasting my breath, but I told him about Sathrik's plans after baby brother Chigaru was dearly departed—murder, invade, and enslave elves. Rache wasn't a patriot unless he was paid to be, but there was a first time for everything. Then for good measure, I told him what Taltek Balmorlan had planned.

For me.

When I finished, Rache didn't say anything, but just because he wasn't talking didn't mean he hadn't been listening. He'd heard every word I said, and now he was measuring what he'd been paid to do with what the son of a bitch who was lining his pockets would be paying mages to do to me.

I hoped the scales in Rache's head wouldn't call that deal even. Yes, I broke up with him. Yes, I'd hurt him. He'd hurt me, so I called that even.

"You want to take out a hit on Balmorlan?" Rache asked.

"I wouldn't shed any tears if he washed up at low tide tomorrow morning."

Rache laughed, low and soft. "You're asking me to do him for *free*?" He, like Mago, was a firm believer in the power of currency.

"I'm saying you might want to be more selective who you take money from."

Rache met that statement with silence. I'd just as much as said that Balmorlan had been the man who'd hired him. Rache knew that in addition to his competition's name, I wanted confirmation on Balmorlan being his latest client.

"Quite a few of my clients have deserved killing more than the target they were paying me for," Rache said quietly.

That was as close as I was going to get to a confirmation. I'd take it.

I set my drink on the bar. "You give me your word, your blood oath not to kill Chigaru Mal'Salin, and I'll do everything I can to make sure your competition takes the fall for you."

"And just how do you propose to do that?"

"I'm a Benares, Rache. We can set people up in our sleep."

"You can say that again. It's not like I'm going to forget what happened in Laerin anytime soon."

"*That* wasn't my fault and you know it." I leaned toward him. "Rache, we were no good for each other; you know that, too. I hurt your pride; you broke my heart. I'd call us even."

He arched an eyebrow in surprise. "I broke your heart?"

"I cried at least twice."

"Impressive."

"Believe it."

Rache ran his finger idly through the ring his glass had made on the bar. "My client was going to pay me a bonus if I took out the prince within four days."

"Let the prince live and you'll get your bonus," I said.

"From you?"

"An interested party."

"Interested in what?"

"You don't need to know."

"Let me decide that."

"Not a part of the deal."

Rache shrugged. "Very well. If you can find the bastard, all the better for me. He's a goblin by the name of Nisral Hesai."

"Never heard of him."

"You just don't run in the right circles."

"Meaning hired killers."

"He's young, not much experience, but by all accounts shows extreme promise."

"Apparently he's good enough that Sathrik has hired him to kill his baby brother."

"He's not an assassin," Rache said, "though he does it when the money's right. Nisral Hesai's a thief. The best. He's a decent enough assassin, but you don't need much skill when you can get close enough to touch your target. Anybody could kill like that."

I think I might have stopped breathing. "A thief?"

Rache nodded. "The bastard can change back and forth right before your eyes. And if he can study his target for a while, their own mother couldn't tell the difference. An exact copy even down to the voice and mannerisms. That trick alone makes him the best damned thief in the kingdoms. Better than some of your family even. They don't call him the Chameleon for nothing."

The goblin wasn't stalking Mychael to kill him. He was *memorizing* Mychael. Sarad Nukpana didn't send him only to kill Chigaru.

He was here to steal the Saghred.

And glamoured as Paladin Mychael Eiliesor, he could walk in to the citadel and take it.

Chapter 17

I had to warn Mychael.

I had to find that goblin before he became Mychael and stole the Saghred. Or before he killed me, and converted his pencil sketch into a memorial painting.

"From the look on your face, I'd say the Chameleon has his silvery fingers in more than one pie," Rache noted.

"And on a couple of poison strawberries," I muttered.

"Pardon?"

"Doesn't matter; I'm not going to be eating either one." I looked him in the eye. "I know this probably goes against your professional ethics, but you wouldn't consider lending a hand to find this Chameleon, would you?"

"Old time's sake and all that?"

I shrugged. "If that's what you'd do it for. I was going to give you money, but if you want to—"

Rache's grin reached his eyes. "What old times?"

"How does goblin gold to catch a goblin work for you?"

"If the gold's goblin, it works just fine."

"It would be," I said.

"Then I would be interested. I take it the prince will be paying?"

"Not if you try to kill him again."

"I suppose you want assurances of some sort."

"A plain old promise would work for me."

I actually got to see surprise on Rache's face.

"You'd take my word?" he asked.

"I don't know if I'd take it, but I'd certainly consider it. Do you know where the Chameleon is?"

"Don't have a clue."

"Do you think you could get one? Turn that energy of yours from killing a prince to hunting a lizard?"

Rache laughed. "I don't think he'd like being called that."

I didn't laugh. "He can bite me."

"After what you did yesterday, I don't think he'd want to try."

I didn't move. "What do you know about yesterday?" I didn't think Rache was involved in setting up Balmorlan's demonstration of death and destruction, but if he had been, I wanted to know about it. Rache had taken Balmorlan's money to assassinate Chigaru. Yesterday most definitely qualified as an assassination attempt. Killing hundreds of people to take out one prince was heavy-handed, but . . .

"I know what I heard," Rache said.

"You weren't there?"

"I know what you did, if that's what you mean."

"Who did you hear it from?"

"People."

"Was one of those people named Taltek Balmorlan?"

"No."

"When was the last time you talked to him?"

"The day you and your paladin chased me into the elven embassy."

"He didn't pay you extra to run herd on some firemages?"

"Present company excluded, since when do I associate with magic types?"

"Since pretty much never," I had to admit.

"Exactly."

"Does that mean you weren't involved?"

"That's exactly what it means," Rache said. "I'm an assassin; it's what I do. But I do my work quick and clean. What happened at that hotel yesterday wasn't either one. I take pride in a job well done, but I don't get off on it. They did. As far as I'm concerned, what you gave them was everything they deserved."

I looked at him in something approaching shock. "Thank you. I think."

Rache shrugged. "A man draws his line somewhere. Even me."

"Did your people tell you that Taltek Balmorlan arranged it all for some cartel out-of-towners as a demonstration of what the Saghred could do?"

Rache said nothing for a few heartbeats. "He set you up."

I nodded. "He knew I wouldn't let all those people die. And now there's a convenient price on my head. The elven ambassador has already laid claim to me if I'm brought in."

"The ambassador isn't in charge over there."

"I know. Balmorlan is. He sells me to the highest bidder, arranges a demonstration of the goods, and then gets me arrested. You assassinating Chigaru Mal'Salin is simply another part of the same plan. You still want to line your pockets with his gold?"

Rache's answer was drowned out by raised voices in the tavern common room.

I recognized the loudest one.

Phaelan. A very drunk Phaelan.

I did not need this now. What the hell had happened to Uncle Ryn sitting on him?

My cousin was in the middle of a gaggle of highbred young elves spoiling for a fight, or as they were calling it, a duel. Apparently Phaelan had offended one of them, and for my cousin, being offensive came as naturally as breathing.

Dammit, Phaelan. Not now.

One particularly offended young lord had thrown a glove with a fancy embroidered gauntlet at my cousin's feet.

Phaelan looked down. "You dropped something," he slurred.

"I dropped nothing; that was a challenge. My seconds will contact your seconds for terms."

"Terms for what?"

"A duel at dawn tomorrow—to the death."

Phaelan staggered to his feet. "No, no. There's not going to be any of that 'duel at dawn' crap. See, I sleep late, so why would I want to get up early to kill you when I could sleep in tomorrow and kill you right now? If you want your seconds to watch, I can wait a few minutes. Now or five minutes—your choice."

"Now." The elf lord's lips twisted in a sneer. "And right here."

"Fine with me." Phaelan tossed the gauntlet back to the dandy. "Come on. Let's get you over with."

Then things got ugly. Really ugly.

There are three things that a pirate crew won't let their captain do alone. Plunder, pillage, and brawl are all pirate-sanctioned group activities.

The door shut behind me.

"Good luck, love." Rache and his voice receded down the hall.

He was running out on me. Again.

Bastard.

Or jak'aprit, as Vegard had so astutely called him.

The fancy elves outnumbered Phaelan and his crew, but most pure-blooded elves learned to fight in a salon. My cousin and his men learned on decks and in streets.

The three men huddled at the table weren't huddling anymore. They'd also sobered up entirely too fast.

I definitely didn't need this.

Being glamoured as Rache was about to come in handy. My fists weren't made for brawling, but Rache's were. Better yet, Tam and Imala had seen to it that I was armed like an assassin.

No one had drawn steel yet, and I wasn't going to be first. Unless it spilled out onto the streets, the city watch would ignore a brawl with fists. If you drew steel, your little party immediately got upgraded to a riot. At that point, watchers would draw their steel—both blades and handcuffs. I was understandably nervous around the latter. Both Rache Kai and Raine Benares had their pictures posted around town with tempting amounts listed below. I wasn't going to give the local law any excuse, but at the same time, you don't abandon family in a fight.

You pulled your hat down lower to hide who you were and waded in.

I didn't like glamouring, and I certainly didn't like being a man, but I really liked having a man's fists. I pulled one elf off of Phaelan and landed an incredibly satisfying right hook to his temple. His baby blue eyes rolled up into his highborn head and he dropped like a rock.

One thing a good fight did for Phaelan—it sobered him up real quick. As I tossed an elf over a trestle table, I wondered if Phaelan's grin was sparked by imagining the elves he was beating the crap out of having the face of a certain highborn elf mage or inquisitor. I visualized Carnades's face on the next elf I punched and felt myself grin. Oh yeah, that worked for me, too.

I expected Vegard and company to charge through the door any minute. Actually I was kind of hoping for it. I was sure the shouts could be heard outside, especially after another chair crashed through the front window.

The fight kept getting larger as men either chose sides or just wanted an excuse to hit someone. I barely ducked in time to avoid being crowned with a tankard. A man who was neither elf nor pirate aimed a bottle at Phaelan's head. I grabbed my cousin by the collar and snatched him back; the bottle flew by where he'd been an instant before.

I grinned. "Great fight, cous—"

Phaelan's look was pure murder. *"You!"*

What the hell?

"You son of a bitch!" Phaelan roared. "You've hurt Raine for the last time!"

Oh shit.

"Phaelan, wait. I'm not—"

My cousin's fist embedded itself in my gut. I've never been on the receiving end of one of Phaelan's punches. They hurt. I heard Rache's voice grunt, and then I doubled over headed for the floor. The floor could be good; maybe there was air down there.

When I hit the floor, the knuckles that were bleeding belonged to me, not Rache.

I'd lost my glamour.

And I was wearing a goblin secret service uniform.

Oh crap.

I really should have changed back into my clothes before I left the goblin embassy.

Phaelan's eyes nearly bugged out of his head. "Raine?"

Uniformed city watchmen came out of nowhere to break up the fight. I couldn't get enough air to warn Phaelan about the watcher about to knock him over the head.

With the pommel of an elven embassy dagger.

My last thought before I got knocked over the head myself was that Taltek Balmorlan had been buying himself more than firemages.

I hurt.

My head felt like someone was inside taking a perverse pleasure in trying to pound their way out with a hammer.

I groaned and tried to move.

And heard chains clink.

My eyes blinked open on a room with a pair of light-globes set in the wall on either side of a doorway. It was barred and then some with wards crisscrossing just beyond the bars like a fine net.

I was in a cell.

My wrists were chained above my head to the wall, the weight bearing down on my arms heavier than any metal. A heavy chain that was wrapped around my waist was likewise bolted to the wall. Cold panic surged through me. The pounding in my head just got faster and I got sicker. My eyes flicked down to my ankles. Chained. Power lay dormant in the metal, just waiting for me to use my magic—or to try. Magic-sapping manacles. That power would stay dormant unless I tried to use my magic to escape.

Or to protect myself.

I was in the elven embassy. Oh hell, and then some.

Did Phaelan get away? I winced. Even thinking made my head pound harder. I dimly remembered somebody tossing me, none too gently, over his shoulder. That and the cudgel love tap would definitely account for my splitting skull.

"Would 'I'm sorry' even begin to cover it?" came Phaelan's entirely too loud voice from the shadows. He had to be whispering, but it didn't sound that way to me.

My cousin was trussed up like a holiday goose against the opposite wall. Not chained to the wall, but still chained fore and aft.

"The elven embassy?" I asked, desperately wanting to be told I was delirious from being konked over the head.

"Afraid so. Sucks, doesn't it?"

"You don't know how much."

Phaelan shifted and winced in pain. "Everyone's favorite inquisitor dropped by to check on us about ten minutes ago, and I—"

I froze. "How long have we been here?"

Phaelan managed a clanking shrug. "Half an hour, no more. The city bells were chiming one when we were brought in."

"You were conscious?"

"Not the whole time, and not that they knew." He

grinned. "A knock over the head doesn't put me out like it used to. Guess my skull's gotten thick."

Considering that what he'd done had resulted in us being where we were now, I agreed with him. I vaguely remembered being carried out into the dark. The air stank, too. The stink of too many things you didn't want to know about concentrated into too small of a space. An alley. They must have taken us out the back door of that tavern. Being a neat and tidy megalomaniac, Balmorlan ordered that Phaelan be brought to the elven embassy along with me—no witnesses, no rescue.

Vegard might not have seen me carried out of there, but he had to know where I was now—and if he knew, Mychael knew.

Mychael. I had to warn him about the Chameleon.

Cancel that. I had to warn him when I got out of here. The pessimist living in my head chimed in with "if you get out of here." I slammed the door on that part of my head. Though my resident pessimist wouldn't say what I hadn't already thought. The embassy was elven soil, and even though Mychael was an elf, he couldn't get in here unless invited. I didn't think Mychael would wait for an engraved invitation. If Tam or Imala tried to blast their way in, it'd be an act of war. I didn't see that stopping them, either.

"We have to get out of here," I told Phaelan. Nothing like stating the obvious.

"I know, I'm working on—"

"I hoped you would be awake by now, Raine. I was beginning to get impatient." A cool voice came from beyond the wards. It was the voice of an elven inquisitor who had me right where he'd wanted me since the day I'd set foot on Mid.

"It wasn't like I was taking a nap," I said.

"It was unfortunate, but my men took a necessary precaution."

I rattled my chains. "Like these?"

"Precisely." Balmorlan turned his head toward the guard

standing behind him. "Lower the wards and leave them down for now; others will be joining me."

The guard wasn't just a guard; he was a prison mage. He could not only guard, but construct complex wards. It took nearly two minutes for him to disarm the lethal netting that crisscrossed in front of the cell door's bars.

Balmorlan came inside. "I didn't go to the trouble and expense of acquiring you only to have you leave us before I get what I want. The cell is lined with Level Twelve wards, detainment spells layered for strength, and magic-depleting manacles—and you—bolted to the wall. I must say, you are a beautiful sight."

Sick bastard.

Balmorlan's smile was lascivious. "The goblin uniform suits you."

Really sick bastard.

I'd thought that being helpless in Taltek Balmorlan's dungeon would be the most terrifying thing that'd ever happened to me.

Being chained to a wall with magic-sapping manacles, forced to wait while elf mages were somewhere nearby working up the courage to bond with me in one of the most intimate ways possible made the short list of my personal nightmares, but that was all.

I probably should have been scared. Scared would be smart.

I'm sure that on some level I was, but Taltek Balmorlan had schemed, threatened, bribed, tortured, burned, and murdered his way to his goal—to have the Saghred's power at his command. And while I was chained here, the Chameleon would be morphing into Mychael, waltzing into the citadel and out with the Saghred, and there wasn't a damned thing I could do to stop it. The Saghred would be in goblin hands, Mychael would probably be executed for treason, Justinius would be politically ruined, and Carnades would quickly move to take charge. Then there was the subsequent war, death, and destruction.

I was the only one who knew about the Chameleon. The one act of stealing the Saghred would start an avalanche of events that would essentially carry the world to hell in a handbasket.

One of those greedy power-grabbers chaining me up was just the last straw.

I was furious. I didn't know what qualified as more pissed than furious, but that was what I was; I was positively shaking with it. I wanted to tear Balmorlan apart with my bare hands—no magic involved, just me.

"Afraid, Raine?"

"If that's what you want to think, go right ahead."

The manacles only kept me from using magic. There were no chains on my wits. I had to calm myself down enough to use them. If they couldn't come up with anything, we were all screwed.

Balmorlan winked at me. "After waiting so long for this moment, it's a shame that I can't take the time to truly savor it."

"No time to share the extent of your evil master plan?"

The inquisitor showed me his teeth. "Something like that. Though I can tell you about your first assignment."

"Assignment implies I'd get a choice."

"Very well, my mages' first assignment. Since you were so impressive in preventing my firemages from dispatching Prince Chigaru, we'll have to use my backup plan. A simple implosion of the goblin embassy should ensure that our building isn't damaged."

Oh no.

"The beauty of the plan is that only one woman could pull off such a feat. You'll provide the power and my mages will direct it. Just think, you'll be a hero to the elven people." Balmorlan's eyes glittered. "And as the goblins die, they will know that you betrayed and killed them."

There had to be a way out that didn't involve me using magic. I needed a way out using what wits weren't now screaming and running in panicked circles inside my head.

I'd been chained with magic-sapping manacles before. Tam and his dark mage school buddies had put in an appearance just in time. I wasn't counting on "just in time" now. It looked like this one was up to me, though if someone wanted to charge in here, kick some bad guy elf ass, and cut me loose, I'd kiss whoever or whatever it was right on the lips.

Getting out of these manacles was my only chance. Problem was my hands were stretched over my head and I couldn't feel my arms anymore, aside from a painful tingle.

"If the goblins don't already know that you've been taken, they will soon," Balmorlan said. "Time is of the essence." A twisted eagerness flickered in his eyes. "I would tell you not to worry, that my mages bonding with you and the Saghred won't hurt, but I have no idea how it will feel. I'm sure you'll let me know."

A chill ran through me. "You want me. Okay, you've got me. You don't need Phaelan anymore; let him go."

"Oh, but I do need him. For bonding with my mages, the Saghred deserves the reward of a good meal."

I froze in horror.

"Though a common criminal is many steps removed from the magic user the stone would prefer," Balmorlan noted. "Beggars can't be choosers, can they?"

Chapter 18

"Has the Saghred ever spit anyone out?" Phaelan asked. "Because I think feeding me to a rock that eats mages would just piss it off. From what I've seen, that's not something you want to do."

Balmorlan smiled a nasty smile. "We won't know until we try. Even a gourmand would eat moldy bread if he were starving."

I knew Phaelan would like to shove moldy bread down the inquisitor's throat, but he had to know that we were in a bad situation with an even worse outcome, so he didn't let his violent urges show on his face. The consummate card player, my cousin. I didn't know what my face looked like, but I was going for neutral.

"I heard that all was ready for me."

My skin did a quick crawl, not at the sound of the voice from just outside the cell, but at what it probably belonged to. One of Balmorlan's elf mage imports.

Calm, Raine. Keep it calm. Yeah, you're scared, but scared won't get you out of here, and these two would love

to see you shaking in your boots. Don't give them the satisfaction. Keep your wits and find a way to keep your sanity.

The mage walked into the cell, though a more accurate
description would be that he swept in. Pure-blooded high
elf—cut from the same silky cloth as Carnades. Tall, blond,
green eyed, with cheekbones that looked like they'd been
carved out with a chisel. Unlike Carnades who'd never
stopped looking down his aristocratic nose at me, it was
just my luck that this mage took one look at me and obviously liked what he saw.

I tried to steady my breathing and went for aloof bore-
dom. "So, you want to go first."

The elf mage didn't answer; he just looked me up and
down and took his sweet time doing it. He was trying to get
a reaction, preferably a terrified and cowering one. I'd met
the type before. This guy liked it when women were afraid
of him, but he could only do that to me if I let him. I met
his green eyes and let the corner of my mouth curve into
a smile. Time to see if I could rattle his cage. "Been told
what's going to happen to you?"

I was betting goldilocks wasn't all that eager to die—or
worse.

I sensed his arrogance bump up a notch. Someone was
feeling defensive. Not all that eager to find out what Death
had waiting for him on the other side.

Balmorlan gave me a cold smile. "Nice try, Raine. The
Saghred bonded her with the goblin chancellor Tamnais Nathrach and our esteemed paladin," he told the mage. "They
are both quite well and in full control of their faculties."

"Meaning they haven't gone nuts," I added. "Yet."

Balmorlan ignored me. "The Saghred wants to be used.
It will not harm you."

I just smiled at the mage and shrugged as much as I was
able with my arms stretched over my head. "Your funeral.
The Saghred likes certain people and doesn't like others. I
don't know why and unfortunately none of the 'others' are
around for you to ask. Obliteration does that."

"You will be silent," Balmorlan hissed. "Or I will make it so you can't speak."

In the past, whenever I was up to my pointy ears in trouble and couldn't punch either with a fist or a spell, I'd go with words. Most times it'd gotten me in more trouble than I was already in. Yeah, it was stupid, but I couldn't seem to help myself. I'd always justified stupid by telling myself that I might die, but I'd go down insulting. Dying quietly was just wrong.

"Someone's edgy," I noted. "You won't do it because you've waited too long to hear me scream."

The cool inquisitor was back. "For all the trouble you've caused me, I am due some small compensation."

I eyed the mage. "Has he paid you yet—all of it?"

"The balance of your fee is in my office down the hall," Balmorlan calmly assured the elf. "Keep your end of the bargain and I'll keep mine."

The simple truth was I was stalling. I didn't want that elf mage to touch me. The Saghred had taken me in the street outside the hotel. I didn't know if a mage taking me in a dungeon would tighten the stone's grip on me even further. I remembered Rudra Muralin's journal only too well. Once he'd taken a sacrificed soul through himself to feed the Saghred, membership in the evil madman club hadn't been far behind. Phaelan was first in the chow line. Somehow I had to stop this.

The elf mage reached out and ran one long finger down my chest, but he stopped just short of making contact, smiling at me the whole time.

I held my breath.

The Saghred did nothing, absolutely nothing.

Interesting. I didn't know if it was a good or bad interesting, but I was all for the rock staying unimpressed, and I didn't care why. If the Saghred didn't deem him worthwhile, there would be no effort, no bond, no meal, no imploding goblin embassy. And my sanity and I would get to be roommates for a little longer.

I did some smiling of my own. "When someone asks for volunteers, it's usually because no one else in their right mind would want to do it."

"I know the risks," the mage murmured. "The reward will be worth it." He reached out, barely brushing the skin at the hollow of my throat, continuing downward until the tips of his fingers were between my breasts. His green eyes glittered. "I like the leather."

That did it. If I got out of here alive with my mind intact, I was going to have a long talk with Imala about designing some new uniforms for her agents. This getup was a pervert magnet waiting to happen.

What didn't happen was the Saghred. The mage had touched me and the Saghred hadn't touched him back.

"And why am I waiting for the others?" the mage asked Balmorlan.

The inquisitor laughed. "You never have been one for sharing, have you?"

"And I won't start now."

I saw something out of the corner of my eye that gave hope a boost.

Phaelan winked at me.

It was quick, subtle, and I almost missed it. I kept my eyes on the two elves. I'd seen Phaelan; they didn't need to.

My cousin had a true knack for ruining a person's day. It didn't matter who or what they were, Phaelan was an equal opportunity offender. I had no idea what he had planned. I did know from past experience that it had to be borderline suicidal.

Sometimes crazy was good.

Chained to the wall without an option to my name, I just wanted crazy to work.

Shouts and the sound of running came from the hall, room, or whatever was outside the cell door. A guard stopped just outside, careful not to touch even where the wards had been. The man was wild-eyed and out of breath.

"Sir, the mages. They're . . ." He stopped and tried to pull in some air.

"Late," Balmorlan snapped. "Tell them I don't tolerate—"

"They're dead."

"What?"

"Murdered, sir. Every one of them stabbed through the heart."

"That's impossib—"

"The major said it was a thin blade, probably a stiletto."

Quick and clean.

Rache.

When he'd left the bar, he must have come straight here. I bit my bottom lip against a smile. Rache figured I could handle a barroom brawl; he went where his skill set would be the most useful.

For the first time in years, I wanted to kiss my ex.

"How long ago?" Balmorlan asked.

"The healer says within the past hour, no more."

"You've locked down the embassy?"

"Of course, sir." The guard pulled a folded piece of parchment out of a pocket in his uniform. "The killer left this next to one of the bodies." He started to step into the cell then stopped, looking uncertainly where the wards had crisscrossed the opening.

Balmorlan walked to the door and snatched the paper from the guard's hand. "Oh, give me that, you cowa—" He started reading and stopped talking.

Rache had once written some poetry for me, but somehow I doubted he'd left a love sonnet with a freshly dead body that he'd just made that way.

The elf stepped away from me. "What does it say?"

Balmorlan's face reddened in fury. "The deal's off, but I'm keeping the gold."

Definitely Rache.

The mage took the note. "Release the seeker or you're next," he read.

How sweet was that?

Rache didn't make idle threats. At the same time, I'd heard of him making a threat then taking his time making good on it. One poor bastard spent years jumping at his own shadow until the one day when that shadow was Rache. His threat would at least make Balmorlan think twice about my part in his evil master plan.

It was all I could do not to laugh, but the last thing Balmorlan needed to know was that I not only knew who killed his mages, wrote the note, and kept his gold, but I'd almost married him. Rache Kai was a killer, but there was decency in there somewhere, even if it was a little twisted.

The elf mage suddenly closed the distance between us and gripped the leather just above my breasts in his fists. Leather ties laced the front; they might break or they might not. He bent his head toward me, his face mere inches from mine.

The elf smirked. "My competition's gone; let's see what I've won."

I'd just won a way to ruin Balmorlan's night.

I didn't want the bastard touching me, but I wasn't passing up an opportunity to touch him.

I slammed my forehead down hard on the bridge of his aristocratic nose and was rewarded with a clean break. Clean for me; bloody for the bastard. The mage screamed and staggered backward, the hands that were about to tear me out of my clothes now clutching his broken, bloody nose.

That'd put a damper on his libido.

I froze. Oh, hell. No, no, no.

Blood.

Blood on the hands that'd just been on me.

I sucked in my breath at what I'd just done. Stupid, Raine, stupid. The Saghred needed a victim's blood to fall on it and then actual contact to complete the sacrifice. If the mage touched me again, the rock would take him, sucking his soul through me—a still-living, breathing, and screaming-my-lungs-out me.

My body was meant to contain one soul. Mine. No travelers passing through, just me.

The mage pulled his hands away from his nose and looked at them. Blood covered his fingers.

"You bitch!" he screamed.

An instant later, he backhanded me with his bloody hand, and I tasted my own blood in my mouth. My blood, his blood, and . . .

The Saghred throbbed to life, quivering in anticipation, eager, crouching . . .

The mage brought his hand back for another strike.

"No!" Balmorlan barked. "Conscious. We need her conscious."

The mage hissed and turned on him. Balmorlan didn't flinch.

"Once you've bonded with her, and proven to me that you can use the Saghred alone, the need for her will diminish considerably." Balmorlan stood perfectly still and watched me, his eyes glittering with anticipation. "At that point, I wouldn't be opposed to you exacting appropriate revenge."

The mage slowly wiped the blood from his face with the back of his hand, never taking his eyes from mine. I locked eyes with him; I had to.

Phaelan was moving.

To glance at Phaelan would be to draw attention to him, and that couldn't happen. The mage could get his revenge without ever laying a hand on me—he could kill Phaelan right here and now.

A chill went through me that had nothing to do with what the mage wanted to do to me. It was for what the Saghred wanted to do to him. I didn't care if the mage died, but I didn't want him dying *through* me.

The rock was crouched like the predator it was, ready to

take, to consume. The mage thought he was the predator. He was wrong. Dead wrong.

I knew there was air in the room; I just couldn't get any of it. "Touch me and you're a dead man."

The mage laughed. "I'll be doing more than touching you—"

Idiot. "You're bleeding!" I screamed. "The rock—"

His blood-streaked fingers grabbed my throat, pinning me against the wall. Behind him, Balmorlan's eyes widened in realization and panic.

He knew. He knew the one mage he had left was going to die and all of his plans along with him.

Balmorlan was too slow.

I couldn't stop the mage from choking me or the Saghred from taking him.

I couldn't breathe; I could only pant as a single tendril of white light sliced through the center of my chest, snapping around the elf's wrist like a steel vine, anchoring him where he stood. It engulfed the hand that clenched my throat as I whimpered and gasped for air. More tendrils uncoiled in my chest like a nest of snakes, writhing inside of me, desperate to get out. A scream tore its way from my throat as the Saghred did the same to my body, the tendrils ripping their way out of me, lashing at the mage. I screamed and he screamed, raw and agonized, until there was no air left and black flowers bloomed on the edge of my vision. I was blind to everything but the darkness coming for me and the blazing tendrils that shot up the mage's arm to his shoulder, coiling and constricting, racing hungrily to consume his body. A high-pitched strangled shriek came from inside the column of white flame that was the elf mage.

The Saghred fed and I screamed.

The stone was a living thing inside of me, its weight crushing me, filling my screaming mouth and nose with the sharp, coppery taste of blood. More blood than one body could hold, the blood of hundreds, thousands of screaming victims.

To the Saghred, the mage was just one more.

And I felt it all.

His body dissolving, his soul torn from disintegrating flesh, all that he was or had ever been was pulled inside of me. The mage's soul struggled, writhed in terror and helpless panic.

It didn't know yet. It didn't know it was worse than dead.

My scream became one of the thousands as I fell into darkness.

Chapter 19

I came to and heard groaning. I think it was me.

Strong arms wrapped around my waist, lifting me up. That definitely wasn't me.

I was hanging by my wrists, my shoulders on fire, and the contents of my stomach threatening to leave.

"I've got you," a familiar voice assured me. He made it sound like a good thing.

The voice was familiar, but my head was throbbing so hard it couldn't find a name to go with it.

Hands on my wrists . . . the rattling of chains . . . where was . . .

"We're getting out of here, cousin."

Cousin? Cousin . . . cousin . . . *Phaelan.*

I tried to fight my way out of a cold fog that didn't want to let me go, a fog with soft tendrils, faintly glowing, comforting, caressing, promising safety . . . forever. I sank into a woven blanket of them. I was so tired . . . sleep . . . just for a little while.

"Raine!" the voice shouted from far away. "Stay with me!"

Sharp metal bit into raw skin. My raw skin. Tendrils gently touched my wrists, soothing the pain, a dark power seeping into me, carrying away the pain and fear and replacing it with an eager hunger. I felt a body next to me, a warm body with blood surging through its veins; a living body containing a vibrant soul. The tendrils that held me wanted that soul.

I wanted that soul, and I would have it.

A low growl of need rose in my throat in anticipation of wrapping my arms, my tendrils around that soul, to feel it struggle in vain against my power, as hunter to prey, the body encasing it helpless to stop me from taking what was mine. It was my right; it was how it should be. How it would be again.

"Raine!" A hand slapped me sharply across the face.

I snarled, striking out. With a shout of shock and pain, the body's arm released me. I dropped in the chains, agony searing through my muscles. The arms lifted me again, shaking me. I gasped, waking, trying to pull myself up through the fog. The tendrils pulled me back. I got my eyes opened, and a pair of dark eyes stared into my own. Frightened eyes. Familiar eyes. I blinked a few times to focus.

Phaelan.

The weight pulling me down was manacles on my wrists and me hanging from them. I was in a cell.

"Where?" I rasped, my voice hoarse from something. What had I been . . .

"Dungeon," Phaelan said, his hands working quickly over my head, the scratching of metal on metal.

Picklocks.

I dragged my eyes to a man sprawled on the stone floor. Memory slowly surfaced. Taltek Balmorlan, the elven embassy, the elven mage.

The Saghred. The tendrils trapped him and the stone

took him. Through me. His soul went inside of me, was inside of me now. I tasted the metallic tang of my own blood in my mouth, the coppery . . .

Blood. A sacrifice.

I gasped, choking on my own breath. "No!" I tried to get away from Phaelan, to get away from myself, but he just held me tighter.

"What the—"

I panicked, thrashing and struggling. "Get away!"

"It's all right, I'm—"

"Don't touch me!"

Phaelan's grip tightened. "The rock doesn't want a damned thing to do with me. I'm not bleeding, and you heard him"—he jerked his head toward Balmorlan lying motionless on the floor—"I'm moldy bread. And since I'm not a magic user, I can pick the locks on these things."

He was right. The Saghred didn't want him. It had wanted *me* to do it, to make me take him.

I barely got my head turned away from Phaelan before I threw up.

He held me through all of it, making comforting sounds against my hair until my gags turned to sobs.

"Raine, easy, shhh. I know, I know. I need you to be still for me." Phaelan worked faster at the manacles' locks. There was a sharp click, and my right arm dropped to my side. The only feeling I had was a cold, sharp tingle, stabbing like tiny needles on every square inch of my arm.

I tried to swallow, but just ended up panting. "No, you don't know—"

Phaelan quickly looked away from me, concentrating on the other manacle, but I'd seen his eyes, haunted by what he'd seen. He was scared to death. Nothing scared Phaelan. What happened had. I had. And he'd had a front row seat for all of it.

Then he looked me squarely in the eyes. "I'll tell you what I know; I know you'd never hurt me."

Fear and the other thing I'd felt—what the Saghred had

made me feel—twisted in confusion inside of me. "I'm glad *you* know it."

Phaelan took a handkerchief from his doublet and gently wiped my mouth and chin. "You don't have to." One corner of his mouth curled into a crooked smile, Phaelan's smile. "I know it enough for both of us."

"Thank you." My voice was so quiet I barely heard it myself. My throat was as raw as my wrists. I didn't think I could scream anymore, but that didn't mean one stray thought about what I'd done to that mage and nearly done to Phaelan wouldn't make me start again.

I swallowed, forcing down a rising scream with it. "Guards?"

Phaelan shook his head. "I didn't see or hear any. They're probably hunting for Rache. A couple of them saw what you did . . . what happened, and ran like their asses were on fire. Unlikely they're coming back."

"We need to hurry," I managed.

"Goes without saying." He gave the picklock a sharp twist and the manacle clicked open. My other arm dropped. My body tried to do the same thing, but Phaelan was faster than gravity.

"Gotcha."

I rested my forehead on his shoulder. I'd survived. The Saghred had fed and I was still alive. The rock had taken a man, an actual living man, reduced his body to vapor and inhaled his soul, right in front of me.

Through me.

I was still here, and so was Phaelan.

I chuckled, though it came off more like a running start toward hysteria. My sense of humor must have been marginally intact. Good. Hopefully my sanity had not only come along for the ride, but was going to stick around. If the Saghred had one or two more meals through me, I had no doubt I'd qualify for a padded room. I wasn't going to think about that, either.

Phaelan unlocked the chains around my waist and eased

me down to the floor, a floor that had never felt so good. I breathed slowly, in and out, trying to convince my stomach not to mutiny again. Taltek Balmorlan lay in a motionless heap. Phaelan wasn't bleeding, but Balmorlan was, across the back of the head. My cousin was making quick work of my ankle manacles, but he glanced up and saw where I was looking.

"The rock doing its thing with that mage made for one hell of a distraction," he said. "Let me pick my way out of those manacles and make good use of the chain—right across the back of the bastard's head."

"He's dead?"

Phaelan went back to work. "Don't know, care less."

A split second later, he had me out of my ankle chains.

"Got a blade on you?" Phaelan asked.

"Check my boots."

He did and I didn't. He looked at Balmorlan and growled in frustration.

"What?" I asked.

"I'm not leaving him alive."

As much as I wanted Taltek Balmorlan no longer breathing my air, killing him would just get rid of him; it wouldn't get rid of his allies, his spies, and his lackeys. If Balmorlan was found dead, they'd just regroup and continue as planned. It would delay them, but it wouldn't stop them. Leaving Balmorlan alive—and able to talk—would give us the best chance to end his war-monger operation once and for all.

I told Phaelan what I was thinking.

Phaelan's expression said loud and clear that he didn't like what I was thinking. However, his vicious and frustrated kick to Balmorlan's ribs said he agreed with me. Under extreme protest.

"Get his keys," I said. "I want in his office."

Phaelan's eyes lit with soon-to-be-fulfilled avarice. "That's my girl. The mage payroll—enough to pay six." He nodded in approval. "We'll make a card-carrying Benares out of you yet." He flipped the inquisitor over like a sack of grain. "Rest for a minute," he told me then proceeded to do a very professional job of plundering the body.

I wasn't interested in gold. If that was Balmorlan's only office in the embassy, he probably kept things there that were even more valuable than gold—documents, financial records, anything that would make being in this hellhole and force-fed an elf mage worth my while.

When Phaelan finished his ransacking, he had a full purse, a gag, which meant Balmorlan might have made good on his threat, and a ring of keys.

But no weapons.

"Can you scoot over?" Phaelan asked with a vicious grin. "He made those magic-sapping bracelets, now he's gonna wear 'em."

I got myself against the far wall as Phaelan dragged Balmorlan's body across the stone floor to where I'd been chained to the wall. Limp arms or not, I wasn't about to take a chance on the rock eating Balmorlan.

"Those manacles were custom made for me," I told Phaelan. "They won't fit him."

Phaelan's eyes had an evil gleam. "One way to find out." He cuffed a manacle around one of Balmorlan's wrists, and barely got the thing to lock. "Look at that, it fits."

I smiled. "Someone's going to be uncomfortable when he wakes up."

Phaelan grinned. "Ain't it a shame?" He got the other manacle on, then had to put his own ankle manacles on Balmorlan; mine wouldn't go around his boots.

While Phaelan was making sure Balmorlan wasn't going anywhere, I was making sure that I could. I braced my feet on the floor, leaned my back against the wall, and pushed myself up with my legs. It went slowly, but it went.

"Can you walk?" Phaelan asked.

I did some careful breathing, forcing the nausea down and keeping myself up. "Try and stop me."

"I won't, but you can bet someone—"

"Else will," I finished. "I know. I'll bite the bastards on the kneecaps if I have to."

"Hasn't been a jail built yet that can hold a Benares once we've decided to leave." Phaelan went to the open and wardless cell door and checked both ways. "We're still clear, let's—" He looked back at me and his eyes widened. "Um . . . your eyes are glowing."

The bottom dropped out of my stomach and I suddenly felt sick with fear. Just because the rock was digesting didn't mean it wasn't paying attention.

"Trust me," Phaelan said. "There's nothing wrong with my eyes."

"Then let's put me to good use." I looked back at Balmorlan. When Phaelan wanted someone unconscious, he didn't fool around. Chained in his own custom-made iron with the practical addition of a gag. "I must say you're a beautiful sight," I muttered.

Once in the corridor, Phaelan walked like a man with a purpose—and a man who knew where he was going.

"Uh . . . been here before?" I asked.

"Just on paper. When Balmorlan started threatening you, I figured blueprints for this place might come in handy. Tanik sold me a set. Included the layout, and everything we need to avoid to get out of here. Guaranteed."

Tanik Ozal was a smuggler. Though the goods he dealt in didn't end up in a dusty warehouse or back alley trading room. Tanik's source of his considerable income was the choicest merchandise for the wealthiest clients. I didn't trust him as far as I could toss him, but he'd helped me and Phaelan in the past.

"He gave me the family rate," Phaelan was saying. "Only charged me half a fortune."

"What a sweetheart."

Fortunately, it didn't take a genius to find Taltek Balmorlan's office. It was the only locked door that wasn't a cell.

I let Phaelan work the keys in the lock while I kept

watch. Problem was there was nothing to watch. Don't get me wrong, I loved the possibility of having five full minutes without the need to fight for my life; I just didn't believe it. Lady Luck wasn't speaking to me, and Fate had apparently decided to write me off. But neither of those changed the fact that no one was down here, at least not right now. The guards had seen what the Saghred had done to that mage. To them it'd looked like I'd done it, and every last one of them had run like hell and hadn't come back. Maybe they'd gone for reinforcements, and a freaking platoon was going to come running around the corner any second now.

Now that would be more the way my luck was running.

"Can you work faster?" I whispered.

Phaelan never took his eyes from the lock and keys. "Would if I could," he said in a singsong voice. He tried one key after the other. "You know, this'll be a nice haul for getting knocked over the head and chained up. The mages are all dead, so their money is all ours."

My plan for that pile of dirty money was to give it to Imala and Tam for Chigaru, that is if we got out of here with our lives—and after I got my strength back and wrestled Phaelan for it.

There was a click.

"Yes!" Phaelan hissed in celebration.

It wasn't a large office, just enough room for a desk, two chairs, and a cabinet. Taltek Balmorlan was a tidy megalomaniac. Retentive, actually. Writing quills arranged in a wooden rack in order of size. Inkwells were capped with no dribbles down the sides of the bottles, and there were no papers out anywhere. That was just wrong. Though if everything was in its proper place, then the proper place for what both Phaelan and I were looking for would be a safe. Now we just had to find the damned thing.

There was nothing hanging on the walls and no rug on the floor for a safe to hide behind or under.

"Walls are stone," Phaelan noted.

"So's the floor. See any seams?"

"Nothing. You?"

"Nada."

We looked at each other. "Ransack," we said together.

We went to work. Phaelan was a pirate and I was a seeker, so both of us had extensive experience making short work searching a room without getting caught. I opened a shallow cabinet, put my hands against the wood panel on the back and pushed it back and forth, testing for some give in the wood. And give it did. It slid to the right, exposing a not-so-solid part of the wall. A safe that wasn't very safe. Bad for Balmorlan and best for us, it opened with yet another key on the ring. It only took Phaelan two tries to get it open.

Inside was a strongbox and papers—lots of papers.

"Get the box out of my way," I said. My arms were functional enough for paper, but not a box of gold, even if it was probably the lightweight goblin variety.

Phaelan reached over my shoulder. "With pleasure."

I'd also had experience doing a fast scan of paperwork, but the thing we needed to do faster than that was to leave. I didn't want to risk leaving anything behind that might put Taltek Balmorlan away for the rest of his life.

I started snatching the papers out of the safe. "See anything to put these in?"

Phaelan was incredulous. "You're taking them all?"

I just looked at him. "You're taking all the gold?"

"Good point. Stupid question." He looked under the desk and held up a leather satchel, a nice one. "This do the trick?"

"Yeah."

Phaelan tossed it; I caught it and started stuffing. A ledger slipped out of my hand and fell on my foot. I bent over to get it, and nausea reared its ugly head.

"Damn," I muttered, slowly lifting my head up and forcing the contents of my stomach down.

"Easy," Phaelan cautioned.

"Later." I got the ledger and stood up. It'd fallen open.

To Carnades Silvanus's signature.

I felt dizzy again and it had nothing to do with the Saghred and everything to do with taking down everyone who'd supported the bastards who wanted me and everyone I loved imprisoned or dead. I scanned the document, flipped the page, and did the same, again and again.

They were pledges, signed pledges of support, monetary and otherwise. I recognized enough of the names to know that Taltek Balmorlan had secured as allies some of the most powerful men and women in the elven government, military, and aristocracy.

Signed, sealed, and witnessed.

At least half of them had been witnessed by Carnades Silvanus.

I held all of it in my hands.

If I'd had the strength, I'd have jumped for joy. For now, I'd settle for not throwing up again.

"I can see risking your life for money, but you're taking a book for booty." Phaelan shook his head as he emptied the last of the gold in what had to have been his last pocket. "Where did we go wrong with you?"

"It's not a book. It's a leather-bound payback."

No one was going to stop me from getting out of here and getting these papers into the hands of the right people, people who knew how to use them to inflict maximum damage on Balmorlan and his generous new friends.

I fastened the satchel's buckle, slung its long strap over my shoulder and across my chest, and peered out into the hall. Still empty. "We need weapons."

Phaelan stepped around me and out into the hall. I followed. "Blueprints say there's a guard station at the next right turn."

We heard it before we saw it, but not before it'd seen us. It was waiting, between us and a guard station we weren't going to live long enough to reach.

It scuttled out in front of us, stopping less than ten feet away, massive eyestalks locked on us. I knew now why there were no guards down here. They could just turn this thing loose and know that the prisoners would either stay put or get eaten.

Phaelan recovered his voice before I did, though it was higher than normal. "What the fuck is that?"

It was a crab, an enormous crab. Pinchers the size of my head and a shell that came way past my knees. Unblinking black eyes glittered on the ends of eyestalks as thick as my forearms. Black eyes that were fixed on us.

Phaelan froze. "This wasn't on the blueprints. Tanik, you bastard, I want my money back!"

Chapter 20

Where were a claw cracker and hot butter when you needed them?

I'd eaten crab. I loved crab. Now I faced the very real and immediate irony of a crab eating me—or at least pinching off my leg. I thought crab legs were delicious. I wondered in a moment of giddy panic if giant crabs felt the same way about people legs.

Years ago, I'd run into a werehound in a goblin prison. I was there as an unwanted visitor helping a valued guest leave. There was an explosion two cell blocks over, and the guards had run to put out the resulting fire. The explosion had been my doing; releasing a werehound to patrol in their absence had been the guards'.

I'd been expecting a werehound. One drugged treat and two minutes later, it'd been dozing like a puppy.

Right now, I didn't think we had minutes, and I had no idea what the hell a giant crab ate. Though from the way its claws were clicking and clacking, I think it knew exactly what it wanted.

I'd be willing to bet those pincers weren't its only

weapon. Its shell had a dull metallic sheen, more like armor than anything else, and the shell's edges looked razor sharp and were actually dripping with strands of green slime. Poisonous? Probably. I couldn't imagine green slime being a good thing.

"Do crabs have ears?" Phaelan whispered.

"How the hell am I supposed to know?"

The eyestalks swiveled toward us. Apparently were-crabs did.

Yeah, I know, but at least werecrab sounded remotely dangerous, because being snipped into big-sized chunks by a mere crab, even a giant one, would be beyond embarrassing. I didn't know if the thing was something else between sunup and sundown, and right now it didn't matter.

Werecrab, it was.

Run away was my impulse, but it wasn't an option, at least not with a hungry crustacean standing between us and what Phaelan's blueprints said was freedom. One of us could distract the thing while the other darted around it. Problem was the crab's shell with its dripping slime almost extended from one side of the corridor to the other. There was no room to get around it, and the only way we could distract it would result in one of us losing an arm or leg. I wasn't eager to try either one, but the crab didn't look inclined to go back where it came from, and as to us going back to where we came—

"Is there a way out behind us?" I asked.

"Would I still be here if there was?" Phaelan was bouncing on the balls of his feet, ready to move in any direction, including up. "What are you waiting for? Do your thing."

"My *thing*?"

Phaelan wiggled his fingers in the air. "Magic. You can move things. Move that."

"Don't know if I can."

"What do you mean you don't—"

"Magic doesn't always work on magic."

"It ain't magic; it's a crab."

"If it's a construct, anything I do won't dest—"

"What the hell's a—"

"It means it doesn't really exist. Looks real, feels real, but ain't real." My voice was edging toward panic, and the rest of me wasn't far behind.

"Well, that *construct* wants to take a bite out of my leg. That real enough for you?"

My borderline anxiety attack wasn't just because my only way out of this hellhole was blocked by a werecrab. My magic could tell me if the werecrab was real or not. The real problem was that I couldn't tell.

My heart pounded absurdly loud in my ears.

My magic wasn't working.

Nothing, not even a spark. I never believed that blood could actually run cold, but mine did.

The few times that I'd actually used the Saghred, I'd been winded afterward, sometimes knocked on my ass, but I'd never lost my magic. Could it have been the manacles? Were there aftereffects from being locked in them after a certain length of time? Or could the Saghred have been pissed off at not getting Phaelan's soul and decided to suck out my magic instead? I didn't know, had no way of knowing, and it didn't matter.

A werecrab was here and my magic was not.

And we *were* getting out of here.

Did I need magic to ruin Taltek Balmorlan and Carnades Silvanus? No. The only thing I needed was the documents I had. Documents that I would get out of here in one piece and us along with them. The only thing Phaelan valued more than his skin was the goblin gold stuffed in every pocket he had. I wasn't about to tell him that gold wasn't his to spend. If avarice and the urge to spend Balmorlan's hard-stolen gold was enough motivation to take down a giant crab, I'd let him think every last coin was his to have, to hold, and to spend.

I actually heard Phaelan swallow next to me. "So do your seeker thing and—"

"It isn't working."

"What?"

"My magic isn't working." I said it without moving my lips. Hell, I wasn't about to move a muscle. I stayed frozen to the spot. If I moved, the werecrab would move, and if the werecrab moved, chances were that I'd go from frozen elf to tasty treat in two clicks of a claw.

Realization dawned on my cousin at the same time that all the blood seemed to run out of his face. "You're just running low on juice, right?"

Phaelan didn't want to hear that this was more than a momentary inconvenience. He didn't like magic, but he'd never objected to me using it to save his ass.

"*No* juice," I said.

"Shit."

The crab hadn't attacked us yet. That was good, but it could also be bad. The thing could have been trained to keep escaping prisoners right where they were until the guards could get there. I didn't know if this was what was keeping the crab at pincer's length, but I wasn't going to ask too many questions.

I risked moving my head and looked around for something, anything we could use as a weapon. The dungeon was lit by lightglobes, not torches, so there was no handy fire on a stick. Nothing on the wall or on the floor . . . wait a minute. A metal tray with the remains of a meal sat outside of a cell door. It was a pathetic excuse for a weapon, but if you didn't have what you needed, you made do with what you had.

I carefully backed up and bent down for the tray without taking my eyes off the snapping claws. I had no idea why the thing hadn't rushed us by now, but I wasn't going to look a gift werecrab in the mandibles.

The tray wasn't heavy, which was good for a seeker with numb arms. The metal caught the light and I damned near blinded myself. Crap it. What kind of dungeon had fancy, shiny metal . . .

Shiny?

That could work . . . only one way to find out. I carefully stepped forward. I didn't have to be close, just close enough.

Phaelan caught a glimpse of light reflecting off the tray, and a slow grin spread over his face. "Can you make the thing back up past the armory door?"

"That's the plan."

"We arm ourselves and then have some crab shish kebob."

I could be in the mood for crab.

I caught the reflection of a lightglobe just behind the werecrab, and carefully angled the tray toward its eyestalks. I got a reflection, bright and blinding.

On the freaking wall.

At that moment, the werecrab got tired of waiting.

The crab scuttled at me faster than something that should be served with melted butter had a right to. I squealed before I could stop myself, thrust the tray out in front of me, and scurried backward, Phaelan right there with me. The only thing between us and being pinched and picked to death was a flimsy, shiny tray.

The werecrab stopped, eyestalks flinching backward in what would have been surprise or fear on something that didn't have eight legs. Then it backed up, virtually tripping over those spindly legs trying to get away from that tray. What the hell was it—

Its reflection.

It was probably the thing's first look at itself, and it clearly didn't like what it saw. We weren't the only ones scared of that crab—it was afraid of itself.

"That's it, you ugly beastie," Phaelan murmured from beside me. "Back up."

The werecrab did.

"Nice and slow," Phaelan told me. "Too fast and he might fight back."

I shot Phaelan the mother of all shut-up looks.

"Sorry, that was obvious, wasn't it?"

"Yes."

We continued walking forward and the werecrab continued cooperating. For now. Scary things had a tendency to be less scary if they didn't immediately try to bite your face off. A werecrab probably had a tiny brain, but I didn't want to find out how long it'd take him to figure out what he saw in that tray wasn't a scary thing and that he was running from himself—or worse, decided to kill his reflection.

"Just a little farther," Phaelan murmured.

I risked a quick glance beyond the werecrab and saw blades, blessed blades hanging on the wall of a room with the miracle of an unlocked and open door. If Lady Luck wasn't speaking to me, maybe she at least wanted to leave Phaelan alive long enough for a chat.

The werecrab backed up past the door, and Phaelan darted inside. After a few seconds of clanging and commotion, my cousin came out of that room with enough steel to start his own war. He slipped a long dagger through my belt at the small of my back, and I swear my heart rate dropped by half at the weight of some good, sharp steel.

Phaelan didn't waste time making use of what he'd pilfered. He clutched a huge elven broadsword in both hands and lunged.

The crab's claw shot out and snapped it in half.

The blade clattered loudly to the floor. Tempered steel cut like paper with scissors.

That was bad.

Phaelan dropped what was left of the sword, drew a pair of short swords, and rethought his strategy.

The long dagger Phaelan had given me wasn't long enough for me to risk my arm by getting inside that thing's snipping-in-half distance.

Phaelan and I immediately went with a tactic that had served us well in the past—distract and destroy. I made use of the tray for the distraction part, but unless I got my magic back—or my hands on a really long spear—the destruction was up to Phaelan.

I didn't think crustaceans had tactics. I was wrong. The crab had two pincers and poisonous shell edges, and was doing its best to pin one or both of us against the wall so it could use any of the above. The werecrab maneuvered with amazing agility, darting in to attack with its pincers, and quickly scuttling back when Phaelan lunged with his short swords. He didn't want to try his luck stabbing anywhere on that armored shell. He needed to get a blade in its belly, without getting his hands snipped off.

The damn thing's eyes could swivel on those stalks, and nothing we did caught it off guard.

Wait a minute.

Eyes. On stalks.

Saghred-induced exhaustion must have made me dimwitted.

"The eyestalks," I told Phaelan.

"Yeah, the damn thing sees me just fine," Phaelan growled.

"Cut them off!"

The crab could still kill us if it couldn't see us, but blinding it would at least give one of us a chance to get the heel of a boot under its shell and flip it on its back. Then Phaelan could drive a blade into its vitals. Of course severing its eyestalks and flipping it onto its back meant going in between its pincers. Distract with the tray, take out the eyestalks with the blade, then kick and flip. Sounded simple. It also sounded like something we'd better get right the first time.

I feinted to the right with the tray, and the werecrab slammed a claw dead into the center of the tray, just like a boxer's punch. At the same time, Phaelan lunged for the eyestalks.

And the crab's other claw neatly clipped the short sword in half.

The blade clattered to the floor to join the other. I used the tray like a combo of a shield and club, beating the claw back and hitting any other part of it that I could. Phaelan was still moving, and a split second later had sliced through both eyestalks using his other blade with a yell that sounded more like a terrified girly scream. I caught the bottom edge of the crab's shell with the toe of my boot and kicked with everything I had left.

The crab was a lot lighter than it looked and flipped right over. Only now its legs and pinchers were flailing madly over its vulnerable underside. Phaelan did some evasive darting and weaving, and when he saw an opening, drove his sword in up to the hilt. The legs slowed their flailing, and the pincers faltered in mid pinch mere inches from his face. Phaelan jumped back, pulling his blade back with him. It was coated with something icky that bubbled and sizzled on the steel. He dropped the sword before the bubbling reached his hand.

The werecrab twitched twice then was still. I wasn't about to turn my back on it, dead or not.

I stared at the tray. It was almost bent in half and in the center was a jagged hole where the claw's edge had punched through the metal.

I slumped against the wall, breathing hard. Apparently pounding a werecrab with a tray took it out of a girl. "Gimme a minute," I panted.

Phaelan ran into the armory and replenished his weapons, and got a sword for me. "We don't have a minute."

"How 'bout a second?"

"How about I carry you?"

I made myself stand up. "How about you just find the way out of here."

Phaelan looked down the hall beyond the dead crab. He wasn't seeing the hall; he was remembering what was on Tanik's blueprint. At least I hoped he was remembering.

"Follow me," he said.

For once, I was happy to do what he said, no questions asked.

Turned out I should have asked questions.

"How much farther?" I asked after we'd gone up one floor and through another ten minutes.

I was more than a little uneasy. Not that I wanted to find out that the werecrab had backup, or all of the guards were waiting for us in the dark just ahead, but a dungeon without any guards—while nice—wasn't right, and I didn't trust our good fortune or believe it for a second.

"Uh . . . I'm not exactly sure," Phaelan admitted.

I blinked. "What do you mean you're not sure? Where are we?"

"I'm not sure of that, either."

Phaelan looked slightly embarrassed. It wasn't a look I'd seen on him often, and considering what it implied, I didn't want to see it on him now.

I gaped at him. "We're lost?"

"I didn't say that."

"You didn't have to. You don't know where we are. That's called lost."

"The blueprints didn't include this floor. Besides, I prefer to think of it as temporarily misplaced."

I took a breath and let it out slowly. I told myself we were fine and we were going to stay that way. At the moment no one was trying to kill us or clip us in half. So it was all good. It still didn't alter the fact that we were lost with an exit hopefully still somewhere ahead of us. It also didn't change the spooky silence behind us—silence I didn't trust.

The silence didn't stay silent for long.

At the pounding of heavy boots on the stone floor, Phaelan and I ran like hell for the first open doorway we could find. Thankfully, the room was not only empty, but dark.

A trio of embassy guards ran past us. I adjusted my grip on my sword, held my breath, tried to think invisible thoughts, and hoped Phaelan was doing the same. While I didn't want to go in the same direction as a bunch of elven guards, they appeared to be going up to the embassy's main floor. Coincidentally, up for them happened to be out for us. We trailed them at a safe distance.

The embassy's entry hall was packed. Mostly with embassy employees, but I gave a silent cheer when I caught a glimpse of burnished steel Guardian battle armor just inside the massive embassy doors. I wasn't close enough to see who they were, but the fact that they were here was enough.

No one had seen me and Phaelan, and for now, we wanted to keep it that way. We ducked behind one of the absurdly big columns around the edge of the room. We were far enough away from the crowd of curious onlookers not to be found, but close enough to hear what was going on.

A man was speaking. Loudly. He wanted everyone to hear every word he had to say. I knew that voice. I only heard the last part of what he was saying, but those words made my day, week, and life.

"Ambassador Giles Keril, in the name of Her Majesty, Queen Lisara Ambrosiel, I relieve you of your post and place you under arrest for aiding and abetting the kidnapping and torture of elven subjects, obstructing justice, and treason against the elven government."

I grinned like I hadn't grinned in weeks. It wasn't just that Giles Keril, patsy to Taltek Balmorlan, was about to be locked up in his own embassy. It was the beautiful sound of a voice from beyond the grave.

Duke Markus Sevelien picked himself one hell of a time to return from the dead.

Chapter 21

Duke Markus Sevelien was the chief of elven intelligence. For the past few weeks, Markus had been officially—though not actually—dead. Taltek Balmorlan had arranged for his boss to have the kind of housewarming present that really warmed the house—by blowing it up then burning down what was left. As a result, Markus had found it advantageous to let Balmorlan and his allies inside the agency continue to believe that he'd died in that explosion. He thought he could better clean his agency of rats if they thought he was dead and came crawling out of the woodwork to take over the house.

As always, Markus's timing was impeccable.

Markus wore his usual black, looking unusually elegant for a man who had been considered by most to be dearly departed until mere minutes ago. Though to ex-ambassador Giles Keril, the elven duke probably looked like Death himself with a newfound sense of style.

As the chief of elven intelligence, even one newly back from the dead, Markus had the right to take over the embassy and everyone in it. And with a grim-faced Vegard and at least four dozen Guardians armed to the teeth and beyond at his back, he was not only exercising his rights, but daring anyone to say or try to do anything about it. No one looked inclined to do either.

Vegard looked like he really wanted someone to try.

Giles Keril's mouth hung open in shock. "Your Grace," he managed. "I protest these charges."

Markus gave him a chilly smile. "You deny that Raine and Phaelan Benares are at this moment imprisoned in the dungeons of this embassy with the intent of torture and death?"

The little man drew himself up to what little height he had. "I not only deny the charges, I demand to know the identity of my accusers. It is my right."

If that wasn't an entry line, I didn't know what was. I looked at Phaelan. "Are my eyes still glowing?"

"Not as much as they were, but you still look scary as hell."

"Bet you say that to all the girls."

I walked and the guards parted. I even heard a sword drop. I gave them what I hoped was an evil glare. I hoped it wasn't what I felt like, the grimace of a woman who was about to throw up on her own boots. Throwing up on myself wouldn't exactly be intimidating. Phaelan stayed right by my side, his swagger telling every guard or embassy official we passed that "We're wanted fugitives and you can't do a damned thing about it." I glanced at Phaelan, half expecting to see him sticking his tongue out.

Once the last of the gawking embassy bystanders parted and there was nothing between me and Giles Keril but a gratifyingly small section of empty floor, I got the satisfaction of seeing a man literally shake in his boots. I didn't know if it was the shock of just seeing me upright and breathing, or the terror of seeing me upright, breathing, and with glowing eyes. It didn't matter; I enjoyed it anyway.

"Good to see you, Raine." Markus's smooth greeting

would have been right at home at an embassy cocktail party. He graciously inclined his head to Phaelan. "Captain Benares."

"Good to be alive to be seen." I stopped when I got close enough to Giles Keril to make him start to hyperventilate. I didn't think Markus wanted him to faint quite yet. "Where's Mychael?"

"The citadel, ma'am," Vegard said. "We have a situation there."

I felt a little sicker than I already was. "The Saghred?"

"The rock's still where it's supposed to be, but we have a thief in the house. The boss is trying to find him before he makes a try for it."

"That thief's a master glamourer."

"He knows."

I blinked. "How did—"

Vegard cleared his throat awkwardly. "He got a message from . . . uh, a mutual acquaintance of yours."

Rache Kai.

First he killed Balmorlan's mages, and then he warned Mychael about the goblin thief. If he thought that meant we owed him, he had another thing . . .

I stopped and smiled. Yeah, we did owe him. I was sure Rache had a reason for doing what he did, and there was even a remote possibility that reason didn't have anything to do with Rache. He could have merely been thinking about someone else besides himself for a change. Yeah, and he probably had some mountain property to sell me in the Daith Swamp. I chuckled, and instantly three pairs of eyes were on me. Worried eyes.

I held up my hands. "I just thought of something funny; I haven't gone over the edge."

Markus stepped in close and kept his face neutral. Vegard was right behind him. "You don't look well," Markus murmured without moving his lips.

"Flirt," I told him.

"Raine."

Nothing like a joke you didn't feel like making falling flat. "I . . . ate a mage."

Markus didn't so much as bat an eye. "I see."

A master of understatement, my erstwhile employer. Truth was, if I let myself so much as think about what did happen and what nearly had happened, I'd want a cozy padded room all my own that I could curl up in the corner of.

"You might say I have a bit of indigestion right now that I'm trying really hard not to dwell on."

"Understood."

I was also trying really hard not to look at Vegard. I knew I'd see every flavor of pain and guilt in my big Guardian's big blues. If I saw that, I just might lose what little grip I had. I think he knew.

"Ma'am," he said, his voice tight. "This wouldn't have happened if I—"

I raised my hand to stop him from finishing. If he finished, my grip on sanity might be the same. "Nothing you could have done. Shit happens."

"Not to you and not on my watch," Vegard growled. He paused uncomfortably. "Are you . . ."

Vegard wanted to know, but didn't want to ask. Was I still in my right mind? Considering everything that'd happened since the Saghred had latched on to me like a soul-sucking leach, sanity was relative.

"Don't worry," I told him. "I'm still sane, whatever that means. And if I don't think about the alternative, I won't go skipping down that path."

"In that case, you didn't hear me ask."

I gave him a curt nod. Denial has always worked great for me. It'd never made a problem go away, but I was in denial about that, too.

"You saved me the exertion of looking for you," Markus said. "Though I confess I was rather looking forward to releasing these gentlemen to find you by any means possible."

The men behind him didn't look gentle in the least. They looked a bit disappointed, too.

"They can go collect Taltek Balmorlan, if they'd like," I said. "That way their trip won't be a complete waste."

Markus's dark eyes gleamed. "And where is my wayward and also soon-to-be-ex employee?"

Phaelan spoke up. "Special-built cell, Level Twelve wards, chained to the wall in magic-sapping manacles." He glanced at me. "Did I get it right, cousin?"

"Perfectly." I handed the satchel full of documents to Markus.

"What is—"

"Documents I found in Balmorlan's office," I told him. "Protect-with-your-life kind of documents. Promissory notes, deeds to property—I think I even saw a will—all signed by Taltek Balmorlan. He's collecting money and anything else of value to fund his own war against the goblins and anyone else who gets in his way. I couldn't take the time to go through the lot of them, but a couple of the documents I saw were witnessed by Carnades."

For the first time in my life, I heard Markus Sevelien whistle.

Giles Keril picked that moment to faint.

Phaelan stepped aside to avoid Keril's head hitting his boots. "Looks like he's impressed, too."

Markus raised his voice so that the entire embassy staff could hear. "Sir Vegard, I would like to formally request that your knights remain here to ensure a smooth and uneventful transition of power."

The big Guardian grinned. "We're here to serve, Your Grace."

"And if you would be so kind as to select a few of your men to escort—or carry, as the case may be—ex-Ambassador Keril to a maximum security cell and see to it that he and ex-Inquisitor Balmorlan are not allowed to communicate in any way."

Vegard inclined his head. "On behalf of the paladin and archmagus, the Conclave Guardians are honored to render any assistance we can to ensure the security of this island

and the protection of its *law-abiding* citizens." At the last part, he shot a dark look down at the sprawled Giles Keril.

"Nice," I murmured.

Vegard flashed a grin. "Sounded good to me, too."

Markus's sharp black eyes scanned the room like he was memorizing every guilty face, at least half of which were trying to be casual while noting the nearest exits. "Raine, my apologies, but I need to remain here. I've found through unfortunate experience that after a person of power is removed from their post, the underlings have an annoying habit of vanishing along with evidence that may connect them to crimes their superiors may have committed."

"There looked to be plenty of vacancies in the dungeon," Phaelan suggested brightly.

Markus smiled. "That was to be my next request to Sir Vegard."

The big Guardian's eyes fell like a slab of granite on the nearest pack of bureaucrats who suddenly found the floor beneath their boots simply fascinating. "I'd recommend starting with the senior embassy staff and working our way down until we run out of cells."

Markus nodded in approval. "Eminently practical."

Vegard smiled in a quick flash of teeth. "I think you'll be pleased with how many lackeys my men can fit in a cell."

"Just leave me enough people to operate the embassy."

"How many is that exactly?"

"More than myself."

"Done."

Vegard issued orders and the Guardians started herding bureaucrats in silly pseudo-military uniforms down the same stairs that Phaelan and I had sneaked up.

"There's still a price on my head?" I asked Markus.

"Oh, yes. But I don't believe any man who saw you right now would be foolish enough to attempt to collect."

I snorted. "The citadel's packed with fools."

"You're referring to Carnades?"

"The very one at the top of the Seat-of-Twelve heap."

"Then you'll want to know that when I left the citadel to come here, Carnades was being escorted to the archmagus's office for questioning."

"Questioning?"

Markus's dark eyes glittered and he lowered his voice. "A result of your *other* cousin's activities, I believe. Tell Mago that should he ever wish to change careers, I would gladly offer him a position in intelligence."

As a testament to Phaelan's determination to stick to me like glue, he did something even more terrifying than fight a werecrab.

He rode a sky dragon.

Speed was critical. Going by ground, even on the fastest horses, was out of the question. Less than five minutes versus half an hour or more equals no contest. I was on the second saddle behind Vegard, and Phaelan had a white-knuckled grip on the horn of his saddle behind a Guardian dragon pilot. My cousin sat rigidly upright, staring straight ahead, unblinking, unmoving, either from terror he was having now, or the fear of the terror he would have if he looked down. Phaelan had sailed into the teeth of the Straits of Mourning with half a crew and storm-ripped sails, but apparently taking him off the ground took away every bit of daredevil he had.

I didn't like being on a sky dragon, either, but I liked the thought of Sarad Nukpana getting his hands on the Saghred—and thereby his hands on me—even less. Unlike Phaelan, I felt better if I kept my eyes on the ground. That's where I wanted to be, and if I kept looking at it, maybe my stomach would believe we were actually going to make it there. The sun had not yet come up as we banked over the harbor on our approach to the citadel, and our dragons announced their landing intentions with deafening shrieks.

One of them sounded suspiciously like Phaelan.

I grinned, then started to laugh. I couldn't help it, and I—

Choked. Did a bug fly in my—

My throat constricted as if a giant hand were tightening around it, clutching, suffocating me. I panicked and tried to pull air in. Nothing. With the pressure came a presence I instantly recognized.

The Saghred.

I felt close enough to the rock to smell it. Corruption, vile and sickening, like sour bile at the back of my throat. Ancient, rotten, and malignant.

The Saghred was me. I was the rock.

And the thief had both of us.

I didn't see him; I didn't have to. The bastard's hand was wrapped around the rock, around me. He'd gotten past the guards and the wards, and had stolen the Saghred.

The rock wasn't doing a damned thing to stop him.

It wanted to be taken.

The edges of my vision were going dark. Holy hell, I was going to pass out flying over the city. I clutched the saddle horn in front of me with one hand and pounded desperately on Vegard's back with the other, grabbing at his shoulder.

Vegard turned, saw my face, and his eyes went wide. He shouted something I couldn't hear. The roar I heard wasn't the wind; it was my breath rasping, absurdly loud like I was trapped inside a box with no air, no light. I knew I wasn't locked inside a box, and not only did I have plenty of air, I was flying through it. My body didn't believe it, panicking, fighting to escape. My legs jerked with a mind of their own and did something very bad.

I kicked off the leg restraints, also known as the only things strapping me to a giant airborne lizard.

I fell off.

I clawed at the saddle as I slid from Kalinpar's back. My hands, still weak from the manacles, slipped off of the smooth leather edge, my other grasping for something, anything.

Vegard's big hand closed like a vise around my wrist.

"Shit!"

Vegard didn't mince words. I couldn't make them.

Vegard fought to keep Kalinpar steady, struggled to haul me back into the saddle or at the very least not drop me, while trying to keep from falling off himself. The morbid pessimist in the back of my head wondered if I fell, would I die instantly on impact, or would I get to feel myself break and/or splat into a million pieces; and if so, what would it feel like?

That made me scream, or at least try to.

"Give me your other hand!" Vegard bellowed.

My hand, arm, and the rest of me was dangling at talon level with Kalinpar. The dragon's talons were the length of my hand. Had Kalinpar been trained to pluck a falling person out of the air without a fatal puncture?

"Raine!" Vegard screamed.

His grip was slipping.

Vegard didn't have the leverage to pull me up, and I didn't have the strength. The thief was on the move, carrying the boxed Saghred in a pocket or pouch. His pace was smooth and unhurried. No, he wouldn't want to attract attention. I had a link with a rock that did nothing but destroy, and I couldn't so much as burn a hole in the bastard's pocket.

I wasn't the Saghred. I was me, and I was dangling above the city, and the only thing between me and a messy death was getting back on a flying lizard. Thick leather straps crisscrossed underneath Kalinpar's gray-scaled belly, strong enough to hold two saddles and two men.

Strong enough to hold a desperate-not-to-die elf.

A gust of wind caught my legs; Vegard's gloved fingers slipped again. I screamed, this time in rage, and sound actually made it out. I was not going to fall. I was not going to die. I was going to get on the ground, run down a thief, take that rock away from him, and club him over the head with it. Hard. Repeatedly. I hooked the edge of my fingers under Kalinpar's belly strap, then up to the second knuckle, then wrapped my fist around it with a white-knuckled death grip. Which was exactly what it was going to take to get me to let that leather strap go. Death himself would have to come and pry my fingers off one at a time.

"Hang on!" Vegard shouted.

I shot him a look and got a grin in return.

The grin widened. "You're about to get a lift."

What?

I looked down. There weren't any buildings or streets, just a big, broad, scaled back. Phaelan's pilot expertly guided his dragon up beneath where my legs dangled, staying just out of the way of Kalinpar's powerful wings. The sky dragon's back was as good as solid ground. Phaelan's hands steadied my legs just below the knees. Vegard got a firm grip on my arm, and between the two of them—and a pathetic amount of assistance from me—got me back in the saddle. I wasted no time strapping my legs back onto Kalinpar's sides where they belonged.

"Let's get you on the ground," Vegard shouted back at me.

I gasped for breath, and the rushing wind tried to take it away. "Thief . . . has the rock . . . not in citadel."

Vegard's eyes narrowed in fury. "Where?"

"Moving."

"Can you track him?"

I only felt like I was riding in his pocket. I nodded.

Vegard signaled to Phaelan's pilot to go to the citadel and get reinforcements.

I stopped fighting the contact with the rock. I couldn't see where the thief was, but I could feel him, like an invisible string bound me to him. As we circled back from the citadel, the string tightened. I had no clue how I could sense the rock, yet couldn't tap one iota of magic. I'd just add it to the absurdly long list of crap I didn't understand.

"Down!" I shouted. "Need to be closer . . . to the street."

"Hold on."

I'd heard that sky dragons were nimble enough to fly

and land pretty much anywhere. I'd never seen it, and I sure as hell didn't want to be in the saddle of one while it happened.

Vegard sent Kalinpar into a full dive.

Kalinpar shrieked in pure joy.

I just shrieked.

The sky dragon leveled out just below the rooftops in an entirely too small street. I got an up-close look at the goblin thief wearing what I guessed was his own skin, and he got the same view of the three of us. His eyes widened, right before he darted down a too-narrow-for-Kalinpar side street and out of our reach.

Vegard pulled back hard on the dragon's reins and banked back up into the sky. My stomach tried to do the same. He leveled off just above the rooftops.

"Still sense him?"

The only sense I had was the need to be sick. I shoved it down, literally, and focused on the rock with everything I had. I might not have magic right now, but I had something even more powerful.

Stubbornness.

That thief wasn't getting away. He couldn't get away. If he did I'd wish I was dead or sharing the Saghred's link with a bunch of pervert elf mages. They'd get to share the sensation of having people slaughtered and feel like they were being slaughtered on them, feel their souls being torn out of their dying bodies, those bodies disintegrated under the Saghred's destructive magic.

Over and over again.

Dozens or hundreds or even thousands of times. Until the Saghred was full. Until it was at full power. And Sarad Nukpana and his king could turn that power against anyone they chose. Unrelenting. Unstoppable.

"Left!" I shouted.

I followed the thief and guided Vegard to an intersection that might be big enough to land in. Not that we had a choice. The thief was there, so we were going to land.

It wasn't the worst part of town, but it was far from the best. We were less than a dozen or so blocks from the citadel, but we weren't close enough that they'd come running if I screamed loud enough.

The sun wasn't up, and the dregs of Mid's society were still out. They scattered when Kalinpar swooped in for a landing, claws extended.

Vegard swung a long leg over the dragon's neck and smoothly dismounted.

I smoothly fell off.

"You look green, ma'am."

"Feel green."

"You gonna make it?"

"Not if we don't get that rock back."

He gave me a hand up and I took it. Behind us, Kalinpar snorted.

"Stay," Vegard told him. "Signal."

In response, the sky dragon tossed back his head and sent a plume of blue flame straight up above the rooftops. Any Guardian pilots in the air couldn't miss that.

The plume also lit the outlines of some less-than-scrupulous individuals closing in on Kalinpar or at least thinking about it. The dragon turned his massive head in their direction, and I swear he smiled.

Vegard saw it, too. "Signal first. Play later."

Kalinpar stopped smiling and sent a short, miffed plume in the air, angled slightly toward the nearest thug. The thugs jumped back. The dragon smiled.

We left Kalinpar to his amusements.

We had to catch a thief.

Chapter 22

Dawn was less than an hour away. We didn't have an hour.

"Which way?" Vegard asked.

I hesitated. I hadn't told Vegard that my magic was gone. I especially hadn't told him that I'd damn near taken Phaelan's soul. That wasn't the kind of comment you casually tossed out there before going into a place where we'd be trusting each other with our lives. I didn't think the Saghred would try anything with Vegard. When my magic had gone, so had my soul-sucking urges. At least I thought they were gone. If they weren't, it wouldn't be the first time that the Saghred tried to pull a fast one.

I'd hoped my magic would be back by now. It wasn't, and we were going after a master glamourer who had a rock of cataclysmic power in his pocket. The goblin couldn't use it, neither could I; but the rock, however, might take offense at me wanting to take it back to the citadel.

Big, messy, soul-sucking offense.

Right now, I could barely sense it, and without my

magic, I couldn't tap the thing even if our lives depended on it, and they probably would.

I gave Vegard the short and not-so-sweet version of my magicless state.

To his credit, he didn't put his fist through the wall we were standing against, even when I told him it was all the fault of Taltek Balmorlan and his magic-sapping manacles.

Or the Saghred.

Or all three.

I had no clue and I desperately wanted one—along with my magic back.

I'd never lost my magic before, and had never heard of anyone who had lost theirs, so any reason I came up with would be nothing but a guess. But any guess I made wouldn't alter the fact that magically speaking, I was as naked as the day I was born.

"Can you get a general direction from the Saghred?" Vegard asked.

"Think so."

I reached out. Not with the magic I didn't have, just with a link to a cursed rock.

The Saghred was here, close by. I knew that much. What I had no clue about was which way the goblin had gone with it. Now that we were on the ground, my sense of the rock was spread thin, as if the trail had been smeared over the whole block. Naturally, it wasn't a block with only one or two buildings; it was a rat's warren of narrow, twisting streets and alleys, recessed doorways and darkened windows. Perfect for seeing without being seen. Perfect for a goblin who could see better in the dark than a hundred cats combined.

My life, soul, and sanity depended on going into that dark and finding that goblin and the rock he'd stolen. A diluted trail from the Saghred meant only one thing—magic of the interfering kind. That meant our thief wasn't alone. I couldn't see a master glamourer and thief conjuring a ward complex enough to mask an object as powerful as the Saghred.

A Khrynsani could. I already knew from the two suicide

bombers in the harbor that there were Khrynsani on Mid. Well, those two particular Khrynsani weren't anywhere anymore, but they didn't travel only in pairs. Like rats, if you saw two, simply check the dark corners. There were more; you could count on it.

I quietly told Vegard what I'd sensed—and what I couldn't.

"Don't worry, ma'am," he assured me. "I've got a trick or two up my sleeve."

"You might need more than that," I whispered. I quickly told him about the thief's arsenal—darts and strawberries— one eatable, both poisonous. I didn't mention the box the poison came in or the itty-bitty portrait of me in it. If Vegard knew he'd take me back to Kalinpar and order the dragon to make *me* stay. At least he'd try. By not telling him, I was saving valuable time. Vegard wouldn't have seen it that way, but then Vegard wasn't going to know.

Ten minutes ago, the goblin thief had been wearing his own skin. For a man who could alter his appearance in the blink of an eye, ten minutes was an eternity. The goblin had the Saghred, was on his home turf, lurking in the dark, and could look like anyone by now.

I didn't have diddly-squat.

No sleep, no strength, no magic. I'd been kidnapped, chained, choked, force-fed a mage, and fallen off of a sky dragon.

The thief had changed into a beautiful girl, had a kinky-fun evening, and an hour ago had taken an early-morning stroll into the citadel to pick up and carry out a rock.

I was on my last leg. He was just getting warmed up.

And to top it all off, he knew we were here.

"Ma'am, I don't suppose you'd stay here and let me take care of this?"

I just looked at him.

"Didn't think so." Vegard took what to him was a short sword from the harness across his back, and offered it to me. To me, it was massive.

"As much as I'd love to take that," I told him, "right now I couldn't hold it up, let alone run anyone through with it. Got something smaller?"

Vegard flashed a quick grin. "That's something I never thought I'd hear you ask."

"Me, either."

He handed me a pair of long, slender daggers.

"Aren't those a little . . . dainty for you?" I asked.

"I'm not always a brute. I can do subtle."

"Vegard?"

"Ma'am?"

"Bring the brute."

"Don't worry, ma'am. He's right here." The big Guardian bared his teeth in what might have been a grin. If so, it was one the goblin thief or any of his Khrynsani friends didn't want to see.

A sky dragon roar overhead nearly made me jump out of my skin.

We looked up. Two dragons glided past just above the rooftops, wings slightly pulled back for landing. One of the pilots raised an armored hand at Vegard.

"Reinforcements," Vegard snapped. "About damned time. Let's move; they'll catch up."

I held my daggers out in front of me. If someone or something came at me out of the dark, it'd be met with steel.

We moved as fast as I could detect the Saghred's trail, and as cautiously as our sense of survival demanded. The rock's presence grew stronger, though not any more definite. It wasn't moving and we were; you'd think that would be called progress.

I estimated it was about half an hour until dawn. There should be lights in some of the windows; people should be up, even people who stayed up all night waiting to jump on people like us.

No one. Nothing.

I didn't need my seeker instincts to tell me that was a bad thing.

Every step I took was like sticking my head into Kalinpar's mouth while he was feeling playful.

It was suicidal and I knew it. We should be running in the opposite direction, not sneaking forward. The goblin and whatever friends he had were somewhere ahead, waiting until we got close enough to do something we really weren't going to like. The Saghred was with them and wanted to be with them. I didn't need magic to know any of it; my instincts were working just fine, and they were screaming at me to run and not stop until I hit the harbor, and once I got there to start swimming.

Instincts had a way of thinking you had a choice. I didn't.

The look on my face must have said all of that loud and clear. The big Guardian's only response was a grim nod. I guess surviving something that was suicidal but necessary made you a hero. Failure just made you dead and posthumously stupid.

I stopped—and stayed stopped.

The Saghred's presence rang like a bell. An evil bell, but still a bell. Loud and clear.

And close. Too close.

I inclined my head ever so slightly in the direction the rock's come-hither was coming from. Vegard saw and calmly drew his battle-ax from where it rode across his back, the blade glowing blue with restrained magic. He started to step in front of me. I put a hand on his arm and shook my head once. It didn't look like an evil hideout; the only thing it looked like was abandoned. The worn, wooden door looked like any other door. Though if the Saghred and that body-morphing thief were in there, absolutely nothing would be what it seemed.

I took a breath and made it a good one, in case it was my last, and carefully wrapped my hand around the metal latch. I made no move to turn it, but stood perfectly still, willing the essence of the last person who opened it to come to me.

Nothing.

I resisted the urge to growl and kick the door. It wasn't the door's fault that when the Saghred had fed it'd sucked out my magic along with that elf mage's soul.

There, I'd said it.

I'd been in magic-sapping manacles before; my magic came back almost immediately. I'd been telling myself that since I was in Balmorlan's longer that it was taking longer for the effect to wear off. I didn't believe it, but I didn't want to let the possibility of the alternative so much as cross my thoughts.

The Saghred had taken my magic, whether by accident or spite. I didn't want to think about it, but I couldn't ignore what it might mean. An old door with a rusty latch would be just that and no more. No sense of who last touched it, how much power they were packing, no warning of what waited on the other side. I'd be going in blind.

I inhaled sharply through my nose and clenched my teeth, willing myself not to scream in impotent fury—or cry. I didn't have time for either one. Though if I survived this, I'd treat myself to one, the other, or probably both. Vegard's strong hand tightly squeezed my shoulder, that one touch telling me he knew what I was thinking, and he was there for me. I knew it was a mistake, but I glanced up into his eyes. I couldn't see them all that well because my vision had suddenly gone blurry. I sniffed, clenched my jaw, and swallowed hard. Vegard laid his big hand next to mine against the door, and his lip curled back with distaste.

"Khrynsani?" I asked.

Vegard nodded tightly. "And a hint of a repel ward. Just enough to make people pass by or not notice it at all." He took his hand off the door. "We're waiting for backup."

"We don't have time to—"

"Ma'am, do you feel the Saghred moving?"

"No, but—"

"Then we wait."

Less than two minutes later, four Guardians silently emerged from the dark on the opposite side of the street.

Mychael was one of them.

Yes, running across the street and launching myself at him would make me a target, and it took everything I had not to do it. Another reason to survive and not screw this up. I didn't know the other three Guardians. They might be Mychael's men, but there was still a warrant out for my arrest. It might have been rescinded, but until I heard that from Mychael's own lips, I'd be wary of any armed man I didn't know.

If those were Mychael's lips.

I normally wasn't this paranoid, but I wasn't normally this powerless, either.

The Saghred was somewhere inside the building behind us. I could feel that; I knew it for a fact. The goblin thief had run in there with it. He sure as hell wasn't going anywhere without it, so logic said loud and clear that the goblin was in there with his prize, not glamoured as Mychael standing across the street from me.

"Who are those—"

"Trustworthy men, ma'am," Vegard assured me.

I saw the faint glow of shields as Mychael and his men darted across the street to us. The three Guardians went to the opposite side of the door. Mychael came directly to me, and I stepped back from him.

Mychael's expression went from confused to hurt in the time it took me to take that step back.

"Raine, what—"

"Prove you're you." My whispered demand didn't carry past the two of us.

"Who else would I . . ." Realization dawned. "I'm not the thief."

"You're wearing full armor, so it's not like I can check you for freckles."

One side of his mouth curled in a quick grin, an all-too-familiar grin. "If we weren't standing in the middle of the street in the worst part of town, I'd drop my pants, armor and all, and let you inspect to your heart's content. Would that convince you?"

I smiled. "Won't know until I see it."

"You're a bad girl, Raine Benares."

"You bet I am." I said, stepping into his arms.

Words couldn't describe how good it felt to hold him, to be held. Best of all, Mychael smelled like Mychael. Though there was something that I couldn't feel. Our link was gone. It made sense. No magic, no magical link. Dammit. I might be having that good cry sooner than I wanted to.

I swallowed against the sudden lump in my throat, and gave Mychael a whispered, thirty-second summary of my magic being gone and my theory on how it left.

Mychael pulled me to him again; my head nestled into the warm hollow of his neck. I felt the pounding of the pulse in his throat, the anger. He quickly released me and stepped around Vegard, one hand extended to check for wards. He frowned and moved his hand closer, then looked at me and Vegard and shook his head once.

No wards.

"Let's hope it's not a buka on the other side this time," Mychael muttered. He carefully turned the knob, and the door opened.

No lock, either.

Step into my parlor, and all that.

Maybe when you got your hands on the most powerful magical object in the world, you forgot the little things like locking doors behind you. I didn't believe it, but it was better than wasting time dismantling wards and picking locks. On the flip side, I'd been around powerful magical talents long enough to know—by learning the hard way—that when it came to outwitting one, there was no such thing as good luck. More than once, what I'd thought was good luck nearly turned out to be good riddance.

Mychael led the way into a big room, or at least one big enough that the Guardians' lightglobes didn't reach into all the dark corners. The place was covered in dust and empty bottles. The dust was everywhere, except on the bottles that were scattered across the floor just a little too evenly to be happenstance. Drunks don't usually abandon an empty bottle every three feet to completely cover a room. These were strategically placed to make the most noise. Sometimes the best alarms were the most basic. The Saghred was here, somewhere below my feet, on the next level down. We were on the ground floor. That meant the Saghred was in the basement.

Naturally.

Scary, evil, bite-your-face-off, suck-out-your-soul magic. Of course it was in the basement.

I pointed down.

Mychael silently mouthed a word that summed up my feelings perfectly. Though actually knowing where the rock was did simplify the plan.

Find the stairs. Find the rock. Get out.

Though the plan did have an unspoken fourth step— try not to think about everything that could and probably would go wrong during steps one through three.

With a few gestures, Mychael ordered two Guardians to guard the door and the other one the stairs. Then he looked at me and mouthed, "Stay here." The look I responded with didn't need any words, mouthed or otherwise, to get my message across. Mychael raised my look and gave me a glare.

He scanned the door to the basement and silently raised the latch. No wards, no locks, no goblins. My stomach stayed clenched in terror, just in case.

The stairs were steep and narrow. Beyond that, my expectations were knocked flat.

There wasn't a lot of light, but there was enough to see that there was nothing to see. No Khrynsani and no Chameleon— unless he could glamour himself as a brick wall.

The air was stale and damp like nothing had been breathing down here for years. The only thing that could qualify as living was the mold. We reached the bottom and near the far corner of the room was a single, battered chair.

The Saghred was on it.

It wasn't in a casket; no wards held it. An armored glove lay on the chair next to it. The Saghred was just sitting there, its surface a flat, lifeless black.

I knew better.

So did the rock.

I had to get it out of here.

The rock knew that, too.

I looked around. The goblin hadn't carried it out of the citadel in his bare hands. The Saghred had been in its casket, unwarded, but still in its casket.

"Do you think it ate the goblin?" Vegard asked quietly.

"I wish," I muttered. "Even without my magic I'd have known."

"Right, no burp," Vegard agreed solemnly.

That made me crack a smile.

"Can you sense where . . ." Vegard stopped himself. "Oh, ma'am, I'm so sorry, I—"

I snorted quietly. "I might have to get used to it." People asking me to use the magic I no longer had.

Bottles clanked and something hit the boards above our heads hard enough to shower us with dust.

I got an even more white-knuckled grip on my daggers, and the glow of Vegard's ax doubled. Mychael drew his sword.

It didn't glow.

No glow. No magic.

No Mychael.

Oh hell.

There was a single pop and Vegard's eyes rolled up in his head as he crumpled to the floor. The goblin thief glamoured as Mychael stood over him, a small dart gun in his other hand. He smiled and pointed it at me.

"This promises to be a very profitable day."

Chapter 23

Vegard wasn't moving. I couldn't even tell if he was breathing.

I started to go to him, but was abruptly nose to muzzle with the goblin thief's poison dart gun.

"The Guardian's alive," he told me. "I only kill when need demands it." The thief smiled and pointed the gun at Vegard's exposed throat. "However, a second dose would be sufficient to kill a man of his size." His finger tightened on the trigger.

"No!" I shouted, loud enough for the Guardians upstairs to hear.

Silence.

I didn't think that was good.

The thief still glamoured as Mychael pointed the gun at me. "You on the other hand are rather small. It may be too large a dose." He took a few steps back, keeping his eyes and the gun on me. "Dalen," he called, his voice entirely too casual. "What was that?"

"Cahil tripped, sir."

The thief chuckled. "Human eyes in the dark are worthless."

"Permission to drop our glamours?" the goblin called back.

"In a few minutes."

Oh crap.

"Khrynsani," I said. So much for help—at least for me.

He smirked. "You catch on quickly, but not quickly enough."

Three Khrynsani glamoured as Guardians. Two had been glamoured as elves in the harbor. Who knew how many more there were in the citadel and around the city? No one knew.

And no one knew I was here.

With the Saghred and a goblin master thief glamoured as Mychael.

Something wasn't adding up. Like how the hell he was in two places at the same time—running from us with the Saghred one minute, then landing on a sky dragon as Mychael five minutes later? Not to mention, the longer I got him to talk, the longer Vegard and I got to keep breathing.

"You stole the Saghred and brought it here," I said. "We saw you and chased you. Then you fly in here on a—"

Mychael smiled. The goblin might have looked like Mychael, but he didn't bother to copy Mychael's mannerisms any longer. His smile gave me ten different kinds of the creeps. "Did you actually see me on the dragon?"

"No, but—"

"Or any of my men?"

Realization dawned, and I thought it might just be worth taking a poison dart in the gut to get my hands on him. "Four Guardians flew in . . . you and those Khrynsani were there waiting. You killed them."

"You make it sound simple," the goblin said. "I assure you it was not. However, their arrival saved us a great deal of trouble."

"You got what you came for," I said. "So now you're hiding in a basement?"

The thief winked at me. "Not hiding, Raine. Merely

awaiting transportation." He looked over my shoulder. "I've sent the signal that I have the Saghred; within minutes, we'll have direct passage home. What would we do without magic?" He laughed. "Though it looks like you may be finding out; what a pity."

Bastard. I took a quick glance behind me. Nothing there but a brick wall. I froze.

A Gate.

The bastard had just ordered a freaking getaway Gate.

A Gate was a tear in the fabric of reality. Stepping through one was like stepping through a doorway, except that Gates covered miles instead of inches. Black magic made them, and torture and death fueled them—the more the merrier.

Once that Gate was open and stable, the thief would have all the help he needed dragging me through it kicking and screaming. The Saghred would just be happily going home.

If that happened, it was all over—or I'd wish it was. At that point, the best thing I could do for myself would be to fall on one of Vegard's dainty daggers. I wasn't going to do that, because I wasn't going through that Gate. To keep that from happening, all I had to do was get the Saghred, get past a fully armored man with a poison dart gun, then dodge three Khrynsani. And I'd have to do it all without magic. Just me and mine.

Help wasn't coming. Vegard was unconscious, the real Guardians who'd flown in from the citadel were probably dead in an alley, the dragons were snacking on thugs, no one knew I was here, and I had no magic.

But I had desperation in spades.

Think, Raine. Think. Keep him talking.

"That's why you came forward first out there in the street. You didn't know I'd lost my magic, until . . ."

"You told me. Again saving me much trouble." The thief gestured toward my daggers with the gun's muzzle. "Drop the daggers, Raine."

I made no move to comply.

The thief pointed the gun at Vegard, then back at me. "Your choice—the Guardian takes a fatal second dart or you take your fatal first." His sea blue eyes glittered coldly—Mychael's sea blue eyes. "Drop. The daggers."

I dropped them and rethought my strategy, such that it was.

The thief kicked my daggers across the room to the base of the stairs, keeping the gun aimed at me the entire time. "I didn't think I'd get the chance to take you alive. Put your hands behind your head and stand against the wall."

Like hell anyone was putting manacles on me again. I began to circle him. When in an impossible situation, keep your goals simple. Circle until I reach my daggers. Get them without being shot. Simple. Right.

"Come with me without any trouble and you need not die." The thief started circling me with a saunter as if he had all the time in the world. "My employers would rather have you alive, but they'll be fine with dead."

I kept my eyes on his, my peripheral vision on that gun. I didn't need to look at the stairs, not yet. I knew where they were. "Yeah, Sarad Nukpana would be an extra happy psycho if he could kill me on a Khrynsani altar."

I had only a few minutes to prevent that from happening.

The thief drew a dagger—long, thin, with a needle-sharp tip. That wasn't Guardian issue.

I kept circling. "Let me guess. Poisoned."

"You don't have to find out." His voice became low, coaxing. "Come now, little elf. Let's not make this hurt any more than it has to."

He didn't want to kill me, but I didn't care what I had to do to him. Problem was, if I didn't do it quietly, I'd have to do it three more times to the Khrynsani who'd come running down those stairs.

There were no winners in a knife fight. This was especially true when your opponent was wearing armor and had a poisoned dagger. He didn't need to stab me; a scratch could kill me just as dead. Either I won or Sarad Nukpana won me, and I got a long and painful death, followed by the destruction of civilization as we knew it.

No pressure.

Nukpana could feed the rock just fine without me. All he'd have to do is sacrifice victims so that their blood fell on the Saghred. The rock would take the sacrifices, and I would feel every last one of them; it didn't matter if I was in the same room or hundreds of miles away. I'd taken one mage already and he hadn't even been murdered first. I'd be stark raving loony within the first hour.

"Though you may welcome death," the thief said. "If I don't kill you now, you'll beg for it later—or do it yourself."

My mind was racing even faster than my feet. Okay, Raine. He was a thief, a thief who could make himself look like someone else. Big freaking deal. That was all the magic he had. If he'd had any more he'd have used it by now. The only advantage he had was that he was bigger than me. You've dealt with that before and come out on top. Literally. Come on, girl, time for some ugly.

I darted my eyes to the right like I was going to make a run for the stairs.

He bought it.

I ran straight at him, driving my shoulder into his midsection. The impact with that armor hurt like hell. Better to hurt like hell than to be dragged there. The gun fired, the dart went wide, and we hit the floor together. His head and hands were the only parts of him without armor. I sank my teeth into the wrist of his dagger hand. He swore, but held onto that dagger. Dammit. I didn't kid myself into thinking that I could reach anything vital, but I knew extreme pain made me drop my glamours. If it didn't work on him, at least I'd go down biting.

A thief and a glamourer did his job by hiding and sneaking, not direct confrontation.

My fist directly confronted his temple.

The thief dropped the dagger—and his glamour.

He had the high cheekbones and fine, straight nose of a

pure-blooded goblin. He wouldn't have either for long, if my fists had their way. Mychael's armor vanished with the glamour, leaving the goblin wearing his own clothes with leather armor covering only the most vital of areas. Hurt a man badly enough in a non-vital area and it'd turn vital real quick.

He was bigger and stronger. I was desperate and terrified and exhausted. But desperation trumped terror and exhaustion every time. It had to. The thief pivoted his body, trying to pin my arms, my legs, pin anything he could to get me to stop kicking and punching. I didn't have long nails, but I used what I had on the upswept tip of one ear and sank my teeth into the other.

He screamed. I snarled.

Next to nuts, the tips of a goblin's ears were one of their most sensitive parts.

I growled and shook my head like a terrier with a rat. I didn't have much, but I used what I had. It was an ugly fight, but I wasn't in it to make it pretty. I was in it to win, or at least survive. I used every trick in the book and wrote a couple of new pages right there on the spot. The damned rock just sat there watching, or waiting, or whatever.

I had to hand it to Imala's uniform design—skintight also meant impossible to hold on to.

The air grew heavy with power, like air just before a lightning strike, prickling my skin like thousands of hot needles.

Not yet. Please, no, not yet.

I was facing the back wall. A long, narrow part of the bricks shimmered. The sickly sweet, coppery stench of blood came from beyond.

The Gate.

It opened simply, no mouth of Hell, no brimstone stench, just a parting curtain of silvery fog. The smell of blood came from the Gate and the chanting of voices came from beyond it. The chants and what was feeding the Gate were worse, much worse—the screams in the background proved it.

A tall figure appeared just beyond the opening.

Sarad Nukpana. Now in his uncle Janos Ghalfari's body.

Sarad Nukpana had been consumed by the Saghred, escaped, and attempted to regenerate his body by ingesting the life forces of the most powerful mages he could hunt down. Desperate for a body to inhabit, Nukpana took the corpse of his recently dead uncle, the nachtmagus Janos Ghalfari.

Sarad Nukpana considered it all my fault.

In a way, it was.

Now he was going to make me pay.

Nukpana was lean and lethal. His black hair gleamed in the light of the torches burning behind him. Like many a serpent that'd slithered out of a dark place, Sarad Nukpana was beautiful to look at; but unless you wanted to die, you needed to stay out of striking distance.

I was within striking distance. I knew it, and so did he.

So did the thief. He planted his fist in my gut.

I folded double in a red haze of agony. I couldn't breathe, couldn't speak. I was facing the Gate, curled up and panting on the floor less than ten steps from being at Sarad Nukpana's feet.

He smiled, fangs gleaming in the firelight. "Mine," he purred. He whispered as if I were his lover. "Even my dreams were not this good, little seeker."

He had me right where he wanted me, or he would as soon as he stepped through that Gate and claimed what he saw as his—the Saghred and me.

"Give me the Saghred," Nukpana ordered the thief. "Then bring the girl."

Nukpana didn't step through the Gate.

He couldn't.

An instant later, I realized why.

The thief had only called for it less than a half hour before. Nukpana would have had to work fast, and apparently fast meant one-way. The thief could go in, but Sarad Nukpana couldn't come out.

Hope flickered. It didn't flare, but at least it hadn't been stomped out.

Though nothing—especially me—was going to keep the thief from taking me through that Gate with him. I managed a gasp and a little air. Heavy breathing on the bastard's boots wouldn't exactly be a defiant gesture.

The torchlight from beyond the Gate glinted off the goblin thief's dagger on the floor not two feet from where I was curled up. Both of my hands were busy clenched in agony around my stomach. If I could persuade one to move, I could just reach the thing. Though reaching was a long way from using. Hell, breathing was a long way from happening. Every time I tried, it was like pushing a white-hot poker through my own guts.

The thief pulled on the armored glove lying on the chair next to the Saghred and picked up the rock. He was bleeding, but was careful not to let any of it come in contact with the Saghred. Just my luck.

I wasn't just going to lie there and wait for the bastard to come pick me up like so much baggage. If I did nothing, I was going to die. If I did something, I'd probably still end up dead, but I'd have my self-respect—like that was going to do me any good once Sarad Nukpana started his fun and games. I unclenched my right hand and slid it along the floor toward the dagger. I thought the pain would knock me unconscious. I bit my lip against a scream until I tasted my own blood, but my hand didn't stop moving. I closed my hand around the dagger's grip.

Then all hell broke loose.

An explosion from upstairs shook the floor under me as if a giant fist had splintered the door and the walls it'd been attached to. Goblin voices shouted, followed by the ring of steel on steel, screams, falling bodies, and more dust falling from the ceiling.

The thief looked up and swore. He yelled something up at his men. At least I think he was yelling. Everything sounded the same and all of it was too loud, like I'd been kicked in the head instead of the gut.

"Give me the stone and *get the girl*!" Nukpana shouted.

The thief crossed the distance between us in three strides, and I did the only thing I could do with the dagger in my hand—I drove it through the top of his boot and into his foot.

The goblin howled in pain and kicked me with his other foot, the tip of his boot landing a vicious blow to my shoulder, the movement ripping the dagger out of his foot, but not out of my grip. The fighting upstairs got louder and the goblin snatched me up by the arm, the Saghred in one hand and me in the other. I struggled to get my legs under me and to get that dagger into him.

Eight steps to the Gate.

The thief quickly exchanged his grip on my arm for his arm tight around my throat. The harder I fought, the tighter he squeezed, until my vision started to go black.

Six steps.

I desperately tried to dig my heels into the dirt floor. The thief just dragged me.

Four.

"Raine!" shouted voices from upstairs.

Mychael. And Tam.

Sarad Nukpana extended his armored hand as far as he dared toward the Gate opening, his glittering black eyes locked on the Saghred.

Three steps.

"Give it to me!" Sarad Nukpana screamed.

Then he'd slam the Gate shut. He'd give up the chance to get me to get the rock.

"And leave me here," the thief growled.

Two steps.

I desperately slashed at the thief's forearm that was locked around my throat. It was covered in leather, but that didn't stop me. I cried and screamed and slammed the point of the dagger past my throat into whatever I could stab. The tip sank into skin, once, twice, three times, and the goblin's hold loosened for an instant. I twisted and brought the dagger up from below, underneath the leather chest plate, and buried it up to the hilt in soft flesh.

One step to the Gate.

Time slowed and stretched.

I looked up into the goblin thief's eyes. The dagger wasn't long enough to have reached his heart, but it didn't have to be.

The goblin's eyes were fixed and staring. Flecks of foam were at one corner of his mouth. The dagger *had* been poisoned.

The thief began to fall backward toward the Gate, taking me with him. Sarad Nukpana's black-armored hand punched through the Gate inches from me.

How the hell did he—

The thief's hand went limp in death and the Saghred began to fall. I didn't think; I just reached for it. Sarad Nukpana extended his arm through the opening, the power from the Gate heating the metal of his glove to molten red, like armor on a forge. Nukpana snatched the Saghred out of the air, clutching it and howling in mindless agony. His hand being cooked alive in that armored glove didn't stop him from reaching through the Gate with his other hand, his bare hand, clawing at me, his flesh burning, the skin melting away from his fingers, his hand.

Black-robed figures rushed up behind Nukpana, pulling him back. He fought them, lunging toward me. They dragged him back and Sarad Nukpana screamed. His words rang through the Gate and slammed into me with physical blows. "No! She is *mine*!"

A blast of heat threw me halfway across the room as the Gate closed.

Sarad Nukpana was on the other side. In Regor.

I was lying on my belly in a dusty basement gasping for air.

Sarad Nukpana had taken the Saghred.

I was still here.

But part of me had been stolen along with it.

Chapter 24

Whoever said waiting was the hardest part must not have been waiting on much of anything.

I was waiting for people to die.

On me. Through me. Talk about living from one breath to the next.

Just like Sarad Nukpana's goblin mage prisoners were doing right now.

His injuries were probably all that was keeping him from starting the slaughter. With any luck, he'd never be able to hold a dagger again. No one had made him stick his hands through that Gate, but that didn't matter. He'd blame me for that, too. That'd be fine with me; I'd gladly take the credit for crippling the bastard.

Now I was all that was standing between him and full control of the Saghred—he either needed me captured then dead, or just dead would be perfectly fine with him, though I know he'd rather have the fun of doing it himself.

The Gate had closed with Nukpana and the Saghred on the other side nearly twelve hours ago. I dimly recalled another sky dragon ride to the citadel that had been thankfully uneventful. I had no recollection of Mychael carrying me to his apartment or putting me to bed. Exhaustion would do that to you. I'd only been awake for about an hour. From the way my back ached, I think I'd spent nearly the entire day sleeping, or whatever, in the same position. Unconsciousness didn't count as real sleep, but right now I was grateful for what I'd gotten. Every minute I could spend essentially out cold was one less minute wondering if any sudden chest pain was an impending heart attack or an incoming Saghred sacrifice. I think I'd rather have the heart attack. Generally those only happened once. That it could be fatal might actually be a plus.

Vegard was going to be fine. He was conscious within an hour after the Gate had closed, and was as sick as Mago in rough seas for the next five. Mychael hadn't declared him fit for duty yet. Vegard was probably ready for what most Guardians considered duty. Mychael was saying Vegard wasn't ready to return to duty guarding *me* yet. I didn't think any man was truly ready for that.

Not going after the Saghred was not an option. Getting to Regor the normal way would take weeks. We didn't have weeks. We might not even have days.

Mychael had come to see me when he'd been told that I was up. He'd been in emergency meetings all day with the archmagus, the Seat of Twelve, and half the Conclave trying to find a way to stop what Sarad Nukpana had set in motion the moment he snatched the Saghred through that Gate. But his main concern was doing what every paladin down through the centuries prayed he'd never have to do—protect the citizens, students, and mages of Mid from imminent invasion.

Sarad Nukpana had said he was coming after me, but the students weren't being evacuated just to protect them from being killed—at least not in the normal way. Sarad Nukpana was many things, most of them evil and insane, but he wasn't wasteful. The Saghred gained more power from magically talented sacrifices. Nukpana wasn't only coming to Mid to get me, he was coming to power up the rock, to prepare it for conquest. Taking the lives of Mid's students and mages would give him everything he needed and then some.

The Guardians who'd flown the reconnaissance mission to the plains outside of Regor had returned a few hours ago and reported a massive magical buildup as well as the construction of a framed platform that looked to be wide enough for at least a hundred men to go through standing shoulder to shoulder.

Wide enough for an army.

A hundred. Then a hundred more and hundreds after that, waiting on that plain outside of Regor for their turn to step through that Gate directly into Mid, an elven city, or any damned place the goblin king or Sarad Nukpana wanted them to be.

Even if we had a way to empty the Saghred of the souls it held now, unless we could destroy it, Sarad Nukpana would simply sacrifice more to feed it. Starting with Tam's parents, Chigaru's allies, Mid's students, the Conclave's mages.

The only people capable of stopping him.

Though as a silver lining to our catastrophe, we'd done some stopping ourselves.

With Carnades and Balmorlan laid low, their entire criminal network was crumbling or running like hell, some straight to their lawyers.

The documents I found in Taltek Balmorlan's office would ruin them all. The fruits of Mago's labor had been enough to get Carnades charged with treason, not to the elven government, those charges were still pending, but to the Conclave. The Conclave of Sorcerers was a neutral governing body. Neutral organizations frowned on its members starting wars.

Mago had a lawyer-to-lackey chat with Carnades's two yes-mages on the Seat of Twelve—at least that was the profession Mago had chosen for the occasion. Living in a man's pocket was enlightening. And if that man was the arrogant sort, he gave his lackeys no more consideration than the furniture. Furniture with ears, alert ears. Carnades's yes-mages had heard things, seen things, and knew things. These mages were willing to ride Carnades's robe hem to power, but not to the prison Mago convinced them they were going to. They sang. Two members of the Seat of Twelve laying down proof of extortion, bribery, misappropriated Conclave funds, and treason, carried enough weight to get a search warrant for Carnades's office and home. More evidence was found, charges were brought, and the people rejoiced. Well, I was rejoicing.

I would have enjoyed it a lot more if Sarad Nukpana hadn't been breathing down my neck from hundreds of miles away.

My ex-fiancé had vanished just like he'd appeared—without a trace. No one had seen Rache Kai, and no one was really looking for him. One killer on the island was an inconvenience; hundreds was an invasion. His note to Balmorlan said the deal was off and I believed him. And me sticking a certain poisoned dagger through a boot had eliminated the need to protect Prince Chigaru against a master glamourer/thief/assassin armed with the Nukpana family poison, a box of poison that Imala had taken into custody. I would have felt a lot better if she'd destroyed it. Though Imala, always the secret service director, said it would be a waste to destroy a weapon she hoped to soon put to good use. I knew exactly what she was thinking. Sarad Nukpana killed by his own family's poison. It'd be ironic as hell.

Goblins loved irony.

Taltek Balmorlan was imprisoned in his own dungeon by the one man who could get him to admit everything he'd done and rat on the powerful and influential people he'd convinced to help him do it. People who also knew how and where to buy the services they needed to clean up the mess Balmorlan had made—starting with Balmorlan. Rache might soon find himself besieged with work offers.

We'd taken down the bad guys, but the evil ones had gotten away.

I'd glanced outside the apartment door once since getting up. It looked like Mychael had posted half a platoon of Guardians. I guess that was what it took to make him feel I was safe.

I'd had a bath. I was having a meal.

I had a visitor.

A visitor who insisted I finish eating before he'd give me any more news. He told me I had to keep my strength up. I was surprised he didn't tell me to eat my vegetables.

Dads were like that.

After that, all similarities between my dad and every other dad in the seven kingdoms ended.

"Sarad won't begin feeding the Saghred immediately," he told me. "He has no reason to hurry and every reason to proceed with caution."

If anyone else had been in the room, it'd seem odd for them to hear that kind of calm assurance from a kid who didn't look old enough to buy himself a drink in a bar, even if he was a kid in a Guardian uniform. The young, blond elf sitting across from me was my father.

Arlyn Ravide, the young Guardian in whose body my dad's soul lived, had died at the hands of the demon queen, the Scythe of Nen plunged through his heart. She'd wet the blade with his sacrificial blood, then stabbed the Saghred with equal ease to open the stone for her demon king consort to escape. The demon king was still trapped inside the Saghred, but Sarad Nukpana and five other inmates he'd plotted with while inside had escaped. My dad's soul had escaped and occupied Arlyn Ravide's lifeless body.

Dad's real name was Eamaliel Anguis, a beautiful silverhaired, gray-eyed, pure-blooded high elf. He had been the Saghred's Guardian and bond servant before me.

Nearly a thousand years before me. He was 934 years old.

Running for your life carrying the Saghred did that to you. I guess the rock didn't want to be alone.

I'd only been stuck with the rock for three months. Dad had the Saghred and the people who wanted it chasing him the better part of a millennium. It had cost him his body when the rock turned its bond servant into its next meal.

It'd cost my mother her life.

"Sarad knows what it's like to be inside the Saghred," Dad continued. "He'll want to be entirely sure of the ritual before he conducts it in public. King Sathrik will gather those of influence who oppose him but whom he dare not act against, to witness the sacrifices."

I pushed my plate aside, appetite gone. "To take the fight out of every last one of them."

"Exactly. So we have a little time." Dad smiled. "Besides, it wouldn't look good for Sarad to get sucked inside the Saghred again, only this time in front of the people he's trying to impress."

This wouldn't be the first time the Saghred had been taken from a goblin king and a mad Khrynsani. Dad and an elite team of Guardians had done it that time, too. Now he was talking about doing it again.

Like I said, goblins loved irony.

I didn't.

"Okay, what's the fix?"

He arched a brow at me. "Pardon?"

"The fix. The way we're going to get there. You're talking like getting to Regor before Nukpana starts feeding souls to the Saghred isn't our biggest problem."

"It's not." He paused, the pause of a man who was about to say something he knew I didn't want to hear. "We'll be using a mirror."

Oh hell.

I just looked at him. "You know I hate mirrors, right?"

"I'm not fond of them myself, but it's our only option. The entrance mirror is here in the citadel. The exit is in a cave ten miles southwest of Regor."

We would be there in seconds. Step into one mirror, step out of another. We'd be in the goblin capital in time for a midnight snack. Easy, fast, hopefully not fatal.

"The team will have to be small by necessity," he continued. "No more than ten people."

I took a breath and tried to let it out without it shaking. I failed.

Dad studied my face for a moment. "Raine?"

"My magic's gone," I said slowly. "You know that, right?"

"I know." His eyes were steady. "I've talked to Mychael about it and we want you to be on Phaelan's ship out of here on the morning tide."

Running for the rest of my life. Dad had been doing it for almost a thousand years. How long until I was caught? Or just got tired of running and let them catch me.

No. No more.

It wasn't going to end like that. *I* wasn't going to end like that.

I wanted to live, and dammit, I wanted a life. A happy one. If anyone deserved all of that and more, and to never have to look over his shoulder again, it was the man sitting across from me. And all of it—my life, his life, the survival of everyone Sarad Nukpana wanted dead—depended on us doing this and not failing.

Dad sat there, watching me, probably reading my mind.

"You want to go." He stated it simply, no question.

"Walking through a mirror to Regor to take on Sarad Nukpana and the goblin army with no magic? Hell, no, that's not what I want. No one in their right mind would want that. But I'm not running and I won't let anyone else risk death or worse while I go sailing with Phaelan." I stood up and looked around for my gear. "Kick someone off that team of yours. I'm going."

"Are you sure?" Dad asked quietly. "No one would blame you. Actually, it'd be a relief to all of us to know you were safe."

"No, I'm not sure, but I'm doing it anyway. I can still do something that none of you can. I can sense the Saghred. Do you have any idea how I can sense the rock, but can't tap my magic?"

"You're treading untrod ground, Raine. No one knows."

"Sarad Nukpana's going to know I'm not packing."

"Safe assumption."

I snorted. "Glad assumptions are safe. I'm not."

"It's entirely possible that your magic is simply in shock from what you went through and should be coming back."

"Should?"

Dad shrugged. "It's a theory."

"Theories aren't going to keep Sarad Nukpana from frying me where I stand."

His lips turned up at one corner in a crooked smile. "Then I'd suggest you keep moving."

"Story of my life," I muttered, finishing off the rest of my coffee.

The smile turned into a grin. "Story of both our lives."

There was a knock on the door, then it opened and Vegard stuck his head in. The big Guardian was still a little pasty, but he was smiling.

"Good to see you up and alive, ma'am."

I raised my mug in salute. "Same to you, darlin'."

"Are they ready for us?" Dad asked him.

"Yes, sir."

I looked from one to the other. "Ready?"

"You'll see, daughter. Follow me."

"Where are we going?"

"Justinius Valerian's office."

"The goblins will kill me!"

I knew that voice. It belonged to the best mirror mage on Mid—and the Conclave's newest criminal.

Carnades Silvanus.

"Shit," I spat.

We were listening at the door outside of Justinius's office. We hadn't gone in yet, and I was giving serious thought to going right back to Mychael's apartment and crawling under the bed.

Dad chuckled. "Couldn't have said it better. Unfortunately, he's also the best. And that's his getaway mirror in that cave outside Regor."

"Carnades was the emissary to the goblin court a handful of years ago," Vegard said. "It was Archmagus Valerian's first try to get rid of him. The goblins hated Carnades and the feeling was mutual, so . . ."

I nodded. "He had a getaway mirror waiting nearby, though you'd think he'd have put the thing closer."

"Ten miles was as close as he could put it without it being detected," Dad explained.

"And all of this is good, how?"

"Beggars can't be choosers," he murmured. His eyes sparkled with barely contained mirth. "And Carnades has definitely drawn the short straw today."

The Lower Hells were officially frozen over.

I was going to Regor using a mirror with Carnades Silvanus as my tour guide.

I gave a second's serious thought to going sailing with Phaelan. A lifetime of running wouldn't be that bad. I'd be in fabulous shape.

Justinius snorted and laughed. "You don't have to go to Regor to die," he told Carnades. "You've got people on this island lining up to kill you. The advantage to Regor is they won't know you're there—if you don't screw up. You get the team there and safely back again. Every. Last. One. Do it and you live—behind bars, but your head will still be attached to the rest of you. If you don't . . . well, you'd be better off staying with the goblins. On your return, your level of cooperation will be taken into consideration at your trial. Understand?"

"Perfectly." Icicles hung off of that one word.

I decided to add the cherry on top of Carnades's bad

day. I stepped into Justinius's office and let Carnades see me. The expression on his face made the risk of death and dismemberment in Regor worth it.

The elf mage was still wearing his usual sumptuous black velvet robes, but now they were perfectly accessorized with a pair of magic-sapping manacles. Though they were bright and shiny and looked more like jewelry than restraints. I guess high-class criminals got the good stuff.

Carnades's face turned a most unattractive shade of red. "You!"

I smiled. "Me."

I thought I'd make his day even worse by confirming what he'd long suspected. I walked over to Mychael and got myself a good hug and a kiss. I deserved it—and so did Carnades.

I looked up at Mychael, his arms still around me. "So when do we get this show on the road?" I nodded toward my dad. "I've been told the big picture." I wasn't about to say "dad" out loud around Carnades. Maybe it'd scare him into behaving if he knew—or kick him one step closer to more betrayal. Some secrets were best kept that way.

"The mirror we'll be using is downstairs in the containment area," Mychael said.

That was surprising. I'd have figured Carnades would have kept it in his house. But I guess if he came screaming through a mirror with a hundred pissed off and racially offended goblins after him, he'd want Guardians for backup, not his butler.

"We'll leave as soon as we gather our gear and the rest of the team arrives," Mychael told me.

"Who's the rest of the team?"

He gazed down at me. "You're going?"

"Not my first choice for a romantic getaway, but yeah, I'm going."

Mychael tightened his arms around me. "The two of us, Carnades, Tam, Imala, Prince Chigaru, and four others."

I knew Dad was one of the four others. For Tam and Imala, now was the time to move against Sathrik, and prevent their people from being slaughtered to feed the Saghred. I knew that Prince Chigaru was determined to rescue his fiancée before she was forced to marry Sathrik. After that, Chigaru only had two goals: take his brother's throne, then take his brother's life.

"Carnades can take ten people through that mirror," Mychael was saying. "In weapons and supplies, we'll essentially be limited to what we can carry."

Vegard stepped forward. "Sir, what about—"

"I need you here, Vegard."

"But, sir—"

"As acting paladin."

You could have heard a pin drop.

"I need to know that you're here," Mychael told him, "working in my stead if we fail—"

"You won't fail," Vegard said vehemently.

"If we do, I want you to get the students off of the island."

Justinius put a hand on Vegard's shoulder. "I'll make the announcement to the full Conclave within the hour. It would be good if you were there beside me."

"Evacuate the students first, youngest to oldest," Mychael told him. "Phaelan and Commodore Benares have offered their ships as transport."

My throat threatened to close up. "And they'll be damned fine guards," I managed.

"Yes, they will," Mychael agreed quietly.

Justinius dropped his hand from Vegard's shoulder and motioned to me. He went to the far corner of his office, out of earshot, and I followed.

"Any sign of your magic?"

"No, sir."

"It should have come back by now."

"I was going with 'if I don't say it, it won't be true.'"

"Doesn't work like that."

"I know." I glanced at Carnades; he was glaring at me. I turned away so he couldn't read my lips. "Does Carnades know?"

"Not from me or anyone else here. You play cards, girl?"

I knew where he was going. I nodded. "And I know how to run a convincing bluff."

"Make this one your best."

"Thank you, sir, but that goes without saying."

Mychael was talking to Carnades. "If you want to destroy goblins, there are two in Regor that you're free to cut loose on. Only on my command. You will not endanger the lives of this team, or we'll gladly walk home from Regor."

"You wouldn't dare!" Carnades snarled.

"No, I wouldn't dare," Mychael replied mildly. "I would *do*; and as I just said, I would do it gladly."

Carnades lunged at Mychael.

Mychael met him with an armored forearm against his throat.

A blue-white spark flared to life at the tip of my finger. It didn't grow. It just pulsed there. As far as magic went, it was smaller than tiny.

But it was mine. I didn't know how, but I'd made it.

"You don't have a choice, Carnades," I said, hardly daring to breathe for fear of blowing that spark out. "And neither do I."

The elf mage's stare was silent and icy.

"Yeah, it sucks to be us. If Nukpana wins, the two of us will be at the front of his kill line. Are you with us or not?"

His stare didn't melt. "Yes."

And the tiny spark didn't vanish. Its glow was fierce and bright. Determined.

I looked at Mychael over the spark and smiled.

"Let's go steal ourselves a rock."

About the Author

Lisa is the editor and quality control manager at an advertising agency. She has been a magazine editor and writer of corporate marketing materials of every description. She lives in North Carolina with her very patient and understanding husband, one cat, two retired racing greyhounds, and a Jack Russell terrier who rules them all.

For more information about Lisa and her books, visit her at www.lisashearin.com.

From the #1 *New York Times*
Bestselling Author
PATRICIA BRIGGS

RIVER MARKED

Car mechanic Mercy Thompson has always known there is something unique about her, and it's not just the way she can make a VW engine sit up and beg. Mercy is a different breed of shapeshifter, a characteristic she inherited from her long-gone father. She's never known any others of her kind. Until now.

An evil is stirring in the depths of the Columbia River— one that her father's people may know something about. And to have any hope of surviving, Mercy and her mate, the Alpha werewolf Adam, will need their help . . .

Available now from Ace Books

penguin.com